CHAIN GANG
ELEMENTARY

A Novel

Jonathan Grant

Thornbriar Press
Atlanta

Copyright 2011 by Jonathan Grant

Published in the United States of America by Thornbriar Press, Atlanta, Georgia. www.thornbriarpress.com.

Publisher's Cataloging-in-Publication

    Grant, Jonathan, 1955-
    Chain Gang Elementary : a novel/Jonathan Grant.
    p. cm.
    LCCN 2011926123
    ISBN-13: 978-0-9834921-0-8
    ISBN-10: 0-9834921-0-7
    ISBN-13: 978-0-9834921-1-5 (eBook)
    ISBN-10: 0-9834921-1-5(eBook)

    1. Elementary school principals—Fiction.
    2. Parents' and teachers' associations—Fiction.
    3. Education—Fiction. 4. Parenting—Fiction.
    5. Suspense fiction, American. 6. Public schools—fiction.
    I. Title.

    PS3607.R3638C43 2011
    813'.6 QB111-600105

Printed in the United States of America

Cover Design by Michael Mullins at Anything Design
Interior Layout by AuthorSupport.com

Books are available at quantity discounts. For more information, contact Marketing Department, Thornbriar Press, 3522 Ashford Dunwoody Road Suite 187, Atlanta GA 30319.

In the first place God made idiots. This was for practice. Then He made School Boards.

—Mark Twain

I will not waste chalk.
I will not waste chalk.
I will not waste chalk.
I will not ...

—Bart Simpson

For Judy, Laurel, and Nathan
and all the teachers who teach

ONE

In the twelfth year of his marriage, sixteen months before the shooting, twenty-one shopping days until Christmas, and eight hours before he reckoned for the tenth time that his wife didn't love him, Richard Gray met a woman who would have roughly the same effect on his life a tornado has on a trailer park.

There was no storm on the horizon as he walked to Malliford Elementary to pick up his son that balmy December afternoon, however—not even a cloud in the sky. A slight breeze rustled the last withered leaves clinging to oaks and poplars surrounding the suburban school as Richard stood on the sidewalk, towering over the children flowing past him like he was an upended boulder in a stream. Nick trudged out the door. Upon seeing his father, the brown-haired second-grader shouted a greeting and quickened his pace.

After a short walk home and a snack of Nutter Butters, Richard took Nick to Gatebooks, one of their favorite places. In the store's parking lot, a stiff wind rose from nowhere, swirling trash around and sending an empty paper cup dancing to the sidewalk. Richard climbed out of his old silver Audi and stood still, like a dog sniffing for trouble. Winter was coming, for him a heartless season.

He took Nick's hand, grateful for the warmth, and squinted reproachfully at the receding sun. "We've got an hour," Richard said, holding the bookstore's door open. "You know the drill: Don't read the one you want to buy."

"Go get a robot book," Nick commanded, and then raced to the kid's section and plopped cross-legged on the floor with *Captain Underpants*. As Diana Krall sang seductively in the background, Richard ambled over to the

Science and Technology section, giving a wary backward glance. Nick was already absorbed, head bowed, a monk in the midst of monkey business.

Richard found the book he wanted and leafed through it as he shuffled across the tan carpet, dodging a coffee-sipping college kid, also read-walking. The fellow was short, with dark hair and black glasses—a younger version of himself. Richard turned to watch his imperfect doppelganger recede from view.

He spotted the woman just past the Bestsellers and New Arrivals displays, in the Fiction section, squatting in the aisle beside a stack of paperbacks—a Malliford mom in funky retro glasses with angled frames—something Lucille Ball might wear. He passed by and doubled back for another look, peering around the bookcase like a bumbling spy. Her auburn hair was straight, not quite to her shoulders, her face oval, pleasing, with slightly close-set eyes and sharply sculpted brows. Standard-issue nose, neither button nor beak. A nice look—quirky, amusing, even intriguing. He could imagine her as Vera the steno gal in a pale green DeSoto convertible, wearing a billowing pink scarf, honking and waving as she drove by.

She glanced up and gave him a kiss-off look, nice and hard. Then a look of recognition lit her face. "Oh, hi." She slipped him a smile, then put it away and pushed down her dress with her palms as she stood. She was three inches shorter than him, about five-six. He guessed she was thirty, ten years his junior.

"Hey. I'm Richard Gray. From Malliford. I, uh—"

"I know. I've read your work."

He gave her a puzzled look. "My work?"

"You *are* Malliford's faithful scribe, after all."

"Newsletter editor."

"I like scribe."

He grimaced. "It makes me think *circumscribed*."

She cocked a finely arched brow. "*Are* you?"

"*Really.* I hardly know you."

She grinned. "You're on the Parent-Teacher Organization board, right?"

"Yeah. My second year."

"I heard the PTO is sitting on a pile of money," she said with a slight Southern accent, more magnolia-honey than moonshine-banjo.

He laughed. "Hardly. We nearly went broke last year. We're just now recovering."

"Thanks to Miss Glamour Shot," she said, meaning Barbara Hodges—PTO president, cosmetics addict and real estate agent, whose yard signs could double as Clinique ads.

"As far as money is concerned, I stay out of it. I'm a spender, not a fund-raiser."

"What do you mean, 'As far as money is concerned?' Any issues I should know about?" Her eyes pierced his as she waited for dish.

Well. He certainly had opinions and didn't want this bright, shiny new person to think he was part of the problem. "The PTO should be a stronger voice for children. It's dreadfully status quo."

"You ought to be president."

He'd been hearing that lately, but still, her bluntness took him by surprise. In any case, the prospect seemed unlikely. His gender was jinxed. Barbara had told him that Malliford's first (and last) male PTA president had committed an affair with the principal and absconded with the group's considerable wealth. The PTA chapter had been disbanded and the principal fired, replaced by Miz Rutherford and an independent PTO, along with an unwritten rule forbidding men from holding the organization's top office.

"I'm not part of the ruling clique," he said with a shrug. "There's outer circles and inner circles."

"So you *are* circumscribed."

He laughed. "I love a good math joke."

"Don't sell yourself short. The newsletter makes you a big shot."

"There's bigger shots."

"Like who, besides Barbara? She's not running again, is she?"

"Not likely. She's done her duty, especially after she stepped in to salvage last year's disaster. There's always Susan Gunther." He shuddered slightly as he said the name.

"She lives two doors down from me," the woman said. This meant she lived on Summerwood, in the school district's ritziest subdivision, where houses were worth twice as much as Richard's remodeled ranch.

"Well, smart money says she's the next president," he said.

"I don't think so. Not with her problems."

"What problems?"

"Didn't you hear? Archie moved out yesterday. I saw the truck."

"Why? What happened?"

"Something to do with his pregnant secretary, I suppose."

"I'm shocked," he said, figuring that acting aghast was his best defense. "Absolutely shocked."

"That's what I heard. Susan and I don't talk much. By the time we met, her husband had already hit on me. Then he got a look at Carl and backed off."

"Carl? Is that your husband, or a Rottweiler that goes on adventures with your kids?"

"Dog *of* a husband."

"I see."

"Susan irritates me."

"She has that effect on people," Richard noted.

"So why should she be PTO president?"

"No one else wants it."

"You should want it. She's not going to be able to function. She'll be just like Denise Coley last year. I predict nasty times ahead for her and her asshole husband."

"I wouldn't know," Richard said, although it wasn't hard to see it getting ugly with those two, especially since Archie was a ruthless divorce attorney and Susan had a take-no-prisoners attitude, herself.

"No, you don't look ruthless." She gave him a beguiling smile. "Quite the opposite. I hear you're a stay-at-home dad, and—"

"I have a business," he interjected. It was crucial that people know he wasn't just a househusband. "Corporate newsletters."

"A pro. That's why *Duck Call* is so good. Best newsletter in the state. And taking care of your son. It's great, what you do. ...Why is it named *Duck Call*?"

"Long ago, someone decided that Malliford was a mallard."

"That totally makes sense. Not." She glanced around, then fixed her gaze on Richard. "Are you happy with the school? It's my first year. I just know it's got four stars, whatever that means."

He shrugged. "Better than most. Nick's teacher is good. Mrs. Leland."

"What do you think of Miz Rutherford?"

"She is what she is."

"She needs to lighten up. And she's got a face you could use for a chisel." The woman fingered the spine of an Alice Hoffman novel. "I need to be more involved. Caitlin's in first grade and Amber Ellen starts kindergarten next fall. They're here somewhere," she said, glancing around in mock distraction. "Actually, Caitlin's babysitting for me right now. Anyway, I'll have more time, so I'd like to help. Does Miz Rutherford want parents to take part in decision-making, or just obey her commands and be good suburban zombies?"

Unfortunately, the hills were alive with suburban zombies. Richard tried to be diplomatic but truthful. "She can be difficult, but there are always things you can do."

"So how do I get on the PTO board?"

"Just move slow. They'll catch you."

"A wise guy. I like you." She nudged him with her elbow and kept it there for a tantalizing moment before pulling back. He averted his gaze and saw a book on the floor: *To Have and Have Not*.

"What do you like to read?"

"Today, I want a murder book with tough, cheesy people making hard, stupid choices. I want to read about dames," she said with a twinkle in her eye.

"Dames. Hmm. You should read Raymond Chandler."

"Really?"

"His dames are damier," he assured her.

"What about you?" She tipped her glasses and gazed over them at *Build Your Own Robot*. She made an "O" with her mouth. "I'm impressed."

"It's for a holiday project with my son."

"That's nice. I wish Carl would do things with the girls. Of course, he travels all the time."

A child called out, "Mommy!"

"Mine," the woman said. She proceeded to the children's section. Richard tagged along.

He found Nick sprawled on his belly, deep into his "read two, buy one" spree, *Underpants* books scattered about. Auburn-haired Caitlin, in jeans, T-shirt, and a red jacket, was holding a Dr. Seuss book. She looked up wide-eyed. "Mommy, can I get *Horton Hears a Who?*"

"My favorite Seuss," Richard said. "Quite political. You must listen for each tiny voice."

The woman smiled warmly at him, and then turned to her daughter. "Sure, sweetie. Where's Amber?"

"Amberella!" Caitlin shouted.

A smaller brown-haired girl in a lacy dress jumped from behind a display of dinosaur books and shouted "Bumbershoot!" The two girls began dancing to a song only they could hear.

"Come on, girls, let's pay for the books. What did you get, Bumbershoot?" Amber produced a paperback picture book with a kitten on the cover. "Good talking with you," the woman told Richard over her shoulder as she herded her girls toward the cashier.

After a minute, he sauntered after them and watched through the front window as they walked to a red Chrysler Town and Country minivan. Most mommies didn't move that way. He decided right than that she was really quite beautiful. And she smelled like lilacs, his favorite scent. He felt a pang of frustration when he realized he hadn't got her name, nor had he noticed the book she'd picked out.

He gathered up boy and books, paid and went home, hoping he made a good impression—not that it should matter, of course. But for some reason, he couldn't get the conversation out of his head.

*   *   *

Dusk was fast approaching as they pulled into their brick ranch's garage, and Nick wanted to play outside in the waning light. Although Applegate Way was a nice, quiet, relatively crime-free cul-de-sac nestled in the middle of Windamere Heights, cocooned away from major traffic and the urban jungle to the south, Richard still worried. The boy sprinted outside, and Richard stooped to yell beneath the closing garage door: "Don't help anyone look for their lost pet! Tell them their pet is dead, yell 'Fire!' and run inside."

Nick turned. "I thought I was supposed to yell their *pet* was on fire and run inside."

"Whatever!"

Richard went to his cluttered office, where memos, flyers, e-mail print-outs, letters, official notices, unofficial notes, and jotted-down phone numbers—most without names—were spread over file cabinets, the computer table and floor. Three milk crates contained stacks of unsorted papers. A mess. He claimed he thrived on the chaos of his office, though his wife would disagree—about the thriving, not the chaos.

One message on the machine. Anna Lee, from her office at the Chamber of Commerce: "You probably don't remember, but I have a banquet to attend," she reminded him in her clear, sharp voice. "Fend for yourselves." As executive vice president-public affairs, she attended many such events (and kept getting new titles instead of raises).

Not having to fix dinner meant he could work on the PTO newsletter and finish *Duck Call* so he could focus on his paying clients, both of them. He plopped into his leather office chair and scooted up to the work table. It was so burdened with computer equipment and papers there was barely room for a legal pad and a coffee cup—another cup that is, since there were two half-full/half-empty cups left from the morning. He moved both to a bookcase shelf, and then dialed Glamour Shot, chuckling at the PTO president's new nickname.

"Hi, Rick," Barbara Hodges purred when she picked up. "I was just thinking of you."

"Ever since my name came up on Caller ID. I need two articles, 'Volunteer of the Month' and 'Upcoming.'"

"Susan's the volunteer."

"No way."

"Why not? What do you have against her?"

"Nothing," he lied. "But she got it last month. How about Jane Baumgartner? She did all the work on the Fall Festival."

"Fine. Write her up."

"That's your job. I've got five pieces to do. Plus Miz R didn't write anything. *Again*."

"I've told you, writing isn't her thing, especially not for you. And don't even *think* of running a blank space like you did last year. You humiliated her! If you only knew what I have to do to keep things patched together with all these petty feuds going on. You're lucky you're so good. Just don't do it again! She'll kill me, or worse."

"I just did it when she broke a promise. This time Mrs. Baines is supposed to write something, but I'm not holding my breath."

"I don't trust you. What are you running if it falls through?"

"Maybe something from *Everything I Need to Know I Learned in Kindergarten*."

"That would be nice. Oh, one other thing, and this is bad. Miz R told me today the school board wants to redraw lines and put Chantilly Arms Apartments in our district."

"Where do they go now—Hanover? It's way overcrowded."

"Not the issue. Anyway, irregardless, this is a potential catastrophe. You know what we're dealing with."

He knew the party line, at least. Apartment kids lowered test scores and therefore property values. To Barbara, it was the ultimate moral issue, even more important than voting Republican.

"They've got to go somewhere," he pointed out.

"Not Malliford. This is bad for the community. But you wouldn't understand. Your house was below market, a fixer-upper, so you don't have the same sensibilities."

Richard heard a noise and decided to use it as an excuse. "Something's banging on the house. Termites, maybe. I gotta go."

"You should call Bond-it Pest Control. Tell 'em I sent you. Look, we'll talk. We need you on this, with your connections and journalistic skills. Maybe you could write an article—"

"Gotta go."

"All right," she semi-groaned. "Have a good weekend."

"I will when you e-mail me those articles. And bye."

Another BANG! on the garage door. Although soccer season was over, Nick still had a few kicks left. BANG! He'd perfected a power kick, shoelaces to ball. Anna Lee wouldn't allow such mayhem, afraid the house would fall. Even Richard wondered how long the garage door would last. Still, it seemed a small price. BANG!

"He shoots, he scores!" Nick yelled, his voice carrying through the crisp fall air.

Although Richard had begun his career as a reporter, banging out stories on deadline in a crowded room filled with ill-mannered people, it was impossible to work with the house under attack.

BANG!

He rushed outside. "Hey, boy. You want a piece of me?"

"Yeah."

Richard took a goalie's stance and they played their 895th Championship of the Known Universe, standard format. Nick won, 10-7.

"You're getting good," Richard wheezed. "And I'm getting old."

An oak leaf landed on Nick's hair as he stood triumphant, arms stretched exultantly over his head. He danced and howled in the light of the setting sun, then picked out the leaf and tossed it on the driveway. Richard leaned against the garage and caught his breath.

"What's the matter?" Nick asked.

"I love you, that's all."

"It happens." They had a flippant way of dealing with each other's affection. They told each other all the time, rejoiced in it, shrugged it off. *I love you. I loved you first.*

"Nicholas, Nicholas, Nicholas."

"That's my name. Don't wear it out."

They played outside until it was dark, wrestling and putting each other in atomic head locks. *Life is good*, Richard told himself. With winter coming, he needed the reminder.

That evening, they feasted on peanut butter and jelly sandwiches and orange juice, with ice cream bars for dessert. Afterward, they watched a Goes Fast, Blows Up movie. After putting Nick to bed, Richard worked on *Duck Call*. Anna Lee got in just past eleven o'clock and poked her head in the office door.

"Is Nick down?" she asked softly.

"Of course. How was the meeting?"

"It was about economic development. Some guy ..." she trailed off as she walked away. Fine. He didn't care. Chamber functions were boring beyond belief, and he was no fan of Gresham County's economic development. The area was horribly overdeveloped already, as far as he was concerned.

To be sociable, he shut off the computer and followed her. She stripped off her black business suit in a few deft moves and was naked—a slender, raven-haired woman of thirty-five. She had a smooth, unlined face, warm brown eyes, small breasts, and a trim ass. When she tossed her shoulder-length hair, he felt his heart lurch.

She acted surprised to see him admiring her. "Move along," she said. "Show's over."

Ouch.

Walking toward the bathroom, she brushed by him. He reached for her in hopes of making something happen, but ending up clutching air. He wasn't giving up. They'd had a dry spell, but there had been positive signs. A sly smile. A willingness to let him rub her back Thursday night while they watched a movie. Those things had to count for something. *Please.* He was desperate. He'd even offer to wash her Caravan if ...

After taking a couple of minutes to ponder the situation, he stripped, too. Why not? He stood naked and patted his belly. Sure he could stand to lose ten pounds, but he wasn't repulsive. Women sometimes told him he was cute, or that he was cute sometimes—he didn't remember which, exactly. Didn't Rita Malloy make a pass at him on Volunteer Day? He was pretty sure she did.

As he tossed his Buddy Holly glasses on the bedside table, he noticed a cockroach on the wall. *Danger! Mood-killing argument ahead.* Whenever Anna Lee saw a roach, she'd pitch a fit and demand that he call an exterminator. However, he hated the cure worse than the disease, since he knew that the chemicals used would only serve to create a super breed of mutant roaches that would take over the world. Anyway, they didn't have the money—and wouldn't until he started working full time. To keep the mood alive, he knew he must destroy the evidence of his failure as a hunter/gatherer/housekeeper/bug killer.

First the roach had to move off the Seascape Green flat latex paint onto the more washable Ultra Dove White enamel trim, two colors it had taken Richard and Anna Lee months to agree on before he'd been able to start painting.

"Move, damn you," he hissed. A standoff *la cucaracha*—human crouched naked by the wall, fist raised, bug twitching its antennae for an interminable moment as it debated its next and last move. The vermin broke for the window with doom-defying speed. Richard tracked it until it reached the windowsill, pulping it with a mighty blow that sent a wave of pain up to his elbow.

"*Ewwh.*" Anna Lee stood by the bed in her yellow robe, her wet hair in a pink towel turban. Her look of raw disgust suggested she'd caught him doing something else with his fist.

Richard winced and shook off the pain. "Sure I killed, but I killed for you," he drawled.

"You're bug naked."

"Ha, ha." He went to the master bath, washed his hands, and returned with a soapy tissue to clean up the mess.

"Use Lysol," she commanded. He bit his lip and complied. When he returned, she was in bed. Snug as a bug in her own rug, covers pulled tight.

"I'm going to take a shower." His second of the day. When he came out of the bathroom, the room was dark. He slipped into bed and tried to embrace her.

"I don't think so," she said, pushing him away.

It had been five weeks since they'd last made love. Unfortunately, the less sex he had, the more Richard thought about it. He didn't need constant sex—just regular sex, like rain in a temperate zone. But all he'd gotten lately were clouds. Erroneous predictions. And the illusory sights and sounds of storms on the Internet. Over time, his advances became feebler, her rejections more efficient. Tired, don't feel good, period, don't have time.

Two weeks ago, he'd merely said, "You look good."

Her response: "I've got a lot of things to do."

"Fine," he'd retorted. "Look ugly, then."

Now their relations were reduced to cruel dismissal: *I don't think so.* Next time, she'd probably say, *Go ahead without me.*

Anna Lee propped herself on an elbow. "What's the story about the guy who turns into a roach?"

"Metamorphosis," Richard said. "Franz Kafka."

"I hate that story. They made everyone read it in Lit class."

"Well, some people can't accept the premise. To others, no explanation is needed."

"You're definitely one of those."

This was true. He could see waking up as a giant insect, and it wouldn't be so bad if only he could have a ladybug. Now, wide awake and resentful, he got up, put on his robe, and went into the family room to watch Letterman, slamming the door on his way out.

She was snoring lightly when he returned. Streetlight filtered through the cell shades, softly brushing her face and making her hair seem like a shadow on the pillow. He lay down, careful not to touch her. With the scent of Lysol hanging in the air, he tried to distract himself and ended up thinking about the woman in the bookstore. Funky Glasses. He attempted to fantasize about her, but for some reason he couldn't. Nameless and unimaginable she remained.

* * *

The whomp of Saturday's *Sentinel* hitting the driveway woke Richard from a nightmare: Miz Rutherford had been sucking his brains from his skull through a garden hose, pausing to spit and belch. His old grade-school principal, Wilkerson—a certifiable pervert and denizen of his dreams—lurked nearby, zipping and unzipping his pants, somehow looking strict and forbidding with his dark glasses and ageless platinum hair.

That wasn't his worst nightmare about Wilkerson, however. There was the one he'd had a hundred times: The white-haired principal was chasing him, and the ground crumbled at his heels and fell away with every step. With the world disappearing behind him, he looked back to see Wilkerson turn into a huge raptor and fly after him, closing in with impossible speed. Then there was one about a door. In that dream, he woke up and went to check the front door, only to find it unlocked. As he reached to secure it, the knob turned against his grip. Impossibly thin, strong fingers found their way through the cracks and pried the door open, broke the hinges, bending them and popping out the screws with a noise as loud as a tree cracking in a lightning strike. Knowing Wilkerson was on the other side, he woke before he had to confront that evil. Then there was the one where his parents threw him off a cliff, but he hadn't had that one in a while.

As the news carrier's ancient car buzzed off, Richard lay in grateful, dull surprise at the interruption. It was good to be awake, alive, human. Not a bug, like Gregor Samsa. He glanced at his sleeping wife and recalled her rejection. A surge of hostility quickened him. He put on his glasses and squinted at his clock: 5:30 a.m. He had time to work on *Duck Call*. He would be a latter-day alchemist, turning animosity into achievement. The Chinese cookie fortune pinned to his office bulletin board declared: "You Can Let Each Day Build or Destroy You." Today would be a building day. There would be progress, by God!

He stumbled into dirty jeans, took a leak, and trudged to the dark kitchen, where he accidentally flicked on the garbage disposal instead of the lights. His mistake was exacerbated by a fork in the disposal's maw. He cursed, but his words were drowned out by the hellish clatter, which died down after a few seconds to a clunk, clunk ... clunk. Not good, since Nick was easily roused. He switched on the overhead spotlights, giving the kitchen what Anna Lee called an Eastern Bloc interrogation-room look—not what she'd had in mind when he started remodeling. He heard faint skittering and turned to see a roach crawl beneath the microwave, the lucky bastard.

After grinding beans, he started a pot of coffee and fetched the paper, pitching its wrapper into the recycle bin inside the garage. When he turned on the light over the kitchen table, his eyes popped open at the headline along the bottom of the *Sentinel's* front page: "Do Stay-Home Dads Cause Gay Sons?"

He poured a cup of coffee, strong, with sugar—no way could he take this unfortified—and read about the arch-conservative Southern Freedom Foundation study claiming a "distinct correlation" between fathers like Richard and sons who grew up to like other fathers' sons:

> ... While the numbers are still mercifully small, there's indisputable evidence that these overactive fathers create an imbalance in their sons' lives that causes gender-orientation confusion due to inappropriate role modeling and physical contact," said foundation Executive Director Jack Desmond. "It also shows that in many instances homosexuals are made, not born. These boys need deprogramming. We're here to help."

> Desmond added, "These results bolster our bedrock Christian belief that the best child-raising scenario is a full-time mother at home, with a father serving as the family's loving provider.

Richard pounded the table with his fist. Bullshit! Who the hell was this fascist, father-hating, homophobic Jack Desmond? People were born gay. Anyone who was the least bit enlightened knew that. Back when Richard worked at the *Sentinel*, the paper never would have printed such crap. "Liberal bias, my ass!" he hooted.

Although the reporter quoted a child psychologist who dismissed the study as "a half-baked, right-wing attempt to mold the American family in the foundation's own reactionary image," the SCUD had landed in his kitchen. Where he did the cooking. Ka-blooey!

He had to do something. Things were bad enough with Anna Lee already. She thought he was warping their son's personality and had expressed fear that Nick was on his way to becoming just like Dad, whatever that meant.

Actually, he knew what it meant. She'd told him several times that he was, at heart, a wounded child. Once, she'd called him "an emotional cripple with no real friends"—which made it sound like he was well on his way to Troubled Loner territory.

Of course, Richard had a different take: Under constant bombardment from hidden transmitters in the Chamber of Commerce offices, Anna Lee became more conservative, moving from independent to Republican—the better, Richard supposed, to reflect her bosses' views. She now watched Fox News, and if that wasn't bad enough, also called him a left-winger because he voted Democratic. Only she called it "Democrat." Surely that was grounds for divorce.

But he didn't want to leave her, and even at their worst, they were at least civil to each other. Most importantly, there was Nick, whom they both cherished, to hold them together. Clearly, it was time for some protective censorship. He turned the page and saw a tire store ad backing the article. That's the ticket: He needed tires, anyway. Richard got scissors and paused, paper in hand, wishing he and Anna Lee had a relationship in which they laughed at such stories, but they didn't, so he snipped.

TWO

Anna Lee pecked Richard on the cheek, gave him her trademark sigh of regret, and left for work Monday morning, causing him to wonder what she was disappointed in this time—besides him in general, that is.

Five minutes later, father and son began the quarter-mile trek to school. Richard shaded his eyes against the rising sun as he shouldered Nick's backpack. The boy huffed and watched his foggy breath dissipate in the air. To the west, Richard could see the city skyline through bare tree branches. They walked to Applegate's dead-end at Windamere Way, then up the sidewalk to the school crossing at the hilltop.

The journeys to and from school with Nick were Richard's sweetest moments. While they often held hands, their ungloved fingers were stuffed in coat pockets this morning. They bumped each other and acted goofy, skipping and whistling, keeping watch for dog poop. A neighbor had just walked his cocker spaniel and a steaming load stood in their way. "*Ewwh!* Look out!" yelled Nick. "It could go at any moment!" Richard sidestepped just in time. They stopped to visit the black-and-yellow garden spider that lived in the hedge by Scroggins's mailbox, but there was only an empty web, shiny with dew. Too cold for spider blood.

They tromped by the flashing yellow school-zone light and Malliford's ancient, original *School of Excellence* sign, which was attached to a metal post. Walking briskly, they could outpace the sluggish river of SUVs and minivans queuing up for drop-offs. Mrs. Perkins, the grandmotherly crossing guard (hero to walkers, bane of drivers) stepped into the street to halt traffic before they reached the crosswalk. They said howdy as they scurried by, joining the river of students walking past the sixth-grade safety cadets (essentially, valets with yellow belts and badges) who chirped "Have a nice day" as they slammed car doors. An older boy, skateboarding while carrying a trombone case, rattled toward them out of the rising sun. In a single motion, he stopped, flipped the board with his foot, and deftly caught it in his free hand. Nick was awed.

"He should wear a helmet," Richard loudly declared. Before them—just beyond *another School of Excellence* sign, this one monumental—stood Malliford, a good school with four stars by its name in the *Sentinel*'s latest *Practical School Guide*. The long, low forty-year-old grey brick building's design was undistinguished. A metal awning stretched from a side door to the sidewalk, supported by rusted posts in dire need of paint. Richard had mentioned this at September's PTO board meeting. Nothing had been done as a result. It seemed that nothing ever was. The first rule of schools, Richard had learned.

In the back parking lot sat three classroom trailers. Barbara wanted them hidden from public view, but the county wouldn't move them. Besides, the only way the school could meet the state requirement for lower class sizes would mean *more* portable classrooms, although the mandate now looked like nothing more than an empty promise, since school systems could get waivers simply by asking. Meanwhile, closets had been converted to classrooms to comply with the governor's Better Schools initiative—"BS" for short.

The campus was well-laid out, bordered on three sides by tall trees, but the grounds needed work. Weeds dominated the flowerbeds by the front doors. A well-trampled mound of red clay sat in the middle of the yard, left from a drainage project either completed or abandoned months ago. Many would-be kings fought over this hill when teachers weren't watching; Nick stared at it longingly as they passed.

Before them, ramrod straight, stood Estelle Rutherford, Malliford's patrician principal, in a powder blue suit and trademark pearls, her silver hair permed perfectly into a Pattonesque helmet, clipboard in left hand, walkie-talkie in right. Richard gave her the slightest of waves; she nodded a half-centimeter in response, watching him carefully before unlocking her gaze and targeting the next miscreant.

Miz Rutherford had the strong support of most parents and would keep it as long as the school's four stars shone, but she had her detractors, chief among them Stan McAllister, whom she'd blacklisted from the PTO board; longtime maverick board member Rita Malloy, who was certain the principal was the devil; and Richard, whose high opinion of the school's leader had fallen since becoming newsletter editor. Recently he'd told Rita, "Getting to know her is like peeling an onion. Each new layer brings more tears."

Three and a half years earlier, Richard wouldn't have thought he'd ever say that, though he'd never been fond of principals. That's when he and Anna Lee met Miz Rutherford, during their frantic search for a decent school following the legendary drug-related shooting at Bonaire Elementary, when their address became an embarrassment. No way would their child attend Bonaire after *that*. Anna Lee wanted Nick in private preschool; Richard insisted on public pre-kindergarten. Their lack of money decided the debate, but they had to move, of course. Noticing Malliford's combination of high test scores and reasonable housing prices, they contacted real estate agent/cheerleader Barbara Hodges. During the Grays' visit to her school, Estelle Rutherford came across as a strict, no-nonsense commander, flicking her pen like a riding crop to punctuate her message: Malliford was a place of learning. Misbehavior was forbidden. No guns, teacher-beatings, or graffiti like there had been at Bonaire. The old-school headmistress's authoritarian manner was just what Anna Lee wanted. Richard couldn't argue with the stars. For Anna Lee, there was only one problem. The trailers. *What kind of people learned in trailers? And even more disturbing, possibly—what did they learn?*

"Don't be concerned about that," Miz Rutherford had instructed her. "Trailers show that people like you are moving in, which will make the school better. We're a School of Excellence, you know."

They knew. Barbara had proudly pointed out the sign, though she wasn't sure exactly when Malliford earned the honor. Richard hadn't been able to find out since then, either. Rita said it predated Miz Rutherford's tenure. Once a school of excellence, always a school of excellence. Another rule of schools.

To Richard, even at first glance, something was amiss. "It reminds me of my first school, somehow," he'd said on the way home that day.

"That's good," Anna Lee had replied.

He squinched his face. "Not exactly."

"Well, it's either here or stay at Bonaire and pay for private school."

And so Malliford it was, since Richard had no intent of turning Nick into a preppie.

Time passed. The onion unraveled. In Richard's rookie year on the board, the principal tried to exercise prior restraint over *Duck Call*'s content, telling him he couldn't run an article about a parent volunteer (Stan) who had criticized school policy. The former big-city reporter said, "Nonsense," shocking the principal into silence. He prevailed, she pretended the newsletter didn't exist, and a propaganda war ensued. Staunch Rutherford ally Susan Gunther blamed Richard's "headstrong attitude" for hastening PTO President Denise Coley's breakdown and midyear abdication. Upon resigning, Denise pulled her children from Malliford and disappeared, just like the guy who boinked the principal and stole all the money. Richard refused to accept the blame for her abdication; he held that her recent divorce and addiction to painkillers led to her downfall and Vice President Barbara Hodges's subsequent rise. Rita claimed Denise had told her (and apparently no one else) that "the bitch in the principal's office" had driven her to the edge of madness. Clearly, with the world thus stacked against her, poor Denise was doomed to fail.

In the middle of this turmoil, Susan and Miz Rutherford put out a principal's newsletter to compete with Richard's effort, but only one issue of *View from the Top* was ever distributed. It was then, when Miz Rutherford refused to submit her monthly letter to *Duck Call* for publication, that Richard ran a blank space underneath her name on the front page. Embarrassed, the principal grudgingly went back to allowing him to print her propaganda along with the PTO's. Their relationship hadn't risen above cool civility since then. Then *Duck Call* took top state honors, and President Hodges was stuck with him, since no one else would take the job. Barbara's idle threats to fire Richard became a constant joke between them.

Rita declared that an independent press marked the beginning of the end of Miz Rutherford's "reign of error," but the principal remained firmly in control and showed no signs of relinquishing power. Stan bitterly called her "Principal for Life." No one knew how old she was, but surely she was nearing Gresham County's mandatory retirement age. Richard thought her most ungracious to withhold her retirement plans, which would bring such joy to Rita, whose hopes of outlasting the principal were dimming now that her youngest child, Bertie, was only a year and a half away from his sixth-grade graduation.

Consequently, it surprised neither Miz Rutherford nor Richard when he walked by that December morning without stopping to chat and she barely acknowledged his existence, even though she had business to discuss with him.

Father and son stepped through the schoolhouse door into a closed-in world of stale air, happy chatter, sneakers, T-shirts and blue jeans. As three moms huddled in the foyer to share a secret, a line of early-bus kindergartners marched to their classroom, index fingers to lips. Richard signed in at the office in compliance with Rule No. 1 of *Malliford Manners*. School secretary Polly Bedford—pale, thin, blonde, and dour—glanced at him, then turned her attention to mail on her desk.

"Why are you taking me all the way to class?" Nick asked, wrinkling his nose.

"I don't need a reason," Richard replied. Truth was, he hoped to see Funky Glasses again because, face it, she was fun to look at.

Children streamed past them in the front hall; three second-graders hovered around the water fountain like camels at an oasis. Teachers smiled at him—so good to see a father who's involved. And he liked the teachers, most of them. Malliford had a veteran faculty, considered above average by parents, though there had been troubling defections to other schools and professions recently. Rita would be happy to explain why. (And Barbara would be quick to call Rita "a crazy, headstrong old hippie.")

There was tension ahead in the darkened hallway. A heavyset mother seeking an unscheduled conference—a violation of Rule No. 5—grabbed Mrs. Greene's arm and nearly spilled her coffee. The teacher had seen the woman and tried to flee, but a clot of first-graders blocked her escape. Just past them, Mrs. Cates stood with a heavy hand on the shoulder of a stocky black boy with a shaved head. The sullen youth wore baggy denim jeans, an Oakland Raiders jacket, and a Usual Suspect's expression. She lowered her voice and gave Richard a *Keep Moving* glance as he approached.

In accordance with Rule No. 3, Richard stopped outside Mrs. Leland's classroom as Nick slipped in. Roberta Leland, sister of PTO stalwart Jane Baumgartner, gave him her smile, one that seemed to never disappear completely. Pretty and plump, she got almost as many hugs as the kindergarten teachers who lived in their magical world of bright primary colors and constant affection.

As he turned away from the door, Michael Hostetler clipped Richard on the left kneecap and darted into the room. His older sister stopped to apologize. "He's a really bad brother," Stephanie explained. "And a really stupid person."

"Oh, come on. I know Michael. He's very bright," said Richard.

This statement irked her tremendously. "My mother says he tests well, whatever that means. But he's an idiot. He forgets to wear socks." She shook her head in disgust. "Tests are the stupidest thing ever invented. If they tested for socks, he'd flunk."

Richard looked down at his own feet as he stepped away.

"Look up when you walk," a guttural voice commanded. When he did so, he came face-to-face with the infamous Avon Little, a tall, stout, forbidding black woman who taught third grade and was—according to word on the sidewalk, where mothers shared gossip—Malliford's worst teacher, to be avoided at all costs.

Before he could respond, two fifth-grade boys passed by. Thinking himself out of earshot, one of them called out, "Bullfrog Eyes!"

"If I'm a bullfrog, you a fly," Mrs. Little shouted after the miscreants.

The boys hustled away. Mrs. Little stood with her arms akimbo, glowering after them. "We need discipline around here," she muttered.

Richard considered this a strange statement, since Miz Rutherford had a reputation as a fierce disciplinarian. Then he realized one of the boys was Brandon Hodges, Barbara's son. "Does he get away with that?"

"I just work here."

"Let me know if you ever see my boy act that way. After you do what you gotta do."

"Thank you, Mr. Gray. I will."

As he walked toward the office, Richard heard running water in the boys' restroom and went in to investigate. The bathroom was clean, but in desperate need of renovation and repair. Two toilets had been flushing constantly for weeks.

He returned to the hall as a statuesque blonde exited the office. Ms. Bailey, a fifth-grade teacher both stunning and stylish, had been, among other things, first runner-up in the 1975 Miss Texas pageant. "Good morning, Mr. Gray," she said, flashing an incandescent smile.

"Good morning, Ms. Bailey. That's a beautiful dress."

"Thank you. By the way, Miz Rutherford is looking for you."

"She's already seen me."

"Very well."

The bell rang, and Mrs. Bailey's high heels clicked away around the corner. When Richard went outside, Miz Rutherford was checking off a bus arrival. He sauntered up and waited for her to speak. She looked away from her clipboard and off into the distance before fixing her gaze on him. "Are you coming to the meeting tomorrow night?" she asked.

"What meeting?"

"A special meeting of the PTO board."

"What's it about?"

"A county issue. I can't be actively involved." She gave him the slightest of smiles. "We need you on our side. Your journalistic skills. To state our case to the media—we have a good one. Our reputation, most importantly."

"Speaking of reputation, the toilets won't stop running in the boys' front restroom."

"I am aware of the problem, Mr. Gray," she said in a tone meant to quell discussion.

Richard was not easily quelled, however. "One thing to be aware of it, another to do something about it. We're not being very green, are we?"

She snorted and turned toward the entrance. Richard scoffed and turned away from the school, only to see the object of his desire pass by, pulling Caitlin and Amberella behind her, leaving a scent of lilac in her wake. She wore black Capri pants and—God bless her!—a huge pair of shades that covered nearly half her face. "Good morning, Richard," said Funky Glasses, flashing a bright smile.

"Another thing, Miz Rutherford," he called out. "When they gonna get rid of the dirt?"

"I'm doing the best I can, Mr. Gray," Miz Rutherford said as she opened the door just ahead of Funky Glasses. An instant later, both women were gone, leaving Richard slightly thrilled, vaguely disappointed, and somewhat pissed off.

When he got home, there was a message on the machine. Barbara, using an automated calling system, was raising an alarm: "Please attend a special meeting of the Malliford PTO Board Tuesday night at seven p.m. in the media center. Our school's future is at stake!" There was a brief ad for Food Town Supermarket, then her message repeated. Still irritated at her sloth, he called her.

"Hey, Rick-ee," she sang. "Don't lose that number."

"I went ahead and wrote the pieces you were supposed to."

"Good. I have more important stuff to worry about. Our school's—"

"Future is at stake. I know. I got the message twice."

"How'd I sound?"

"Repetitive."

"Damned ad. Those things are so commercial. Other than that."

He laughed at her unintended irony, since she was on a constant quest for corporate sponsors. "Like a cross between Paul Revere and Chicken Little. Is this about that redistricting?"

"Well, the sky *is* falling. Just when we were clear of lawsuits and getting back to neighborhood school status, this comes along. Did you know home prices around Malliford have gone *up* in the past two years? It's the only zip code in Gresham where that's happened. Well, one of three. And now—*shing!*—stabbed in the back. The county says it wants to relieve overcrowding at Hanover, but don't you believe it."

"I heard Hanover has eighteen trailers. We've got three."

"There will be more. Anyway ... *Hell-o*. We're talking Chantilly Arms

Apartments. They'll crowd the classrooms, drive down test scores, and ruin the neighborhood. Simple fact of life: Single-family homes good, apartments bad. And they are *not* part of our neighborhood. Drive over there and see for yourself. There's furniture strewn all over the parking lot, dogs running loose, junk cars. It's Section-Eight. *In the ghet-to*," she sang à la Elvis. "Half the people don't speak English. Crack dealers own the place. This is a back-door plan to get around the Freedom Foundation's lawsuit against affirmative action. Susan says, 'Look out! Here comes diversity! Doncha just love it?'"

Richard bristled at the mention of the right-wing outfit that accused him of perverse parenting. "Did you see the article in Saturday's paper?"

"Don't worry. Your boy has several good years left."

It wasn't funny. It was bullshit. Everything about the Freedom Foundation was bullshit. Bunch of white folks with too much time and money trying to turn back the clock on civil rights, gay rights, women's rights—hell, men's rights, for that matter. And she could write her own articles next time. He fought to control his outrage and prepared for an eloquent outburst. "You—"

"Gotta go. See you tomorrow night."

He hung up, shuddered in revulsion, sighed heavily, and penciled in the meeting on his calendar, wondering how she got away with it. He recalled her son's misbehavior. Apparently, Parents Who Count and their children did as they pleased.

As he was preparing to email the newsletter file to the printer, Rita called, demanding to know what the hell was going on—her basic, all-purpose question. "Have you heard anything about a meeting tomorrow night?" she said in her trademark rasp, which she had once proudly claimed she'd developed from years of yelling at her kids.

"Yeah, it's a pitchfork-and-torch meeting about the county's proposed redistricting." He gave her the details, such as they were. "You should have gotten a call."

"Barbara took me off the list."

"You should complain."

"I *do* complain. That's why they took me off the list. Notice I said 'they,' which may be giving other people more credit than they deserve. Another example of rampant Rutherfordism. I don't like what they're up to. I bet it's a White Citizens Council meeting, a gentrified Klan."

"Rutherfordism? That's a new word."

"You like it? I'm getting a copyright. It means pomp for the principal and obedience for everyone else. And more rules, of course. The woman's a martinet, not an educator."

"Marine Antoinette," he riffed.

"Good one! I'm stealing it."

"Take it, along with the cake."

"She's got no intellectual integrity. She's so full of herself she can't even see what a big hypocrite she is."

"You're starting to carry on."

"And you're not half as funny as you think. You don't love me, so what do I care?"

"Sure I love you."

"Liar. You don't send me flowers, and you never make a pass at me."

"I'm married, remember?"

"When did that ever stop a man? It's 'cause I've got grey hair and a fat butt. Admit it."

Richard admitted nothing.

"OK, OK. You've got a beautiful wife and a wonderful marriage and my asshole husband ran off with a graduate assistant and only comes back to my bed when he's so drunk he can't recall where he lives, so I should be quiet. Sorry I brought it up." She said goodbye and hung up.

Poor Rita isn't aging gracefully at all. Richard looked out his office window and squinted at the morning sun. The looming apartment battle reminded him of something that happened three and half years before, when they moved to Applegate. After he'd locked up the old house for the last time and drove the yellow Ryder truck past overwhelmingly black Bonaire Elementary, he had stopped for coffee at the local Dunkin' Donuts, where four old white men sat in a booth holding their daily bullshit session. They were bitter over the decline of neighborhood schools. One man, a skinny guy with a big silver belt buckle, said something that haunted Richard: "It's a shame when one race pulls all the others down with it." The others nodded in agreement.

Richard saw them as raging hypocrites—the voters who'd kept segregationists in power well into the 1960s, voting early and often for the Southern demagogues who wrapped themselves in the Confederate flag and blocked school entrances, shouting states' rights defiance to black children who dared darken their doorstep. They'd held the region back for decades, just like their daddies and granddaddies before them. People said "Fergit, Hell!" about the Civil War, never remembering anything right in the first place.

The men had lapsed into murmuring racial epithets. Richard ate his donut, slurped his coffee, and then hopped in the truck and fled the school and neighborhood. Not due to blackness, of course, but because test scores were abysmal, graffiti stained the walls, obscenely loud hip-hop music bludgeoned the neighborhood, and the echo of a gunshot hung like a curse in the air.

He'd felt like a cowardly soldier deserting a great battle when he drove away. After all, he'd been raised a liberal, though that was a dirty word around Malliford. As a small-town newspaper editor in Ridalia, his father had fought the good fight on integration (and otherwise been an asshole, unfortunately). Now that old battle had reappeared on his doorstep.

At dinner that night, Richard mentioned the meeting but not its purpose, fearing his wife would support Barbara's position.

"I might have to work late," Anna Lee said.

Richard said he'd take Nick to the board meeting if he had to. It wouldn't be the first time. Still, he was irked. "It's weird that you cover for me less than other board members' husbands do."

"I work long hours to support us. What part of that don't you understand?"

He didn't argue. He was already due for a holiday depression. No need to make it worse.

"Dad," asked Nick, reaching for a roll, "What does 'gay' mean? An older kid called you that. He said 'Your dad is so gay.' I think his name is Hodges."

THREE

Tuesday brought a cold, hard rain. Anna Lee drove Nick to school, and Richard tried to work on Healthnet's newsletter, but he felt unmotivated on this dismal morning. He stood in the darkened kitchen, nose pressed to patio door, gazing out on the back yard. Winter approached; yesterday's golden leaves were now brown clumps of rot. They depressed him; so did everything else. He was suffering from seasonal defective disorder or some such shit. He no longer thought his dark moods resulted from a chemical imbalance, being now quite sure they were event-based. His life sucked and death was imminent, even if it took its time to claim him. It wasn't fair. He should be in the summer of his days, with a wonderful son ... and an increasingly Republican wife. Who didn't love him. Hell, he wasn't sure he loved himself half the time. But there was always Nick.

Lately—and ironically, from his point of view—Anna Lee had spoken about having another child. The other day, she'd told him about a friend who had been impregnated artificially. Now he suspected she was conspiring to have a child without sex. No way would he be party to such a perverse arrangement, though party was hardly the appropriate term. He would, at the very least, demand one last salmon-frenzy run before the sluice gates slammed shut and he was left to flop to death on a rocky shoal or get his meat pounded into a can. This was his great fear: Once safely pregnant for the second and last time, she'd never make love to him again. Wham, bam, thank you, *sir*.

It chafed, this lovemaking—horribly unfair, on her paltry terms. Infrequent. Inconsequential, just a moment of release. Perhaps artificial insemination was a better fit for their sex life, but he'd resist the procedure as long as possible. Still, there was an inevitability to her demand, and he knew that, one way or another, they'd have another child. They'd made the deal long ago: two kids. And a deal is a deal, until death does its part.

Bah. Enough of this self-indulgent bullshit, he told himself. Not every day is a good day, so get over it. He pulled away from the window and forced himself to work. He remained uninspired, but at least he was moving.

It was still wet that afternoon, so he drove to pick up Nick, parking on Windamere's shoulder slightly more than halfway to Malliford, feeling stupid for bothering to drive. Once inside school, he tunneled through the dark front hall to Nick's classroom, where he found his son with his nose pressed to the glass of Mrs. Leland's twenty-gallon aquarium, imitating Percival the goldfish.

That goofy sight cheered Richard immensely, and he realized he'd been kidding himself. He wasn't raising and protecting Nick. The boy was raising and protecting him, keeping him alive, pulling him from the pit time and again. "You are always with me," he said as they walked outside.

"Wherever you may roam," Nick agreed. This was their basic call and response, how they found each other in the dark. On the drive home, accompanied by windshield wipers, Richard sang *Me and Bobby McGee*.

In the kitchen, Nick said, "I'm hungry. I signed up for a sub at lunch but got nachos. I hate nachos."

"I'll fix you a sub for dinner."

"You da man!"

"No, you da man!"

They danced around the counter, shaking fingers, proclaiming themselves da men.

And so, thanks to Nick, Richard's depression abated. It would be back, of course, for the boy could only do so much, being outnumbered seven billion to one.

*   *   *

Anna Lee got home at 6:55 p.m., barely giving Richard time to glare at her as he brushed by on his way out. "You're late," he said.

"I have a job. I guess you forgot."

He didn't have time to argue over who had a job. "Nick's fed, done his homework and played piano. There's a sub in the fridge. I gotta go."

"A sub?" She grimaced in distaste.

"You're worse than a guy," he muttered to himself.

Richard moved like a shadow along Applegate and Windamere, walking by minivans and SUVs parked in the school's loop. A decent turnout on a nasty night, though the steady rain had slowed to drizzle.

Barbara popped out of the media center door as he approached, loafers clicking. "Would you get the podium from the cafetorium?"

When he returned with the rolling lectern, Bessie Harper (who oversaw Room Mothers) loomed over the sign-in table. The huge, happy woman took two of every handout, waddled over to the window, and heaved herself onto a seat beside Susan Gunther (VP-Fund-raising), who wore her usual expression of slight displeasure, no doubt fueled by the departure of her rat-ass husband. She looked like she'd put on weight.

Miz Rutherford sat at a table to the left of the podium. She pursed her wrinkled lips and surveyed the scene with bright eyes, quietly conferring with the long-suffering and exquisite Ms. Bailey. The former Almost Miss Texas winked at Richard as he took a seat at a back table beside Candace Josey (Special Events) and Cindi Lou Reed (Hospitality). The two short-haired brunettes—inseparable best friends and next-door neighbors—looked and acted alike and finished each other's sentences. Barbara claimed they were lovers. Which made this the gay table, he supposed. He would sit here with pride.

Adopting a scholarly air, he looked over his glasses at a petition on the table and began reading: "We, the undersigned concerned parents of Malliford Elementary School students—"

He felt a hand clap on his shoulder, and a moment later, Stan McAllister sat down beside him. Susan looked over and snarled, "He can't be here."

Ah, but there he was—short, chubby, rumpled and opinionated, forty years old, in ill-fitting clothes, with thin, stringy hair that would be gone before long. His brown plastic-framed glasses constantly slipped down his nose. Stan was a seedy gnome, a curmudgeon who knew what was wrong with the school and loved to share his opinions, especially in newsletter articles, which Richard published after toning down Stan's harsh criticisms into something more diplomatic and constructive.

Stan ignored Susan, whom he knew all too well. Their kids were in the same first-grade class, and she was room mother. They clashed over everything from volunteer reading to class parties.

"Did you get my article?" he asked Richard. Specifically, his anti-TV article, part of his crusade against the idiot box and its negative effect on children's intellectual, physical, and social development.

"Yeah," Richard said. "I put it on page three. Scary stuff. The average kid spends more time watching TV than in school—that's a real eye-opener. And half of them have a TV set in their bedroom. What are their parents thinking?"

"They aren't. That's the problem. They're using it as a babysitter. I'm glad you're with me on this. You're my only ally here. There should be a No-TV Committee, but Barbara won't put me on the board just because I don't get along with the principal. What an ass."

Richard wasn't sure if Stan was talking about Miz Rutherford or Barbara, since both women conspired against him. Barbara refused to list houses on Balsam Court because of Stan's carport, which, she said, "looks like a cross-section of a Dumpster."

Susan, loudly: "He's not on the board."

Barbara pounded her wooden gavel to call the meeting to order as Rita Malloy (Cultural Arts) rustled in and pulled up a chair next to Richard. "Hey, good lookin'," she said.

"Madame Chairman, point of order," Susan called out.

Barbara gave her friend and likely successor a bemused look. "The chair recognizes Susan Gunther. And kudos for your great success on the Fall Festival, Susan."

F women applauded, while Richard glanced around for the absent Jane Baumgartner, who had done most of the work on the festival.

Susan stood. "Thank you, Madame President."

"I hear her husband is leaving her," Rita whispered behind her copy of the petition.

"He already did," Richard said. "Moved last week."

"I hate when a man knows stuff before I do," Rita hissed at Candace.

"Madame President, is this a board meeting?" said Susan, glaring at the rowdies in back.

"Yes. It's a called board meeting," the president said.

"A special called board meeting," said Candace.

"A special emergency called board meeting," added Cindi.

"A very special emergency called board meeting," finished Candace.

As women tittered, Barbara smiled wryly. Miz Rutherford shifted slightly in her chair.

"If so, then why are non-board members in attendance?"

"We'll all be bored by the time this is through," Stan observed.

"If we're going to conduct board business—"

The plop of a notebook on the table interrupted her as Richard opened the bylaws he kept handy, experience having shown him that Barbara's sense of democracy dimmed during crisis.

"—there's no need for people who aren't on the board to be here," Susan concluded.

"It's not that I need to be here," Stan said. "It's that I want to."

"Point of order." Richard said, then read aloud: "All Parent-Teacher Organization meetings, both of the board of directors and general membership, shall be open to the public."

"Case closed," Rita said. "He has a right to be here."

"It's Miz Rutherford's building," Susan said. "It's up to her."

"Let him stay," said the principal, giving Rita a dyspeptic glance.

"It's the county's building," Rita said. "Ergo, our building."

"She said he could stay," said Flora Frederick (Volunteers). "Let it go."

"That's not the point."

"She could throw us all out, if she wanted," Flora observed.

"Why don't *you* let it go, Flora?"

"How about you both let it go, and let's move on," Barbara said after she glanced at Miz Rutherford, who looked like she'd suffered too much debate already.

"All parents are equal. Some are more equal than others," said Rita, paraphrasing Orwell.

"That's true," Flora said.

Barbara knew how to quell the disturbance. She placed her hand over her heart. "I pledge allegiance—"

Everyone jumped up in surprise at the patriotic ambush and finished the recitation. Stan shouted the last two words, then muttered, "I hate it when people ignore the part after 'flag.'"

"On to business," said Barbara, taking a deep breath. "If you haven't heard already, the county wants to redraw attendance zones and place Chantilly Arms Apartments in our district. This means between fifty and a hundred additional students. No way to tell exactly how many, and that's just part of the problem. I don't want to sound like the wicked white woman here, but this is bad for our school. We'll have horrible overcrowding."

Richard looked around the library. While the school's student population was about 20 percent black, its PTO board was 100 percent Caucasian, making it the perfect place for a wicked white woman to strut her stuff. "Are we overcrowded?" he asked.

A murmur swept through the crowd. The Parents Who Count (PWCs) were certain Malliford was bursting at the seams. "There are more students than optimal," Miz Rutherford said.

"I can think of a few we could do without," Bessie chirped.

"By county and state standards, are we overcrowded?" Richard asked, looking at Miz Rutherford, who averted her gaze.

"It's not like they're bringing in Arborgate," said Flora.

"I wish," Barbara said wistfully. Arborgate homes were typically worth more than a half million dollars.

"These new kids will drive down test scores," Susan said. "You know what that means."

"Yeah, Barbara will have to drive a Volvo instead of a Mercedes!" Rita exclaimed.

The room half-roared with laughter. Stan laughed loudest; Richard smirked. The women at Susan's table glared at Rita. Miz Rutherford acted like she'd been poked with a needle, and Barbara looked like she'd been whacked by a bat. She'd called a meeting of wicked white women, and the left-wingers at Richard's table were taking over—none of them fund-raisers, mind you. There was no hope for Stan, of course, and Rita was nothing more than a troublemaker, but Richard should know better. After all, his wife was a high-ranking chamber official.

The PTO president gritted her teeth and said, "We need to preserve our local schools. Look what's happening in Gresham. Schools decline, committed parents move away, it gets worse. We don't want that here, do we? No way should the county favor Hanover over us."

"Say that last part three times fast," Cindi Lou whispered to Candace.

"We'll have crack houses in five years," Bessie Harper declared.

"Should we vote whether we want crack houses?" Stan asked.

"You've got the closest thing to a crack house around here," muttered a woman at the next table. Stan wet his index finger and raised it to signal that a point had been scored.

"Madam Chairwoman," Susan said. "Even if he is here, he can't participate in the discussion or vote. Our amateur parliamentarian neglected to mention that part."

Richard turned to Stan. "She's right. You can watch, not speak."

"Isn't this a public forum?" he asked.

"No. It's an extra-special called board meeting," said Cindi Lou.

"This is crap," Stan said.

"They don't pay taxes," Susan declared, ignoring the sideshow. "Half of them are illegal."

"They do pay taxes," Richard insisted. "A penny sales tax for school construction and property taxes through their rent, not counting all the other sales and income taxes they pay. How do you think the complex's taxes get paid?"

"I doubt Chantilly Arms' taxes *are* paid," said Barbara. "I think the owner is in default."

"Bogus point," Stan muttered.

"I can't believe we debate whether people in apartments have the right to breathe," Rita huffed.

"They're not like us," Flora said.

Stan suggested they had gills, off the record.

"Is the point that black kids live in those apartments?" Richard asked, surprising even himself. The bottom of Miz Rutherford's face dropped. She looked like she could swallow a rabbit whole.

"I think it's Hispanics, mainly," said Connie Parker (Student Recognition).

"I resent the insinuation that we're racist," snapped Susan.

"White folks can be so sensitive," Stan said.

"It's simply a demographic question," Richard claimed. "If you want, we can go on record. All in favor of not being prejudiced, raise their hands."

"I move that we celebrate diversity," Rita said.

Barbara banged her gavel. "That's enough. This isn't about race." After all, a racial appeal wouldn't sway the school board, which was required by law to educate all children in Gresham County regardless of race, creed, country of origin, square footage, or period of occupancy.

"Good," said Richard. "Here's my point. Every child is entitled to an equal opportunity. I'm concerned that we're being close-minded about people we don't even know."

"Richard is right," Barbara said. "We must present the right reasons for being against this to the school board. Richard, you're such a good writer. Could you formulate our response?"

Richard shook his head in bemusement. "Don't think so, Madame President. I've seen Hanover's enrollment, and I understand the county's position. They've got, like, twenty trailers. We've got three. If you look at this from a countywide view—"

"It's not our job to take a countywide view!" Susan bellowed.

However, Richard's point had created doubt. Motives were being questioned, and questions weren't being answered. Rita spoke up: "Like Richard, I think we need a *moderate* response. Hanover Elementary has serious overcrowding problems, and even if we oppose it, we've got to understand what the county wants to do. This makes more sense than what they typically come up with. We should ask ourselves, would we fight the redistricting if we got Arborgate subdivision instead of apartments?"

Bessie said, "That's what we should do. Tell 'em we'll take Arborgate, and let the apartment people stay at Hanover. They're set to handle ESOL students over there," she said, referring to the program called English for Speakers of Other Languages. "Half the teachers there can't speak English themselves, for that matter."

"Compared to only one of ours," whispered Connie Parker.

"Which one are you talking about?" whispered Mary Anne Batterson (Grounds).

"Miz Ebonics." Meaning Avon Little.

Richard frowned. The meeting was turning ugly. "I move we table discussion."

"We need a plan of action," said Flora.

"Why don't we burn a cross?" Rita said.

"Rita!" Barbara snapped. "That's completely out of order. It's divisive." The ultimate put-down, since being divisive violated the basic unspoken PTO rule: consensus good, division bad. Four bedrooms good, two bedrooms bad, for that matter.

"We need to have a protest meeting about what the county is doing," said Bessie. "But we're not the Klan!"

Rita leaned over and whispered to Richard, "The Klan's more up-front about its politics."

Brenda Carroll (Bake Sales) said, "I think Richard's right. We need a resolution that says we're not prejudiced, 'cause *I'm* not prejudiced, and I don't think anyone else here is, either."

Richard spoke up. "All in favor of not being prejudiced—"

"Shush," Barbara said, unable to suppress a smile at her bad-boy board member. "I'm squashing that motion. It sounds—"

"Silly," offered Rebecca Ashley-Chastain (Gift Wrap).

"It's *quashing*, anyway," Stan said.

After Stan's motion to buy a welcome mat was ruled out of order, Susan made a motion calling on Barbara "to write a letter to the county on behalf of the PTO outlining its concerns."

Richard flipped through the bylaws while the board voted overwhelmingly to approve Susan's motion. He then stood and announced, "Madame President, point of order. The vote is illegal."

"Lordy, we're all goin' to jail," said Bessie. The room erupted in laughter.

Richard grinned. "Just a misdemeanor. However, bylaws require posting notice forty-eight hours before a called meeting before any action is taken. I don't believe that was done."

"I called every board member!" Barbara protested.

"Ha!" Rita shouted. "You didn't call me!"

"We can go out and post it right now," Bessie suggested. "The way this meeting is going, we'll be here long enough to make it legal."

"Furthermore," Richard said, "The board shouldn't take action on behalf of the entire organization. If we want the PTO to speak with one voice on this matter, let's take it to the general membership."

"Why are you fighting me?" Barbara cried out in frustration. "I'm trying to save this school!"

"I don't want to debate people's motives," Richard said. "But if you're going to do something, you need to do it right. Just play by the rules."

"What do you want?" Susan asked. "A bunch of crack dealers in the neighborhood?"

"Look, that school is overcrowded. The county is trying to provide an adequate education for those children. I'm not going to tell them they're not welcome. I have a rule: If it's not good enough for my child, then it's not good enough for anyone else's either. Based on what I'm hearing, it isn't that more kids are coming that bothers us, but *who they are*."

"That's a lie!" Susan bellowed.

Bessie was outraged. "Lord, he *is* callin' us the Klan!"

"What I believe is a lie?" Richard scoffed. "I hear the code words around here all the time. Low test scores. Section Eight housing. Crack dealers. Minorities. ESOL. Ms. Ebonics. The only people you're fooling are yourselves. We should accept the decision graciously and welcome the new students. Since this meeting is illegal, I'm leaving."

"You're being hypocritical," Susan charged.

"If that's true, it's because I have standards I failed to live up to. Now is a good day to change that."

That seemed like a great pissy-righteous note to end on, so he made his exit.

Rita hurried after him and tugged his arm to slow him down. "That was beautiful. You were the real leader in there. You should be PTO president."

"That meeting was a prime example of the Rutherfordism you've been talking about," he said.

"You see what's in store."

They walked out the front door. A fog had settled over the schoolyard, giving it an eerie, conspiratorial feel.

Bessie Harper came out a minute later. "Ha! Caught you. Plotting to fluoridate our water, I'll bet." The big woman shambled by them and turned back. "You should be ashamed of yourself, blocking the will of the majority on a technicality. I suppose the county will do what it wants anyway, though, so none of this matters, except I missed my favorite show. I hope my boys are in bed when I get home. Goodnight!" she sang, ending on a pleasant note, as was her style.

"You're this school's only hope," Rita whispered to Richard. "Malliford is going down the tubes, and it's got nothing to do with apartments. The county just recognizes it for what it's become. If she was a good principal, this wouldn't be happening. Or she'd make the best of it if it did. But I know her. She'll set up scapegoats for future failures. You and me, if she can. She's that vindictive, mark my word."

"I'm curious. If you feel so strongly, why didn't you ever serve as president?"

"Because she's the principal, obviously. You can, though."

"I'm not sure the clique would want me. Actually, they wouldn't."

"They shouldn't be calling the shots. Besides, they're stupid. Witness tonight. They're easy to outmaneuver," she said. "We can take 'em. Besides, you'll have the helicopter parents on your side. A lot of them don't like this mean-spirited shit. Think about it." With that, she walked off into the fog.

Richard started walking the other way, barely avoiding the rush of PWCs that burst out the front door. Their angry chatter echoed in his ears as he strolled through the mist past lonely streetlights. To amuse himself, he imagined helicopter parents: platoons of battle-hardened mommies rappelling from choppers onto the roof of the school to save their children from the evils of Rutherfordism.

When he got home, Nick was awake in bed, awaiting a lullaby. Anna Lee was reading. She didn't ask about the meeting; he didn't tell. They scarcely said a dozen words before going to bed; once there, they didn't touch. Five weeks, four days, and counting.

*   *   *

Over the next few days, there was a flurry of e-mails, tossed like punches in a prize fight. "The excessive influx of apartment population into Malliford would *further* skew our demographics, lower test scores, and devalue property," Susan wrote in an article she sent Richard for *Duck Call*. "Diversity is one thing, but Section 8 housing is too much!"

After ten seconds of careful consideration, Richard replied: "Hi Susan, No way I'm running this. Trying to keep black and brown kids out of our school is not a worthy effort."

Susan replied: "That's not what we're doing, and you damned well know it."

Richard's response: "I damned well don't."

He didn't bother telling her that she'd missed the deadline and *Duck Call* was already printed. He figured it was better to get the battle over with so he wouldn't have to fight it next month. Susan threatened to appeal her case to Barbara and Miz R, but Richard heard nothing more about it—or the Apartment War, for that matter. If there was a clandestine operation being waged, he figured he'd been completely closed off from it, circumscribed *and* out of the loop at the same time.

FOUR

For Richard, December proceeded like a chained beast dragged through mud. Usually he felt weary and defeated as Christmas approached, but this year a spark of anger lit his way against the darkness. The more he considered the xenophobic war against apartment kids being waged by the principal and PTO, the brighter it burned. Perhaps sensing this stirring in his soul, Rita constantly tugged his sleeve, demanding he step up and join the battle for the community's soul.

A week after the board meeting, Rita accosted him in the school hall at dismissal. She wore faded jeans and a black sweatshirt emblazoned with words, PHILOSOPHY: I'M IN IT FOR THE MONEY. "I meant what I said last Thursday," she said. "The PTO's goal should be to replace Miz Rutherford and bring the school into the 1960s."

Her favorite decade, no doubt. "I don't know—"

"She's a closet segregationist. Another reason to despise her." She adopted a pensive expression. "Then again, I've hated her for ten years, at least."

"That long?" Richard recoiled in amazement. "What happened?"

"I was breastfeeding Bertie in the cafeteria. Don't look so shocked. It was empty, no big deal. I'd been working with Catherine's fourth-grade class. Bertie was four months old and hungry. What could I do? I took the blanket I carried around and shut the doors behind me, went to a corner, and turned my back, hunched over, meek as a mouse. Ten seconds after Bertie starts, I hear the door creak like in a horror movie. *Her.* My blood curdled. Hell, my milk curdled. 'What are you doing?' she asks, real cold. 'Nursing my baby.'" Rita wagged her head back and forth as she recounted. "'You can't do that here. What if a child saw it?' 'Every child *has* seen it.' 'I don't allow it in my school. You must leave.' Just like that. That's how it started with me."

"I see. She's a baby-starver."

"Exactly!" Rita cried out. "You know, I've got a confession of sorts. Bertie was Stanford's going-away present. I was forty-two. Ah, such memories. Did you know we named him after Bertrand Russell? Everyone thinks he's named after the Sesame Street character. The gay one."

"You were divorced right after that?"

"More or less. Don't look at me that way. OK, we weren't big on formality. We're not really divorced because we never really married. You must think I'm just an old hippie."

"Old hippies are cool. Got any Grateful Dead concert tapes I can borrow?"

"Shut up. When I told him he'd knocked me up he said, 'That which does not kill us, makes us strong.' I said, 'Bullshit, asshole. That which does not kill us makes us sick.'" She sighed. "He still comes by sometimes, when his grad student du jour locks him out. What can I do? I'm a sucker for a bald philosophy professor who's always late on child support. He's ... familiar. It doesn't seem odd to crawl into bed and—"

"Too much information, Rita."

"We'll probably end up together, old and toothless. I hate sleeping alone. So, any time—"

"I need to get Nick," Richard blurted, then saw the principal approach. His Detention Avoidance Reflex caused him to step away from Rita. Miz R gave them a warden's smile, as if they were a pair of bumbling inmates caught trying to escape. Richard kept moving, leaving the two women who had long ago abandoned attempts at civility staring at each other. When he returned with his son, both were gone.

* * *

Thursday, December 16, brought a cold snap, stirring Nick's hopes for a white Christmas. That night, Richard sat through the PTO's general meeting expecting to hear Barbara's battle report in the Apartment War. Wouldn't it be *precious* if the PWCs used the meeting to showcase their unchristian attitude? *Suffer the children to come unto us. NOT!*

However, redistricting wasn't on the agenda, and Barbara didn't mention the issue. He was surprised; it was as if they'd given a war and nobody came. After adjournment, she introduced "our esteemed principal." To polite applause, Miz Rutherford took the podium. She spoke briefly about Malliford's wonderfulness, wished everyone season's greetings, and then introduced *Holiday for Ducks*. The curtain rose to reveal red-shirted second- and third-graders. In the middle of them stood Nick, looking splendid in his turtleneck. The music teacher, Mrs. Spinelli, stepped forward, baton in hand, red elf hat on head. "One and two and three and four—"

The children sang as Mrs. Leland played piano. Voices teetered on high notes, fell off and cracked, amusing and charming parents. The night's theme was twisted around humanity's undying need to sing another song. The Kwanzaa Karaoke Chorus sang about fruit juice and family as the loudspeaker—stuck in the beak of the huge painted Malliford Duck on the back wall—belted out the backbeat. Then came songs long on Santa and short on Jesus, courtesy of the fourth- and fifth-graders. Former breastfeeder Bertie Malloy pranced around the stage in a red and white outfit, cotton beard wisping off his chin. Rita beamed.

Eight antlered kids wore red suits that made them look like they'd been skinned. They fidgeted, waiting to perform "The Reindeer Cheer." One of them, Candace's daughter Samantha, held her red bulb nose on her face with her hand. When the big moment came, five reindeer advanced toward poster boards lying on the stage as their colleagues waved ersatz hooves over their heads and shouted encouragement. Antlers bumped and cameras flashed as the fourth-graders stooped to pick up cards. When they snapped up the boards in unison, audible gasps and bursts of high-pitched laughter rang throughout the room.

The reindeer had spelled out S-A-T-A-N.

Mrs. Spinelli furiously duck-walked to the stage and tugged feet to correct the sacrilegious spelling. The reindeer stood cluelessly for a moment, and then the last *A* saw the problem. Grinning, he switched places with his neighbor, spelling SANAT. Mrs. Spinelli gestured furiously until they had SANTA.

Shortly after that, Bertie's beard fell off. 'Twas a program to remember.

Afterward, Richard gathered up his son. Funky Glasses, alone at the moment, approached them. Her tight red dress revealed a drop-dead figure. "Hi Teresa," Richard said, glad that he'd snooped around and learned her name from Rita.

She sidled up to him, brushing her cleavage against his right arm. "Tell the truth," she teased. "Did you switch the cards? Do you have it in for Santa?"

Anna Lee appeared at his side and elbowed him sharply. In a harsh whisper, she said, "Kids are here, remember. Ixnay on your heartwarming Anta-

Say story," ignoring the fact that Nick was more fluent in pig Latin than either of his parents.

"You have no idea," he told Teresa with a pained smile. He was going to introduce Anna Lee, but his wife had turned away to greet a neighbor.

"Well. Happy all-purpose holiday greeting, Teresa."

"Happy all-purpose holidays to you, too, Richard." Teresa gave him a mistletoe smile and retreated into the crowd.

Scowling, Anna Lee turned back to Richard. "Who was *that*?"

"Teresa Keller," he said, trying to sound nonchalant as he cast a wistful glance at the woman sashaying out into the hall.

"Sure is friendly," Anna Lee said, narrowing her eyes.

"I hadn't noticed."

"Liar. I saw the way she looked at you."

"What way?"

Nick chose that moment to separate from his parents.

Anna Lee chased him down. "We're going to have to call the North Pole," she warned, reaching into her purse for the cell phone. The ploy had worked so far, but Nick was showing signs of agnosticism, which his mother blamed on Richard.

On the way out of the cafetorium, Richard saw Miz Rutherford in animated conversation with Mrs. Spinelli. The principal looked furious. Could it be ... *Satan*?

They walked home. After Nick was tucked into bed, Anna Lee stuck her head in Richard's office door, *Forbes* magazine in hand, and hissed, "You can't wait to tell him about Santa and ruin everything, can you?"

"By the time I tell him, everything will already be ruined."

"That's a nasty way to look at it. Admit it. You loved it when the reindeer spelled Satan."

"I can't help it if I'm an emotional cripple with no real friends."

She turned on her heel, leaving him to stare at the wall. Yes, he did have a story for Nick. After all, how many people could say they'd watched Santa die?

* * *

"Quit being a mopey bastard and help us get a tree," Anna Lee told Richard after dinner Friday night. "Call a cease fire in your war on Christmas."

"Cease fire?" he said, his expression incredulous. "If anything, I'm a prisoner of war."

"Only because you're an enemy combatant."

Nevertheless, he relented, and the three Grays piled into the Caravan for the drive to a nearby strip mall, where a man named Shepherd sold trees in the parking lot. Richard walked around with his hands in his pockets and surveyed the darkness beyond the reach of portable spotlights. Anna Lee and Nick picked out a bushy green spruce. Shepherd's assistant, a young Latino—a boy, really—wore a yellow nylon windbreaker and blue ski cap. The long-haired youth tied the tree atop the minivan. As the Grays drove off, he warmed his hands over a barrel fire.

Back home, Richard hauled the tree inside and set it up, leaning it this way and that until it was just so. He tightened the set-screws and retreated to his office, having declined to help with decorations. Anna Lee followed. "Your lack of holiday spirit is your deepest, darkest character defect," she told him from the door as he stared at the computer screen, reading news of a distant conflict. "One of them, anyway."

He waved her off like a fly, but she wasn't going. "Sometimes I think you're deranged," she said. "It's sacrilegious. Christmas is not 'the whoring of Christ's legacy.'"

She'd given up long ago trying to get him to appreciate the birth of her savior, so he didn't see why she was revisiting the subject. "I can't help how I feel," he said. "I'll try to behave and not use my mental illness as a weapon of mass destruction."

She shook her head. "This joking about mental illness isn't good." She drummed her fingers on the door frame. "Nick thinks you've been drinking lately, the way you talk to him."

That stung. He'd quit drinking when Nick was still in the womb, to show solidarity with his pregnant wife. He'd never gone back to it, since father-hood required the alertness of a fireman on call. His father had been a mean drunk, though not a constant one, and he'd vowed never to let Nick see him under the influence. Bad enough to be a loser without being a surly, snarling one. "I hope you didn't give him that idea."

"I tell him you're not yourself."

"Who do you think I am?"

She sighed in exasperation. "It's supposed to be the happiest time of the year, and you go out of your way to drag everyone down."

"Just think of it as the flu. I'll be well by Groundhog Day."

"I wish our insurance paid for counseling."

"I have work to do."

After all, his father always said work was the best therapy, the crazy bastard.

*   *   *

That evening, Richard got the phone call he'd been dreading—his mother's annual entreaty for him to come visit for the holidays. Beth and Roy Gray had recently moved back to Ridalia, Missouri, where Richard had spent his first five years. Their younger son had no intention of returning to that place. "No," he said when his mother repeated her request.

"Come on. I don't get to see enough of my grandchildren, especially Nicky," she said.

"You can come down here. You're retired."

"I did. It's your turn to come up."

"Not this year."

An awkward silence followed. Finally, Beth said, "Roy's somewhere around here. You want to talk to him?"

Of course not. What part of *estranged* did she not understand? "No, I'm good." More silence.

"He says to say Hello." Beth said.

Richard stifled a laugh. "I'm sure you'll tell him I did the same."

They said goodbye and Richard heaved a sigh of relief.

Not surprisingly, Anna Lee was glad Richard didn't want to travel to Missouri. After listening in on the call, she leaned on his office doorway and said, "It's a horribly long road trip. And I'm not comfortable around your father."

"Just because he's a bitter, cynical man who gives you the creeps and says nasty things about the Chamber of Commerce and only talks to me when he has to walk past me to get where he's going?"

"Well, yeah. And I'm not terribly fond of your brother, either. He's on his third wife and can't stop talking about how he's going to take over Ridalia in revenge for something only a Gray would understand." After a moment, she added, "I like your mother, though."

*   *   *

Sunday morning, Christmas Eve: Richard looked up from the *Sentinel* across the kitchen table to Anna Lee and announced, "I'm not going to your parents' house for Christmas, either."

Her eyes widened. "Why?"

"I need time to myself. There's stuff to do around here. I could paint the halls." That had a nice holiday ring to it. "Maybe feed the hungry."

"Feed the hungry." The ploy he'd used last year to avoid Thanksgiving at her parents' house. He'd gone down on the south side of Gresham County, past Bonaire, to the Church of Light Shelter and cleaned up after a bunch of homeless people. "I recall the reward for your good work was a nasty bout of flu. Charity begins at home."

Nick showed up at the breakfast table, prompting his father to say, "I don't drink."

"I never said you did."

Richard gave Anna Lee the evil eye. "I'm just not feeling good lately."

"I hope you feel better soon," said Nick.

"Thank you."

"He'll cheer up when we go over to Grandma and Grandpa's house. Won't you, honey?"

Richard resented her use of the kid as a crowbar. "I'm not going. Like I said."

"You have to, Daddy! Uncle Raymond and Uncle Joe don't come any more." This was a consequence of divorce, which Richard blamed on the disagreeable natures of Anna Lee's sisters. "Who will put the toys together if you don't?" Nick implored.

Richard laughed. "My boy. You put everything in perspective."

Moments later, while Nick was eating cereal, he paused with spoon between bowl and mouth. "Daddy, did you believe in Santa when you were a kid?"

"I wasn't a good boy," Richard said, "so I always had doubts." Anna Lee looked askance at him and shook her head. "If you don't believe me, ask my dad," he added.

"About your doubts, or being a good boy?" his wife asked.

"Either."

There was a momentary silence, then came the sound of drumming fingers on the table. Anna Lee's. "Didn't you get a movie for Nick?"

"*My Favorite Martian.*"

"Why don't we let him watch it after breakfast?"

The voltmeter on Richard's psyche twitched. This was as close to making a pass at him as she came. It seemed to come out of nowhere, but who was he to complain? Still, how could he trust her? It had been so long since they'd made love he didn't know the signals any more.

As soon as he finished eating, Nick grabbed the DVD and put it in the player before anyone could think of chores he hadn't done. Anna Lee stood in the hall and beckoned Richard to follow her to the master bedroom. She clicked the door shut, but the look on her face was more anxious than amorous. She sat on the bed. Her clothes stayed on.

"What?" he asked.

"Let's talk."

Ick. He felt betrayed. "Talk? Why?"

"Why not?"

He hemmed and hawed his way through the answer, but her little double cross put him in a foul and truthful mood. "I'm not sure you—I don't know. I just don't feel right. You're down on me so much, it seems like a permanent thing." After a deep breath, he said, "Like you don't love me."

She blinked, her eyes wide in surprise. "What gave you that idea?"

"What doesn't?" This seemed like a defining moment. He just wished he knew the word he was looking for. He felt like he'd taken a wrong turn and gotten lost in the conversation. Maybe he didn't mean this. Maybe he didn't know what he meant, or what he wanted.

"I'm sorry you think I'm your problem, but I do love you. You don't act like you love *me* most of the time."

"That's because I'm an emotional cripple with no real friends."

She pounded the comforter with both fists. "Will you quit saying that?" She took a deep breath. "Look, I'm sorry I ever said that. I take it back. Please stop beating me over the head with it. I'll never say it again. Gawd."

He started to leave. She grabbed his arm and tugged him off balance; he fell back on the bed.

"I'm sorry," she said, nuzzling him. "Sorry." She kissed his lips.

She broke away and unbuttoned her blouse. Was she preparing for pity sex? Make-up sex? Save-the-marriage sex? He wasn't sure which, but at least it would be sex. Or was she going to take a shower? Distrustful, he waited until she stripped completely naked before he took off his clothes. She hugged him, kissed him lightly, no tongue. When they coupled, she put more effort into it this time, even throwing in a few new moves, or ones so old he'd forgotten them.

"I love you," she insisted in the middle of the act.

"I love you, too," he retorted.

Thus was their leaky tire of a marriage patched, and Richard knew he'd be making the crosstown trip to her parents' house the next day. That was the wordless deal.

Still, he felt so ... *used.*

He reclined with his hands behind his head. "Do you realize it's been eight weeks since we made love?"

"No way."

"Yup."

She regarded him as though he were daft. "That can't be right."

"Not right, but possible. Halloween, while Nick was at Ethan's party. Didn't you know you cut me off for two months? Jeez, you didn't get any pleasure from it. What a wasted effort."

"Don't be hateful."

"You must have me confused with someone else."

She gave him a dirty look. "Don't even joke about that."

"*Hmmph.*"

An awkward moment passed before she said, "Let's talk about something else."

Both of them stared at the ceiling for a minute before Anna Lee said, "Tell me more about Santa Claus. I mean, all I know is that a dime-store Santa died when you were five, and supposedly that was a traumatic event. I always thought it should have been one of those things you look back on and laugh. I mean, especially you. Instead, it ruined your life somehow."

"It's what happened afterward that makes the tale ... *interesting*." He shuddered. "And call no life ruined until it's done, dear."

He took a moment to reflect, then pulled his hands from behind his head and pointed fists toward the ceiling as he started blurting out the tale. "OK, so Santa's an old drunk on his last legs, back by the dairy case at the IGA supermarket in Ridalia, cotton beard and a cheap suit, sneaking a drink. I ask him for a Tonka truck or whatever it is I want that day. He says, 'Take my bell.' So I'm ringing it, doing his job. A few seconds later, he clutches his chest and says, 'Help me, boy,' and keels over at my feet. Then there's this nasty smell I'll never forget. I guess everything inside him was coming out."

Anna Lee wrinkled her nose. "Then what did you do?"

"Mom shows up and drags me off just as everybody's gathering around. Somebody says he's dead. I cry. She lets me keep the bell. I'm thinking it's the only thing I'll get for Christmas."

"So Santa's death permanently scarred you? I don't see it."

"There's a difference between finding out Santa doesn't exist and watching him die, that's all I'm saying. The next day, Show and Tell in kindergarten. Last day before the holiday. Guess what I bring?"

"Santa's bell."

"There are things those five-year-olds need to know, and I'm the one to tell 'em. I got the proof and I'm gonna be like Daddy, the big-shot journalist. This is where things get strange and ugly. I stand up and tell my classmates Santa Claus is dead and they won't get anything unless they work a deal with their parents, like I did. No one wants to hear this, especially not Mrs. Selck, the old bitch. She tries to muzzle me—"

"What do you mean, muzzle you?"

"She clamps her hand over my mouth."

Anna Lee sat up. "That's terrible! How could she—"

"Back in the day, you know. Anyway, I bit her."

"Ouch."

"*Ouch me*. Even though she started it, I'm the one who has to go see the principal ... but not until after school. Very cruel and unusual, to make me dread that trip unto the end of my day, but she wants to make me sweat. Or ... she's got a deal with the principal. Wilkerson." He spat the name. "This I realize later, of course."

"A deal?"

He waved his hand. "You'll see. Eventually, the dismissal bell rings. Outside the kindergarten classroom window, big fat snowflakes are falling. It's a friggin' winter wonderland. I should be out throwing snowballs. Instead, Selck marches me to the office, and there I sit while other kids flee the building. Wilkerson comes out of his inner sanctum, looks at me like I'm food, gets on the PA and tells employees to go home, because of the weather. He puts me in his office, leaves again. My teeth chatter. I'm very afraid."

Richard took a deep breath before continuing. "Wilkerson turns out all the lights and locks the doors. He sits down beside me and tells me I'm very bad, and he's going to punish me and it's going to hurt. He lets that sink in. Then he grabs me and tells me he's taking me to Corey and no one will ever see me again. How do I like that?"

"Who's Corey?"

"Don't know. But I think he and Corey are going to hurt me. Cause he was being scary, way beyond old-school scary. Then he tells me to pull down my pants."

"Oh God."

"He takes off his belt. At that point, I'm thinking it's just a normal, everyday whipping. But then he starts taking off *his* pants."

She grimaces. "So you're both—"

"I keep my pants on. I decide he doesn't have a right to spank me."

"That is *so you*."

"He grabs me by the scruff of the neck, and then ... a bell buzzes. This breaks his concentration and I run for it—I had a lot of experience running away from whippings—and I get out of the office and into the hall. I see the mailman, Mr. Parker, standing at the door. Wilkerson yells for me to come back. He can't follow me, because he's trouser-challenged. I run to the door and open it. The mailman asks what's going on, but I don't stop to tell him. I run all the way home, which was only two blocks away, thank God."

She stared at him wide-eyed. "Wow."

"I had no idea what he was up to until I got older and figured out how perverted people could be. He wasn't even a nice molester. No candy. Fear was his deal. He got off on causing fear. Anyway, I'm in trouble for coming home late. I tell Mom the principal is going to whip me for telling kids about Santa Claus. She calls Dad, and they have this big argument. Mom's yelling that Wilkerson can't do that, and I'm thinking I might be getting out of a beating from the principal, and on the other hand I might get one from Dad when he gets home. She tells me everything's going to be all right. Famous last words. A little while later, Dad pulls into the driveway. It's around dusk, and I'm up on the front porch throwing snowballs at Nazi soldiers."

"Doing *what?*"

"Fighting Hitler. It's a constant battle, believe me. At the time, he was staging a comeback. This was before the Russians showed off his skull."

"Uh-huh."

"The soldiers were imaginary, of course."

"Good. I was worried. Go on."

"Dad stomps up the steps and turns toward me. I realize it's an attack and decide to be somewhere else. I'm boxed in by the porch railing, so I start to climb over it. Before I can break on through to the other side, he kicks me with great force and violence. I fly off the porch into a bush." He paused. "I fell out of the bush onto my head and I saw stars so I wasn't clear on what happened next. Mom came out and there was yelling. I thought he was beating her, too, but he wasn't."

"You said he got violent when he got drunk, but if he was coming home from work—"

"He was fired that day."

"What? Why?"

"Who, what, when, where, why. A lot of stuff I still don't understand. It was a dark day all around. Apparently, Wilkerson got him fired—which is ironic and evil, but nobody would talk about it. As near as I can figure, it was some kind of preemptive reaction."

"So that's why your family is so ..."

"Fucked-up is the term you're looking for. To complicate matters, Dad had been writing pro-civil rights editorials, and he wasn't popular with the Chamber of Commerce types." He gave her a reproachful smirk. "Then again, maybe he was drinking on the job, although that was common back then. Anyway, he blamed me for pissing off the principal and running away, not taking my punishment like a man. I guess I *would* have taken it like a man if I'd stuck around."

She groaned. "That was so wrong of your father."

"He had his reasons. Not good ones, but reasons nonetheless. Once when he was drunk he said, 'You're not the hill I wanted to die on.'"

"What does that mean?"

"I wasn't worth fighting for. But he got caught by shrapnel anyway, I reckon."

"That's horrible."

"Yeah. I keep my distance and he keeps his."

"What about Reggie?"

"Dad channeled whatever fatherly feelings he had toward his oldest son."

"And you carry all this around with you."

Richard gave out a dry chuckle. "Yeah," he said ruefully. "It is always with me. I dream about it all the time, what would have happened if I hadn't made a run for it."

"What?"

"Dying. I dream of dying. They say if you die in your dreams you die in real life, but I've died a thousand deaths in my fitful sleep."

"I guess you wish you'd kept quiet about Santa Claus."

"Not really. Couldn't do that anyway, dear. Not in my nature. You should know that by now."

She shrugged. "So what happened then?"

"Dad took a job as a supervisor in a printing plant about thirty miles away. Not as much prestige, but it was a living, I guess. We moved over the holidays. I didn't go back to Warsaw School. Later, we found out Wilkerson left town about the same time we did, so—"

"In the middle of the school year?"

"Must have had skeletons in his closet."

"You need closure," Anna Lee said, sitting up and then reaching for her bra on the floor. She put it on backwards and spun it around. "But how do you get it?"

"Don't know," Richard said. "Don't know. ... Now the rest of my family is back in Ridalia. Reggie wants to restore our good name. That's why he moved there and started taking over the town. That and greed."

"And your parents moved back into the old house last year."

"At Reggie's urging, after Mom retired from teaching."

"And you've never gone back to Ridalia?"

Hmm. Some things were best left unsaid. "Too many ghosts."

"I have a question. You picked the name Nicholas. Why?"

He thought for a moment and bit his lip before saying, "Maybe I wanted Santa Claus to live, after all."

FIVE

Thursday, January 13, was chilly with slate-grey skies, cold enough to hint of snow. After lunch, Richard pulled on his parka and walked up to Malliford to attend Nick's second-grade honors assembly. Polly was pecking away at her keyboard when he entered the office to check the mail in his PTO file. After pocketing a note from Brenda Carroll about the upcoming bake sale, he glanced at the office wall. He squinted and then tilted his head like a puzzled dog, having noticed for the first time that the four stars painted above the school's name were lopsided.

While he waited for two parents to sign the visitors' log, he asked Polly about this oddity.

"We're holding a space for a fifth star," she said, sounding like she expected its delivery any day.

"Oh," Richard replied, making his mouth into a circle.

When he turned his attention to the logbook, his eyes bugged out. Sitting fat and squalid at the bottom of the day's first page, was Joey Armstrong's signature. Years ago, Richard had worked with the *Sentinel* photographer, a grizzled Vietnam vet with rumpled khakis, a rank old safari vest, and two Nikons hanging from his neck. *Sentinel* education reporter Deanna Richardson had signed in, too—during that morning's fifth-grade assembly, according to the schedule taped to the counter.

What was going on? A 300,000-circulation newspaper didn't cover grade-school assemblies during the course of a normal business day. Richard had no time to ponder this mystery, however. Nick's assembly was due to start. He signed his name and hustled out into the hall.

"Richard!" Rita's grey-streaked ponytail bobbed and her sneakers squeaked as she ran up to him, catching him outside the computer lab. Her eyes danced with gleeful outrage. "She's *really* done it this time!"

Richard looked over his glasses at her, awaiting further explanation.

"Rutherford found out who switched letters at the holiday program," she said.

"Ah. I always suspected foul play."

"Spencer Hadley, in Bertie's class. She put him on the chain gang."

"Chain gang?"

"That's what Stan's calling it. Spencer has to work outdoors, in public, with a shovel and wear an orange vest like he's a criminal. She's calling it 'community service.' He began yesterday. Our principal, Lizzie Warden, pointed him out to kids, who took her cue and started taunting him while she watched and laughed. His mother is livid. He was working in the parking lot, and he almost got hit by a minivan. Can you believe she's putting kids out in traffic? It's an outrage. I can't believe you didn't know. What do we do?"

"Well, *someone* did *something*. A reporter was here during the fifth-grade assembly."

"Get out!" She punched Richard on the arm. "You're kidding."

He shook his head while rubbing his arm.

"Hold on." With a Captain Kirk gesture, she whipped out her cell phone from a jacket pocket and speed-dialed. "Sally, it's Rita. Did you see a reporter here this morning? No, I didn't make it. I had to—"

Her eyes widened as she listened. She stuck her finger in her free ear when a line of first graders passed by. "OK. I gotta go. Talk to you later. *I gotta go.* Bye. *Really.* Later. Gotta go." She rolled her eyes and shuddered. Her eyelids fluttered, too. For a moment, Richard thought she was having a seizure—or perhaps an ecstasy of contempt.

"I *knew* I should have attended Bertie's assembly," Rita said. "You were right. Somebody called the newspaper. Sally thinks it was Spencer's mom, but I bet it was Stan. Spencer smuggled his orange vest into the assembly and then, when he got to the stage to receive his Academics Award, he slipped it on. They'd already stripped him from the Principal's Award list even though he's made all A's since first grade. He's too smart for this place ... maybe too smart for his own good. Anyway, Mrs. Cates didn't see it in time, and Mrs. Baines handed him his certificate. He pounded his chest and said, 'I wear your scorn like a badge of honor,' like he's Patrick Henry—"

"Or Dan Quayle."

"—and Mrs. Cates got in his face, yelling at him to take it off, just as the photographer took the picture. Sally said it should be a great shot." She paused to savor the anarchy of the moment, and then frowned in disapproval. "This is a publicity nightmare for Marine Antoinette."

Richard glanced at his watch. "I'll miss the awards," he said, backpedaling toward the cafetorium.

When he entered the cafetorium, Miz Rutherford was speaking: "Please give Mrs. Vandenburg an extra round of applause, since she's our Teacher of the Year." Richard clapped unenthusiastically; Joyce Vandenburg had never impressed him, and he was glad Nick had Mrs. Leland instead of her. Rita had claimed the flat-faced, childless second-grade teacher won the award because she did and thought as her boss commanded, adding mind control to the principal's ever-growing list of sins.

Unlike the fifth-grade fiasco, the second-grade assembly went smoothly. Nick got all A's and made Principal's List for academics and good behavior. The boy gave a gap-tooth grin from the stage as Richard snapped a photo of him accepting his certificate from Miz Rutherford.

On the way out, Richard ran into Jane Baumgartner, sister to Nick's teacher and therefore an invaluable source of high-quality gossip about the school. Jane, a strawberry blonde with one of the world's great button noses, gave him background: Miz Rutherford and the Hadleys had feuded ever since Spencer was in kindergarten, when the principal was forced to substitute teach in his class and he corrected her for calling a spider an insect. Neither party ever got over the confrontation.

"So does she know a spider isn't an insect now?" Richard asked.

Jane shrugged. "Don't know. She told Spencer's mom he was too smart for his own good back then, and again this year. And she's determined to prove it."

"Does this latest act of mischief justify turning Spider-man into Cool Hand Luke?"

She laughed. "Cool Hand Luke. I like that."

Richard went home and e-mailed his photo to Anna Lee at work. She promptly replied: "I'll pick up pizza on way home to honor The Boy."

That afternoon, when Richard returned to school to pick up Nick, he saw an ill-humored Spencer Hadley storm out the door in his road-crew vest, along with a similarly attired tall black kid with a blank expression. Two other African-American boys in orange vests followed, their breath steaming the air. All were fifth- or sixth-graders and carried shovels. Another black kid appeared around the corner of the building, pushing a wheelbarrow. They were heading toward the dirt pile left by county workers. Suddenly Cool Hand Luke didn't seem so cool. Richard had always considered Miz Rutherford a by-the-book principal. Turned out the book was *I Am a Fugitive From a Georgia Chain Gang!*

Casting a worried glance over his shoulder, Richard entered the building. Lizzie Warden stood by the door wearing a triumphant smile and gazing out upon the detainees.

"Miz Rutherford," he said, nodding toward the work crew. "I don't like what I see out there. This is a school, not a prison."

Her smile dissolved, her jaw muscles bulged, and her lips parted, but she didn't speak. Instead, she gave him a malignant stare that had no place in an elementary school—or anywhere outside a war zone, prison, or mental hospital. Her crazed-bitch look, Rita called it. As the dismissal bell rang, a grimace of horror replaced it, and she said, "What the ..."

Richard turned to follow her gaze as a white Ford Crown Victoria hurtled through the loop, nearly sideswiping a parked bus. The car hit the inner curb with a *clang* and a wheel cover rattled off, rolling between buses, up onto the sidewalk. A rangy white safety cadet in basketball shoes kicked at it awkwardly in self-defense. A horn honked as the driver double-parked beside a bus, blocking traffic in a fascinating mix of poor timing and bad driving.

"I don't believe it," Miz R growled. "He never comes here."

Spencer, loading dirt into a wheelbarrow in desultory fashion, stopped and leaned on his shovel handle as he regarded the heavyset black man in a dark suit barreling up the walk. The other chain gang members did likewise. The man stopped to stare at them in disbelief, then hustled toward the building. The principal mustered her outrage as he lunged in. "You can't park—"

"In your office, Miz Rutherford!" he roared. "Now!"

She meekly complied. Richard marveled at this most unlikely sight even as he was pushed to the wall by the daily river of bus riders streaming by: first kindergartners, then primary students, and finally older kids, in a rising flood bursting through a levee.

Mrs. Leland appeared beside him. "Did I see what I think I saw?"

"I think so. Who is he?"

"Her boss," said Nick's teacher. "Curtis Blodgett, district supervisor. He never comes unless there's trouble."

"He was unhappy. Threw a hubcap and blocked the buses."

"I hear there's going to be something in the *Sentinel.*"

He nodded. "Bad news travels fast."

*   *   *

The next morning, after waking Nick, Richard shuffled out into the frosty morning to retrieve the paper. The Malliford story was on the front page of the *Sentinel*'s local section, with Joey Armstrong's absurdly comic yet dreadful photo of the ample Mrs. Cates grabbing Spencer's vest, looking like she was shaking a bobble-head doll. Over the picture, a bold headline: "Chain Gang Elementary?" Under it, in smaller type: "*School's Hard Line on Discipline Racist, Critics Say.*"

According to Jeannette Hadley, her son's punishment was "barbaric and inhumane." Stan gave the story its racial context, pointing out, "The chain gang is 80 percent black, and you can bet it will stay filled up with black kids." Miz Rutherford claimed she was only doing what the community wanted her to do and that the vests were for the students' safety. She cut the interview short "to attend another assembly for our wonderful children, who have done so well."

The county's position?

"I may have problems with this," said Superintendent Harold Johnson.

I'll bet you do, once you see the coverage. Richard left the paper folded so Anna Lee could see the article. She came into the kitchen a few minutes later and fixed herself a bagel with cream cheese and a glass of orange juice. She stopped chewing when she saw the story. Richard sipped coffee and watched her read.

She looked up. "I don't think Miz Rutherford is doing anything wrong."

"Of course you don't, dear."

"Kids need to learn consequences."

"So do adults."

The phone rang. Richard got up to answer it. "Hello?"

"Fight the power!" Rita declared. "Just had to say that. Gotta go!" Richard heard a car horn blare just before she hung up.

"Who was that?" Anna Lee asked when Richard returned to the table.

"Communist Party. They want me to join."

"*Hmmph.* Usually they just want old clothes."

*   *   *

That afternoon three TV trucks were parked on Windamere, disrupting school traffic. The chain gangs failed to appear, however, having been hastily abolished by central office edict. Channel Six's Trevor Medford and his colleagues were no doubt tremendously disappointed to be interviewing parents instead of prisoners—law-and-order parents, at that. Barbara and Susan stood on the sidewalk along with two other PWC wannabes who held placards saying WE LOVE MALLIFORD and SUPPORT OUR SCHOOL. Richard crossed the street by the dingy old *School of Excellence* sign to avoid the counter-protest and cameras.

That evening, Richard watched "Are There Chain Gangs at a Local Elementary School?" on Channel Six's *Headliner News*. Lacking current footage to go with the story, a news producer with a wicked sense of humor set up the piece with grainy old newsreel footage of a real chain gang. Barbara and Susan looked like racist idiots for endorsing Miz Rutherford's "alternative sentencing." While the beleaguered principal was unavailable for comment, Stan was more than happy to repeat what he'd told the *Sentinel* reporter. On camera, he looked like a radical union organizer or an angry left-wing professor, gesturing vehemently and speaking loudly. A little unsettling, in fact.

The coverage died quickly once the chain gang was abolished, but Malliford was stuck with that horrible nickname from then on. And it would not be the last the world would hear from the brilliant, maladjusted Spencer Hadley. Miz Rutherford had made a crucial error when he was in kindergarten and compounded it by refusing to learn the lesson he'd tried to teach her back then: Never mistake a spider for a fly.

* * *

January's *Duck Call* contained a reformist editorial by Richard entitled "What Will It Take to Make Malliford a Five-Star School?" Basing his piece on what he'd learned at December's Northside Parent Council meeting, he called on the school's administration and teachers to begin the practice of discussing standardized test scores with parents, implement a reading enhancement program, remodel the media center, and work with the PTO to improve library holdings. He modestly placed it on the lower half of page three.

While Miz Rutherford did not speak to Richard about his column, Barbara was sputtering in rage when she called him the afternoon the newsletter came out. Usually cordial, the PTO president started by saying, "I should just be done with this madness and fire you!"

"Go ahead," said Richard. "Make my day."

"You! You're more trouble than you're worth. Submit your resignation. Right now!"

"No, you have to fire me," he insisted.

She whimpered in despair. "I don't know how to. And I don't have anyone to take your place."

"You could do it," Richard suggested brightly.

"You'd like that, wouldn't you? Let me tell you this: You are a disruptive, negative influence, young man." She sounded like she was talking to her son, although they were about the same age. "We didn't push Chantilly Arms at December's general meeting because we were afraid you'd do something embarrassing and nasty."

"Well, what's nasty depends on your point of view, I suppose."

She sighed. Or huffed. "I met privately with the superintendent, but it didn't go well. Listen up, Buster. If this school goes straight to hell, I'm holding you responsible. And for the record, Miz R is quite displeased. She called you 'a loose cannon on a rolling deck.'"

"At least she admits the deck's rolling."

*   *   *

Richard didn't make it to February's sparsely attended PTO board meeting, which had what he considered a boring and dangerous agenda. The only major item on it was selection of a nominating committee for next year's officers. Serving on this panel was a thankless—even hazardous—task, since committee members were often forced to cannibalize their own ranks to come up with enough willing victims ... uh, new leaders ... to manage the organization in the coming school year. Richard knew from experience that it could take a while to talk skittish board members into serving on it. Therefore, Barbara and Miz Rutherford must have been alarmed when Rita Malloy popped out of her chair and immediately volunteered to chair the nominating committee. Although some PWCs grumbled, no one challenged her.

The next morning, Rita caught up to Richard in the hall at school and hummed "Hail to the Chief" in his ear, then pinched his ass.

"Oh no you didn't!" he shouted after her as she bustled off.

"Not yet," she called out over her shoulder. "But I will."

*   *   *

In mid-February, the Apartment War ended. The Gresham County School Board—having held hearings and listened to protests from throughout the county, including a few from Windamere Heights—unanimously ratified its redistricting plan. Residents of Chantilly Arms would attend Malliford next year, and that was that. Miz Rutherford was left to sputter in her office and figure out how to make room for this Malliford boatlift and to limit the damage the hip-hoppers and Hispanics would cause to her precious reputation.

* * *

On the afternoon of February 24, Rita called Richard at home and said, "The PTO presidency is yours if you want it. And you want it."

"I—"

"You'd better, after what I went through. It's either you or Susan Gunther, who was being pushed hard by *certain people*. It was a four-three vote for you, recast to make it unanimous. Like Barbara puts it, 'Consensus good, division bad.'" Rita grunted these last words.

Silence.

"So, will you accept? ... Hello, Richard?"

"I'd be crazy to do it."

"Of course you are! Barbara's gonna *love* this. Not! You know what's funny? The swing vote was Arlene Bailey. She thought it would be good to have a man in the position. I think she has a crush on you. That makes me wonder what kind of position—"

"Stop."

"You stay away from her. That's not what you're here for."

"You have a filthy mind. She's old enough to be my—"

"*Sister*, Richard, *sister*. For God's sakes, she's my age."

"Really? *Hmm*."

"*Hmm* to you."

"Isn't she worried about how her boss will react?"

"Lizzie Warden has done everything she can to make Arlene miserable, so our Miss Bailey has nothing left to lose. Besides, she's working to get certified as an administrator. I think she's qualified to be a principal already. That's why Miz Rutherford doesn't trust her. She fears a coup. If we can get rid of her and get Arlene in her place, I'd die happy. And Arlene would be *sooo* grateful to you."

"Quit. I mean it."

"I know. You're a happily married man."

"Yes, I have been lately. And I will continue to be one until I tell Anna Lee I'm the new PTO president."

"Good luck with that. Well, I've got to round up some usual suspects slash willing victims to fill out the slate. Now that we've got you, everything else will fall into place."

"Bye," Richard said. After he hung up, he stared at the wall, thinking about how to break the news to his wife. He knew she wouldn't be happy to hear her underemployed husband had taken on another non-paying job. Should he apologize? Or maybe he should gloat: *Take that, o ye of little faith! Someone actually believes in me!*

Rita called again an hour later to say that the nominating committee had finished its business and Mrs. Vandenburg, its most troublesome member, reluctantly reported results to Miz Rutherford. "As I stepped outside, I heard a howl of anguish from the principal's office. It was inhuman, I tell you," Rita declared. "I love it!"

"You're having way too much fun with this," Richard said.

"Helen Bagby agreed to serve again as recording secretary. Candace Josey is vice president, Cindi Lou is corresponding secretary. They're on the nominating committee and ended up volunteering for next year so they could go home and fix dinner. They agreed after I assured them these were easy jobs. You have my permission to work them to death."

"You're evil, you know."

"I get that a lot. And you'll be interested to know that the new treasurer is—drumroll—Teresa Keller."

Richard's pulse quickened. His throat went dry.

"She talks about you all the time. Thinks you hung the moon. That's why she agreed to serve, to work with you. Hell, she came up to me a week ago when she heard I was on the nominating committee and said she'd be treasurer if you were the boss man. It was the easiest position to fill. She's got the cutest little girls. One's nicknamed Umbrella, or something ... Richard. Richard! You all right? Are you still there?"

* * *

When the time came, Richard neither gloated nor apologized to Anna Lee. He simply mentioned his nomination and his acceptance of it in a straightforward manner, curious to see how his wife would take the news of his honor/burden.

Not well, as it turned out.

"Are you insane?" Anna Lee shouted, standing in the kitchen that evening, dressed in her best blue business suit. She drummed the blue laminate countertop with her fingers and glanced around. For a moment, Richard feared she was looking for a butcher knife, but she stuck with words. "This isn't going to work. I can't believe you didn't talk to me about it!"

"It's my decision," he said, trying to sound calm and authoritative.

"I should have some say. What about your business? You're supposed to be building it up. We're going to have another child."

Richard's voice rose. "We are?"

"Well, eventually. Next year ... and that's soon, at least for people who bother to plan as opposed to merely screwing. I'm thirty-six. My clock's ticking. What you're doing runs counter to everything we've talked about." She shook her head. "God, they'll suck you dry. All volunteer organizations do. You can kiss next year goodbye."

Richard thought a chamber official should be more civic-minded, but he wasn't going to argue the point. "I won't do the newsletter next year, so it won't take much more time. No difference, really," he added in a near-mumble.

"Bullshit. Was this your idea?"

"Not exactly. More of a vast left-wing conspiracy."

She rolled her eyes in exasperation. "I don't see how you're going to be effective. You don't even like Miz Rutherford. I mean, you've got some mixed-up childhood issues—deep, dark issues, if you ask me—that I still don't even understand."

And never will. "Those are irrelevant. Anyway, I'm a guy. I don't have to like someone to get along with them."

"You think schools are prisons."

"I also think they shouldn't be."

The argument continued for a while. Anna Lee told him he was leading a doomed, quixotic protest; he claimed he was heading a genuine reform movement in the name of what was right and fine and fair, or something like that.

She didn't buy his lofty claims, so he changed tack, weighing his words carefully to say the wrong thing the right way: "We could use some clout next year, when it comes to class placement." (He felt guilty saying this, because teacher-shopping was very PWC-ish, not typically his style at all.)

She pursed her lips. "*Hmm.* I hadn't thought of that. It would be worth it to know Nick's going to have a good teacher next year. Makes all the difference in the world. Anybody but—"

"Now you don't have to worry about that," he said, refusing to believe they'd stick the PTO president's child in the worst teacher's classroom. Nobody was *that* stupid.

"This better work. But I have my doubts."

"You always do, dear."

"You sure there's no way out of it?"

"A deal's a deal," Richard said. "I gave my word."

"There's got to be something."

"Somebody could run against me and win, I suppose. But that's never happened."

*   *   *

The school seemed different the next morning. A red scar had replaced the dirt pile out front. Now it looked like someone was buried in the schoolyard. Richard made a mental note to see if Mrs. Vandenburg was alive, since Miz Rutherford seemed like the kind of person who would kill the bearer of bad news. Ms. Bailey, on bus duty, winked at Richard as he and Nick walked by. Like this was some kind of joke. If so, he didn't get it—unless *he* was the joke, being played on the principal.

Inside, the school seemed dingier and darker than usual, more oppressive now that this burden of bricks, this Malliford, had been placed on his shoulders. Nick scurried to his class, rushing by Rita, who was holding court in the foyer, within crowing distance of the principal's office. Her eyes lit up at the sight of Richard. With a speed and strength that surprised him, she reached out and dragged him into her circle, which included two stocky fifth-grade mothers he didn't recognize and the new treasurer, alluring as always. Teresa's funky glasses were gone. She wore jeans and a sweater, along with hiking boots. She looked athletic. Actually, *sporting* might be a better word. "You look different," he said.

"I had surgery."

He glanced down.

"Laser surgery on my *eyes*, silly."

"Oh, oh. Of course." He turned red as the women laughed.

"For myopia," Teresa said. "Is that what you have?"

"I have cornucopia," Richard said. "I see too much."

More laughter. "He's going to be great," one of the mothers told Rita.

Rita grinned at her protégé and reached up to massage his shoulder. "The best president ever."

"That makes me sound like the title of a Richard Scarry book." Pronounced *Scary*.

He was thinking maybe he should kill Rita and toss her in the shallow grave with Vandenburg when the click of high heels broke his concentration. Barbara Hodges, real estate nametag on her red blazer, skidded to a stop by the office door, and then tiptoed over to visit the rival faction. Her painted-on face looking harder than usual, as if she'd used enamel. "Hell-o, people," she said uncertainly. "Congratulations, I suppose." She offered a hand to Richard. "If you need anything, you know where to find me."

"On your cell phone, weaving in and out of traffic?"

"You're so bad," she said, grinning as she swatted him on the chest. "That's why I love you."

She turned and waved to the group with the back of her hand as she proceeded to the office to commiserate with the grieving principal.

Teresa looked Richard in the eye and said, "I'm glad we'll be working—"

The morning bell rang, causing her to shout.

"—together."

When the group broke up, Rita, Teresa, and Richard walked outside. Rita said she needed a moment with Richard. Teresa smiled and said goodbye. He watched her walk to the parking lot.

"Isn't she cute?" Rita asked.

"I hadn't noticed."

"Liar. I'll bet she's got a tattoo. If you're lucky, she'll show you."

That gave him something new to think about.

"Hey. Did you hear me?" She punched him on the arm.

"What? What?"

"Just be careful."

"I'm a happily married man."

"That's what they all say. To me, anyway." She glanced around for spies. "Have you gotten any feedback?"

"My wife isn't thrilled. What have you heard?"

"Those who still talk to me think it's great, though that number has dwindled since yesterday." She nodded toward the office. "Silence from the bunker. I think I nuked her winter. Maybe she'll retire."

"Dream on."

"Not a dream. A plan. Regime change is definitely on the agenda."

"That again? Look, I'm going to be president and you're going to help me, since you got me into this mess. But getting rid of her is above my pay-grade. Getting her to work with me, that's my agenda."

"You know the place would be better off without her."

"I'll fight her on the issues if I have to, not on whether she should be here or not. Not the hill I want to die on."

She gave him a piercing look, then softened her gaze. "You'll come around." After an awkward pause, she glanced at her watch. "Well, I've got to be at the gallery early." (Rita received a meager salary to manage the non-profit Prometheus Art Gallery in the city's trendy loft district.) "Let me know if you need anything."

"A way out of this would be nice."

She chuckled and turned away. He watched her swagger down the side-walk. She could be such an ass. That made him the leader of a rump government, he supposed. He wondered what Barbara thought, now that the uncool kids were taking over, and Stan and Rita would have their day. He needed the cool people on his side. Well, maybe not the cool people. The hardworking ones. He was afraid what he'd get instead would be misfits and cranks stumbling across his yard with their so-called great ideas. *Night of the Living Dead* meets *Revenge of the Nerds*. That would really suck, since he'd always wanted to be *The Road Warrior*—that is, until Mel Gibson turned out to be such an asshole.

SIX

Word of a Susan Gunther presidential candidacy roiled the waters of Malliford. PWCs were prepared to put her name forward in opposition to Richard's when the PTO's general membership voted. The rumor-fueled scenario called for a packed cafetorium and a bitter, divisive election in April, filled with name-calling and accusations—the most fun in years.

In hallway conversations, timid board members worried about the effects of an internecine war, but Rita dismissed their concerns with a brawler's laugh. "We'll be ready," she said. "Set the election for high noon." Then she tunelessly whistled the theme from *The Good, the Bad, and the Ugly*.

And so the stage was set for April's general meeting. Stan stood at the cafetorium door that evening handing out No-TV Week flyers to parents and students filing in. Despite a lack of support from the PTO and school administration, the gadfly had taken it upon himself to educate people on the pernicious effects of watching too much mindless fare: lower student achievement, obesity, increased violence, unwholesome sexuality. In short, TV made people fat, stupid, angry, and horny. Stan was diplomatic enough to avoid putting it that way. Barely.

Anna Lee was a no-show due to a work conflict. Richard was disappointed, even resentful, over her absence. Then again, she hadn't fully accepted his decision and half-joked she wasn't sure she'd vote for him.

Anxious about the coming showdown and feeling feisty, Richard grabbed a handful of flyers and stood across the entrance from Stan, urging people to turn off their TVs during the last week of April and "rediscover the real world." He figured he should have a platform, and No-TV Week was as good a cause as any. He'd given it prominent play in *Duck Call* and promised Stan PTO support next year, if elected.

Near the stage, Mrs. Vandenburg bent over and whispered to Miz Rutherford. Glaring at the leafletters, the principal rose from her seat and started toward them. Vice-principal Baines reached out and put a restraining hand on her boss's shoulder. Barbara then hustled over and huddled with school administrators. The PTO president pointed to the podium. The principal sat down, turning her back on the troublemakers and stiffening her shoulders.

"They won't support me on this, even though it would do more good for families and children than anything they've accomplished," Stan said, a defiant gleam in his eyes. "I'd like to see her come out against me. Just tell me to shut up and sit down and go on record in favor of mindless sex and violence and intellectual bankruptcy."

From the podium, Barbara wagged a finger at Richard and mouthed "bad boy" before she spoke into the microphone: "A quorum being present, I hereby call this meeting to order. Let all political activity cease."

"Ha!" Stan said loudly.

"Come on," Richard told him. "We'll give it a rest for now."

Stan handed out two more flyers and stepped away from the door, scowling.

Richard took a seat beside his fidgeting son. As they stood for the pledge, he looked around. No sign of Susan. He watched both entrances carefully, and after a few more minutes, concluded his would-be rival was a no-show.

Midway through the meeting, Rita announced the nominating committee's slate of officers. Following protocol, Barbara called for nominations from the floor. Silence. And so Richard became president-elect by acclamation. *Take that, PWCs!* Teresa smiled at him across the aisle and gave a thumbs-up. When Miz Rutherford took the podium, she congratulated Richard and the other newly-elected officers. As far as the average parent was concerned, Malliford was one big happy family.

When the meeting adjourned, Rita rushed over to Richard and said, "I thought the principal's face was going to crack when she smiled. Think of it! We won!"

"One battle does not a war make," Richard said.

"Cool it, Yoda."

Richard accepted congratulations on his way out of the cafetorium, and Nick endured several hair-touslings. During the walk home, Nick asked how much money his father would make as president and was disappointed at the answer.

Anna Lee was there when they returned to Applegate, and Nick gave her the news. "It was unanimous!" the boy exclaimed. "Everybody likes Daddy."

"So Susan didn't run," Anna Lee said, sounding mournful. "Congratulations, I guess."

Richard gave her a worried look. "Are you OK with this?"

"Oh, of course," she said, sarcasm seeping into her tone. "Thanks for asking."

*   *   *

April's No-TV Week was a disappointment to Stan. Only a few teachers cooperated with him, including Mrs. Leland and—surprise!—Bullfrog Eyes, Avon Little. The Grays participated, but Nick barely noticed, since he didn't watch much TV during the week and soccer season was in full swing. When Stan reported via e-mail that only thirty students turned in pledge cards, Richard said, "That's not so bad, considering."

"It's horrible, like a five percent turnout," Stan wrote.

"Next year will be better. It will be a really big deal," Richard assured him.

*   *   *

The giant mallard on the yellow cinder-block wall mural stared out balefully over the cafetorium crowd that had gathered for the May PTO meeting. Richard stood beneath it, accepting compliments and condolences from parents and teachers, then made his way toward Nick and Anna Lee, who sat in the middle of the room near the aisle. "Door hinge," Nick said as Richard took a seat.

"What?" Anna Lee asked.

"Everybody thinks that nothing rhymes with orange. Door hinge does, especially if you say it fast. Orange, orange, orange. Door hinge, door hinge, door hinge."

"This is good to know." She smiled at her husband and squeezed his hand. Such a cute couple. And happy, sort of. After Richard added a client and promised to get more next year when he gave up *Duck Call*, their love-making schedule was back to heartworm medication frequency, or better. Often enough to keep him alive, at least.

The cafetorium was packed, but PTO business was of no consequence to the parents, grandparents, and children who sat on the green molded plastic chairs, stood in the door blocking traffic, or skittered around on the polished floor. They were there to see fifth- and sixth-graders, currently rustling on stage behind the green curtain, who would perform *Rhapsody in Orange: A Musical Extravaganza.*

Mrs. Spinelli had performers in place at 6:30 p.m., and they would begin after a brief PTO meeting. Barbara rushed in late, patted her hair and smoothed down the skirt of her red suit, pulled a folder out of her satchel and gaveled the meeting to order. "Have I got a pledger?" A sixth-grader in a lime-green zoot suit appeared from behind the curtain, hand already placed over heart. After that, minutes were approved, and then Treasurer Sandra Cauthorn reported that the PTO wasn't broke. People applauded this good news, since solvency was by no means certain after the prior year's fiscal disaster. Then came the ceremony to install new officers. When his name was called, Richard stood beside Barbara and gazed out over the crowd at the big duck. He was sure the barnyard Big Brother was watching him, its eyes following his every move

The new officers recited the oath in unison, more or less. Miz Rutherford sat primly on her front-row seat, her silver hair in a perfect Ann Landers 'do. Mrs. Baines appeared with several bouquets of flowers—yellow daisies, red carnations and white mums with babies' breath. She handed them out to the outgoing officers, who accepted with smiles. Richard figured he should say something—perhaps along the lines of Winston Churchill's "Blood, Sweat, and Tears" speech—and turned to the audience.

Before he could open his mouth, Bessie Harper erupted from her chair. "Madame President!" She trundled down the center aisle holding a silver gift bag with red yarn handles and white crepe paper sticking out the top. When she reached the speaker's podium, she said, "I have a special presentation to make." She paused to catch her breath. "On behalf of the Malliford PTO, I want to present President-elect Gray with a special gift to welcome him to his new office."

Bessie offered him the bag, and he accepted it. "Thank you."

"Open it!" Susan Gunther shouted from her front-row seat.

He hesitated. Others joined in, playfully heckling him.

"All right, all right," he said, pulling out a package. A flicker of pleasure on Richard's face dissolved into fury.

"It fits your personality," Bessie said. "A yo-yo for a yo-yo."

Some people laughed, but not everyone. Miz Rutherford wore a cruel smile. Richard felt a hitch in his breath at this PWC-style slap in the face. "It's nice," he said, buying time. "Real nice." Indeed, it was a beaut: a Duncan Vintage Jeweled Tournament Classic, made of hard maple and painted black, in a clear plastic case. A championship yo-yo. Its beaded sides flashed in the light. He removed it and slipped the string loop over his finger. He yo'ed three times while he tried to think of something to say, let it hang for an instant, then dropped it to the floor, letting it roll. "I guess I'd have to say that what has gone down—"

He deftly snapped the string; the yo-yo returned to his hand.

"—can come back up." He heard someone make a loud finger-in-mouth *pop* to indicate a home run. He returned to his seat accompanied by a smattering of applause. The reform movement was alive and kicking ass, taking names, and walking the dog.

After the meeting, Anna Lee, angry over his mistreatment, suggested that he tell his detractors to go to hell. "Or maybe we should move," she said.

"That's for losers," Richard said. "I'm in it to win it."

* * *

The school year ended on a hot afternoon in May, when an air conditioning breakdown threatened to melt the kids and stick them to their seats. Richard came before dismissal to inspect Malliford's grounds, his trusty yo-yo in the pocket of his khaki shorts. He grumbled softly to himself about the school's rundown condition, and he'd already made campus beautification a top priority, along with the academic improvements he'd advocated in his controversial January newsletter article. The flowerbeds needed a complete overhaul, the lawn needed reseeding, and dead trees needed to come down, though the latter task was the county's responsibility. A parent had suggested building an outdoor classroom of benches and a podium under the oak on the front lawn. A lot of work, but worth it. He'd put it on the list.

As buses pulled into the loop, Richard stomped around, jotting notes on a small pad and swatting at the yellowjackets that buzzed around his sweaty forehead. The safety cadets, fifth-graders newly trained for next year, took their stations. Miz Rutherford walked out the front door, stately and elegant in bright sunshine. Her radio crackled; the ageless leader snapped commands as she ran the year's final dismissal.

She turned to Richard and waved. She seemed chipper, though they'd spoken little since his inauguration. Her good cheer was short-lived, however. She scowled at something behind him. He turned and saw Stan coming up the walk from the back side of the school. The gadfly passed the principal without speaking. As he disappeared into the building, a crooked smile took over her face. Creepy.

"Is everything going well, Richard?" she asked as he approached.

"Just fine, Miz Rutherford."

"I hear Mr. McAllister wants to be on the PTO board. Not a good idea. He has problems dealing with people, you know."

So do you, Richard thought. Her problem had been Stan since the first day of school two years ago, when he barged into her office to complain about the unhygienic, unsafe, unsanitary and code-violating washrooms on the kindergarten hall. He ended up reporting Malliford to the county health department, but the only result of that was assured mutual enmity between the two of them. "He's a dedicated volunteer," Richard said. "Everything will be fine."

"He needs a steadying hand so he doesn't get out of control."

"Out of whose control, Miz Rutherford?"

"I'm thinking of the good of the school."

"We all are. By the way, we should set up a meeting—"

The bell rang and Miz Rutherford's radio squawked, commanding her complete attention. A moment later, the river of bus kids rushed out. Her withering stare was no match for the nuclear explosion of youth into summer. Book bags and hats flew into the air, legs and arms churned. An Alice Cooper moment—truly awesome to behold. Richard stumbled out of the way as the flood washed by. A couple of minutes later, Nick sauntered out with his perfect grin, dragging his backpack like an animal pelt. Oh, for a camera! The boy whirled around in a seven-year-old's glorious celebration of freedom.

"Congratulations, my boy! Let's get summer started."

As they walked away, Nick cast a backward glance at the school. "Miz R gives me the creeps," he whispered.

"She's a principal. That's her job."

"Well, she's real good at it."

"Yup. That she is."

*   *   *

Miz Rutherford agreed to sit down with Richard on the first Monday of summer vacation—while Nick was at science camp—and discuss the coming school year. Since the PTO's finances were a mess and the principal would rather abolish the organization than deal with him, he wasn't expecting great results from the meeting. When he returned home, he pulled out his cell phone and called his treasurer—with whom he'd quickly developed an excellent rapport—to give her his report. "Our principal is a pluperfect bitch," he told Teresa.

"Which old bitch, the big-word bitch," she sang.

"Pluperfect means—"

"I know what it means. She's way past bitch. She was on the road to bitch but it wasn't fast enough, so she took a hard right and got on superbitch highway, but it wasn't fast enough either, so she got on superbitch superhighway and she's speeding down it, and you two just had a wreck."

"Very astute."

"So what else is new?"

"She's quite proud of the new security cameras they're installing. They pivot by remote, giving her increased command and control from her bunker."

"Sounds like she's bracing for armed conflict."

"Yeah, a rearguard action in the Apartment War. Something's brewing. That's what Jane Baumgartner told me. A bunch of new restrictions, supposedly. Anyway, I went up this morning to *finally* meet with her—actually, *confront* is a better word—for the first time since I took office. I had to force the issue before she left for the summer. She'd been putting me off."

"Dilatory tactics. There's your vocabulary word for the day."

"And once we met, you know what she did? She immediately demanded new furniture. She handed me a catalog and a list that includes a fancy desk and a Persian carpet, and the price—"

"Persian carpet?"

"—is over nine grand."

"Is she nuts? Where we supposed to get the money, even if we wanted to buy her a Persian carpet? Which we don't. Does she think this is the Pay Tribute Organization?"

"Yes. She claims we have tons of money. All we have to do is find it—like it's lying around."

"Did she tell you where? I can't find any records earlier than the crappy ones my predecessor left me. Do you have any old documents? No? Helen doesn't have anything before she was secretary. There's no history—no budgets, audits, nuttin'. Denise Coley is gone, her treasurer's gone too, nobody knows where, and Barbara only knows what happened second semester, after she took over. We're a PTO without a past, I tell ya. If there is any money, it's lost in the Malliford Triangle."

"I'll ask Rita. She's been around forever."

"I did. She'd heard of the 'Treasure of the Sierra Malliford' but it was before her time. We've got a hundred and ninety-two dollars in the bank with bills still coming in. We can't bounce checks like they did last year. We'll be screwed from the start."

"Well, Marine Antoinette said we got it tucked away, she was promised new furniture, and it's my job to get it. I said if we had money, I'd spend it on kids. She said a promise is a promise and I'm duty-bound to keep it. I said her request was inappropriate."

"Oh no you didn't. How'd she take that?"

"Like she'd been slapped in the face. Them's fightin' words."

Teresa sang, "Richard bitch-slapped the prin-ci-pal! Then what happened?"

"It got real quiet. She sat there like she was frozen. Just to liven up the death march, I handed her my five-page mission statement for the coming year."

"Ah, yes. Single-spaced. Impressive."

"Thanks. I tried to talk about August registration. She cut me off, said talk to Mrs. Baines. I told her I want parents to know on registration day who's teaching their kids. Ninety percent are pre-registered, anyway, so it's no big deal. Great opportunity to meet their teachers. You know what they do, instead? They post class rolls at the last minute, after they lock the doors on the Friday before the first day at school. That way, they don't deal with requests or problems. Monday morning they say, 'School's in session, can't make changes.'"

"What did she say?"

"She thought my idea '*lacked merit.*' We stared at each other for a while. I got up to go. She handed me her furniture request and that big catalog and said, 'Take this.' Then she held up my mission statement between her thumb and forefinger like she had a rat by the tail and said, 'Do you want this back?' I said, 'No, it's yours.' As I walked out, I heard it clunk in her waste basket. So I dropped her stuff in a metal trash can by the office door. It made a nice plunk, louder than hers. Ten minutes after I got home, she called and we *really* got into it. She accused me of yelling. I said she started it. She said Rita Malloy wasn't going to run *her* school, and I wasn't going to get rid of her. That really pissed me off, because I didn't want to get rid of her—not until today, when she told me she needs to approve my budget *ideas* and my board *suggestions*. I told her that *I* pick the committee chairs with input from the officers. She asked what gave me the authority to pick committee chairs, and I said, *the bylaws*. She said that's not the Malliford way. I said she can suggest officers and propose changes to the bylaws. Now she's pissed, too."

"I can't believe she puts herself above kids. Don't principals have an oath or something?"

"Just the Pledge of Allegiance. What a nasty woman. And unprofessional. I'll tell you right now I'm not quitting. It would give her too much pleasure. Of course, that's probably what she says, too. So we're stuck with each other."

"We'll do great, and she'll look bad for not working with us. I'll help you with anything you need," Teresa said. "*Anything.*"

"Well, thanks. I'll see what I can come up with."

She laughed. "You do that."

As soon as they'd finished talking, Richard's home phone rang. "Hello?"

It was his older brother. "Now you have to come back to Ridalia," Reggie said, pausing a beat. "Dad died."

SEVEN

The Grays departed Applegate late Saturday morning and spent the night in Paducah. Shortly after noon Sunday, as Richard approached the Ridalia city limits on U.S. 65, Nick asked, "Daddy, what's a Corey?"

"A corey?"

"I just saw a sign that said Old Corey Road."

"*Quarry.* Where they dig up rocks to use for building things."

"Did you ever go to the quarry?"

"No," Richard said. *Corey.* A troubled expression crossed his face.

"What's wrong?" Anna Lee asked.

"Stab from the past." He shook his head, but the thought that was sprouting could not be uprooted.

They drove by a dying strip mall facing off against a hulking grey and blue Wal-Mart. Further on, Main Street appeared to be gripped in a struggle between death and life. On one block sat a row of vacant buildings. On the next stood a gift store, an upscale bike shop, and a bakery/sidewalk café accented by a green awning over patio tables. Reggie had told Richard his bank was financing a downtown revitalization. If this was his brother's doing, perhaps there was hope for Reggie, after all.

Richard recognized two buildings from his early childhood: Whittier Drugstore (home of the World's Best Chocolate Soda), now abandoned, its windows posted over with yellow and black concert notices; and the *Ridalia Independent*, housed in a run-down three-story brick building, its name in black letters on a cheap white plastic sign, now cracked. Once upon a time, Richard thought the newspaper was the universe's center and his daddy its king. Now it seemed second-rate. Maybe third.

Ridalia's old-town streets ran straight and true; within two minutes, they were in the tree-lined world of Richard's early childhood. He glanced at Warsaw Elementary as he drove by.

"Is that where you went to school, Daddy?"

"For a little while. In kindergarten."

"Where you went to the principal's office over Santa?"

"Oh dear," Anna Lee said.

"Reggie told him," Richard said.

She craned her neck to face Nick. "You know the Santa Claus Daddy saw wasn't real."

"None of them are, Mom."

"Glad that's over," Richard muttered to himself.

His old house stood at the four-way stop on Candler Street. The brick sidewalk was crumbling; the pear trees lining it were ancient and gnarled. He remembered climbing up into ... *that one* to sit and wait for the mail on sunny days.

The two-story white house at 897 Warsaw with black shutters looked like it did when he moved away thirty-five years before. The wraparound porch was surrounded by boxwoods, its roof supported by fluted wooden columns. Then he noticed something was missing. The porch railing was gone. He glanced at Anna Lee. If she noticed the discrepancy, she didn't show it.

Richard parked in dappled patch of asphalt on the narrow street. He climbed out into the warm, still air. He shuddered in an ecstasy of relief at having reached his destination. A lawnmower droned in the distance. As two old women in a Buick drove by, the passenger waved. He waved back, completing the small-town ritual.

"What a neat tree!" Nick stared in awe at the willow that dominated the front lawn. "It looks like it sweeps the yard. A sweeping willow." He laughed as he ran around the tree. "Hope it's not a whomping willow."

"I can see why they moved back," Anna Lee said. "It's beautiful."

A bright-red cardinal flew low over the yard and landed in the lilac bush next door. Its blossoms had withered; Richard felt a pang of longing for their scent. Nick bounced up the steps onto the porch and rang the doorbell. His parents trailed behind.

"How do you feel?" Anna Lee asked.

"I remember. I don't feel," he said, misquoting *Robocop*.

Beth Gray appeared at the front door, her salt-and-pepper hair in a bun.

She wore black slacks and a blouse covered with small blue flowers. Her round, puffy face brightened at the sight of visitors. Her older sister Sally, with hennaed hair and a large beaded necklace, loomed over her.

Beth reached down to hug her youngest grandchild. "Nicky, you've grown so big!" Richard stepped onto the porch, and his mother embraced him. "I'm glad you're here."

Anna Lee kissed her mother-in-law's cheek. "I'm so sorry. I can't imagine how terrible it must be."

"Thank you, honey. Where are your things? Bring them inside. We've got plenty of room. *Ut, ut,*" she said, watching Richard's expression change to a frown. "You're staying here. I don't care what you say."

"You sure?"

"This is where you belong. Especially since you snubbed us at Christmas." She shook her head sadly. "Missed your last chance—"

"You know the deal," Richard said gruffly. "Hostile territory."

"Don't be churlish. He can be so churlish, can't he?" Beth asked her daughter-in-law.

"I tried to get him up here," Anna Lee said, "but you know how he is."

Richard cast a sidelong glance at his wife before retreating to the van, chuckling at her disingenuous attempt to curry favor. The older women escorted their guests inside, showering Nick with praise over his good looks, height, and intelligence. Aunt Sally hadn't seen the boy since he was three, and it had been nearly two years since Grandma Beth flew south—alone—to visit for a week.

When Richard finished lugging in the last bag, he found everyone at the kitchen table eating chocolate cake. "I cut a piece for you," his mother said.

He turned around in a slow spin, marveling that the bleak house of his childhood was now a place of light and life. The newly remodeled kitchen had blue granite counters, light maple cabinets, and a white double sink. He'd expected a dark, closed-in, old-folk smelling place, but several screened windows were open, and ceiling fans created a pleasant breeze.

The remodeling was courtesy of Reggie, who had insisted his parents reclaim their former home when it came on the market. Richard's older brother also had issues with the past; with Reggie, they seemed to involve buying it up and changing it to suit his needs.

Aunt Sally poured Richard a glass of tea, and his mother talked about Roy Gray's death. He'd passed away peacefully in his sleep of a heart attack. Really a surprise, even though he was seventy-eight years old, and Gray men didn't live so long, anyway. She *tut-tutted* to Anna Lee, who responded with the right touch of gravitas—a sad shake of her head.

Beth then went over funeral details. She and Reggie were handling arrangements, which was more than fine with Richard. "What kind of service is it?" he asked.

"Baptist. I know what you're thinking, so stop it," she snapped.

Richard happened to be thinking his father would attend a Baptist service only if it was held over his dead body.

"Anyway, Reverend Ballew owes Reggie a favor. And he's really a nice man. You just missed him. He wanted to know about Roy, of course. I told him about his work on the newspaper. Anyway, Roy told me last year to do it however I wanted. I wonder if he knew. ... Well, he didn't care about ceremonies in the first place, and he sure doesn't now. I'm not sure what I believe, but this is what I want."

Anna Lee, the Methodist, bit her lip and looked away.

"Fine," Richard said. "Where's Reggie?"

"He likes to play golf at the club on Sunday afternoons. You can probably reach him on his cell phone."

"Wouldn't want to mess up his swing," Richard said, drawing a chuckle from Aunt Sally.

Nick, having finished his cake, slipped off his chair next to his grandma. "You, I don't get to see so much," Beth said, grabbing Nick and hugging him before letting him go. She turned to Richard. "Actually, I don't get to see enough of any of my grandchildren. Your brother divorces badly. Christine and Sara moved away, to Kansas City and St. Louis. No, St. Louis and Kansas City. And Reggie's so busy he hardly ever sees his kids himself. Mainly he writes checks. Good thing he's got money."

"Do you still take care of Nicky all day?" Aunt Sally asked.

"When he's not in school," Richard said.

"Tag-team parenting," Anna Lee said, fumbling with her napkin. "I'd like to take a turn at home with our next child."

The older women's eyes grew wide in unison. "Are you expecting, dear?" Aunt Sally asked.

"Oh, no, no," said Anna Lee, crisscrossing her hands in denial. "Next year, that's the target."

Richard considered it a moving target, however.

"You're the opposite of your brother," Beth said. "You take care of your children. Reggie takes care of his parents."

If that was intended to make Richard feel guilty, it didn't work.

"They're not twins, that's for sure," Aunt Sally chimed in.

"Reggie's been such a great help," Beth said. "He saw the house for sale and talked us into moving back here. I know you don't like it, but it suits me. I never wanted to leave. I had to agree to pay for it with my teacher's retirement before your father would move. There are a few people here I knew from before. You were too young to remember them. The Boones, you might. John and Arlene. Their boy disappeared one day. Never came back. Do you remember him?"

"Oh yeah." Richard took a deep breath. "Allen borrowed Reggie's bike and never came back. It was the summer before I started kindergarten. I was sitting in the pear tree, and I was mad at you because you took me to the doctor for shots. Allen rode by, and I jumped down and chased after him to the stop sign, which was as far as I was allowed to go. The end of my world, as I knew it. He turned and laughed at me, flashing that silver tooth of his, and rode across, standing up and pumping. Reggie's Sting-Ray was the coolest bike in the world. High rise handlebars, banana seat. I was hoping I'd get to ride it some day."

Beth stood up and left the room without saying a word.

Richard looked at Aunt Sally, then Anna Lee. "What did I say?"

His wife shrugged. The older woman pursed her lips and said, "You'll see."

A minute later, Beth returned with an armful of folders and journals. She set them on the table and slipped on her bifocals. Wisps of hair along her neck stood out in the light from the hooded lamp hanging from the ceiling. She scrutinized papers briefly before calling out to Nick, who was staring out the window, "Would you like to play with some toys I keep for special visitors?" Nick nodded enthusiastically.

Beth whispered, "I don't want him to hear this. It could upset him."

She took her grandson upstairs and returned to her papers. "Ricky got his shots August twentieth that year," she declared, looking at a page of medical records in an old scrapbook. "You hated shots. That's why you remembered. Look at this." She shoved a photocopy from a thirty-five-year-old *Ridalia Independent* across the table. Aunt Sally leaned over, blocking Richard's light. Top of the front page, August 21: "9-Year-Old Boy Missing." A headline Roy Gray had most likely written. There was a black-and-white picture of Allen Boone flashing that silver smile. "Last seen playing in his back yard," Beth said.

"No," Richard said. "Last seen riding across the playground of Warsaw School." Old memories and new connections crashed into place like the rusty iron couplings of old, overloaded baggage cars.

Beth looked at him wearily. "You didn't tell us."

Richard shrugged. "I didn't—"

Beth hit the table lightly with her fist. "You were the last person to see him alive! Of course, now we know Wilkerson killed him. We were protecting you from a deep, dark secret and we should have been saving Allen."

"Well, thank goodness you put a stop to protecting me."

"Don't be bitter. Not now."

"I'm not. So what do you know now?"

"Well, they never found the body. Or Wilkerson. I knew something was going on when Roy ..." She paused and looked up. Tears welled in her eyes. She gave Richard an imploring look. He didn't think they were tears of sadness, though. And he was right. After she wiped her eyes, she gave her son a penetrating stare. "They would have caught the bastard!" she cried, slamming a fist on the table.

Richard wasn't sure exactly what was going on, and he wanted to distance himself from the problem that was blossoming like a toxic weed. Was his mother trying to put the burden on him? What could he have done back then? What could he do now? *I'll let go of it if you do, Mom.*

There was no use dwelling on something awful that happened so long ago, no use magnifying and multiplying a case that would never close, a wound that would never heal.

OK. If he had said *something* about Allen Boone that afternoon, Reggie's best friend might still be alive and everyone's life would have been better, and they wouldn't have to live with a ghost. Richard needed to get out from under the weight pressing down on him. "I'm going for a walk," he said. He rose from his chair and called upstairs. He needed his life preserver. "Nick! Wanna check out the park?"

Nick skipped down the stairs. "Is it the one you used to play in?"

"The very same."

"Cool! Let's go."

With a curt goodbye to the three women, Richard turned to leave.

"I'll pass," Anna Lee said, acting like he'd asked her if she wanted to go, but no doubt reading the signals. "I need to rest. Be careful."

He walked out the front door. Nick bounded past him and ran down the sidewalk, stopping to wait for his father to catch up.

"The toys aren't any good," he confided. "Everything's missing pieces."

They walked down Warsaw to its dead-end at Park Avenue three blocks away and stopped to admire the dark green holly trees surrounding Memorial Park's gate.

"This is a neat town," Nick said as they walked through the entrance. Nick sprinted across a broad lawn toward two play forts floating in lakes of pine bark. The metalwork of Richard's youth had been replaced with yellow and red plastic, wood beams and decking. The lagoon was still there. A stone bridge arched across to an island populated by honeysuckle-laden trellises. Richard plopped down on a bench and watched a young family of four feed the swans. His gaze drifted to the trellises, and he remembered chasing butterflies on the bank. It was amazing he hadn't pitched over the embankment and into the lagoon and drowned. It required a great deal of luck just to survive childhood. Poor Allen.

Richard looked around and sighed. There were too many secrets in this town, too many ghosts. He wanted to bury them deep, but he realized that he did owe something to Allen, who died because the little boy in a pear tree didn't tell anyone where he'd gone. Richard checked his watch. He knew where to look, but there was no time to go there now. He heard a distant cry, high and faint: *Catch me if you can!*

* * *

A handful of neighbors attended the viewing at Weatherby's Funeral Home Sunday evening, along with Beth's people. Richard's mother, wearing a simple black dress, sat in a wingback chair by a wall near the mid-priced aluminum coffin and received condolences. Nick, child of duty and decorum, stood beside her in his blue suit and held her hand.

Some local Chamber of Commerce types were there out of respect for Reggie, since Richard's paunchy banker-brother was a big fish in this little pond. Earlier, while sipping whiskey at their mother's house, Reggie had bragged about his latest plans and tried to pull Richard into his schemes, saying, "I could use your help running the newspaper when I buy it." And Anna Lee could run the Chamber of Commerce when he took over completely—which, by his estimate, wouldn't take long. A year, at most.

"The fools at the *Independent* don't know their butts from a tin can," Reggie said. "They need an online edition, too. I'll get a radio station, and we'll go multimedia and clean up. Your wife would do ten times the job at the chamber Tommy Harkel does, the fucking hick."

Richard, unmoved, had gazed warily into the hazel eyes of his brother, who was taller by three inches, older by four years, with a mop of strawberry blond hair. "And all this would be in Ridalia, correct?"

"Yeah, sure."

"That's the problem."

"Think about it."

Now, in the funeral home, Richard kept his distance from the coffin and Reggie. He stared at the red carpet and contemplated the prospect of having his brother as his boss, sitting on his chest and telling him what to do, hiding his paycheck where he'd never find it.

The elderly woman who waved at him that afternoon came up to him and squeezed Richard's arm. "I know how you feel," she said.

How could she, if he didn't? He considered the issue. Something was missing, of course, absent so long it should be declared lost. That was the theme of the day. Other than that, he felt a dull emptiness, a vague grinding of parts inside. It seemed like tears should come, but they didn't. Why couldn't he mourn his father properly? How should he mourn such an improper man? *Mourn that, then.* But in truth, it was a blow, reminding him that his time wasn't so very far off. He felt numb, that's how he felt. Did she know that? He gazed into her face, weathered and worn. Perhaps she did.

"Are you from out of town?" she asked.

"Hmm? Oh, yes, ma'am."

"Were you here during the earthquake the other night?"

"No," Richard said, shaking his head. "There was an earthquake?"

"It rattled my china." She turned and saw a new arrival. "Ernestine!" she called out, then turned back to Richard. "You take care, now," she said, already drifting away.

Reggie sidled up and took her place. In a low voice, he said, "On the way over, Mom told me about your conversation this afternoon. I guess at five years old, you were out of the information loop. Who knew? Maybe if somebody had asked you that night, they might have found Allen tied up in Wilkerson's apartment. Alive."

Richard gave his older brother a Get Lost look. Reggie stepped back and adopted an innocent tone. "I just found out the other day. I was talking to a detective. He's about to retire now, but he was a rookie patrolman back in the day. He said they searched Wilkerson's apartment after he didn't show up at school in January for winter term—we were gone already due to our own set of problems." He nodded in deference to the coffin. "Anyway, police found a blood-stained shirt matching the one Allen Boone wore the day he disappeared. That day you were in the office, you were probably going to be Wilkerson's third victim. Or fourth, or fifth. Seems he was a serial killer. Before he came to Ridalia, he was in Montana and his name was Wilson. He killed a boy in Billings the day school let out for summer and moved to Missouri to start over with a new identity. The police here found out about it, along with Allen's shirt, when they searched his apartment after he left town. They think he got the hell out of Ridalia the night he tried to molest you—dirty dishes still on the table. A miracle you got away."

"Did they ever catch him? Mom—"

Reggie shook his head. "Not that I know of. Apparently, no one has seen Wilkerson since. Probably changed his name, like he did before. And he got away with murder. Ever since I told her, Mom's been trying to stir things up. Like she's going to solve it with a bunch of old newspaper clippings. Wilkerson would have to be a hundred. Well, maybe not that old. He wasn't that old back then. He just had prematurely white hair. I gotta admit, I'd like to catch the bastard myself, if he was alive. Be good for the town. Closure, you know. Two birds with one stone, if you know what I mean."

"Why didn't you wait for me that day I got sent to the office?"

"I had a snowball fight I had to get to, I guess." Reggie shrugged and toed the carpet as the room buzzed softly around them. "I'm giving the eulogy tomorrow."

"Mom told me. That's fine."

"The preacher's just there because ... it looks good."

"Appearances are everything."

"Between you and me, I figured I'd have to carry the load," Reggie said.

"Thanks."

"God knows what you'd say."

"I don't think so."

Reggie grinned. "I love you, brother. I know you and Dad never got along, but he was always OK by me. You were as tough on him as he was on you. Just a shitty relationship. Happens."

"Well, it eventually mellowed out to simple aversion."

"You could be hard-headed. That's what kept you going. I tell Mom you're fine, but she worries about you."

"I worry about her."

Reggie gave him a fake pout. "Nobody ever worries about me."

"We worry about the people you marry. I'm going to get some fresh air," Richard said, hoping to be alone.

Reggie followed. They stood quietly in the evening light. Reggie sat down on a stone bench, then got up and paced the sidewalk twenty paces out and twenty paces back. He stood squinting into the sun and spoke: "There's something else."

"What's that?"

"It's about Mom."

"What about her?"

"I don't know how she found out. I guess someone told her yesterday, or maybe Friday night, after Dad died. Real helpful," His voice oozed sarcasm.

Richard was perplexed. "What are you talking about?"

"She's getting a single headstone for Dad. She's leaving him."

"Do what? How can you—"

"Her idea of a divorce. She won't sleep with him any more. I don't care about the circumstances. It's not right, what she wants to do. Nobody deserves that. To spend eternity that way."

"What the hell." Richard shook his head vigorously. "This has to be a joke."

"Mom wanted to confront Wilkerson that day. Dad didn't want to push the issue. Know why?"

"He didn't think I was worth it. He once told me I wasn't the hill he wanted to die on."

"Well, he had his own dirty little secret. He was screwing my fourth-grade teacher—who happened to be the police chief's wife. Wilkerson must have called the newspaper publisher and told him after you escaped, because Dad was fired that day. And Wilkerson took off, too."

"But ... Dad was fired because the Chamber of Commerce objected to his editorials about racism."

"Yeah. His story and he stuck to it." Reggie gave Richard a disgusted look, and then bent down and picked up a handful of dirt. He watched it trickle through his fingers, then threw the rest into the air. "He was weak, and my best friend's murderer got away. When I think about it, I get pissed."

"When did you find this out?"

"The day Dad died. I went to have a drink in his honor after we got him to the funeral home, and I ran into Detective Reynolds in a bar. After a few beers, he laid it out for me. I kept quiet, but some old gossip told Mom. To cheer her up, I guess."

"And now she's not speaking to him."

"Exactly so."

Richard turned on his heel and went back inside. Nick came over and took his father's hand, pulling him to the coffin to pay his respects. Richard looked down on Roy Gray's sharp features. He was now a greyish Gray, framed perfectly in the plush white pillowed padding of the casket. He looked smug, as if he'd died thinking he'd gotten away with something.

Nick said, "I love you, Dad. I hope you never die."

"A bit much to ask for," Richard said, "but I'll try my best."

*   *   *

The next day, after Richard fidgeted through Reggie's self-indulgent eulogy, the small funeral procession proceeded to Bluet, some thirty miles distant from Ridalia. Nick was allowed to play his Gameboy as long as he did it respectfully while Richard drove in silence behind the limo, where Beth rode with Reggie, his third wife, Cynthia, and his two daughters—half-sisters who had traveled far to attend the services.

"Are you all right?" Anna Lee asked her husband.

"Yeah."

"A penny for your thoughts."

"I'm thinking of wounds that don't heal and crimes that go unpunished." Richard shook his head. "I'll be glad when this is over."

"Well, that's something to look forward to."

They lapsed back into silence. After a while, the procession passed Marshallville High School, where Beth taught for twenty-five years and both sons earned diplomas. A few miles on, they drove by Adco Commercial Printing and Publishing, where Roy had retired as plant manager. After another twelve miles, they hit Bluet, population 225. Richard pointed out his old grade school and the house where he'd spent most of his childhood. They left town on a county highway, and after a mile, pulled onto a gravel road. An old white church stood on a hill. Beside it, the cemetery awaited them, a backhoe parked under a spreading maple's branches. Several cars and pickups were parked in the cemetery's semicircular drive. A cluster of people stood beside a green pavilion tent. Richard recognized a few old-timers from the printing plant.

"We're here," he said. "Dad's final resting place."

Anna Lee woke and gazed at a grassy hillside enlivened by the low-growing wildflowers that gave the town its name. "It's pretty."

Nick shut down his Gameboy and tossed it on the seat. "I'm going to be sad now," he said.

"OK," Anna Lee said.

Richard got out and stretched. The sun warmed his face, and a breeze rustled the leaves on the giant maple in the center of the graveyard. Car doors slammed. Across the road, beyond the bluets, a cloud shadow scudded across a rippling field of wheat. The hearse backed toward the tent as two men in baseball caps and overalls signaled directions. Nick bent down to pick a dandelion and blew its grey globe apart. Richard watched the seeds waft away into the late spring air.

Following a brief graveside service, Roy Gray, known skeptic, rational humanist, and rageaholic, was commended to heaven by a young minister who knew him not. During the eulogy, Beth seized Richard's arm and squeezed it. The casket was lowered into its vault and people gathered around the dry-eyed widow to give her their condolences.

As the crowd drifted away, the graveyard tractor rumbled to a start. Richard and Anna Lee each held one of Nick's hands as they returned to the Caravan. Richard listened to the crunch of tires on gravel and the beeping of Nick's Gameboy as he drove. Feeling somber and dull, Richard felt protected by some unfathomable amount of time or distance from his loss—actually something he'd never had, or something that disappeared so early in his life he couldn't even remember it properly. In short, his time for mourning had passed. In his world, Santa didn't go down alone.

Back in Ridalia, mourners ate a late covered-dish lunch at Beth's house. Afterward, Richard went upstairs to the guest bedroom, furnished with Ozzie and Harriet twin beds, and changed clothes, putting on jeans and lacing up his hiking boots.

When he reappeared in the hall, Nick said, "I've been looking for you. Whatcha doin'?"

"I was going to take a walk."

"I want to go."

Richard considered the grim nature of his quest and shook his head.

"I am always with you," Nick chided him. "Wherever you may roam."

Richard laughed. "You got that right. OK, put on long pants. There could be brambles."

"Are we going to the park?"

"No. To a place I've never been."

A few minutes later, they clomped down the stairs, and after a smattering of goodbyes and minimal explanations, they were out on the porch. "So, where are we going?" Nick asked.

"The quarry."

"Corey to the Quarry."

"Indeed."

Ignoring the ninety-degree heat, Richard drove through town with his window open and the air conditioning off, passing by diners sitting under the café's blue umbrellas and a yellow-suited rider with a sleek helmet and futuristic shades straddling his touring cycle in front of the bike shop. Richard turned north on U.S. 65 and went three miles to Old Quarry Road, yielding to a tractor-trailer rig hauling cattle before he turned left.

"P-U," Nick said, holding his nose to ward off the smell of manure.

Richard drove down a cracked and crumbling asphalt lane that cut a narrow channel between encroaching trees, shrubs, and weeds. Branches swiped the van; one reached inside the window and slapped him. The thick, oppressive air of the river bottom reminded him of summer down south.

There were no houses, driveways, or intersections along the service road's two-mile length. An abandoned rail spur ran parallel; weeds grew from its gravel bed. Trash was strewn everywhere; shards of brown glass glittered in the afternoon sun. Richard drove by an ancient, rusting mowing machine, its seat resting on a steel spring. Weed stalks jutted through its iron-spoked wheels. Beyond it sat a bleached-out blue 1965 Ford Galaxie, the same model his parents once drove.

The road ended in a gravel plain a thousand feet across, mostly overgrown with grass and weeds. On each side, cut limestone walls rose about fifty feet. Bushes and small trees clung stubbornly to cliff faces. Richard stopped in the hard-packed clearing. Some recent tire tracks were visible, along with a dozen empty Budweiser bottles. To the right, a car path wound up the slope behind a short cliff. To the left, the distinctive form of a Model A coupe rusted in a clump of weeds.

"We're here," Richard said. "Let's explore." They climbed out, hushing a hundred crickets with a door slam, which sent a covey of quail bursting from the underbrush. After a brief silence, the crickets resumed their concert. The weeds were almost as tall as Nick, but there were large open spaces and paths leading in all directions.

"It's a wilderness here," Nick said. "I can't even hear the highway." He yelled, "Anybody here?" An echo answered: *Here. Here. Here.*

A frog croaked, and Nick ran to the green pond in the quarry's center. A rusted refrigerator jutted from its surface. Richard followed Nick, trying to soak in his surroundings. Something seemed wrong, out of place. Nick threw a rock that skipped twice and disappeared.

"Do you think there's any fish in there?" his son asked.

Richard squinted at the water. "Might be. Somebody might have put them there."

Another frog sounded, then another as a fledgling chorus erupted. A dragonfly flew by. "Dragonflies are magic," Nick said. "They're old like dinosaurs." He chased the elusive creature for a moment, then gave up.

Something caught Richard's attention—the very thing that was wrong with the picture. "Look, Nick. That cliff broke away and fell down." Richard pointed to a pile of sharp-edged boulders, the crushed weeds underneath still green. Scattered atop the rocks: several decades' worth of trash, newer stuff to the left, plastic and paper on top. A jumble of steel buckets and metal parts, fiercely corroded. "A woman told me an earthquake hit the other day. I bet it broke this pillar of rock away from the cliff. Or maybe it fell and they thought it was a quake."

"It's probably a million tons," Nick said. "I'll bet it made a giant BOOM!"

"See how it broke along the base? There was a fissure. A crack. Looks like people used to drive up there and dump trash in the gap between the limestone column and the main wall. A few days ago, it splintered off and crashed."

"Can I climb on the rocks?"

Richard looked at the tumbled-down pile of limestone, then at the short cliff it had come from. "Yeah. But be careful. Stay away from the cliff. Watch out for falling rocks."

"King of the hill!" Nick shouted. An instant later, he scraped his knee trying to get up, but he bravely climbed on. Richard went over to examine the trash, which now made a fascinating archaeological display. The boy hopped from boulder to boulder, peering down at the refuse. He found a stick and poked about, rattling a rusty tin can before flipping it away.

Richard leaned against a boulder and squinted into the late afternoon sun, wondering what the hell he was doing there. Meanwhile, Nick walked along the rocks pointing his stick at interesting pieces of junk. "Hey, Dad, I'm taller than you!" he shouted from thirty feet away.

A few minutes passed, and then Nick called out again. "I see some old handlebars. They're rusty."

"Where?" Richard said. He clambered up and boulder-hopped to his son's side. Nick was pointing at a pair of high-rise handlebars four feet below them near the limestone column's fractured base. Richard climbed down for a closer look. "Toss me that stick, Nick."

"Nick stick coming down!"

Richard caught it and pushed away rotted cloth from the handlebars. He could see the front end of a bike that had been there a long, long time. He could make out enough letters on the rusted brand plate to see that it was a Schwinn. His pulse quickened and he pushed hard with the stick, but the rest of the bike was not attached.

Richard felt a chill. *This could be it*, he told himself. He looked up. The sun was shrinking from the sky. He felt dizzy. He blinked and licked his lips. Then he pulled out his cell phone and made a call.

"Reggie Gray here."

"Hey. It's Rick. I'm at the quarry on Sixty-Five."

"What the *fuck* are you doing out there?"

"Looking for Allen Boone."

"You're crazy as batshit."

"Maybe, but we found something."

"What do you mean? What did you find?"

"Schwinn Sting-Ray handlebars. In an old dump that broke open and spilled out. From the look of the crushed grass and weeds, it just happened."

"Maybe that earthquake knocked it loose."

"Maybe that was the earthquake," Richard suggested, thinking another earthquake was coming.

"I'll be there in ten minutes." Reggie hung up.

Richard took Nick to the van and waited. After a few minutes, Reggie's Town Car approached, its tires popping gravel. It crunched to a stop and Reggie got out, stripped off his coat, and threw it inside along with his tie. He looked like a well-dressed hood in an old *Rockford Files* episode.

Nick and Richard climbed out of the van. "Nick found the handlebars," Richard said.

The brothers gauged each other. The older brother's face was drawn, the usual spark gone from his eyes. "OK. We're both from around here, so show me."

Richard gestured toward the rock pile. Nick led the way, skipping ahead of them and scrambling up among the rocks.

"Given the circumstances, your boy's downright chipper," Reggie said.

"He doesn't know the circumstances."

Reggie stared at the pile of rocks. "Yeah," he drawled. "I bet that's what we heard last week, that cliff falling down. Rumbled like thunder." He looked around. "I gotta climb up?"

Richard cupped his hands to help him. Reggie grunted and flailed clumsily. He had to stand on his brother's shoulders to reach the higher level, digging in his heels as his little brother grimaced. Richard negotiated the climb with relative ease—a benefit of working out twice a week. Like a hunting dog,

Nick pointed at the handlebars. Reggie sauntered over and regarded them, and then turned to Richard. "You think he's here?"

"Who are you talking about?" Nick asked.

Reggie looked off in the distance. "My best friend got lost when we were kids. Maybe he ended up here."

"He could have rode it up there and fallen into the crevice," Nick said. "He might not have been wearing a helmet."

"Yeah, right, no helmet," said Reggie, shielding his eyes. "His parents got worried when he didn't come home by dark. Everybody's lights were on up and down the street that night. You must have already been asleep when we found out he was missing. Nobody thought to talk to you, even though you sat out in the pear tree and watched everything that came and went. And you could have told us, damn us all." Reggie looked around. "What made you come here?"

"I thought Wilkerson said he was going to take me to Corey. And then Nick saw the sign and read it that way. Just a hunch."

Reggie nodded slowly. "You could have been buried here, too."

Richard put his hands on his hips. "So what are you going to do?"

"I'll find him. Maybe not today, but I'll bring some people out and do some looking." He shuddered. "So now I know. This place is haunted. Explains why I never got lucky out here."

"I don't believe in ghosts," Richard said. "At least I didn't."

But he knew now that Allen had been calling to him ever since he returned to Ridalia.

*   *   *

The next morning, as they drove off in the van with Nick, leaving Beth and Aunt Sally waving on the porch, Anna Lee shuddered with relief and whispered to Richard, "Now I understand why you don't believe in God."

"I never said I didn't believe in God," he replied. "I just don't like Him much."

Richard looked out the window and followed Allen Boone's last journey. He saw the nine-year-old riding the coolest bike ever, his silver tooth glinting as he laughed at the little boy who couldn't catch him, then standing up and pumping his way across the schoolyard, into eternity.

EIGHT

On a hot, sunny afternoon late in June, Richard drove past the modest ranches on Balmore Court and entered Attaway Swim Club's gravel lot, parking beside Teresa's red van. Nick, in yellow knee-length trunks and blue swim shoes, jumped out of the Audi and ran ahead, stopping at the pool entrance to urge on his lagging father with a frantic windmill motion.

A boombox played Justin Timberlake as they entered the gate. A lifeguard took two dollars from Richard and crossed out two names on the guest list. As Richard walked past a row of sunning mothers, a pair of tanned women in pastel bikinis called greetings. The pale president in khaki pants and a loud red shirt waved, barely noticing them, because his gaze was attracted to a webbed lounge chair beyond the pool's deep end, where Teresa lounged in a sleek black tank suit. Her arms and legs were golden; the sun had reddened her hair. Her skin was smooth and oiled, her toenails dark red, her breasts more ample than he had imagined—and he'd done a lot of that lately. As he approached, his shadow fell over her. She looked up and smiled from behind huge sunglasses.

"You should have worn trunks, Mr. President. You look like a tourist. Nice shirt, though."

"Thanks, it's Hawaiian."

"I can tell."

She slipped on wedge-heeled sandals and chug-chugged over to the picnic pavilion, where she'd set up office. He could feel his desire for her building up like a static charge. That way madness lay, Richard knew. Thank goodness they were so busy such a union would be impossible to consummate.

But she always smelled of lilacs. How did she know the antidote to the toxins in his life? Each time he saw her, he wanted her more. At this rate, how could he make it through an entire year, working so closely with her?

He turned to see a blonde lifeguard pull Nick from the diving-board line and give him a swim test. His son jumped into the pool and thrashed his way to the other end and back, past waders and horseplayers. When Nick climbed out, he found his father's approving gaze and pumped his fist in the air. Richard watched as he went yipping and dripping to the back of the divers' line.

"He looks just like you," Teresa said.

"Don't tell him. He was hoping to do better."

"Ha. He's handsome. You want a Diet Coke?"

"I do."

She produced a cold bottle from behind her back. "I can read your mind."

"Thanks." He looked around. "Where are your girls?"

She nodded toward the pool's far end. "The tadpoles are in the shallows with their sitter."

After some small talk, they sat down in the pavilion. She handed him a balance sheet, marked in red. "Last year's budget was heavy on teacher tributes," she said. "Actually, it was a friggin' mess. The Principal's Fund is *huge*. Five grand. Fifteen percent of the budget, and no approval slips, just canceled checks. Know what she spent it on?"

"I'm afraid to ask."

"Be very afraid. Parties and gifts. 'Morale boosters.' Catered party for Teacher of the Year. *Five hundred.* Flowers. More flowers. Check this out: two-hundred-dollar gift certificate at Regent's Mall for Sandra Kincaid, deputy superintendent for elementary ed. That's a bribe to her boss's boss. With PTO funds, no less. That should be illegal."

"Boss's boss's boss, I think. I had no idea it was that bad. No wonder she didn't want me in charge. She didn't want me to see the books. She truly is Marine Antoinette."

"Only half of the Principal's Fund went to benefit the kids."

"So let's cut it in half."

"Or eliminate it entirely. The training manual we pilfered from the PTA says to watch out for this kind of thing. Better to set up a miscellaneous fund and grant requests as they come. We also need an independent audit, so we don't end up liable or in jail or some crazy shit." She threw up her hands to punctuate her concerns.

"I like the way you think. We definitely need to avoid crazy shit."

"Thank you." She moved her hand toward his face, then froze.

"Hi guys," called out a Malliford mom in khaki shorts and a tank top, padding by in loose flip-flops. "Having fun?"

Richard recognized the woman's face but couldn't recall her name.

"You betcha," Teresa said. "Fun with numbers."

"Do we have any money?" the woman asked over her shoulder.

"We're looking for it," Teresa said, holding up a handful of papers. "If you find any, let us know."

Teresa laughed. Feeling like he'd barely avoided a collision, Richard exhaled and looked away, only to see Nick in the middle of a cannonball. He chuckled at the skinny eight-year-old's splash.

After looking over finances, they reviewed board assignments, specifically the fund-raising committees. Whatever it was that Teresa was up to, she was still doing it. She rubbed her shoulder against his as they leaned over Richard's list of likely suspects. She swayed to the boombox tune and hummed softly, then playfully bumped Richard's hip with hers. "Hey!" she said, acting like he'd been doing the grinding.

"Hey."

"I know it's going to be tough, with all the new kids coming in and Rutherford being the way she is. But I believe in you. I just want you to know that I'm with you all the way." She flipped up her sunglasses and flashed a beguiling smile and touched his chest just above the top button. "So how you like me now?"

Richard swallowed nervously. "You're my new best friend," he said, although he was beginning to think that they were on their first date.

He still hadn't met her husband and only knew Carl through her constant put-downs of him. He was a smoker who blew rings in her face. She'd told Richard that despite a good income, there were money problems because he was a day-trader, and "thanks to his risky-ass investments," they'd been hurt even worse by the crash than other investors.

Nick appeared beside him. "Can I have money for a drink?"

"Sure." Richard fumbled in his pocket and handed Nick some quarters, then wiped the sweat off his forehead as the boy ambled off.

He peered into the clear blue sky and watched a hawk as it disappeared among the tall trees surrounding Malliford. What was happening was awkward but not entirely unwelcome. Richard didn't know what he should do. Maybe nothing. That seemed a wise choice.

"What are you thinking?" Teresa asked, pressing in so close he could feel body heat, warmer than a summer day.

"I'm thinking it's going to be a tough year."

"Well, you're not alone. You've got me."

"I know. It's just—"

"I don't want you to be lonely."

"I—"

"*Shhh,*" she said, pressing a finger gently to his lips, then gently stroked his arm.

He glanced around, to see if any Malliford moms had witnessed this indiscretion. "That's about all we need to cover today, isn't it?"

"If you say so, Mr. President." She gave him a little pout.

"I guess I'd better be going."

Teresa reverted to a more businesslike demeanor and they finalized the to-do lists they'd drawn up. After that, Richard coaxed his protesting son from the pool with the promise of ice cream. As they were leaving. Richard gazed at Teresa for a second while he fumbled with the gate. No longer unimaginable, she now seemed ... almost inevitable. The thought quickened his heart and slowed his brain. He tripped over some gravel in the parking lot. Whether to look up or down when he walked—that was always the issue, wasn't it?

* * *

Summertime. The lawn turned brown. Richard struggled to put out newsletters. And always there was Nick. Some mornings, they played soccer or baseball at Malliford, retreating home when the sun topped the tall trees beside the school's playing field, which they had all to themselves. In the afternoons, Richard worked while Nick read or played. There was home schooling for math, science, and social studies, along with field trips to museums and Civil War battlefields, ice cream, movies, Chinese checkers, and chess.

And the PTO, of course. The other officers fell in line with his plans, except for Helen Bagby. He didn't bother with the returning secretary much, however, having pegged her as a remnant of the old regime and perhaps a spy. He kept her out of the loop and assigned her the task of chasing down old records.

In July, the Grays celebrated Nick's birthday with a trip to St. Augustine. Later that month, the *Sentinel's School Guide* came out, and Malliford held on to its four stars. Barbara called Richard to congratulate herself, ignoring the fact the rating was based on test scores from Denise Coley's reign—and were more a measure of the school's demographics than anything else. The ex-president also mentioned she'd made a deal with Miz R to place her company's logo on the sign at the school entrance. In exchange, Abacus Realty would become the school's business partner.

Richard didn't protest, having learned there were limits on what he could do after failing to remake the PTO in his image. Case in point: Danielle Morelli, the replacement newsletter editor, was a friend of Barbara's. And while Richard had deep misgivings about Susan Gunther, the other officers (except Teresa) demanded he take advantage of her experience to help balance his grand and heroic budget. He held off as long as possible, but finally, in late July, he reluctantly offered her the fund-raising co-chair with Jane Baumgartner and she grudgingly accepted.

When Rita made her weekly phone call to find out what the hell was going on, Richard informed her about the last-minute appointment.

"Shit!" she yelled. "I told you we needed to keep her off the board and out of the line of succession!"

"You talk like there's going to be an assassination," Richard said.

"I wouldn't put it past them," Rita muttered.

*   *   *

For reasons known only to the Gresham County School Board, the first day of class was set for August 10, smack dab in the middle of summer, even though most schools' antiquated air-conditioning systems buckled under the load. This year would be no exception. On registration day, less than a week before school started, Miz Rutherford stood in the sweltering cafetorium at 10:00 a.m., phone in hand, angrily protesting Malliford's sweltering state.

Richard watched her performance and turned to Rita. "The AC wasn't working on the last day of school. She had all summer to get it fixed."

"She didn't notice because she spent most of the summer sunning on a rock, catching flies. And by the way, the office AC works. Look at her, acting angry over something that's her fault. Disgusting," Rita snorted, then scurried off to spread word of the principal's incompetence.

Miz Rutherford retreated to the comfort of her office. Meanwhile, teachers sat behind tables along two walls of the multipurpose room. Mrs. Baines and Ms. Bailey stood in the center of the room, directing traffic. Richard served a similar role for the PTO, overseeing tables staffed by the chairs of Membership, Volunteers, Duckwear, and Yearbook. Three PTO volunteers at a crowded table sold school supplies. Teresa and Jane Baumgartner worked as cashiers while Candace sought volunteers and donations—"pimping the PTO," she called it. Cindi Lou served by babysitting the other volunteers' kids, including Nick.

Children milled about, renewing old acquaintances, while parents went from table to table, buying this and signing that, intent on escaping the stuffy building as soon as possible. All was routine until two black women showed up and paraded around the cafetorium, shouting and holding signs saying, "Counseling Is Cool!" and "Your Friendly Psychologist."

"What's that about?" Richard asked Candace.

"I don't know," she said, "but they scare me. Apparently, they're in favor of mental health. Not that I ever had any use for it, myself."

Rita broke off her conversation with a fellow dissident and rushed over to apprise Richard of yet another intolerable act: "Do you know what she's done this time?"

"Which she?" He looked around. He was the only man there.

"She who shall not be named, who else? She got rid of our art teacher, Artice Kenyatta! You know, Artice was into Africanism."

"Africanism?"

"Then she combined our half-credit for art staffing and an extra half-credit we earned from the apartment kids to hire a psychologist *and* a new counselor to replace Mrs. Ingersoll when she retired."

"What do you mean, she got rid of the art teacher? It's impossible to get rid of teachers."

"Artice is gone. Just like Jessica Agincart from fourth grade. We're losing our best teachers. This school is going straight to hell."

"They're coming over," Candace whispered.

The two women, plain-looking and young, were dressed in Rutherfordian dark suits. They introduced themselves with brisk confidence: Counselor Cassandra Hardwick and psychologist Donzella James. "Welcome to Malliford," they said in unison.

"I'm Richard Gray, PTO president. This is Candace Josey, vice president, Teresa Keller, treasurer, and Rita Malloy, usual suspect."

"I've been here eleven years, thank you," Rita said. "So I should welcome *you.*"

Ms. James drew her head back and gave Rita a look: *Oh no you didn't.*

"We're professionals," said Ms. Hardwick, giving Rita a practiced smile. "But we were told there was some negativity among the parents this year."

"We're here to help," added Ms. James, softening her expression.

"Then get us our art teacher back!" Rita said.

"A decision has been made by the school leader to improve student life by using our services and talents. You are not the one to make school decisions," declared Ms. Hardwick. Her tone suggested she'd already diagnosed Rita as borderline unruly.

Rita's mouth opened and closed as her engine built up steam. Just before her whistle screamed, Mrs. Baines beckoned the two women to the other side of the room.

"Anger is a disease, Ms. Malloy," Ms. James said as they retreated.

"More like a natural reaction to bullshit," Rita muttered under her breath.

"They're professionals," Candace noted.

"This is insane," Rita said, shaking her head furiously. "And what's this about *Dear Leader?*"

"Mental health is insane," Candace said. "I want that on a T-shirt!"

Richard shook his head. "Having a counselor *and* psychologist without an art teacher *or* a nurse doesn't make sense."

"It's kind of weird," Teresa said from behind the cash box. "Our principal is not touchy-feely. I can't see her buying into the self-esteem movement. Not other people's self-esteem, anyway."

"Not self-esteem," said Jane Baumgartner as she sauntered up. "Behavior modification. That's what Miz R told the faculty. And you didn't hear that from me."

"Behavior modification." Rita spoke the words like a preacher savoring an especially interesting sin. "Sounds like something I should be fighting."

"For the good of all mankind," Candace added. "Before mental health runs amok."

Just then, Spencer Hadley—Mr. Chain Gang himself, dressed in black, with long, stringy hair—threw his school planner against the wall.

"Our little Goth must have just found out Cates is teaching sixth grade," Rita said. "What you wanna bet they torture him until he admits a spider is an insect?"

"He's going to get suspended before school starts," Richard said, watching Mrs. Baines descend upon the problem student.

A minute later, Stan McAllister came in with his equally stubby wife, Janet, and their anomalously beautiful, blue-eyed daughter Karen. Rita hustled over to brief her fellow principal-hater on Miz Rutherford's most recent misdeed. Meanwhile, Janet—a quiet woman who worked as a nurse—towed Karen from table to table.

"Those two are going to cause trouble," Candace said, nodding toward Rita and Stan.

"Good," Teresa said.

Richard watched Rita and Stan exit. "This is going to be an interesting year," he muttered.

Still looking cool and crisp, Miz Rutherford returned and made another loud, angry cell phone call about the air conditioning. Believing the situation to be under control, Richard walked home through a sweltering haze to retrieve a folder he'd forgotten. Upon his return, he saw Stan on the sidewalk—barely off school property—next to the *School of Excellence* sign. A black ribbon was tied around the pole, and a crudely lettered poster taped beneath it said: BRING BACK ART TO MALLIFORD.

"What the heck are you doing?" Richard asked as strode toward Stan.

"Wanna sign my petition?" Stan asked. Richard glanced at the names on it: Rita, Stan, three he didn't recognize, two he did.

"I'll deal with this my own way."

"I also drew up opt-out forms."

"Opt-out forms?"

"To keep them from administering psych tests and interviews without parents' permission."

"Come on," Richard implored. "You're a PTO board member. You're supposed to be on the team. This is registration day. Classes haven't even started. Think how it looks, especially to new parents."

"Like things aren't right, which they aren't. Instead of teaching, they're opening a 'behavior modification' clinic. No art, no nurse, just two bureaucrats intruding on parental rights. We want a school, not an asylum."

"Looks kinda weird, protesting mental health services and counseling if people don't understand it's about getting rid of an art teacher and not having a school nurse. I don't care how many psychologists they hire as long as other needs are met."

"Like that's going to happen." Stan gave him a skeptical look.

"Do it for me, then."

"*Hunh.*" After a pause, Stan grudgingly conceded. "All right."

"Good." Richard turned and saw Miz Rutherford standing in front of the school, arms akimbo, glaring at them. He cupped his hands and shouted: "They get the air conditioning fixed yet?" Without speaking, she retreated to the building's only cool room.

When Richard returned to the cafetorium, the new counselor handed him a memo and said, "The county doesn't provide us with any materials or supplies."

He glanced over her message. Ms. James and Ms. Hardwick wanted the

PTO to buy them $2,000 worth of equipment and supplies, including 650 copies of a pamphlet entitled *Practice Good Mental Hygiene Daily!*

Last year the PTO had given the counselor $400 for materials and supplies, and that seemed like a good number to Richard. He cleared his throat. "Well ..."

"Can we have the money?" Ms. Hardwick asked. "We need it before school starts."

"Not right now. We're kind of broke."

She turned and walked away, shouting across the room to Donzella James, "He says they don't have money."

The psychologist shouted back, "Mr. Gray, this money is necessary for us to do our job!"

"Sorry." Richard gave a shrug worthy of a mime. He then went to the cashier's table and showed the request to Teresa. She whispered in his ear, "Let them earn it. Put them in the dunking tank at the Fall Festival. I have a feeling there'll be a line for tickets."

"We can put Stan and Rita in there, too."

"Why them?"

"You'll see."

*   *   *

Registration ended, but the Art War continued. Miz Rutherford declined to meet with the PTO's executive committee Friday morning to discuss hiring an art teacher. The officers met anyway and signed the letter Richard drafted urging her "to reinstate the school's art program and hire an art teacher for the current school year." Even Helen signed, after much cajoling.

The principal was out when Richard delivered it to the office at noon, so he gave the letter to Polly. "Class rosters up yet?" he asked.

The secretary snorted. "Course not. Mrs. Baines will post them—"

"After the last teacher leaves the building this afternoon, too late for parents to do anything before classes start Monday."

"You catch on quick, for a guy."

* * *

That night, Richard told Anna Lee about his dispute with the principal. She was unsympathetic. "It's her school. Remember that," she said between bites of salad at Rome Pizza.

"No it's not. Sovereignty resides in the people. It's our school."

"Do you want me to sing *This Land Is Your Land?* It's not some folk-song democracy, even if your friend Rita thinks so. I'll bet she doesn't know how much baggage you carry where principals are concerned." She slowly shook her head. "Still trying to win a kindergarten fight."

"It's the people's school," Richard said, taking a slice of pepperoni pie. "And she's alienating the PTO. The people."

"She's alienating *you*. There's a difference. Don't take yourself so seriously. You're there to support the people who do the job. You can't teach the classes. Leave it to the professionals."

"I'd love to leave it to the professionals, but the professionals are leaving. She's getting rid of the best teachers and replacing them with behavior modificationists."

"You talk like a conspiracy nut. *Modificationist* isn't even a word. You should stay away from Stan and Rita."

"Dad's a nut!" Nick shouted.

"Shhh," Anna Lee said. "We don't want people to know."

Staying away from those two rabble-rousers—or were they the rabble, and he the rouser?—was easier said than done, however. When Richard got home that night, an e-mail from Stan awaited him. Fifty people have signed his petition. "There will be more," the parent activist promised.

* * *

Richard woke Saturday to a weird noise—*wang-chung*, like a saw falling on concrete. He heard a car start roughly and rattle off. Then birdsong. Anna Lee grumbled in her sleep. He yawned, stretched, and put on his glasses. School started in two days. With Nick in class, he'd get his life back—at least the part he hadn't given to the PTO.

Once dressed, he went outside. The sun had cleared the treetops and was now scorching the earth. He picked up the *Sentinel* and flung it onto the stoop, having decided to check Nick's class assignment. He figured the boy would be in Ms. Radcliffe's class at best, Mrs. Greene's at worst. Nick wanted Ms. Radcliffe. So did Anna Lee, as did most people who knew the score—and test scores—but Mrs. Greene would be OK. He hadn't bothered to make a special request. That would be selfish, hypocritical, and greedy. Plus he didn't want to beg for anything from the principal. Why should he? Surely they had enough sense to take care of the president's child, for the sake of peace.

As he walked toward Windamere, he thought about stuff he needed to do and what a bitch Miz Rutherford was. At the school property line, he stopped. Something was amiss. Richard cocked his head like a puzzled dog, surveying his surroundings for a minute before realizing the *School of Excellence* sign had been removed from its rusty post. Bolts had been cut. Metal shavings sparkled in the grass: a fresh kill. So that's what he'd heard earlier—a trickster altering the universe. A dissident with a hacksaw had grown tired of the ancient, irrelevant claim to fame. Miz Rutherford would not be pleased. *School of Excellence* signs were hard to come by. With her inherited status symbol gone, she'd have to earn a new one. He doubted that she was up to the task.

He walked on. At least the vandal hadn't knocked over the stone *School of Excellence* marker, although it did look like someone had taken a swing at it with a sledgehammer. The parking lot was empty, but he knew from experience that teachers would come in that day to put finishing touches on classrooms and lesson plans. A yellow security light shone on class postings taped to the inside of the front doors' glass panes, starting with kindergarten on the left. He looked at Mrs. Radcliffe's third-grade roster. A name between Samantha Fowler and David Higgins had been redacted, blacked out like sensitive information in a government memo. He looked at Mrs. Greene's roster. No Nicholas Gray there, either. Odd. He rechecked each list. Nick's name was nowhere—

Then he saw Mrs. Little's roll. His mouth dropped open. Nick's name was penciled at the bottom, following a bunch of names he didn't recognize—strangers and underachievers, no doubt. His child was being left behind, like Hansel in the woods. "No!" he shouted. Obscenities danced in his head. "Fuck me! Fuck me very much. She's taking it out on my kid!" He could see the headline: "Boy Genius Sentenced to Chain Gang for Father's Crimes!"

After he'd spent a few moments dumbly staring at the class lists and failing to come up with a corrective action that didn't involve a major felony, a car pulled up behind him. He turned to see a black Buick Park Avenue stop in the loop. He watched with the amazement of the newly damned as Avon Little hauled her considerable self out of the driver's door. She leaned on the car roof and said, "You're just the man I need."

Remembering his manners, he said, "Good morning," and ambled toward her. She came around the car and gave him a firm handshake. She was wearing a sleeveless pale blue sundress and he noticed a nasty-looking three-inch scar on her upper left arm. A knife wound? As he gave her the once over, she reciprocated.

"You're out early," she said. "You jog?"

"No, just checking on Nick's classes." He paused. "Looks like his class got switched."

"How 'bout that. I saw his records yesterday. Bright. Very bright."

"Uh, thank you."

"It's gonna be a good year." She gave him a toothy grin. "Even if we got Dumpster duty."

"Dumpster duty?"

"When you're low on the totem pole, you get the room by the trash bins in back. On hot days ... *whooee*." She wrinkled her nose and fanned her right hand in front of her face.

"Who had it last year?"

"Ms. Agincart."

"I heard she was a fine teacher."

Mrs. Little's booming laugh scared a nearby squirrel off the lawn and back into its tree. "So am I. Being good got nothin' to do with doin' well, not in this school system." She nodded and regarded him carefully. "So what *you* do to rile up Miz Rutherford?"

"I'm sure there's a list."

"Ha. A list. I like that. Well, she big on sending messages."

"I don't think she should—"

She waved him off—whether diplomatically or dismissively, he wasn't sure.

"Oh, it doesn't bother me a bit," she said, as if she was the one who should be offended. "Somebody's got to be in her doghouse. It's a big doghouse, and she hates seeing all that space go to waste. Might as well be me and you. Come on. And bring your strong back with you. We got some haulin' to do, Mister President. I'll let you in and you open the back door. Had to borrow Miz Leland's key. Miz R doesn't trust me with one." She rolled her eyes. "We all burglars, you know."

She rumbled toward the front door holding the key tightly in her fist. Bemused, he followed.

She looked back and said, "Spozed to be a hundred again today. Be mid-September 'fore the kids can play outside. I hate that. I let children who act right play outside. There's no official recess any more."

She halted abruptly. He almost bumped into her, which meant he almost got knocked down. "Are you all right?" he asked.

"Just writin' a mental memo to myself."

She unlocked the door and rushed into the office, where she studied a card for a moment before switching off the alarm. "*Whew*. Just in time. Don't want the police on us. I reckon a PTO president can be in the school alone for a minute. Maybe not. I doan wanna find out, not today. Things been tense lately. You go back and open the door by the Dumpsters and don't lock yourself out. Put somethin' to stop it."

Avon Little was nothing if not authoritative. Richard did as he was told, propping one of the double doors open with a broken desk left in the hall. He walked to the curb and regarded the school's two Dumpsters anew, like they were monoliths placed there by a higher power. He hummed the theme from *2001: A Space Odyssey*.

Mrs. Little popped open the trunk, which was packed with grocery boxes and several dozen ten-packs of fruit juice. The back seat was filled, too, all the way to the roof. There had to be a ton of food in the car. Its suspension sagged under the weight.

"Did you hijack a grocery truck?" Richard asked.

She scowled, but her eyes twinkled. "Smart aleck. I bet you got in trouble all the time at school when you was a boy. Reason I do this is because they don't give free breakfasts here, so I fill the gap."

"Is this for the whole year?"

"Heavens, no! This may not last to September. I feed thirty kids each mornin' before school, all grades. Be more this year. I got ten Chantilly kids, at least. I see kids aren't getting fed at home, so I make sure they doan start the day empty. I give 'em something to take home, too."

Richard did the math. Ten apartment kids in one class meant nearly two hundred in all. Guilt overcame him. *Why didn't I fight the redistricting?* "How many students from the apartment complex in all?"

"Mrs. Baines says there's fifty-six. I got all of 'em in third grade. Every blessed one. Any more come, I get them, too, I reckon. How's that for coincidence?"

"It's very strange," he said, grabbing four packs of boxed orange juice, fighting back his growing anger. *Taking the weakest students and dumping them in her class—ghettoizing, that's what it was! An outrage!*

Mrs. Little pulled a plastic sack from the trunk. "My husband died in Vietnam a long time ago, back when I was a young thing. I got no children of my own." She looked off toward the pine trees along the school's fence. "So I see them all as partly mine."

"Do you pay for this yourself? I mean, I'm wondering why I haven't heard about this. Seems like the PTO could help."

She gestured for him to put the drinks in the closet. "Miz R doesn't officially admit I do this." She put a finger to her lips. "She doesn't wanna know. Have to admit we need a breakfast program or shut me down or *somethin'*. For me, it's Christian duty. Can't say *that*, though. Some folks think God wants nuthin' to do with public schools, but they His children, too."

He looked around. Her classroom wasn't hideous. Actually it was festive. She'd decorated it in bright red, yellow, and blue. A corner was sectioned off with a standing divider to create activity spaces. An old sofa sat under a green-on-yellow poster proclaiming READING TIME. He told himself it wasn't so bad. Obviously, she had a good heart. That wasn't enough by itself, of course, but it was something.

They hauled in another load, talking as they worked. He peered over two cartons of Pop Tarts and asked Mrs. Little how long she'd been at Malliford. This was her fourth year, same as Nick. Before that, she'd been at Bonaire.

"Bonaire?" he said, incredulous. Had she followed him here? It seemed like cosmic mockery, somehow.

"That's right. I started this when I was there. They need it worse, but I had to leave."

"We lived near Bonaire, then it got violent." He was referring to the drug dealer's murder, of course. How could he forget? He put his house up for sale the next day. "The shooting. You had to—"

She rocked on her feet. "Yes, sir, I took it hard. I wanted *out* of there. They let me pick a school, and I decided on Malliford, Miz Rutherford didn't want me here. She never forgave me for comin' here against her wishes."

Since when did black teachers get to change schools just because someone got shot? He decided it would be rude to pose that question, however.

When he'd finished hauling in the food, Richard asked if there was anything else he could do to help. "No," said Mrs. Little. "But there is something I want you to know."

"What's that?"

"Mr. Gray, I prayed your son would be in my class."

Whoa, way too much church and state in that sentence. "Good day, Mrs. Little," Richard said, torn between atheism and anger at the Almighty. *If there is a God, He has a mighty funny way of revealing Himself.*

In the hall, he noticed the security camera was trained on Miz Little's classroom door, not the back entrance. He paused at the front door to check the class roster once more. Despite his anger, he would not ask for a change. No way. Nick was teacher-proof, he told himself. The boy would learn no matter whose class he was in. Still, this was a deliberate insult, probably intended to provoke a racist reaction. *Well, he was white, but he wouldn't bite.*

Maybe Mrs. Little wasn't so bad. After all, Stan liked her, mainly because she forced her students to sign up for No-TV Week and regarded TV as the Devil's tool. Took it downright personally. For sure, she had some old-time religion. If she turned out to be horrible, he'd work to get rid of her, if such a thing were possible. Perhaps Miz Rutherford was trying to make an ally of Richard, so that he would help her get rid of a bad teacher. Well, that was too twisted to think about. In fact, it made his head hurt.

Wife and child were still asleep when he got home. He left a note on the kitchen table and took the van to run errands—as many as he could think of, seeking to delay as long as possible her recriminations over his failures as man, husband, hunter, gatherer, and now PTO president.

When he returned after lunch, Nick was in the family room, working on a jigsaw puzzle of a tornado. Anna Lee sat at the kitchen table going through an ominous-looking pile of bills. She looked up as he carried in groceries. "Did you go by the school?"

Gulp. No use sugarcoating it. "Yeah. He's in Mrs. Little's class."

Her jaw dropped. "Shit. I don't believe it. I just don't believe it. Could you please explain how this happened? I thought you took the presidency to avoid this." She pounded the table with both fists and cried out, "This is messed up!"

Richard cringed when he saw not just anger but also hatred in her eyes. He tried hating back in self-defense, but he was weak and no match for her. The next thing he knew, he was sitting at the table like a suspect cooking under an interrogation lamp, thanks to the poor design of their remodeled kitchen. He called Nick's reassignment a reprisal for not buying Miz Rutherford new furniture. Or maybe it was the letter calling on her to rehire the art teacher. Or putting Stan on the board, being seen with Stan, talking with Stan—

"Stan, period," Anna Lee suggested drily.

Richard didn't mention Nick's switch from Mrs. Radcliffe's class. That would make it worse. He also didn't mention God, fearing Nick might get caught in a providential riptide if Anna Lee started counter-praying. *It could tear the boy apart, I tell you.*

"If the principal's that petty, she should be fired, like your friends say," Anna Lee declared, slamming her Crystal Springs water bottle on the table. "It's not wise to alienate a PTO president, even if ... whatever," she said, leaving his gross incompetence unstated but implied. "What are you going to do? You have the principal's home phone number?"

"I'm not calling her."

Anna Lee folded her arms and locked eyes with him in a stare-down. "You'd better. I don't want my son in that woman's class."

She then repeated rumors about Mrs. Little that Richard had heard before; actually, he'd told her a couple of them. Now they hurtled back at him like heat-seeking missiles that missed their target and were returning to the launch pad to explode. He had to admit they sounded racist when someone else said them.

Anna Lee told him that if he wasn't going to call the principal, he should call Superintendent Johnson or school board members he knew. Richard considered this unreasonable, since Mrs. Little was a certified teacher with no outstanding warrants, that he knew of (though he did wonder about the knife scar).

He took off his glasses and ran his right hand brusquely through his hair. "Let's just accept this and move on," he said.

"Accept a slap in the face? That makes you as timid as the mousiest housewife. And after you said—remind me again: Why the hell did you take the job?"

"I didn't think our principal would be unprofessional. Look, I talked with Mrs. Little. She's a good woman. Stan thinks highly of her."

"And, as we discussed, Stan is part of the problem."

"I don't know what else I can say."

"Barry wonders why we put Nick in public school," she said, throwing her oily boss into the argument. "He said if Nick was his child—"

"Nick isn't his child!" Richard growled. "We've been over this. No private school."

"That's moot. We don't have the money. Not until you get a job."

"Nick's going to be fine."

"I wish." She grabbed her purse. "I gotta get out of here. I'm going shopping—and buying a lottery ticket. If I win, Nick goes to a private school." She slammed the door behind her.

"Next year," he declared through gritted teeth, "because a man keeps his promises."

He went to tell Nick the news, vowing not to apologize for the way the world worked, even if it worked against the boy, but thanks to his powerful kid ears, Nick already knew Ms. Bullfrog Eyes would be his teacher.

NINE

H is blue backpack bouncing, Nick pranced up the hill Monday into bright sunshine like a pint-sized Pied Piper. He wore khaki shorts, new sneakers, and a Gresham Soccer T-shirt. His hair was neatly parted, a concession to his mother, who wore a white sun dress and brought up the rear of the family procession, trudging along like a condemned prisoner. Between them, Richard strode purposefully, dressed in blue pleated Dockers and Rockport walking shoes. A yellow button with red letters on his grey polo shirt proclaimed his name and rank in the PTO.

He turned to speak to Anna Lee, but she made a point of ignoring him, so he shut his mouth. She'd barely spoken to him since breakfast, when he forbade any mention of Nick's class placement to Miz Rutherford. There would be no special requests or useless begging; negotiating with that dreadful woman was out of the question. As for Mrs. Little, he would keep an open mind *and* an eye on her. "Nick will be fine," he'd said.

"I doubt it," she'd replied, not bothering to conceal her contempt.

There were the typical first-day snafus. At the summit, traffic snarled at the loop entrance. Also, the school-zone lights on Windamere malfunctioned. All summer they flashed needless warnings twice daily. Now needed, they were dead. Richard would call the county—again and again, as it turned out. As he neared the school, a woman waved and called to him. Without recognizing her, he smiled and returned the greeting. Nick waited at the crosswalk, creating a bigger jam, since the guard stopped cars on the rumor of a crossing.

"Morning, Mr. Gray."

"Good morning, Mrs. Perkins."

"Good to see you back, Nick. Third grade?"

The boy nodded.

"The school-zone lights are out," Richard told her, as he waited for Anna Lee to cross.

"I'll call the county."

"How many years is this for you, Mrs. Perkins? Twenty? Wow. Keep up the good work."

She beamed as he walked off. Meanwhile, in front of school, Miz Rutherford stood with radio and clipboard in hand, an obstacle to the flow of humanity. She wore a sleeveless blue dress and pearls. In the morning sun's glare, her aging arms resembled plucked chicken wings. Richard gave himself permission to officially hate her after having practiced all summer, though smiles would be the order of the day.

He stopped inside near the office while Anna Lee escorted Nick to Mrs. Little's class. She insisted on seeing Nick seated, even though Rule No. 3 of *Malliford Manners* stated she should go no further than the classroom door. She had told Richard she hoped there wasn't room for Nick in the class— implicitly suggesting that their son should be the first one out, just because he was the last one in. However, Richard was fairly certain Nick would have Mrs. Little even if he was the *only* student in her class.

Manners contained forty-two rules in all, ten of them brand-new. The restrictions were Miz Rutherford's pride and joy, designed to prevent parents from interfering with "the Malliford Experience." The PTO had dutifully printed up copies (at considerable cost) and distributed them on registration day. Security and Discipline were the school themes this year—an unsubtle response to the invasion of the Apartment Dwellers. Principal, faculty, and PWCs agreed: *Malliford Manners* were especially important as the rampaging horde arrived and threatened to lower test scores, property values, morality, health, safety, and living standards.

In the crowded front hall, first-day dramas played out. Parents were knotted in twos and threes, gossiping. A mother bent down to console a crying kindergartner; another wept as her son ran off to check out the Legos in Ms. Cranford's room. Veteran parents conspired to enjoy their newfound freedom. Cindi Lou ambled along, talking on her cell phone, and bumped into a first-grader, nearly running him over. One parent thanked Richard for doing a thankless job; another he'd been trying to recruit as a volunteer avoided him like he was selling insurance.

Rita sidled up to him and squeezed his arm. "We've got a hundred signatures. Has she responded to the letter? No? Damn her." She pinballed away, blithely unaware Nick was the first casualty of her accursed war. A second later, one of Rita's friends gave Richard a raised-fist salute: Fight the power! *Had it come to that?*

Anna Lee appeared at his side. "I was turned away at the classroom door," she said, sounding like a frustrated civil rights activist. Perhaps she could call the Southern Freedom Foundation and have them file a reverse-discrimination lawsuit on her behalf.

"Standard operating procedure," he said, pleased she was speaking to him at all.

As they walked outside, Anna Lee whispered, "There are a lot of black kids in Nick's class. At least everyone's sitting quietly. She must scare them." She shuddered. "She scares me, for that matter. Well, I've got to go to work. You staying?" He nodded. She gave him a wan smile and turned to go. "Good luck," she said over her shoulder. "You'll need it."

Miz Rutherford saw Anna Lee, lowered her radio and prepared to speak. Anna Lee averted her gaze as she walked by. The snubbed principal wore a look of pained surprise at the affront. To Richard this was the height of hypocrisy. She knew what she'd done and done it on purpose. Did she expect Anna Lee to thank her? Or did she plan to negotiate Nick's freedom with his mother and thereby emasculate Dad? *Whatever.* He no longer cared to guess at the deep, unfathomable motives of the Evil One.

Richard turned into a greeter, all smiles, welcoming parents and children to Malliford. His forlorn wife stopped on the sidewalk to chat with Joan Brewer, whose third-grader was in Mrs. Radcliffe's class—a winner in Malliford's rigged lottery.

"Mr. President!" Barbara Hodges approached in her bouncy, high-heeled walk, wearing a tight red skirt and ruffled cream blouse, towing her younger son. The boy broke away and darted inside, ignoring a spindly girl safety cadet's cry: "Walk, don't run, please." (Her older son—the fly to Mrs. Little's bullfrog—was captain of cadets, a Pupil Who Counts.)

Barbara laid a hand on Richard's shoulder and gave him her let-bygones-be-bygones smile. "You're doing a fantastic job! Registration went so well! You must have put in a ton of work."

With Barbara as a social buffer, Miz Rutherford came over. The three exchanged pleasantries and agreed that everything was wonderful. Barbara said her second-grader had Mrs. Vandenburg.

"A fine teacher," Miz Rutherford said.

"The best," Barbara agreed.

They looked at Richard for a response, but he remained silent on the issue. Neither woman mentioned Nick's class assignment; Richard was sure they'd share a good laugh when he was gone, if they hadn't already busted a gut at his expense.

Barbara went inside; Miz Rutherford and Richard returned to their respective posts. A few minutes later, Susan Gunther, wearing khaki shorts, sandals, and a Malliford Ducks T-shirt, approached with her son and two daughters.

"Hey, Susan," Richard said. She waved—or maybe she was telling him to talk to the hand.

Miz Rutherford's radio crackled. She frowned. Seconds later, a bus packed with rowdy kids pulled into the loop. The dreaded Apartment Dwellers had arrived. Miz Rutherford gave the black, brown, and yellow kids her steeliest eye as they scrambled off the bus. Some bounced; others trudged. A Latino boy led two small twins dressed in identical plaid skirts and white polo shirts. Two black boys scuffled on the sidewalk, ignoring Miz Rutherford's admonition: "Stop that nonsense right now!"

A sullen eight-year-old black boy approached Richard, glaring at him and looking over his shoulder after he walked past. That would be Devonious Saunderson.

The bell rang. Miz Rutherford retreated. Tomorrow she would hand out tardy slips. As cadets sauntered toward school, wily students rushed past them, since those who entered the building after the last cadet were officially tardy. The further from the schoolhouse door, the more wildly children flailed their arms in their flight from doom—or toward it, as the case might be.

The apartment bus didn't leave. Richard saw the driver standing and wagging her finger toward the back of the bus. The middle-aged black woman turned and shouted, "I need help. This girl won't get off."

Richard had a Travis Bickle moment. He looked around and realized she *was* talkin' to him. He walked over and climbed into the bus. In the back sat a petulant little girl with a purple ribbon in her silky black hair, looking like she was going to a dance: lacy white dress, white tights, and patent leather shoes. She would take home a note from Coach saying, "Wear sneakers every day." She was extraordinarily pretty, with dark shining eyes she used to bore a hole in Richard's head before turning her gaze on the window. "Do you speak Spanish?" the driver asked him.

"No." After an awkward moment, he remembered his trusty yo-yo. He pulled it out and tightened the string. The girl turned toward him, her glare softening into a look of curiosity. "This is a special yo-yo. People gave it to me to make fun of me, but they didn't know it had magic. Uh, do you speak English?"

"Sure. I'm not *stupeed*," she said with a distinct Hispanic accent.

"No, of course not. What's your name?"

"Alicia Rodriguez."

"That's a pretty name."

"What kind of magic?" she asked.

"Strength and courage."

"Are you afraid?"

"No," he said. "I've got my yo-yo. How about you? Is something bothering you?"

"I like my old school. My friends are there. And I miss my mommy. I don't have a daddy. He died."

"I'm sorry to hear that. But you'll make new friends here. If you come here and try hard, I'll give you a yo-yo." He knew where he could get them for four bucks a dozen, but she knew quality and held out her hand for the Duncan. "*Whoa* ... not this one."

She didn't relent. After she agreed to return it, he handed it to her.

"This is the PTO president ... Mr. Gray," the driver said, reading his name tag. "He's going to take you to your class."

The girl stood up with her backpack and looked at Richard hopefully. "If I'm good and come to school, you give me a yo-yo I can keep?"

"Sure. Absolutely."

She followed him. He held out his hand to help her down the steps. "What grade are you in?"

"Second."

"Hey," he said, brightening. "I know a girl in second grade. Her name is Karen McAllister. I bet she'll be your friend."

The doors slammed behind them and the bus pulled away. On the sidewalk, Richard showed Alicia how to work the yo-yo. After a couple of tries, she managed to bring it up and down three times before it strung out. "Come on," Richard said. "Let's get you to class."

She grabbed his hand as they walked to the door.

"This is a good school," he said. "It has four stars."

"You are president of the school?"

"No, I'm president of the Parent-Teacher Organization."

"El Presidente."

He liked the sound of that. He stopped at the door to check class postings. She was in Vandenburg's class, poor girl. But so was Stan's daughter, so that much was good. He took her inside, still holding her hand.

Teresa popped out of the office. "Got a new friend, I see. I'm jealous," she said with a wink.

Richard's pulse quickened, but he kept moving. "Gotta get her to class," he said.

Alicia started singing softly in Spanish. A few seconds later, Miz Rutherford began the Pledge of Allegiance over the intercom, halting Richard in his tracks. He assumed the position and pledged to the wall. Alicia dutifully followed suit.

They arrived at Mrs. Vandenburg's room in the back hall.

"It's a nice yo-yo," the girl said, returning it to him. For a moment, he was tempted to let her keep it, but he needed its power. When they entered, Susan Gunther was there, staking her claim as room mother, although Stan would no doubt challenge her primacy.

Susan gave Richard a thin smile. "Mentoring the apartment kids? Great. You should," she said, finishing off with a sneer.

Richard ignored her. "I've got a new student for you," he told Mrs. Vandenburg, who looked up from her desk and motioned Alicia toward an empty seat in back. Stan's daughter waved at Richard. "That's Karen," he said, pointing her out to Alicia.

"I'll take it from here," Mrs. Vandenburg declared firmly.

"Be good, Alicia. I won't forget my promise."

"Alicia, if you're late again, you'll need a tardy slip from the office," the teacher warned.

"There was a problem on the bus," Richard said.

"Have a nice day, Mr. Gray."

Realizing that no good would come of continued conversation, he walked out. He heard Susan say, "Great, another illegal."

He paused, waiting to hear Susan get an appropriate rebuke from Mrs. Vandenburg. Nothing. He stuck his head back inside the room and said, "Alicia speaks English, Susan. And so do I."

Susan looked at him in shock.

Mrs. Vandenburg said, "That nice day, Mr. Gray? Go have it."

A moment later, the heavyset Mrs. Cates, bane of parents and tormenter of Spencer Hadley, appeared to shoo him away. "You need a visitor's or volunteer's tag, Mr. Gray."

He glanced down at his chest to see if he'd lost his identity. He hadn't. "A button saying I'm PTO president won't do?"

"A visitor's name tag shows us you've signed in. Security and Discipline. New rules."

"I'll do better next time." No use arguing with Ms. Chain Gang. Next to Mrs. Little, she was Malliford's most unpopular teacher among parents—the salt to Avon Little's pepper, but Richard thought Nick's charitable, somewhat friendly teacher was superior to this lumpy, churlish white woman. *Shouldn't she be in her room, or did she just police the halls for wayward parents?*

Shaking his head in disgust, Richard left the building. He blinked in the sunlight, feeling like he'd just escaped from a cave. A straggler hustled up the sidewalk at a dead run.

"Don't be late tomorrow!" Richard hollered after the boy.

"I know, I know!" the kid said as he opened the door.

Richard reached into his pocket. The yo-yo felt good and solid. Best of all, its magic worked not just for him, but for little ones, too. He realized right then that everything had changed—from last year, from the summer, from registration day, from the second before he met Alicia. There was a war on, no doubt, and he had to fight. He would say what needed to be said, even if no one wanted to hear it. He'd do what needed to be done, even if he had to do it alone. For Nick and Alicia and every other kid. For Mrs. Little, even if it meant forming an alliance with the worst teacher in the school. It would be good to be the answer to someone's prayer—to be a Yes in a world of Nos. He snapped his cell phone from its holder and made a call.

"Hey, handsome," Rita said.

"You got me into this Mallifordian mess. Now you have to help."

"Name your price."

"Tutors. I need you to recruit ten people, and each of them to recruit two, to start. Do you know anyone who speaks Spanish? Korean? Vietnamese? We need 'em. We're going to make this PTO what it should have been all along."

"I'm with you all the way. Go get 'em, cowboy."

"We need a hundred more signatures on Stan's petition."

"Yes, sir. You sound like a man who found his hill to fight for."

"It's the hill I live on. What better place than that?"

* * *

Three days later, the fight was still on. That sultry Thursday evening, just. before the school year's first PTO board meeting, Candace and Cindi Lou stood in the school's lengthening shadow and watched Richard swing his brown leather satchel as he approached, wearing a puzzled look. "Is the door locked?" he asked.

"Maybe," said Cindi Lou.

"We don't want to go in," Candace said. "We're nervous."

"And scared. She could expel us."

"Send us to bed without our supper."

"Or worse. Look what she did to your son."

"Nick's just fine, thank you!" Richard snapped.

Candace turned to Cindi Lou and said, "Denial. It's the first stage."

"I hope you're right," Cindi Lou told Richard. "I don't know Mrs. Little. Except she isn't. Little."

"All right," Richard said. "Let's get this over with."

"Did you bring copies of the resolution about the art teacher?" Candace asked.

"Yes, enough for everyone."

"Damn," the women said in unison.

"I don't see how it's going to pass," Candace said.

"We gotta try," Richard said.

"We gonna get whupped," Cindi Lou pointed out.

"Ain't nothin' but a thing," he said, borrowing one of Mrs. Little's pet phrases.

"She'll abolish the PTO," Candace said.

"Then we get the rest of the year off. Come on." Richard stretched his arms to engulf them and pushed them inside.

Two hours after he gaveled the meeting to order with his yo-yo, Richard staggered out of the media center. There had been a flurry of motions, counter motions, recriminations, and two confrontations—one between Rita and Susan, the other between Teresa and the "Table of Trouble," as she called it, where Barbara and Susan sat with the other hardcore Rutherford supporters.

Although the proposed budget had been easily approved, Richard's motion calling on Miz Rutherford to hire an art teacher had carried by the narrowest of margins, 13-12, after the principal abstained, glaring at Richard, her hands crossed and clamped into fists across her chest. Following that vote, Barbara made a motion to reconsider, which was defeated because one of her supporters got pissed at Miz Rutherford for not voting in the first place.

Not only had the PTO leadership stood on its hind legs for once, it had also managed to mark some territory while it danced around. After the vote, Miz Rutherford told board members they could pass any motions they wanted, because it didn't matter. "I'm not going to let a bunch of helicopter parents tell me how to run my school," she declared. Then she stormed out.

Stan dove into the ensuing silence to deliver a five-minute presentation on No-TV Week, which wasn't scheduled until April. Richard cut him off to adjourn the meeting, and everyone left in a foul mood—except Rita, who was gleeful at the turn of events. Still, all in all, Richard was pleased with his performance: *gutsy, gritty, with a hint of the young De Niro.*

One thing they didn't do was present Stan's incendiary petition. Richard had persuaded him to bring it up at the general membership meeting, but the PTO president hoped it wouldn't come to that. He also feared reprisals from the school administration against those who'd signed it. There was a widespread fear among parents that educators would come after their kids if they spoke up too loudly or often. And now Richard had seen the proof, up close and personal, with Nick.

Ms. Bailey asked for Richard's help securing the building. Afterward, he walked her to her late-model gold Lexus and thought perhaps teachers weren't so underpaid, after all.

"That certainly was *interesting*," she said. "I've never seen anything like it."

"I didn't want things to work out this way."

"She didn't think you'd go this far. Didn't think you'd have any support."

"*Whoops.* Now she knows."

"She's too stubborn to change. She'll do something, though. Expect a surprise."

"It's hard to expect a surprise."

She giggled. "Oh Richard, I do like you."

"Well, *she* doesn't."

"She saw you as a cruel joke Rita was playing on her. She severely underestimated you."

"I thought the cruel joke was on me. And you were in on it."

She gave him an offended look. "I beg your pardon."

"You were on the nominating committee, remember?"

"Oh, right. Seemed like a good idea at the time. Still might be. I'm afraid you two are locked in battle for the time being."

"I'm just trying to make this a better school."

"I know you are. And so is she. Unfortunately, you frighten her."

"She's got a funny way of showing it."

She patted his cheek and got into her car, showing a shapely leg. She drove off, leaving him standing in the dark beside an empty building, alone with all the stars.

*   *   *

The next morning, Miz Rutherford approached Richard in the front hall. "Mr. Gray," she said. "A word about last night's performance."

He turned to face her. "Aw shucks. 'Twarn't nothin', ma'am. I didn't even rehearse." He toed the floor for good measure, then stuck his hands in his pockets and grasped the yo-yo, his talisman against evil.

She saw no humor in his response. Her expression was hard. "I don't want a repeat during Open House next week. I'm not letting you turn our biggest meeting into a circus, not when the teachers already have to stay late to meet with parents. The issue of staffing is closed."

"No, it isn't. You devalued this school's academics without input from parents, and there are repercussions. In other words, actions have consequences, as you're so fond of saying. This is just the beginning."

"I'll not argue, but I warn you the PTO's status as a school-based organization is not a given."

"You mean you'd drive the PTO underground?"

Wow. That would to be Rita's wildest dream. She'd form a guerilla parent group, complete with Hendrix posters and protest songs: *All we are saying ... is give PTAs a chance.*

"Here's the deal, Mr. Gray: If you misuse your position and PTO meetings to hurt this school, I'll halt the meeting. We don't have time for manufactured brouhaha. Publicly attacking my decisions will only do harm."

"You ignored us when we privately attacked them," he pointed out. "And there's a danger in that."

She was taken aback by his remark. Before she could respond, Polly peeked around the corner and beckoned her. Seconds later, the bell rang, chasing the pissed-off president home.

Richard knew three school board members and the superintendent. Despite their faults and failings, they'd want to defuse the powder keg at Malliford, wouldn't they? He dialed the superintendent's office. The phone rang twenty times before Richard hung up, cursing. He was considering calling school board members and drawing them into the arena of micromanagement when he remembered the hubcap man, Curtis Blodgett. Miz Rutherford's supervisor had been quite agitated over her "alternative sentencing" program last year.

Richard dialed. Blodgett was in. "Mr. Blodgett, this is Richard Gray, PTO president at Chain Gang Elementary. There are things you need to know, and I'm the one to tell you."

TEN

Anna Lee was right: Being PTO president was "an adventure in suckage." Trudging toward Malliford's Open House with his satchel strap slung over his shoulder, Richard knew he was doomed. That afternoon, he'd been called *divisive*. Mrs. Vandenburg hissed the word loudly in the hall while talking to Mrs. Cates. No crueler cut could she deliver: He was part of the problem, not part of the solution. The cancer, not the answer. A smarty-pantser.

OK, he could admit that using the school's nickname wasn't so bright. Blodgett had hung up after interrupting Richard to tell him, "The principal runs the school." His hopes fading, Richard had faxed the board resolution to Blodgett with a note: "Petition with 100s of sigs to come." He followed up on the threat, sending Stan's ten-page masterpiece, but the bureaucrat didn't respond.

Richard had considered it a clever gambit to leave a photocopy of the meeting agenda on the Xerox machine that morning as a final warning to Miz Rutherford. New Business, Item No. 1: *Consideration of Board Resolution re Art Teacher*. He'd hoped she'd call him to make a deal. Instead, she'd sent out her minions to vilify him.

As it turned out, she also called the police. As he crossed Windamere at the loop, he stared in disbelief at a cop standing in front of the school. Was Marine Antoinette really going to shut down the meeting and throw him out? Rita would claim it was Kent State all over again and put a flower in his gun barrel.

There was no gun, however. Richard drew closer and saw it was just a potbellied brown-uniformed Gresham school security guard who couldn't keep his shirt tucked in. No nightstick, even, just a radio to call real cops when the deal went down. The man, reeking of cigarette smoke, nodded sleepily to Richard as he walked by.

In the front hall, silhouettes blocked the sunlight cutting straight through the dirt-streaked courtyard windows. As Richard stopped to chat with his volunteers at the Membership and Duckwear tables, his eyes adjusted to the glare and he realized he was surrounded by county bureaucrats—who seemed to be inching in on him like zombies. Mrs. Baines was talking to a heavyset man in white short sleeves and black tie who looked like a McDonald's manager. By God, it was Blodgett. *He never comes unless there's trouble. Interesting.*

When Richard proceeded to the library to check on the book fair, Blodgett drifted after him like a tethered balloon. "Mr. Gray," the man called out. "We talked recently."

Richard halted and cocked his head. "Really? About what?"

Blodgett offered his hand "You had some concerns."

Richard shook it unenthusiastically. "Nothing came of it, I recall. And the conversation ended badly."

Blodgett ignored the reference to the late unpleasantness. "I want to address your concerns," he said. "Work out a win-win situation."

"Really? What's the score?" He loved *win-win, a hundred and ten percent*—all those irrational sports clichés.

"We understand there are legitimate parental concerns. Tell the truth, all those faxes tore up my machine." Blodgett chuckled to show no hard feelings, despite the trouble this parental unit was causing him. "I started looking at how things looked, and I saw that parents saw things differently from Miz Rutherford, and everyone's right in a way. She's got big challenges ahead with changing student populations, so forth and whatnot, and we need to support her efforts to make all Malliford students good achievers. On the other hand, it shouldn't come at the expense of the quality education the community expects. I see where you see it as a loss, losing the art teacher."

Richard shuffled his feet restlessly. "Yeah, a loss-loss situation."

"To make a long story short, we're considering giving the school another faculty position that can be used to hire an art teacher."

Richard closed one eye and cocked his head as he analyzed this information. "I don't think I heard exactly what I need to hear."

"Somebody told me you used to be an editor at the *Sentinel.*"

"Yes, that's true." He was about to say, "Why?" when he realized what Blodgett was getting at.

"You haven't talked to Deanna Richardson, have you?"

Ah. There is was. "There's a message on my machine." Richard figured all's fair in win-win. Or loss-loss.

"You'll tell her the issue has been resolved satisfactorily, I hope."

Had Richard missed something? He didn't think so. "But it hasn't. You gave me too many qualifiers, while what we need is an art teacher. Until we get one, the problem is unresolved. No one will be happy. Call it a whine-whine situation."

"Believe me, we're working right now to bring Miz Rutherford on board."

"Please do, before she drowns."

"I hear you, Mr. Gray," Blodgett said, forcing a smile. "I hear you."

"Way to go, Prez," said a stocky Applegate neighbor in cargo shorts and a T-shirt, clapping his hand on Richard's shoulder as he passed. "Get us that art teacher. Don't give up."

Richard hoped this timely support would show the bureaucrat that he was dealing not with a mere helicopter parent whirling out of control, but a citizen leader capable of ramming through resolutions, destroying fax machines, playing the media like a harp, and making Blodgett's life miserable.

And this may have been the case, since whatever Blodgett was thinking caused him to scowl.

"Look," Richard said. "I tried to work this out but I hit a brick in the wall. We're moving ahead with ... let's just call it a vote of no confidence in the principal, since she's being this way. If war is what she wants, war is what she'll get. A war-war situation."

"There's no need for that kind of talk."

"Uh, uh." Richard wagged his finger, having surmised that Blodgett really didn't want to do anything other than ride out the storm. "It's on the agenda. We're on the ledge and we'll jump, I tell you. If you want to talk us down, we need a commitment. Tonight. Publicly. That's the win-win deal I need. That's how you address my *concerns.*"

"Oh." Blodgett looked like he'd been caught bluffing without the chips to back his bet.

"You weren't going to do anything, were you? Well, that won't work. Tell her to behave, Mr. Blodgett. ... One more thing. If she threatens to throw the PTO out of the school again, I'll take her up on her offer and make sure Deanna Richardson at the *Sentinel* is the first to know. Don't make us go outlaw. Do we understand each other?"

"We most certainly do." Blodgett seemed quite unhappy, so he probably did understand. "Excuse me. I have work to do."

"Thank you, Mr. Blodgett."

The bureaucrat retreated. Richard let out a deep breath and stepped into the media center, which was packed with parents and kids, several of whom sat cross-legged, reading books in front of portable metal bookcases. Candace and Cindi Lou were busily ringing up sales. His vice president gave him a thumbs-up. Cindi Lou asked, "What's going on? Tawny said you were giving some county guy the business." She punctuated her statement with a right jab.

Richard shrugged. "We'll see."

He wound his way to the cafetorium through the deserted back hall, gathering his wits in the face of the approaching storm. When he turned a corner, he saw a most welcome sight: Teresa and her daughters handing out agendas, minutes, and resolutions to parents at the cafetorium door.

"Hey you," Teresa said. "We need to go over the budget. Amber, Caitlin, keep handing out the papers, please."

"You're great helpers," Richard told the girls.

He and Teresa went onstage and sat on plastic chairs. Richard looked around. "Is Carl here tonight?"

She gave him a bitter chuckle. "No way. He's out golfing. He never comes to these meetings. Giving a damn isn't his style."

Time to change the subject. "Hey, the county sent an army to quell our riot. The area director says they're *thinking about* giving us an art teacher. Apparently, our principal still needs convincing."

"They'd better do more than just think about it."

"Our resolution rattled them. The guy tried to bullshit me, but I told him we were on a ledge and about to jump. I hope they're doing an intervention with her right now. I thought people would come after *me* with pitchforks and weed whackers. Amazing."

"You're what's amazing."

"This is giving me a headache."

"Poor Prezzie," she cooed, touching his forehead. "You'll look back at this and laugh."

He looked in her eyes and saw something he wished he saw in Anna Lee's. He hadn't been imagining it—unless he was still imagining it. How could she look at him that way? Didn't she know it was dangerous? He couldn't tear his gaze away. He wanted to stare into her eyes and smell the lilacs. He managed a crooked smile and said, "I'm looking forward to looking back."

"Speaking of looking." Teresa nodded toward the wall. A security camera was focused on them. It pivoted away when Richard stared at the lens, as if it was ashamed at being caught.

"Creepy."

"Even the robots here are bitches," Teresa said.

They returned to their duties. When Richard glanced up again, the camera had returned its unblinking gaze to them. By then, most of the seats had been taken. Looking around, Richard saw more parents of color than in years past—though still relatively few, considering the influx of black and Hispanic students. A shame, really, since Open House might be the only meeting many of them would attend.

Stan entered with his daughter and took a front-row seat. Richard hopped down from the stage to speak with him. "Where's your wife?"

"She's not into the PTO," Stan said, wrinkling his nose. "Especially not the confrontational stuff."

"Which you live for."

They were discussing late-breaking developments in the Art War when Anna Lee entered with Nick and smiled wryly at her husband as she took her seat. Nick wore a Hot Wheels T-Shirt, shorts, and sandals. He tossed his *Pokémon* book in his mother's lap and sat on his hands, adopting the pained expression of an eight-year-old under strict orders to sit still and be quiet.

Richard flashed him a "V" sign, then crooked his fingers, the international sign for bunny ears. Nick laughed, turned to his mother, got a nod of permission, and scooted away to the book fair.

When Blodgett and Miz Rutherford entered, the man gave Richard an "OK" sign. The principal regarded Richard disdainfully as she took the stage and claimed a seat to the right of the podium. She waved her hand like his queen, gesturing for him to get on with the show. Laughing at her imperious gesture, Richard hopped onto the stage like he was vaulting a fence and took the podium. The fascist duck stared at him from the back of the room. He returned its glare. After all, he *was* the duck! Long live the duck!

He flicked on the microphone, pulled his yo-yo from his khakis, and rapped the podium. "Good evening. I'm PTO President Richard Gray. Welcome to Malliford Elementary's Open House." With a Chaplinesque move, he flicked the yo-yo down and up. Amid a ripple of laughter, he said, "There being a quorum present, I call this meeting to order."

After the pledge and opening remarks, Richard turned the podium over to Miz Rutherford with no exchange of pleasantries, since neither had anything nice to say about the other right then. After her standard welcome, the principal spoke of new challenges confronting Malliford: Security and Discipline, in other words. Then she introduced the teachers, who received a warm ovation. She gave Richard a smug look, as if this show of support for teachers was a setback for him, even though he'd led the applause. She concluded without mentioning the art teacher. Richard gave Blodgett a WTF look and jabbed his agenda. As the principal bent to sit, Richard whispered, "We will vote on it."

She was caught in a crouch, an inch off the chair. "Oh, yes. That."

"That, indeed."

She straightened up and returned to the podium. "I have been informed that the county has *finally* agreed to release funds to allow me to hire a *full-time* art teacher. Apparently, a few parents are under a misapprehension about this," she said, casting a withering glance in Richard's direction. "I'm happy to clear it up."

"When will the new art teacher begin?" asked Richard, acting quite unshriveled.

She turned and looked at him like she'd found him on the bottom of her shoe—in a pasture. She started to say something, then turned to face the audience. "As soon as possible, Mr. Gray."

"So we don't have to consider the resolution tonight. I know parents are happy to hear that. Aren't you, parents?" Applause broke out like a sheet of wind-driven rain on a tin roof.

She reluctantly returned the podium to him, and the meeting moved quickly after that. Teresa's budget was approved unanimously with no debate. Richard watched Susan in the audience, her body rigid as she abstained. And so, with the exception of a tabled agenda item and a brief exchange between PTO president and principal, it was business as usual at a well-regarded public elementary school with four stars by its name.

The meeting was adjourned, and parents gravitated toward classrooms to meet their students' teachers. His headache was gone, and Richard's feelings of doom were replaced by those of sweet victory and relief. A monster had rushed toward him, and instead of clawing him to death and biting off his head, it hurtled by and plummeted off a cliff. Barbara congratulated him with a tight-lipped smile. Parents patted him on the back. He was a local hero, surrounded by his people, now knotted in a tight circle around him, the new PWCs: Rita, Stan, Jane Baumgartner, Candace, Cindi Lou, and most of all Teresa, who stood close beside him. Anna Lee cast a fleeting, indecipherable glance at his entourage as she left for Mrs. Little's room.

Teresa whispered, "You should be proud of yourself, pouring water on the witch."

"That would make me Dorothy."

"Hey, if the ruby red slippers fit ..."

Richard looked at the principal, who was stooping slightly and seemed to have aged ten years in as many days, but hadn't melted. No, that would take time—and heat. She returned his gaze before breaking it off and shuffling out the door.

"Not her night," Stan crowed softly.

A few minutes later, Richard exited the cafetorium, passing under the red, white and blue Celebrate Diversity banner hanging beside the double doors. He stopped to speak with a supporter and then found—and left—Nick at the book fair, under Cindi Lou's semi-watchful eye. On the way to Mrs. Little's room, Richard saw Stan in the door of Mrs. Vandenburg's classroom on the other side of the back hall, angrily whacking the doorjamb with his agenda.

Richard came to the green banner that proclaimed "Mrs. Little's Lair" and stood in the doorway trying to appear serenely presidential. He'd expected to find a classroom jammed with parents, but it was only half full. A dozen people had shown up, and they didn't match the class's demographics. Half of them were white, although Mrs. Little's class was 85 percent minority, in stark contrast to the school's overall population, which was 64 percent white. Anna Lee sat in front near the white dry-erase boards. Some parents discussing a homework issue with Mrs. Little seemed irritated. Richard noticed a small white man sitting in back, wearing a gray business suit, smirking at the exchange.

Mrs. Little broke off the discussion, nodded to Richard, and addressed the parents: "Good evening! I'm delighted to see so many of you here. I'm very pleased with my class and they're gonna to do real good. It takes time to get sorted and straight. I've taught for thirty years, and I know it can be frustratin' when kids get to third grade. This is where it gets tougher, but your kids will do fine. As you may know, they got their syllabuses in their courier envelopes last Friday. If you look—"

Peripheral movement caught Richard's eye. He turned to see Stan storm up the hall toward him, shaking his head furiously, throwing up his hands. Stan pivoted and disappeared into the library hall. Richard turned back to Mrs. Little as she spoke his name: "Thank you, Mr. Gray, for taking the lead in setting up the PTO tutoring program."

"Glad to do it," he said. "That's what we're here for."

After twenty minutes of explanations, questions, and answers, a bell rang, signaling the end of Open House. Richard stepped aside as parents filed out. The weary teacher looked like she could use a kind word. "These twelve-hour days are killers, aren't they?" he said.

"Fourteen. I was here at seven."

"Ah, yes. Breakfast duty. Keep up the good work."

"Thanks. That means a lot, coming from you. Seems like a lot of folks are unhappy."

"They think it's their job."

She broke out laughing and wiped her eyes. "Thanks. I 'specially needed that. You go on home now."

"You, too."

Richard found Anna Lee waiting for him in the hall. She rolled her eyes toward the ceiling and bit her lip. "That went well," she said with a touch of sarcasm.

"I thought it did."

"I'm going to go say hello to Mrs. Leland."

"Hey, find the boy!" he called out after her. When he turned around, the man from the back of the class was standing next to him.

"Congratulations," said the dapper fellow, extending his hand. "Or should I say, my condolences. Being a PTA president in a public school takes courage these days. Where do they get these teachers?" He nodded toward Mrs. Little's room and smirked.

Richard felt protective of Mrs. Little now that his child was in her class and didn't want smartass white guys making fun of her. In fact, he felt an instinctive dislike toward the man.

"I'm Jack Desmond, Christopher's dad."

Jack Desmond? Not the Jack Desmond who with the right-wing group that fought public schools at every turn? Not the asshole who thought Richard was turning his son gay? Nah. Couldn't be.

"Of course, I refuse to join the Parent-Teacher Association because of its opposition to school choice and vouchers."

Yes, *that* Jack Desmond. What was *he* doing here? Why wasn't his kid in private school?

"This is a PTO, not a PTA." Richard did his best to sound condescending, since he'd decided Desmond was thick-headed as well as being a homophobic bastard. "Not that I favor vouchers."

Desmond ignored the correction. "So what did you think of the dog-and-pony show? You know, where the teacher tries to convince parents that everything's under control when it isn't, and that she's qualified to teach them, which she isn't."

"That wasn't my take on it at all."

"Come on. *Curriculums*? We be learnin', we be learnin'." He sang in mock-reggae style.

Richard wanted to bitch-slap him. "Mrs. Little doesn't deserve that kind of response."

"I'm sorry," the man said somberly, then brightened. "We should celebrate our diversity, right? No matter how low the test scores go."

"I don't think we're on the same page here."

"Well, there's no accounting for reading skills," Desmond quipped. "You'll see. Working up close and personal to this mess will open your eyes to what's really going on. Women—they bake cookies, sell gift wrap, buy bright shiny stuff, get the kids out of the house and into college, that's it for them. We want more for our sons, I'm sure you–"

"Out of the house and into college sounds like a plan to me."

Desmond plowed ahead. "There's a war on for the souls of our children, and I've enlisted as a soldier in the fight. My wife recently inherited a house on Bendabar, so I'm new here, which explains how my boy ended up in this class. So what did you do wrong?"

He eyed Richard curiously. The president refused to take the bait. "Join the PTO board if you're such a soldier," Richard said. "There's a couple of committees still open."

"Like I said, not my army. Here." Desmond handed him a business card that said: "Jack Desmond, Executive Director, Southern Freedom Foundation." It was embossed with the silhouette of a vigilant Minuteman.

"People say America needs to hire 100,000 more teachers. Actually we need to fire 100,000 like her." Desmond jerked his thumb toward the room.

"Perhaps you should ask the principal to put your son in another class. Or maybe you should consider private school."

"This is where the war is being fought. Leave no child behind, right?"

"Race to the top."

"Whatever. All I'm asking is just do the right thing and back us at the appropriate time. It will come soon enough. Big things are ahead."

"I consider myself a reformer."

"We have a lot in common, then. We'll talk. Good meeting you." Desmond turned and walked away.

I don't think so. Richard's cell phone buzzed. "I'm in the front hall," Anna Lee said. "Some of us have to work tomorrow."

"All of us have to work tomorrow."

"Mrs. Leland says thanks. I don't know for what."

"The art teacher."

"I thought the county took care of that."

"Under duress," he said, clicking off as he walked toward her. Ten seconds later, she was in sight. She regarded him critically. "Your treasurer is a hot little number."

"I hadn't noticed."

"Liar, liar, pants on fire. Let's find Nick and go home."

* * *

Richard didn't have time to savor his victory in the Art War. Another conflict—unspecified at first—erupted the next day. Friday afternoon, he noticed Mrs. Vandenburg, Mrs. Baines, and the principal huddled in the front office in animated conversation. When he got home with Nick, there was a phone message from Polly: "Miz Rutherford needs you in her office ASAP."

Who did the principal think she was, ordering him around—even worse, ordering poor Polly to order him around? That dreadful woman could go to hell. He wasn't letting her destroy his weekend. When the phone rang, he let the machine pick up. It was Polly again: "Miz Rutherford has to leave. Please come to her office Monday at eight-fifteen. It's extremely important."

When Monday morning came around, Richard held Nick's hand on the way to Malliford. As they approached the crossing, Nick pried free. "What's wrong?" Richard asked.

"I don't want them to see me," Nick said.

"Who?"

"Devonious and Simeon. They'll say I'm gay."

Richard knew Devonious Saunderson and Simeon Dupree, of course. They were bad-attitude apartment kids he'd been tutoring. He considered it horribly unfair that a budding juvenile delinquent like Devonious—trouble from Day One, according to Mrs. Little—should set the standards for behavior. Anyway, it sounded like bullying.

"Well, that's no way for them to talk. And it doesn't mean anything. Don't let the haters rule. We still hold hands when we're not around school, right?"

Nick shrugged. "Yeah, I guess."

As Mrs. Perkins stopped traffic, Richard remembered the principal's edict and decided to stiff-arm her as long as possible. "You go ahead and cross by yourself. You're a big guy. You can handle it."

"Sure. I could walk all the way, but you'd be lonely."

Nick hitched up his pack and jogged across the street. Richard watched him trot to catch up with a friend. He felt a growing resentment toward Nick's classmates for coming between him and his son—he hated being at the mercy of two fatherless boys who knew the latest rap lyrics but couldn't tell him what a verb was.

"They grow up so fast," Mrs. Perkins observed.

"Yeah. By the way, the lights still don't work."

"I told them a dozen times. I'll make it a baker's dozen."

He returned home, intent on ignoring the principal's edict as long as possible. After he e-mailed the files for a client's newsletter to the printer and ate lunch, he walked up to Malliford and nonchalantly checked PTO mail in the office. The inner door was closed, but the light was on. Polly was busy at her computer. The stoop-shouldered secretary looked up and scowled. "Didn't you get my messages? Why weren't you here this morning?"

"Never said I would be. Does she still want to see me?"

"You bet. I'll tell her you finally showed up." She picked up the phone and he heard a buzz twenty feet away. "He's here. ... I don't know why. ... All right." She hung up and shooed him toward the principal's office.

Richard knocked on Miz Rutherford's door and went in. She gave him a wintry look.

"What is your problem?" he asked, his tone hard and flat as slate.

In a word, Stan.

"*Your* Mr. McAllister came in and delivered a letter on PTO letterhead stating your group, quote, 'upholds parents' rights to pull children from school when television is being shown,' unquote," she huffed. "He took it upon himself to put a copy in every teacher's box."

"Really? Can I see it?"

"They've been taken up and destroyed. I'm sure you're familiar with its contents."

"Afraid not. It's news to me. So what's the big deal?"

"He absconded with his daughter. He called her to the door and took her. We have procedures—"

"Was Mrs. Vandenburg in the classroom?"

"That isn't the point."

"Were the kids watching cartoons? That's an issue with him, you know."

"That's not the point, either."

"Well, *yeah. It is.*"

Irritated by his delivery, she jabbed her index finger in the air as she spoke: "The point is that the PTO is being used to disrupt classes. I warned you to control him. Now we have chaos."

"Are you telling me a teacher plops kids in front of a TV and takes off? *That's* chaos."

"You aren't seeing the big picture here."

"No," he said emphatically. "We're seeing different big pictures. Looks like both you and Stan are overreacting."

"I never overreact." She gave him a supercilious smile.

"I'll talk to Stan, but you've got to realize parents can protest what's wrong in the classroom. He has a right to pull his daughter out if the teacher's not teaching. Parents don't have much recourse or input, you know. Sometimes we get frustrated. All we can do is vote with our feet."

"You're so full of rights, Mr. Gray. Despite your end-around on the art teacher, I'm not letting parents run this school."

Richard chuckled, just to irritate her.

"Don't you laugh at me," she scolded. "I'm serious. We can't have anarchy. You talk to him. I've said all I care to say to that man."

"That all?" He wanted to leave before he blew his cool, and laughing on the way out seemed the perfect exit strategy.

"Get him under control. He's a threat to peace and order in this school. You should remove him from the board."

"That's a blatant overreaction."

"Again, *I don't overreact.*" She jabbed her desk calendar. "Up until this year, there's been cooperation and harmony. I was concerned about this from the beginning. That woman ..." She shook her head as she trailed off. Rita would be ecstatic to learn she'd become Rutherford's *She Who Shall Not Be Named*. "From the beginning, you've been difficult. Trying to take over."

"That's not true. I just want what's best for this school."

"And there's little I can do if you're determined to be that way," she declared, apparently ignoring his comment. "Just see that you obey the rules. I don't want the PTO president serving as a bad example. I'd hate—"

"I'm not the one who's misbehaving here. Before you start threatening me again, I'll go."

He went. When he got home, there was a message from Polly: "Please remove PTO stationery from the school ASAP."

Richard had to admit this was a good idea even though the principal thought it was a good idea. He must batten down hatches and secure communications for battles to come. But first he needed to pay a visit to Stan, who lived on the back side of Malliford, not much further from school than he did.

It was a nice day, cool for late August, and a gentle breeze brought a hint of autumn, so he walked. As he approached 1318 Balsam Court, Richard realized Barbara was right: Stan's house was a property-value downer, ugly and ill-kempt, sitting on a piney lot covered by a decade's worth of needles. The queer contempo-ranch looked like it had been dropped on its cracked foundation before conformists filled the subdivision with brick ranches in the 1960s. Stan's battered white Corolla was parked in the drive facing a carport overflowing with junk, much of it covered by dusty blue tarps. It looked like a flea market had been bulldozed against the wall. Richard spotted the washing machine Barbara complained about under a stack of cardboard boxes. Atop an old dresser sat an upside-down barbecue grill, a plaid shirt hanging from its leg.

Richard knocked on a screenless storm door. A huge black creature—part Lab, part seal—wagged its tail and barked happily.

"El Presidente," Stan said, looking puzzled as he held the door open, blocking the dog with his leg. "To what do I owe the honor? Hush, Bones."

"I want to talk." Richard stepped inside. The dog quieted and sniffed his crotch. Richard followed Stan through the kitchen. The table was covered with dirty dishes, and the sink was full of pans. There was a hole under the counter where a dishwasher would go. They walked through the dining room, past a battered antique table covered with family photos, into the living room. The air was musty and dank, an unholy combination of old dog, radon, and something else he couldn't identify.

Richard looked around in vain for a fan before sitting on the sofa. He looked down at green shag carpet, something he hadn't seen since his brother's college apartment. What the hell did Stan do with his time? All the other stay-at-home dads Richard knew either had a home business, took college classes, worked part time, substitute taught, or remodeled and renovated their houses. At the very least, they kept them up, thereby avoiding the stigma of lethargy and worthlessness. Apparently, Stan had no such hang-up.

"How long have you lived here?" Richard asked.

"Ten years, since Janet's mom died. We inherited it along with all her furniture. She keeled over at the kitchen sink one day and was found three weeks later."

OK. Old dog, radon, and dead mother-in-law.

"*Awk.* School of Excellence," said a bright green parrot in a golden cage.

Do what? Richard rose and walked over to the cage. "I had no idea a bird was capable of contempt."

"Contempt? Nah, I just taught Malliford to read."

Richard glanced at the bottom of the cage and saw the missing *School of Excellence* sign, covered in parrot shit.

"Now you know my little secret," Stan said. The parrot dropped a load to punctuate his sentence. "I'll give it back if you insist, but I'm not going to clean it. Maybe I'll present it to her, covered with shit, at her retirement party. A fitting tribute, don't you think?"

"Another reason not to attend the festivities," Richard said.

"Hey, the parrot isn't doing anything to the school's reputation that Iron-pants hasn't already done. You're not going to rat me out, are you?"

"No. I'm glad it's gone. It was embarrassing. It reminded me of this old demented woman who lived down the street in my home town. Long after her yard went to weeds, she kept her *Lawn of the Month* sign up. It was the town joke."

"Then you know how I felt when I took the sonofabitch down. I stole an old demented woman's yard sign because it was the town joke. It wasn't even hers. It was there when she arrived, that's how old it was. She did nothing to earn it. Then she puts up that gravestone marker. They should bury her under it."

"All right." Richard said, retaking his seat and slapping his thighs with his palms. "Let's talk."

"Go ahead."

"Stan, we've got a problem with how you handled the TV thing."

"I've got a right to pull Karen out of class."

"I'm not arguing that. But you used letterhead, and you made up the PTO's position. We like to be ... non-confrontational about such things."

"I'm a committee chairman," Stan declared.

"Even so, you can't speak for the entire PTO when you're pursuing a personal agenda."

"It affects every kid in the class."

Richard was getting exasperated. "What are you trying to do? Sabotage No-TV Week?"

Stan set his jaw and gave Richard a sullen glare. "No, I'm not. Are you?"

"I sympathize with your position, but if you're going to act like this, you'll squander good will and alienate people—including me."

"You're caving. You know, when you took over the presidency, I was so happy. I thought you'd be a man. Instead you cut some kind of deal over the art teacher just to keep the petition from coming out."

Richard took a deep breath to keep from raising his voice. "I'm not going there. This is about how you deal with people. I'm in the middle of this, and nobody's happy. You've got attitude. So does she. I'm just trying to patch things up. I'd like for you to work through channels."

"You're turning the PTO into another damn bureaucracy."

"If you don't watch it, you're going to screw yourself. All the kids will be watching *Nick at Nite* during No-TV Week. You will have defeated your own cause."

"The PTO is so weak."

"Look, build friendships and alliances. That's politics. Make as many friends as possible and keep 'em as long as you can. If I were you, I'd make sure I was one of them."

"What about principles?" Stan asked.

"We're stuck with the principal we've got. For now."

The quip broke the tension somewhat, and after Stan agreed not to use letterhead without permission, the two men parted amicably. Richard then stopped by the school and retrieved the stationery as the dismissal bell rang. On the way home, Nick told him Chris Desmond had been transferred to Mrs. Radcliffe's class. Which meant Jack Desmond wasn't above pulling strings. No surprise there.

"Chris is my friend," Nick whined. "Now I'm the only white boy in my class."

"You've got friends," Richard assured him. "Antonio. Kendrick."

"They're the only two. I hate school."

"It's not so bad."

"What do you know? You're paid to say that."

*　　*　　*

Richard was torn between trying to patch things up and saying to hell with Miz Rutherford. The next morning, after she brushed by him in the hall with a curt nod, he decided to steer clear of her. There were things he needed to do. Kissing her ancient ass was not one of them.

Anyway, there was another crisis to deal with. When he checked the PTO mail, he found a note:

President,

I cannot fulfill the duty as newsletter editor knowing what I know and that is that the PTA and school leadership are suppose to work together, but I do not believe this is the intent or purpose of PTA leadership. Under this circumstances, it would be hypocritical for me to serve. Good luck finding an editor that share your vision tho that will be difficult.

Regrettably,

Danielle Morelli

Sic, sic, sic. You cannot fulfill the duties as newsletter editor if you write *this circumstances* and don't know the difference between PTO and PTA, Richard thought as he stuffed the note in his pocket. And Danielle Morelli was one of the women who called Avon Little *Miz Ebonics!* Did she want him to apologize and beg her to come back? No way would he do that. When she'd accepted the position, she said she could "improve" the newsletter and "make it more relevant."

Excuse me, but Duck Call *won first prize in statewide competition, you idiot.*

Richard's temples throbbed; he felt a huge headache coming on. He searched the front hall for the dumpy, brown-haired, moon-faced, bespectacled woman. The foolish gossip wasn't there, luckily for her. He suspected Susan or the principal of putting her up to this. But not Barbara. After all, a rift at the school could depress real estate prices. No, she'd wish him well even if she hated him and wouldn't let him know if she did. That's what he liked about his predecessor: her friendly duplicity. More likely, Danielle now realized putting out a newsletter was a lot like work. The fool hadn't put out a single issue! She hadn't even written a single article. She was completely incompetent, and the half-baked politics of her resignation letter were nothing more than a weak attempt to cover her illiterate, procrastinating ass.

Of course he could find an editor who shared his views—all he had to do was look in the mirror. Still, it sucked being Atlas, tricked into holding the world on his shoulders. As he was walking out the door, essentially in a daze, the thought hit him: *This is a good thing.* His enemies had ceded control of the media to him, handing him the keys to the strife-torn land's only radio station. Enough defeatism. Time to start broadcasting!

He went home and wrote Danielle a terse e-mail accepting her resignation as editor *and* from the PTO board, stripping her of PWC status. (There would be a battle over this, but Richard would prevail. No work, no power. That was the deal.) Then he started piecing the newsletter together, using the paltry crumbs she'd left. He spent all day on it, becoming so engrossed he almost forgot to pick up Nick after school. Before he knew it, Anna Lee was home.

Richard came out of his office and said, "The newsletter editor resigned. Can you cook dinner while I work on *Duck Call?* I need to finish tonight and pull strings so I can get it out Friday."

"Get somebody else," she suggested. "Tell them you can't do the news-letter, too."

"Sadly, there is no them. Only me."

"I'm hungry," Nick called out from the family room.

"I don't like this PTO overload," Anna Lee said. "Not a bit. You promised."

"Did not," Richard said, retreating to his office.

That night they ate boiled macaroni and cheese served rudely and crude-ly, with clanging plates and silverware. But that was all right. Richard un-derstood that poor rations served under hostile conditions were an inevitable consequence of war.

ELEVEN

Richard sipped strong coffee from an insulated metal mug and gazed up at the silver glint of an airliner crossing a cotton-candy sky. The morning bell had just rung, and he was waiting in front of the school for the hubbub to die down before he went inside to tutor some of Nick's classmates, including the ones who thought he was turning his son gay. He smiled sympathetically at a brown-haired girl who ran by wearing a horrified grimace, her red backpack canting like a compass needle. The safety cadets were all inside. She was *so* tardy. Miz R would have her behind.

"Late September, and the flashing light by Gatewood still isn't working," said Rita, there to tutor the Delgado twins—apartment kids, like Richard's charges.

"The one by my house is out, too. I told Polly twice and wrote a letter to the county. Two, actually, and one to the principal. Hell, I've lost track."

"It's a hazard. Drivers are crazy, even parents going to school. ... Is that dark roast? *Mmm.*"

"Get some from the teacher's lounge or the cafeteria. We pay for it."

"I don't want to *trespass*," Rita hissed.

"You're teaching today. You're entitled."

"Yours is better. Just give me some, boy." She made a two-handed grab for his cup.

"Just take it," he said, once she had a better grip on it than he did.

"I will, thanks." She took a sip. "Strong. Wish you used cream."

"Cuts the effect." He looked down at the weedy flowerbed and scowled.

"What's wrong?" Rita asked.

"Just thinking about Volunteer Day. Know any good gardeners?"

"Don't look at me. I got shrubs died five years ago that I still haven't pulled up. I let rain and birds take care of the toilet paper my daughter's so-called friends put in the trees. My place is old and rundown, just like me. (Rita owned the area's oldest home, a Craftsman bungalow that predated Windamere Woods by fifty years.) Barbara can sue me."

That gave him an idea. He pointed toward the new Abacus Realty sign on the message board and said, "I'll put Barbara in charge of that. Maybe she can bring some money, too."

"Good idea. How's the free labor coming?"

"I'm using Stan's petition to draft people, since the new *Duckectory* isn't out yet."

"Marine Antoinette will just love that. Talk to her lately?"

"Nope. It's pretty frosty."

"I thought there was a truce."

"More of a cold war. It's not so bad, since we just argue when we talk, anyway. When we're anywhere near sharing the same spot in time and space, she looks beyond me and barely nods in passing. I deal with Ms. Bailey and Mrs. Baines. Ms. Bailey, preferably."

She snorted. "Goes without saying. You heard anything about an art teacher? It's been two weeks."

"Mrs. Baines says they can't find any qualified candidates. I thought there were plenty of starving artists. Don't you have some stashed away at your gallery?"

"They need a starving artist with a teaching certificate. Mine just starve." She handed him the empty cup. "Come on, cold warrior. Let's get to work."

They signed in at the office. As they entered the hall, a round-faced woman with a vacant stare breezed by wearing a flowing, light-blue caftan and a weird peach-colored hat: half pillbox, half turban. "Oh, god," Rita groaned. "Bella Donna Landistoy."

"She looks like she came from Hogwarts. Or a Marx Brothers film."

"Named herself after a Stevie Nicks song. She must be the new art teacher. A prime example of those who can't, period."

"She's that bad?"

"They're punishing us. She couldn't be Marine Antoinette's choice unless the woman is completely demented." Rita paused reflectively. "Well, that *is* a possibility."

Richard went to Mrs. Little's room. Although he didn't *feel* tardy, the teacher regarded him with exasperation. "*There* you are. Devonious, Simeon,

Antonio. Go with Mr. Gray. They're in fine form today," she muttered.

"And good morning to you!" Richard said, grinning as Antonio Jarvus, Devonious Saunderson, and Simeon Dupree popped up from their chairs, proud of the attention they were receiving. The three Chantilly Arms residents loved going to the learning resources lab, since computers beat textbooks any day.

Antonio, Nick's friend, wore glasses and wanted to go to college. Devonious, a scowling trash talker, put down Antonio by calling him Erkl, after the nerdy black TV character. Simeon, a somber, watchful boy, often parroted Devonious's macho attitudes.

"Can we do Math Busters today?" Simeon asked as they walked down the hall.

"Thursday," Richard said. "Tuesdays are language arts."

"Oh," the boys said in a weary, disjointed chorus.

"It's all good," Richard said. They entered the computer lab, empty at this early hour. "Today, I'm teaching you how to complain."

That sparked their curiosity. Richard told them they'd be writing letters because they'd gotten cereal boxes that were supposed to contain a prize, but when they opened the package, the box contained no prize, just corn flakes. "What you gonna do?" he asked.

"When they come for you," Devonious sang, from the TV show *Cops*. He didn't want to write a letter. "There should be a toll-free number to call."

"When you get a grade for using the phone, I'll teach you that. For now, we write."

"You trippin', man."

"I assure you, I *am not* tripping."

"I don't need no help to use the phone. I use my mama's cell phone all the time."

"I'll bet she loves that."

"She got unlimited minutes. And I don't like corn flakes."

"It doesn't matter. You just bought it for the prize."

"What's the prize?"

"Super spy decoder ring," Richard said.

Devonious made a face. "I wouldn't buy a box of corn flakes to get a Dakota ring."

"Can it be frosted flakes?" asked Antonio.

"I suppose."

"Why don't we just get our money back?"

"We're going for the prize."

"Not no Dakota ring."

"Fine! Whatever! A computer game."

"That's better. What game?"

"Whatever one you want."

"*Grand Theft Auto!*" the boys shouted in unison.

"Isn't that a game for adults with criminal tendencies?"

"Yeah!"

"They don't put *Grand Theft Auto* in cereal boxes. How about *Sandlot Football?*" The boys were clearly disappointed. "You realize this is just an exercise."

Devonious scowled at Richard and asked, "What good is it, then?"

"You're learning to write a letter. If you'd rather write a letter to a friend, that's fine."

"I don't need to write letters. Like I said since you ain't listenin'. I got a cell phone. We got all kinda money. My old man's a rapper. Big playa."

Antonio shook his head. Devonious gave him a threatening glare.

"That's fine, Devonious. However, we're building skills here. Do you want to go back to class? Didn't think so. Let's get to work. Each of you get on a computer. Spread out. No hitting!" he added, since Devonious had a habit of elbowing Antonio when they sat by each other.

They settled in. Richard showed them how to write a letter and address an envelope. He made Devonious rewrite the sentence that said, "You fools better give me my prize or I come up there and beat on you," but he complimented the boy on sentence structure. The kid was smart, though Richard feared this only made him more dangerous.

He returned them to class with their completed work. Mrs. Little laughed as she read. "You're teachin' 'em to be lawyers. You're gonna give me the vapors."

"I told them knowledge is power."

"You're good, but I think I'll burn these letters. Complaints don't go down so good 'round here, as you might have noticed."

* * *

Richard's victory in the Art War turned out to be not so clear-cut. In addition to Rita's claim that the new art teacher was incompetent, teachers stuck in trailers were displeased that they'd lost a coveted classroom. Nick complained, too. "Ms. Landistoy is weird," he said. "She told us to experience ourselves in art. I don't know how to do that. I just want to draw."

A few days later, Ms. Landistoy approached Richard in the hall. She wore a practical outfit this time—khaki pants and blue smock—no doubt conforming to the iron-willed principal's dress code.

"I heard you're getting the children to experience themselves in art," he said.

"No, we're *actualizing* ourselves through art. And I have great plans for putting living work created by students in the courtyard. That's what I want to talk to you about."

She stared out the hall window into the courtyard, mesmerized for a moment. Richard figured she was actualizing her vision, or maybe pre-actualizing it, actually. "Really."

Her attention meandered back to him. "There's a program a friend of mine runs called Living Artwork," she said, her tone rising as she spoke. "She empowers students to create works from natural materials. Hemp, for instance."

"Hemp? What about the Zero Tolerance policy?"

That drew a blank look. "Of course it wouldn't last forever."

No, the sixth-graders would smoke it. He glanced out on the courtyard, already filled with natural materials—weeds, wooden picnic tables, old bricks. Sprucing it up was at the top of his list of Volunteer Day projects. "You mean we'd put it out there to rot? Why don't we just laminate it and put it in the library?"

"You're kidding." She rolled her eyes. "Anyway, her fee is two thousand dollars, plus materials, for a week. I'm not sure about travel expenses. I suppose she could stay with me while she's in town. We'd need to eat. I'd have to take her out. I don't really cook that much. And she's vegan. I'm only semi-vegan. I suppose the total would be twenty-five hundred dollars. Or more."

"And the kids do all the work?"

"More actualization that way."

"Whatever happened to finger painting?"

"This is another realm entirely. I'll conceptualize my request in memo form for you."

"You do that."

She drifted toward the faculty lounge and he was left to wonder what he'd missed in life, actualization-wise. Could that be the root of his problems?

Later, when Richard recounted the conversation to Teresa, she said, "Declare a victory and move on. If we hadn't fought, we'd have nothing. At least kids are learning to draw."

"I'm not sure drawing fits in with her definition of art, actualizationally," Richard said.

* * *

September's newsletter deadlines rushed by like rocks in an avalanche. Richard worked late for corporate clients and put an even greater effort into *Duck Call*, scouring the Internet for article ideas on parent involvement, parent's rights, and school reform. He would use the PTO's news organ to send a message of hope and freedom to the masses. *Fight the Power!*

One morning as he drank coffee and rustled through the *Sentinel's* Lifestyle section, he found the perfect term: *hyperparent*. Yes, that was him, making sure Nick had everything—a full-time parent on call, soccer, piano lessons—while running a PTO and a business. He'd done everything except let Nick join Cub Scouts—despite the boy's pleas whenever he saw Chris Desmond in uniform. Richard would not stoop to validate the organization's homophobia. He had to draw the line somewhere. Why not at intolerance, if it saved time?

Meanwhile, the principal spent much of her time huddling in her office with the counselor and psychologist. Richard often saw her talking with Jack Desmond and suspected a right-wing conspiracy of unknown vastness.

"She's working on a grant proposal," Ms. Bailey told Richard one morning after she coaxed him out of range of the front-hall security camera. "Could be big money," she added.

"I figure it's for metal detectors," Richard said. "Nothing says security like high-priced hardware."

"Actually, she wants student uniforms next year."

"I'm against that. So are most parents." He hoped they were, anyway.

Despite the war clouds that hovered over Malliford since the beginning of the school year, there were many days when the sun broke through and shone on Richard. More volunteers joined the PTO's ranks. Teachers smiled at Richard and approached him with suggestions and requests. Mrs. Patterson asked if the PTO could get parents to donate books to kindergarten classes, and she did so *while she was standing in front of a surveillance camera!*

The tutoring continued, with Malliford's "ghettoized" classes receiving priority treatment. By the end of September, the other third-grade teachers demanded that Richard and Mrs. Little include their students in their blossoming class newsletter project after they saw young

journalists' pictures and bylined stories. Anna Lee was pleased by Nick's front-page editorial against littering. That same edition contained a poem about baseball by Antonio. Devonious ("call me D") responded to Antonio's claim that rappers were poets by calling him a motherfucker and striking him in the face with his fist. D missed a week of PE for that, but the sentence was as hard on Mrs. Little as it was on the boy.

Richard thought Nick was doing just fine, despite a few rough patches. His cursive writing was illegible, and his homework sometimes disappeared before he turned it in. Nick claimed that school wasn't fun any more, due largely to the aforementioned homework, which sometimes took him an hour and a half to do—up from essentially zero in second grade. "Mrs. Little is way past mean," Nick explained, "heading toward pure evil."

Richard said she wasn't so bad.

"Is too," Nick retorted.

Worst of all, Nick said, he didn't have any friends since Chris Desmond went to Mrs. Radcliffe's class. "Except Antonio," he said. "The other kids call us names, especially Devonious. He calls me a girl."

"Sticks and stones," Richard said.

"Yeah, they use those, too."

*   *   *

Looming large on Richard's agenda was Volunteer Day—the third Saturday in October, which was typically nothing more than an anemic leaf-raking expedition to the school property's back fence. Richard was determined to improve both the school's appearance and the PTO's modus operandi. Malliford's ugliness was daunting, however. The school's interior trim looked like Halloween in a rundown factory: Half the doorjambs were grey, the rest either orange or black. All were badly chipped. Walls were covered with decades' worth of adhesives. Bathrooms belonged in a subway station. The school custodian had been fired for moonlighting during his regular work hours, and Miz Rutherford struggled to find a janitor who would bother to show up.

Outside, the hard-packed yard was dominated by scrawny, ragged bushes and random patches of mutant crabgrass. The trailers' driftwood-colored steps needed repairs. The nature trail needed work. There were dozens of things to do, in addition to building an outdoor classroom.

Richard spent a hundred hours recruiting and organizing volunteers, ordering lumber and paint, wrangling deals at Hilliard's Nursery for plants and grass seed, and persuading local supermarkets to donate drinks, donuts and bagels. All told, his grand vision would cost $3,000. Fortunately, fund-raisers were coming in over budget—with little or no help from Susan.

Teresa was very helpful, although surprisingly, Barbara Hodges ran a close second. The ex-president had readily agreed to supervise landscaping and convinced her bosses at Abacus Realty to pony up money for plants. In addition, half the PTO board members signed up; many committed their husbands to the cause. Rita dubbed his followers *Richardistas*; she claimed she'd heard Susan call them *Dickheads. Whatever.*

Best of all, nearly half the teachers signed up to help.

Even on the brightest of days, there were clouds, however. A redecorating dispute marred the week leading up to V-Day. Richard sent Candace and Cindi Lou to meet with Miz Rutherford, having promised them they could pick the school's trim colors as long as they worked out details with the principal. The two women believed that since parents were buying the paint, the PTO should choose the pigments. They wanted all hues to be "brain-based." (No one really knew what this meant except that such colors raised intelligence and test scores.) However, Miz Rutherford had already picked *her* colors—purple and green—and claimed superior expertise in matters of brain-basedness, though Richard considered her colors more mallard-like than mental. The PTO officers wanted sophisticated shades of mauve and taupe, not "tacky duck colors." They weren't prepared to concede on the issue, Richard having taught them courage of a sort. They marched into the principal's office prepared to take a stand. After a brief, unpleasant meeting, they left in tears and refused to participate in V-Day, threatened to sell their houses, and move away, even if it meant using Barbara as an agent. Richard sympathized but did not intercede on their behalf, being more concerned about drying times than pigmentation. He wasn't going to cry over hue and furthermore, had no intention of dying on a purple hill.

* * *

On V-Day, providence smiled upon Malliford. At dawn, Venus winked at Richard as he piled tools into the Audi's trunk. Leaves were golden orange, the air cool and crisp, the sky clear. When he pulled into the loop, Barbara was waiting for him by her Mercedes. She wore overalls with brass buttons, a light-blue, long-sleeved T-shirt, and Gore-Tex hiking boots. With her broad-brimmed straw hat, she looked like she was going to a sorority Sadie Hawkins Day dance.

"Hail to you, o worthy volunteer," he said. "The first one here. I'm impressed."

"You're the worthy one," Barbara said with a bow. "From you all worthiness flows."

Such conciliatory tones. Richard hoped this would be a great and healing day.

An hour later, Teresa and Bessie Harper took their stations at the sign-in table, routing volunteers to their assigned jobs based on Richard's color-coded charts. Teresa apologized for her no-show, no-good husband.

"At least he's taking care of the kids," Richard said.

"No. Candace has them." (Feeling guilty about quitting on Richard, she and Cindi Lou had offered to baby-sit for V-Day volunteers, though not at Malliford.) "I wish Carl was like you. All this and running a business, too. Is there anything you can't do?"

"I've just got you overly impressed."

"Damn right you do. I've got to pinch you to see if you're real."

"Ouch!" He rubbed his arm. "Let me get back to work before I impress you again."

Besides organizing everything, Richard was team leader of the day's centerpiece project, the outdoor classroom being constructed beneath a gigantic white oak at the edge of the school's front lawn. This entailed building three long, wooden-backed benches surrounding a wooden lectern. Barbara's crew would plant laurels around the benches.

Soon, Malliford was a festive, swarming beehive. A hand-drawn, duck-adorned banner hung on the brick wall and fluttered in the breeze: WE ♥ MALLIFORD! VOLUNTEER DAY RULES! The air filled with buzzing, zinging, whirring, and banging, along with occasional cries of pain in what Richard called "Three Stooges moments." Sixth-graders in Service Club cleared the nature path. Cub Scouts picked up trash and limbs, though Christopher Desmond and his father were noticeably absent. When a kid-count revealed that Richard had achieved his goal of a hundred volunteers, he pumped his fist and woofed like a dog, drawing bemused stares.

Smiles, laughter, fellowship, community—exactly what Malliford needed. Richard vowed to build on the day's success. There were plenty of things the PTO could do to break down suburban walls. They could host a spring cleanup, a parents' softball tournament, a picnic. Why not a neighborhood yard sale? Winning the Apartment War meant declaring a cease-fire, then reaching out and connecting with people and making them part of the community. On V-Day, he believed this was possible.

During her mid-morning break, Barbara, her dolled-up face now adorned with mud, came over, snorting and grunting like Tim Allen from *Home Improvement*, to commend Richard and his crew. She pulled Richard aside and whispered, "I heard about a problem with the paint."

"One I avoided," Richard responded. "Notice she didn't bother to show up today." Although, from his point of view, this wasn't such a bad thing. She'd shown weakness by pulling a no-show at an important event, creating a vacuum of authority. Which would be filled, of course.

Barbara sighed. "Not her thing." On that note, she sashayed off.

A little while later, Richard took a bathroom break. When he returned to the job site, Teresa was waiting impatiently. "I've been looking for you," she said. "Sign these." She held up a clipboard with two blank checks attached. "Additional paint and supplies, line item Building and Grounds, sub-line Volunteer Day. I've got to make trips to Sherwin-Williams and Home Depot."

"Isn't there a rule about signing blank checks?"

She scowled at him. "Get real. I don't know how much it's going to cost. You're not going to diss me after all we've been through together, are you?"

"No ma'am." He signed the checks.

"Didn't think so," she said. She stuck out her tongue and stomped off.

The workday went long, with volunteers laboring well into the afternoon. Interior painting was completed thanks to several teachers and parents who toiled past two o'clock. Richard and his crew were the last to finish, wrapping up at just past four o'clock. When Richard finished cleaning up the area, he had Malliford to himself.

Weary but proud, he toured the grounds and marveled at what he and a hundred of his best friends had accomplished. He sat on a bench that hadn't been there Friday and tapped his boots on new paving stones. He looked over his shoulder and admired the shrubs Barbara's crew had planted. The outdoor classroom—now his favorite place in all the world—would be his legacy, lasting long after people had forgotten him. "I did it and it's done," he declared.

And that was that. He threw his tools in his trunk and drove home.

There was a message on the machine from Teresa: "Hey, your cell phone must be dead, but if you're hearing this, Congratulations! And guess what? Susan is moving out. She won't say where, but her kids are staying at Malliford. Anyway, we need to go over money stuff. Can we meet Monday morning at nine?"

When he returned the call, a man answered. It was the first time Richard had ever heard Carl Keller's deep baritone voice. "Carl? Richard Gray."

"El Presidente. Terry says Volunteer Day was great. Sorry I had to miss it." *Why was that again? Oh, yeah. Golf.* "She was a great help."

"She's something. Spends all her time on the PTO." Carl didn't sound pleased.

"We got a lot done today. It's amazing, really. I'm afraid how much it's going to cost. We have to do damage control. Is she there?"

"Nah. She stepped out with the girls. I'll let her know you called."

A half-hour later, Teresa called back, while Richard was watching a football game. "Hey. Carl said you were worried about money. What's the problem?" She sounded anxious.

"He must have misunderstood."

"He said something about damage control, like we'd gone over budget or something. And so he starts giving me a bunch of shit about how I'm in over my head, how I'm not an accountant."

"Uh ... I thought you *were* an accountant." Hadn't Rita assured him of that?

"I took courses in college," she said, sounding defensive. "I almost graduated with a business degree."

"Oh. What degree did you get?"

"I said, 'almost graduated.' Anyway, I have receipts for the paint and Home Depot. I'll show you."

"Teresa, it's OK. I just called to talk with you. I mean—really, just ... everything's cool."

"So you're not worried about the checks and the money?"

"No, just wanted to share the triumph. Didn't want to wait 'til Monday. You rate higher than that."

"Really?"

"You're my favorite person in the whole damned place."

"What about Rita?"

"That old hippie? I despise her with the heat of a thousand suns for getting me into this."

"You do not. What about Stan?"

"He wandered up one day. I fed him, and he hasn't gone away."

She giggled softly. "You're funny."

"Only because I love to hear you laugh."

"I'm sorry I got bent out of shape. It's just that ..."

"What?"

"Never mind. I can't say right now. See you Monday."

*   *   *

That night, Richard made a pass at Anna Lee, but she rejected him, saying, "I'm tired," and deftly shrugging off the hand he'd placed on her shoulder. Sunday, he didn't try.

TWELVE

Monday morning, perhaps sensing her husband's sexual resentment, Anna Lee left for work without the customary peck on the lips. Richard stared at the door to the garage after she'd walked out, shaking his head in disgust. He called for Nick to brush his teeth and grab his backpack for the walk to school. Nick didn't want to go, however, having decided he was sick.

Richard put a hand on his son's forehead and took Nick's temperature: 99.0 degrees. "No fever. You're going to school."

"I can't," Nick whined. "I don't feel good."

"I didn't hear anything about it until after you ate breakfast. You'll be fine." Richard needed the little slacker to be fine. He wanted to take a victory lap around Malliford, for one thing.

Grumbling, Nick got his backpack and jacket. He hit his forehead to unstick his temperature and cause it to rise to its true feverish level, but Richard wouldn't give him a redo with the thermometer. Nick trudged up the hill to Malliford behind Richard, complaining all the way.

At school, Richard gazed lovingly at the benches and newly landscaped grounds. It was cloudy and storms were in the forecast; the rain that missed them on V-Day would nourish the laurels, grass seed, and pansies they'd planted. More good fortune, there. In the front hall, Miz Rutherford was talking to a young mother. She smiled at the Grays when they entered. Had her attitude softened?

Richard stopped by Mrs. Little's room to postpone the week's tutoring sessions, explaining that he had a lot of work to catch up on.

"You deserve a day off," she said. "And thanks for fixin' up the place. Now it looks like somebody cares."

Richard said goodbye to Nick, who refused to meet his gaze, and walked the halls, admiring the freshly painted doors. The fumes had subsided and the air was breathable—a relief, since people had worried about Toxic School Syndrome, which killed three people in Ohio last month, according to Candace. Teachers complimented him lavishly. Barbara, now his best friend, apparently, hugged his neck in the back hall and told him the school looked "*absolutely gorgeously wonderful!*"

When he returned to the front, the principal approached him and asked, "When do you finish the benches?"

"Beg pardon?"

"When will you put that stuff on them?"

Richard thought for a moment. "Stain? The lumber's pressure-treated. It has to dry out for several months. Probably be summer before we do anything."

Her expression turned sour. "That's terrible. They're so plain-looking. Seems like you could do something."

"Not until then. Too bad you weren't there, by the way."

"I had a busy schedule this weekend."

"I'm sure you did," he said in his best fake-chipper voice.

"And today, I'm attending a conference on leadership. I'm the featured speaker. You see, I'm respected by my peers, no matter what some people think."

Unbelievable. "That's nice." He turned away and rolled his eyes in exasperation.

He stopped in the office and looked at the freshly painted mallard-green walls. The lopsided stars had been covered over. *Ha-ha.*

Polly caught him admiring Stan's handiwork. "When are you going to put back our stars?"

"When she earns them. May take a while, the way things are going."

"God, you're nasty. You'll pay for that."

"You're not the problem. Let's leave it at that," Richard said.

He waved at a security camera on his way out. He was supposed to meet Teresa in just over an hour, but he decided he'd had enough of Malliford for the day. He called his treasurer on the way home. "Look, that meeting ... I could use a break from the school."

"Too many fumes?"

"You could say that."

"You want to come over here?"

Although she'd come to his house on Applegate twice during the summer, he'd never been to her place. "Sure. Why not?"

"Looks like rain. I'll leave the garage open for you. Just pull in."

Richard felt a thrill run up one leg and down the other. He silently chided himself: *No, that's not going to happen. ... But who knows?*

After a cup of coffee at home, a shower, and a change of clothes, he drove over to Teresa's. Halfway up Summerwood, he saw a mountain of refuse in front of Susan's house: boxes, mattresses, old clothes, broken toys and furniture, a king-sized pile of boxes and bulging black bags. A "SOLD" placard slashed across Barbara's glamour shot on the Abacus yard sign. Where had Susan gone? Would the principal protect her strongest supporter from the county attendance police? He'd heard it had been a nasty, brutal divorce. Depending on the rumor du jour, Archie, her rat-bastard divorce lawyer husband, had (A) sandbagged money, (B) claimed to be a day trader who lost millions but actually laundered the cash into an off-shore account, (C) filed for bankruptcy, and/or (D) cheated on his pregnant twenty-two-year old legal secretary/mistress with a college co-ed.

What a guy. He belonged in the Whoredog Hall of Fame. Still, even Susan deserved better. Nevertheless, Richard was glad she couldn't spy on him from her window. And again he felt a thrill stirring, along with a little guilt. But what was wrong with the PTO president going to the treasurer's house? Nothing, yet.

Sitting atop a steep drive, the Kellers' substantial red-brick Georgian screamed prosperity. It had long green shutters and three dormer windows jutting from the roof. The landscaping was sculpted, with carefully trimmed hedges and exquisitely mulched flowerbeds. Teresa said Carl kept busy flying coast-to-coast to pay for it all. Richard guessed he made at least one-fifty a year, maybe two hundred. The garage was open. He drove in and the door dropped behind him before he turned off the ignition. As daylight disappeared, he felt like he was being swallowed.

The house door opened and Teresa appeared, wearing a short-sleeved white sweater and dark slacks. He got out of the car and heard Chris Botti playing jazz trumpet: very *noir* and sultry.

What happened next surprised Richard. Teresa pulled him inside, closed the door, and whispered in his ear, "He's out of town, and there's something I've been wanting to do for a long time."

"I—"

"*Shhh,*" she said, placing a finger to his lips. "Just let it happen. It's meant to be."

She kissed him passionately. How could he resist? Soon they were completely entwined, slumped against the wall, endangering family portraits. Before he knew it—but what did knowing have to do with it?—he was upstairs in the master bedroom on a king-sized four-poster, staring at the mirrored ceiling and wondering (if only for a moment) what he was getting into. Then something inside him broke as easily as a piece of chalk, and the fragments disappeared as quickly as if they'd been washed down the drain.

Sex with Teresa was different than with Anna Lee—at least from what he could remember with his wife. It was exciting, for one thing. Teresa told him she'd once been an exotic dancer and put on a show. He marveled at her toned and shaved body. Throughout their lovemaking, she kept thanking him for caring how she felt. They ended up on the floor, sweating profusely and tangled in sheets.

Afterward, lying on the rug, looking mussed-up and goofy in the mirror, he thought: *Well, it's done.* As if *it* had been destined since that December day he saw her in the bookstore, and now he could quit worrying. This didn't have to change everything, did it? They could just go back ... and pretend. No big deal. He was accustomed to pretending one thing or another.

"You're good," she said.

"You, too," Richard responded, although actually she was much, much better.

After they dressed, they sipped coffee at the kitchen table and went over PTO business, which seemed anticlimactic now.

"Those checks you were so worried about?" She held up receipts from Sherwin-Williams and Home Depot.

He glanced at them. A hundred thirty-five, total. "I wasn't worried."

"Just so there isn't any misunderstanding."

"Uh—"

He was about to say, "Not about this," but shut his mouth. He wasn't sure what to say. What they'd done wasn't a mistake, exactly. But it couldn't go on. Well, maybe once or twice. But there was no future in it. Maybe.

Teresa didn't say anything about the change in their relationship, either. So, he decided to let things be. Happen. Slide.

He left shortly before noon. As her garage disgorged him and he drove off, he felt like he'd gotten away with something.

Wrong.

When he got home, there was a three-hour-old message on the answering machine from Nick, who mewled pitifully: "Daddy. I threw up in class. Can you come get me?"

Damn, damn, damn. Richard stared at the machine and cursed himself for being in *exactly* the wrong place at the wrong time—if not for doing the wrong thing. His concern for Nick was washed in shame, along with guilt for not listening to his boy's complaint in the first place. Face it, he told himself: *For you, sex is a curse.* The words on his bulletin board—"You Can Let Each Day Build or Destroy You"—now seemed like a warning, not a call to arms.

He pounded his desk with his fist as he listened for an update, but the other messages were routine PTO crisis calls about the Fun-Filled Fall Festival. It hurt to listen to such piddling problems. Why no update? Was Nick still at school? It seemed impossible. He rushed outside, slamming the front door behind him. He sprinted to the car, still cursing himself. "You fucked up!" he shouted.

But his anger at the school was growing, too. How could they just let the boy put a message on the machine and leave it at that? They had a complete list of contacts: cell phone, Anna Lee's work, even her parents' number. Richard's in-laws were authorized to sign out Nick, and they had done it once. Maybe Nick was resting at his grandparents' house. But Richard knew he would have heard by now if that was the case.

The first raindrops hit the Audi's windshield as Richard raced up the street. He slammed to a stop in the loop, sprinted up the walk, threw open the schoolhouse door, stepped inside, and skidded to a halt when he saw Nick lying on the couch outside the office. Covered by a jacket, the child looked weak and wasted.

"Where were you?" he moaned. "I called you like yesterday."

Richard felt Nick's head; it was burning. "I didn't know, bud ... I'm sorry. I wasn't near the phone."

"You're always home. I told them," his voice forlorn. "Always with me ..."

"No, not always. They know how to get in touch with me or Mommy. Why didn't you call my cell phone?"

"I don't know the number. Miz Polly made me call. I thought you'd come."

"How long have you been out here?"

"Since I called. Mrs. Little said I was contagious."

Richard groaned. "I'm going to get you out of here. I'm real sorry. I feel real bad."

"I feel worse."

"I know. I'll be back in a sec."

"Hurry," Nick moaned.

Richard strode into the office and stood in front of the sign-out log on the counter. Polly was busy pecking at her keyboard. He glared at her as he picked up the chained pen. "There you are," she said, wearing a blank expression on her sallow face. "Finally."

A dark emotion welled up in his gut as he struggled to keep from yelling obscenities. He hated the school right then, hated it fiercely. "You let him lie there in misery for three hours without making a second attempt to contact me. Is that your idea of making me pay for what I said this morning?"

She seemed at first surprised, then genuinely offended. "What? That's ridiculous."

"Is it? Did you try calling my cell phone? Did you call my wife's work number? Did you call her cell phone? Her parents?"

"I figured you'd be here and gone by now."

He shook his head. She wasn't worth arguing with. The thought burned in his brain: This was payback for showing up the principal on V-Day—a despicable effort to discredit him, putting his sick child on display so parents could see what a sorry-ass bastard Richard Gray was. Obviously. Polly was just an extension of her boss, and that's where ultimate responsibility lay. "Does she know this happened?"

Silence. He threw down the pen. It bounced off the counter and swung by its beaded chain like an executed prisoner. Someone behind him spoke up in an authoritative voice: "You need to get your son home and take care of him."

Richard turned to face Mrs. Cates—Ms. Chain Gang herself. "You have a firm grasp of the obvious," he said. "Unless you want to take responsibility for the school's failure to communicate, this is none of your business."

She blinked in shock at the affront. "Mr. Gray—"

"The last thing you want right now is my full attention."

"I know you're upset."

"You have no idea," he said in an icy tone, "how upset I am."

"Don't expect special treatment because you're the PTO president."

Pssst! The ice turned to steam. "How dare you insinuate that! And if this is standard treatment for sick kids, you should be ashamed. Is it school policy to leave them in the hall without bothering to notify parents?"

"Calm down, Mr. Gray."

"Shouldn't you be in your classroom instead of cruising the halls, looking for trouble?"

"Go take care of your son."

He wanted to argue but she had a point, damn her. The teacher grudgingly made room for his exit. He brushed by her, then pivoted in the doorway and glared at Polly. "This isn't about me. I just want you to know that. If I hear about this happening again to any child, I will make it a public issue." He went to the sofa, put Nick's backpack on the boy's belly, scooped him up, and carried him out.

"Get well soon, Nick," Mrs. Cates said as they passed. "You too, Mr. Gray."

"Goddamn this place," Richard muttered as he kicked open the front door and carried Nick out into the driving rain.

Back at Applegate, after Richard tucked Nick into bed, he tried to write a letter, but he was too angry for words. The best he could come up with was, "Dear Superintendent Johnson: If you need to cut costs and improve service, I know three school employees who will *not* be missed."

When the phone rang, he jumped up and cursed it, then gingerly picked up the receiver.

"I heard there was a problem at school today with Nick," Barbara said.

"And that would be your business *how?*"

"Richard, calm down. You terrified everybody up there. They're talking about hiring attorneys and getting restraining orders. You need to cool it. I was asked to call you—"

"By whom?"

"Mrs. Baines. She thinks things are out of control."

"I'm not sure what they're telling you, but I suspect they're making up a bunch of shit just because I refuse to tolerate what they did."

"Do you actually believe they'd let a sick child lay in the hall just because they had a problem with the parent?"

"Before today, no, because I'd never seen it. Do *you* actually believe they'd let a kid who was puking lay out in the hall for three hours when they had five other numbers they could call?"

"It *is* the government, Richard."

He shook his head. "I can't believe they're dragging you into this mess. Don't let them."

"I guess they needed an ambassador to negotiate a truce."

"What do they want? Have you talked to the principal?"

Silence for a moment, then, "Yes."

"It's not Mrs. Baines, then."

"Well, it was her idea to bring me in. Which was better—"

"Better than what?"

"Removing you as PTO president."

He laughed derisively.

"I know what you're thinking," she said. "You did so much work on Volunteer Day, and this is the thanks you get."

"Actually, I was thinking they don't have the votes to remove me. But trying to do it immediately after Volunteer Day pretty much proves my point, don't you think?"

"They're afraid of you, Richard, afraid of what you might do."

"They? Why don't you be honest?"

"OK. *We're* afraid of what you might do."

"Much better."

"Richard, there are some great things going on. There's a synergy developing, and it's going to mean wonderful things for Malliford. We're afraid that it could be ruined if ... the leadership is compromised. I mean, not on the same page."

"Tell me more about this 'synergy.'"

"I can't."

"So the PTO president isn't entitled to know what's going on."

"Not yet. Look, we need a truce. For everyone's sake."

"Do you understand what happened today?" Saying that made him nervous, since as far as dirty laundry went, his sheets weren't clean, either. But that wasn't the point. They purposely neglected and abused his son, and it was irrelevant that he was fucking a former stripper while they did it.

"Angry parent acting out," Barbara said. "What am I missing?"

"Threats, warnings, and several months of aberrant behavior on the principal's part. Why aren't you telling her to cool it? What's unreasonable about expecting the school to make a diligent effort to contact parents? Do you think it was an accident that my kid was put out on display for three hours? Look at the timing! It couldn't be better for her, to try and knock me down a peg. She didn't say 'Thank you' for Saturday! She just complained about the benches. And what about you? You're not making things better, you're just trying to keep them quiet!"

"I was told—"

"There you have it."

"Damn, you're difficult. I was told to find out what you want to calm things down, OK?"

"Right now?"

She let out an exasperated sigh. "Yes."

"I want a copy of the memo Ms. Rutherford is going to write to all faculty and staff that states the school will make at least three attempts to contact a parent or guardian when a child is too sick to stay at school, if they don't succeed on the first and second tries."

"That's already the policy."

"I want it reiterated and dated today, stating that due to recent problems and parental concerns, yada yada yada. Let me ask you: Do they need lawyers and restraining orders against someone who wants that?"

"No, but I heard what happened in the office, and it was ugly."

"You didn't hear what happened. You weren't there and you only heard one side. I said I'd make it a public issue if they ever did it again."

"Well, that's a threat."

"It's only a threat if what they did was indefensible. It's only a threat to do my job because they're not doing theirs. And the policy better include single-parent families and apartment kids, goddamnit! Don't you see how bad they look? Barbara, whose side are you on?"

"Richard, be careful what you do. Be careful what you say."

"They're the ones spreading lies. Hell, let them hire their attorneys. Maybe for once they'll get some good advice. And have a nice day."

* * *

That afternoon, Richard finished writing the letter—elegant, savage, and legal in its particulars. It would wait for delivery, because there was a bigger problem: Nick was very ill. All afternoon, the boy lay in bed, calling out for juice or his father's hand to hold. At first, Richard assumed it was a simple cold, but when Nick's fever hit 104, he couldn't even swallow the crapberry-flavored fever reducer Richard gave him. When Anna Lee came home, the boy was deathly pale.

She pronounced motherly judgment while standing over the sickbed: "You should have taken him to the doctor today."

"I will," he grumbled. "I didn't know it would be this bad."

Nick moaned. "It's this bad. I had to lie on a couch in the hall for forever this morning. Dad didn't come for me until late."

Anna Lee raised an eyebrow and scowled at her husband. In a sharp tone, she asked, "What happened? Where were you?"

"I was busy. I was out."

She shook her head and bit her lip. "You need to take better care of him than that."

Richard stormed out, his guilt about the morning's tryst replaced by resentment at his wife's shrewishness.

He checked on the boy frequently and watched with increasing alarm as Nick grew weaker and less responsive. The fever stayed high, and at midnight, Richard began to worry that the disease would *win* the way it did in those ghastly fables, when the Mills of God Grind Slowly, But They Grind Our Bones to Make His Bread. Taking his firstborn would be God's ven-

geance for his commandment-breaking, going Old Testament on the hapless
adulterer's ass. Sure, God didn't like him much, either—but why take the
boy? Richard pulled out the old baby monitor and lay awake the rest of the
night listening to his son's wheezing, hoping for each next breath.

In the morning, the boy was so weak that he needed help getting to and
from the bathroom, and then to the car. Richard carried him from the Audi
into Childmed Group's offices.

In the yellow-walled exam room, Dr. Samperson checked out Nick and
said, "There's a nasty throat virus going around, but we'll check for strep. To
reduce fever and ease the pain, you'll need to give him acetaminophen suppositories, since he has trouble swallowing."

On the trip home, Nick groaned and howled at every bump in the road.
Richard went into Riteway Drugs and took his son in with him, walking
along aisles of analgesics and laxatives with the boy against his side like a
wounded soldier. The pharmacist kept suppositories behind the counter. *If
they ever fell into the wrong hands ...*

Back at Applegate, Richard put Nick in bed and prepared to medicate him.

"Those aren't tablets! They're bullets!" Nick yelled when he saw the suppositories in their silver package.

"They're medicine. To help."

"How am I supposed to swallow those? They're too big!"

"You don't swallow them. They go in the other end."

"You're crazy! That's gross! I'm not doing that, no way." Showing a surprising burst of energy, he scooted away like a frightened monkey to the head
of his bed and curled up in a ball.

"It sounds bad, but gross means unnecessary and this is necessary to
make you better. Therefore not gross."

"How is that supposed to make me better?"

"It will bring down your fever and help you to drink the fluids your body needs."

"I can't believe you're doing this to me. Your own son."

"It's necessary," Richard said. He surveyed the room. The mini-blinds
were closed; the world was dim, remote. Nick pulled covers over his head.
"Let's get this over with, buddy."

"I get a sundae when I'm better," Nick said from under the covers. "And
it's still gross."

"We don't have to tell anyone. Our secret, right?"

He did it quickly. Nick yelped more in indignity than actual pain and
claimed it hurt much worse than it did. After washing his hands obsessively,

Richard sat on the bed with his hand on the boy's forehead. Within ten minutes, Nick was sleeping peacefully.

Richard went back to his office and tried to work, but he was interrupted by a phone call from Teresa. "Miss me?" she asked playfully.

What could he, the newly damned, say? He felt too guilty to miss her. "There's been a lot going on," he said, and then told her about Nick, his confrontation in the office, and Barbara's phone call. It was news to her, but she was just as disgusted as he was.

"That's how it is at that fucking school," she said. "They don't do their jobs, then claim it's your fault. They want to get rid of you, but you've got the parents' backing. Take it public."

"I'm not sure how to play it."

He was about to touch on the sensitive subject of their relationship, having planned to tell her it might be best if they dialed it back a few notches, but Teresa beat him to it. "I hate to tell you this," she said. "Carl's back in town for *the rest of the year*. The company ran out of money to ship his ass around the Sun Belt. We have to cool it. Damn. I was looking forward to you. Now he's going to park his large butt here in his office all day, every day."

"Oh," he said, his tone dull enough to suggest both shock and sadness. And he *was* sad. For deserting his son in his hour of need. For breaking his marriage vows. Could they be repaired, or could he just hide the damage? He always believed that if he didn't cheat, Anna Lee would never leave. Now his safety net was torn. But in his gut, he felt much worse about Nick. He also remained pissed off at the school. But as for Teresa, perhaps this would subside—a one-time thing that would, in the long run, be of little consequence.

"It really sucks," she said. "I've been thinking about you. My funny Valentine. That's what you are. I wish you were Carl and he was you—with apologies to your wife. *Oops*. He just pulled in the drive. I gotta go. One thing: I remember you saying if it's not good enough for your kid, it's not good enough for anyone else's. That's why I love you."

She left him to ponder the meaning of this new gift she was offering him, something that didn't fit his life properly. And yet he now felt a tickle, maybe even the beginning of an immunity from Anna Lee's sexual frostiness and frequent criticism. There was an option out there, even if it was a distant, twinkling star in the night sky.

Love. What a concept.

* * *

Nick was out the entire week. When Richard walked into the office the next Monday morning, Polly looked up from her computer. As if by dark magic, Miz Rutherford appeared. Two teachers froze at their mail slots as if they'd been caught in the middle of a bank robbery.

Polly cleared her throat and spoke haltingly. "I'm sorry I didn't try to call the other numbers when Nick was sick. ... I should have done that."

Richard stared at her for a moment, unsure of what was really going on. Then he realized that Polly was taking one for the team, especially since Miz Rutherford just stood there, saying nothing. But he also knew that he was on trial, too. There was only one response if he wanted people to consider him a person of good will. "It's all right," he said. "Apology accepted."

Good will was important. But so was making his point. He pulled an envelope out of his jacket pocket and tore it in half, making sure the two women could see the stamp, so they'd known the message he'd intended to deliver was aimed over their heads.

"By the way, it would be better if the school had a nurse instead of a counselor *and* a psychologist. I guess I can work on that in my second term, eh?"

Miz Rutherford's eyes bugged out slightly. Wearing a stricken look, she returned to her office.

Richard was certain now that this was Rutherford's last year, and that one way or another, he would be the cause of her leaving.

THIRTEEN

L ife went on. Children learned, teachers taught, and most importantly
for the PTO, funds were raised. The Fun-Filled Fall Festival, overseen
by Jane Baumgartner, exceeded its goal by $2,000. The PTO's other money-
makers also did well. Since there was no arguing with success, Miz Rutherford spoke to Richard as seldom as possible.

During the festival, Richard learned from Jane that Susan had been
forced by financial circumstances to rent an apartment at Chantilly Arms.
"Wow," Richard said. "She's become what she hated, an apartment dweller."

"She didn't help organize the festival," Jane said. "So I put her in charge
of the 'go fish' tank."

"That's cold."

While Richard and Teresa met almost daily, it was all PTO business,
conducted in the cafetorium, a sexless place where blood, milk, and love all
curdled under the watchful gaze of Miz Rutherford, her security cameras,
and the beady eye of the fascist duck. Although Richard often pined for his
lovely treasurer, he kept his feelings to himself and wondered if there would
ever be an encore.

When he learned that Miz Rutherford took off on Friday afternoons to
get her hair done, he moved his tutoring sessions to take advantage of her
absence. On Friday, December 1, he read aloud stories from Louis Sachar's
Wayside School Is Falling Down.

After he finished, Devonious had a rather off-topic question. He wanted
to know why a woman's private part was called a pussy. Richard said he had no
idea, and that was a dangerous word to use, especially in an elementary school.

Could he spell *suspension*? Devonious said he just wanted to know. The other boys treated him like he was ignorant, but they didn't know either. "I looked it up," Antonio announced a minute later. "Because it's filled with puss."

"Pus," Richard corrected. "No! We can't talk about it. It's illegal under state law. Cut it out!"

The boys laughed. How did they know he could never send them to the principal's office? "One more swear word and I'll send you back to class!"

"Pussy Pus-head," D snarled at Antonio.

"You're busted, Devonious. Go back to class."

"You ain't cool."

"Buh-bye. Make sure you get back there."

As D trudged away, Richard stood at the door and watched to make sure he headed in the right direction. A few seconds later, the bell rang. If Devonious dawdled, Mrs. Little wouldn't know he'd been booted from lab. He decided not to rat out the boy. Mrs. Little had him permanently busted, anyway. On the first day of school, she'd told D, "You're mine."

Richard returned the others to class, offering Antonio and Simeon praise and encouragement along the way. They held up their printouts with stickers on them for classmates to see. Nick grinned at his father.

"Thank you, Mr. Gray," said Mrs. Little. "Class, get out your science books. Wait a minute. Devonious, where's your work from the computer lab?"

Busted. *Ha-ha.*

Richard proceeded to the library. A plump woman wearing a yellow nylon windbreaker, blue jeans, and white sneakers tore out of Mrs. Cates's room and hurtled toward him, looking distraught. "Each year I pray that God will give me a teacher who won't destroy my son," she said, looking past Richard. "Having a child in this school is like running a gauntlet. You're going to get beaten. You just don't know if you'll survive, or if it will ever stop!" He turned and watched her speed past and take a rear exit. She hesitated in the door and shouted, "It's a horror story!" The door slammed shut behind her.

Next year, alarms would be installed to prevent such escapes.

He heard children yelling and walked down the back hall to investigate. He peered through the glass pane into Mrs. Vandenburg's room, where pandemonium reigned, with no teacher in sight. Several kids surrounded the TV, arguing loudly. He opened the door. In the middle of the room, two kids were slamming each other's heads with textbooks in some kind of stupid chicken-fight. In the back corner, a black-haired girl cowered as two boys pummeled her with their fists. Alicia!

"Stop that!" Richard shouted. As he lunged toward the attackers, they scurried to their seats. He squatted beside their victim, who was sobbing so hard she couldn't catch her breath.

"She's always in trouble," said the girl sitting next to her.

"Alicia is my friend. People are being mean to her."

"Mrs. Vandenburg makes her stand in the corner because she's not very smart."

"She is so," Richard said. "She knows two languages. How much Spanish do you know?"

"Hasta la vista, baby!" a boy shouted in Richard's ear.

"What happened, Alicia?"

"Mrs. Vandenburg made me stand here for the rest of the day. And I wanted to sit down."

"The rest of the *day*?"

She nodded.

"Well, it's all right if you sit down now."

"*Gracias*." she sniffed and wiped a tear away with her T-shirt sleeve.

"That's thanks," said the girl. "I do too know Spanish."

"Where's Mrs. Vandenburg?"

"I don't know," the girl said. "Can you fix the TV?"

Mrs. Cates stuck her head in the door and followed with her massive body, nostrils flaring at the sight of Richard. "What's going on? Your child isn't in this class. You shouldn't be here."

"There's no adult supervision, and kids are being assaulted."

"I'll handle this."

"Actually, Miz Rutherford should."

"You need to leave so we can restore order."

"What do you mean 'we'?"

Fortunately, Ms. Bailey arrived a few seconds later and separated the two adults before it got any worse. Alicia, having returned to her desk, buried her face on her arms. Richard looked around for Karen McAllister, then remembered that Stan would have pulled his daughter out of class early on "Cartoon Day." He touched Alicia's head gently (another infraction of Malliford Manners) and whispered to her. She looked up and smiled through her tears.

"I want you to be nice to Alicia," he told the girl, then turned toward the two little thugs and gave them his evilest eye. "You're Michael Gunther." Michael glared at him. "And you're Jason Hodges," he said to the other boy, who hung his head. Sons of PWCs Susan and Barbara.

Richard turned to Ms. Bailey. "These two were beating Alicia with their fists. A *Lord of the Flies* moment. They should be dealt with." He shook his head in a hyperbolic show of disgust. "This is a mess."

As for the kids hitting each other with books, well, he figured it was a fair fight and didn't mention it. Besides, the Gunther-Hodges gang needed special attention.

Ms. Bailey gave him a hopeless shrug. He gave Mrs. Cates a nasty squint and left. On his way out, he saw Caitlin Keller sitting near the window, watching him impassively. He wondered what she'd tell Teresa when she went home.

Curious about Mrs. Vandenburg's whereabouts, he set out to find her. His search ended in the teacher's lounge, where she was lying on the sofa, the back of her hand on her forehead as if she'd swooned following her many travails. She opened one eye and regarded him suspiciously. "What do you want? This room is teachers-only."

"Time to get up. Your kids are rioting."

Her head jerked up. She swung her stubby legs around and planted them on the floor.

"You can get a report from Ms. Bailey," he said, shouting after her as she scurried away. "Mine will be on file with the county."

When Richard signed out, he asked Polly, "Where does the principal get her hair done?"

"I can get in touch with her. Is there a message?"

"Tell her she's busted."

Once home, he sat in his office and brooded for a few minutes before dialing a number. It rang twice before a voice answered, "Blodgett here."

"Mr. Blodgett, it's Chain Gang."

"For God's sakes, man, don't call it that!"

*　*　*

The following Monday, nearly a year after she'd been selected, a brass plate with Mrs. Vandenburg's name was added to the Teacher of the Year plaque in the front hall, right under Mrs. Cates's. Richard vowed never to look at the plaque again unless he swallowed poison and needed to vomit.

That Friday afternoon, Miz Rutherford was conspicuously present in her office, bouncing in and out for everyone to see. When Richard stopped by to sign in, he complimented her on her "sensible" hair, eliciting her trademark scowl. Ms. Bailey followed him out into the hall and said, "I suppose some-one should tell you there's a new school-wide ban on non-educational TV in the classrooms."

"You're welcome," he said.

*   *   *

The next Wednesday, Richard returned to Malliford after school to retrieve a homework assignment Nick left in his desk. As he clicked down the hall in his loafers, he heard Miz Rutherford speaking in the cafetorium: "Scores have been declining, and we must be proactive to reverse this trend and drive Malliford back into Gresham's top ten. Our counselor and psychologist are working overtime on a plan to deal with at-risk students—"

As Richard walked by the door, the principal fell silent. He glanced in; fifty eyeballs stared back at him. Unnerved, he quickened his pace, vowing to wear sneakers from then on, like Coach so wisely advised.

*   *   *

Two days before the holiday break, just when Richard thought he was going to have some peace, Stan chased him down in Malliford's front hall. Look-ing like a scruffy, crazed Hobbit, Stan breathlessly informed him of the latest outrage. "You hear about the ethnic cleansing?"

"Beg pardon?"

"It's called 'psychopharmacological therapy.'"

"Easy for you to say."

"Two parents complained to Sasha Bramblett (one of the four black PTO board members Richard had recruited) and said the school counselor and psychologist threatened them. If they don't put their boys on Ritalin, they'll stick them in Special Ed, or ship them off to Wildwood, where the kids with behavior problems go."

Richard tried to absorb this. He had wondered what counselor Cassan-dra Hardwick and psychologist Donzella James were up to lately, since were both clueless and hyperactive, an exceptionally dangerous combination in government employees. Had Miz Rutherford's pep talk involved pep pills?

"Donzella James reported a mother to Family Services for neglect be-cause she took her son off Ritalin," Stan said. "Two of the boys are in Van-denburg's class. The other is in Radcliffe's. Somehow they let a black kid slip in," Stan said sarcastically. "Obviously, they're tracking—"

"Are *all* the kids you're talking about black?"

"Yup. Since our counselor and psychologist are African-American, I guess they think that makes it all right. It doesn't. People think Ritalin is a miracle drug, but it's speed, and speed kills. This school is coercing parents to drug their children. It's evil." His eyes smoldered.

"I'll look into it." Richard felt a sickening weight settle in his belly. Yet another call to battle, and he didn't know how to proceed. After all, such matters were confidential. He couldn't just confront two staff members over something he'd heard third-hand. Or was it fourth?

"Happy holidays," said Stan, backing away. "I hope Santa is good to you."

"There is no Santa," Richard said. "I saw him die."

"Shush, Mr. Gray," hissed Mrs. Leland as she walked by. "You are *so* bad."

* * *

Richard survived Christmas without a mental breakdown, and the Grays spent New Year's Eve at home. After they put Nick to bed, Richard and Anna Lee watched a movie. She lay on the couch with her feet in his lap, nibbling popcorn and drinking Burgundy. The *noir* film was about a man who cheated on his wife, then had to kill his mistress in self-defense, but it looked like murder, so the guy went down hard.

After several glasses of wine, Anna Lee was cheering the tragic ending like a crazed sports fan. "Take that, you son of a bitch!" she shouted, jabbing her fist at the plasma screen.

Within minutes, she was asleep on the sofa. Richard, sober as always, retreated to his office.

At 11:48 p.m., his cell phone rang. "Guess who?" Teresa said. "I've got my little black dress on and I'm freezing. I'm all goose-bumpy out here on the patio. Carl's trying to get something going with the hostess. I am *not* doing a three-way. Damn! Kids next door are shooting bottle rockets. *Hey, cut that shit out!* Sorry, sweetie. I've got to get inside before I'm a casualty of war."

"Whose party is it?"

"One of Carl's whoredog clients. He and his wife are swingers, but he passed out, so Carl sees an opportunity to have two women to himself. I hate these people. Whatcha doin'?"

"Nothing. Hiding from a drunken woman who's got her *noir* up."

"I wish I was your drunken woman. I'd get your *noir* up. I think about you every day. I wish I woke up next to you each morning."

He missed her terribly, too, but he didn't know what to say. It didn't seem fair for her to keep telling him "I love you" when they'd had sex just once. There should be only one "I love you" per sex act, no matter how good it was.

"What's wrong?" she asked. "You miss me?"

"Yeah," he admitted.

"It's not just that, is it? Are you hurting inside?"

"Holiday depression. Comes with the territory. There was someone long ago I can't forget, especially this time of year."

"What was her name?"

"Sheila."

"I'm jealous."

"Don't be. Something terrible happened."

"Oh. I'm sorry. I wish I could make you feel better."

"I do, too."

"I gotta go before they shoot me. Happy New Year, sweetie."

"Happy New Year."

He clicked the phone shut and listened to the computer hum. After a while, he checked on Anna Lee, still sprawled on the couch, snoring. He picked her up and carried her into the bedroom, tossing her unceremoniously atop the comforter. Outside, a string of firecrackers exploded in a staccato burst.

"They're shooting at us," she said, rousing herself.

"Just the neighbors."

"*Mmm.* That's good." She looked up at him and a sly smile crossed her lips. "Take me. For good luck." She gave him a sloppy kiss, and then laughed as she ran her tongue down his neck.

Where had she been all year? That's what he wanted to know.

FOURTEEN

The Ritalin policy was a nasty piece of business, a significant evil. The overriding issue was control, and the matter was not open for discussion. Mrs. Baines suggested, in her semi-diplomatic way, that Richard mind his own business when he asked about it on the first day of winter term.

"Aren't there better things for the PTO to do than investigate the school it serves?" she asked.

Richard smiled thinly. "We serve the children, not the school."

"A distinction without a difference, Mr. Gray."

She had no idea how obvious the difference was to Richard, or how deeply he meant what he'd said, but he saw no point in arguing.

Her attempt to stiff-arm him did nothing to quell his curiosity, however. He spoke to Mrs. Little that afternoon, saying, "I heard some disturbing news."

"Always some of that floating around. Go on."

"The school is making parents medicate their children."

"Hmm ... Mr. Gray, they got some big idea about raisin' test scores. We went 'round on that. I wish I could paddle some of these boys sometimes, but pumpin' 'em full of drugs is wrong. There's folks tryin' to turn this school into that Cuckoo's Nest you talk about. And I know some parents don't want their kids takin' drugs. That's their right. Miz Hardwick and James don't think so, and they got the backing of you-know-who. I been fightin' 'em on it. I got three reprimands already this year. This keeps up, they won't let me in the building. I'll be teachin' on those benches you built."

Richard chuckled drily. "What about the test scores?"

"There's a meetin' in the cafeteria tomorrow at one. Just sayin'."

Richard left wondering how he could attend the mysterious meeting.

The answer came in the form of a demand the next day. Polly called at 7:30 a.m. to say teachers were out of coffee and Cindi Lou was out of town: "They need caffeine. Can you get it here this morning?"

He'd always cursed the teachers' dependence on the PTO for coffee, which cost $700 a year. Now he saw an opportunity. "I'm working right now," he said. "I can bring it by after lunch."

"Is that the best you can do?"

Richard was certain she was conferring because he could hear scuba breathing in the background. "Yes."

"All right. Have a nice day," she grumbled.

When he showed up at 1:00 p.m., Polly gave him a scathing look.

"Don't worry," he said. "You don't have to get up. I'll take it to the cafeteria myself."

"I wasn't worrying and I wasn't getting up. What brand?"

"Chock full o'Nuts."

"Ha! Figures. Can't resist an editorial comment, can you?"

He carried the plastic sack containing six bags of coffee to the cafetorium. Both sets of doors were closed. He peered through a small glass pane and saw a meeting in progress. Mrs. Baines, Miz Rutherford, and the school counselor sat on chairs in front of the stage. Psychologist Donzella James stood. He opened the door and tiptoed in. Fifty dark-hued boys sat at tables near the stage. Nearly half Mrs. Little's class was there, including all those he tutored.

"Why don't you just let us take the tests like everybody else?" one kid demanded.

"Ain't no big deal. Not like it's a grade," interjected an older boy.

"We already got a ton of homework every night," said a third. "I ain't even gettin' it done. They won't let us take PE. And they make us sit at the convict table."

Richard figured the boy was talking about what Nick called "working lunches." The kids sentenced to them got only a peanut butter sandwich and an apple—without regard to allergies or braces.

Miz Rutherford stood up and shouted, "Young man, DO NOT call it that!"

Right then, Richard could imagine her wearing mirrored shades, holding a bullwhip as shackled students did homework at the big table. *What we have heah is a failure to educate.*

"Not as bad as last year, when they put me on the chain gang," grumbled a sixth-grader.

"There was no such thing!" the principal fumed. "That was a lie perpetrated by the media!"

She was losing control—and certainly wasn't intimidating them. *Fascinating.*

"How come we got to score seventy on the practice tests or we won't get PE? I like PE!"

As more voices rose in protest, Donzella James looked up and spotted the interloper. From forty feet away, Richard saw the flaring whites of her eyes. She looked like she'd grabbed a bare electric wire.

"Shush!" said Miz Rutherford, who then noticed the psychologist's discomfiture and followed her gaze. Her eyes grew wide, too. She instinctively straightened her dress, as if she'd been caught in a compromising act—like trying to screw fifty black and Hispanic boys.

"May I help you?" barked Donzella.

Richard walked toward the coffee urn, which sat on a metal table next to the wall outside the kitchen. "Don't mind me. Just delivering the teachers' coffee. I heard they were passing out this morning." The boys broke out in riotous laughter. "Now that you mention it, I'd like to find out more about the chain gang."

Miz Rutherford and Mrs. Baines looked like they'd eaten nails.

"Leave," the principal said.

Richard set the coffee by the urn. "I wonder if their parents know what's going on."

"This doesn't concern you."

"I get that a lot. But I represent parents, and there have been complaints, mind you."

He pivoted on his heel and walked out.

Five minutes after he returned home, the phone rang.

"Mr. Gray, I just wanted to clear up any misunderstanding about our Achievement Rally today," said Mrs. Baines. "I'm afraid you have allowed yourself to get some misconceptions about what we're doing."

He knew Miz Rutherford was standing beside the vice principal. Even over the phone line, he could feel a disturbance in the Force. "Ain't no misconceptions. Y'all putting black kids back on the chain gang," he drawled. "What's to misconceive 'bout that?"

"That's the kind of talk that concerns us. We're simply pumping them up for tests next month."

"The Standard Hightower Intellachievement Tests?"

"Yes."

"Do all kids have to take a—"

"Yes!" she interjected. "And please don't use the acronym."

"Pretty accurate description, doncha think? What were they thinking when they called—"

"I really don't know, Mr. Gray."

"Kids have fun with it. Spell it out, you know. S-H-"

"We don't allow it to be shortened. There's a memo from central office on that."

"That, I'd like to see. How to take a—"

"Mr. Gray. Please."

"So what's this about missing PE and getting seventies?"

"We're just encouraging them to be all that they can be."

"You want them to join the Army?"

"No! We're trying to ... upgrade test scores. You know we face challenges this year. With coaching and preparation and a winning attitude, we can turn this thing around."

"Why doesn't *everyone* get the pep talk?"

"We're trying to focus our efforts on at-risk students."

"Forgive me for my bluntness, but I saw the crowd you were pumping up. I think you've got some racial motivations here. You shouldn't have singled out black kids. Everyone—"

"It was the counselor's and psychologist's idea. They're—"

"They're what?"

"They are what they are, Mr. Gray."

"And because they're black, that makes everything OK?"

"You said it, I didn't."

"I didn't say it, I asked it, and it doesn't make it all right."

It was just as Stan suspected. Richard could see Miz Rutherford, still in the mirrored shades, calling her two minions into the office and telling them, "You all have simply *got* to improve your people's test scores," as she chewed on a piece of straw.

"It's demeaning," he said. "It should stop."

"Perhaps you should realize it isn't your concern."

"Your call implies it is. Otherwise, you'd just ignore me."

"We just know you have a habit of causing trouble—"

"'Scuse me? Would you like to try saying that again?"

"We know you have contacts in the media, and we ... we need you to understand it's a positive thing."

"I understand you think it's a positive thing."

"You can be so difficult, Mr. Gray."

"Thank you, Mrs. Baines."

*   *   *

Early Thursday afternoon, the chill air slapped Richard's cheeks and stung his eyes as he stepped out his front door. Slate-colored clouds choked the sky; the oppressive weather matched his mood. He pulled his green parka's hood over his head and pinched its collar tight as he started his trek to Malliford's Honors Assembly, where Nick would receive the highest award.

There was a certain what-the-hellishness in his attitude as he trudged up the hill. Despite his concerns about bio-social engineering, he'd concluded, as a matter of self-preservation, that he was better off lame-ducking this PTO thing. This was the time of year when presidents typically started coasting. Why should he be the exception? Besides, of some 700 parents, only 14 percent cared enough to volunteer, and they already knew what to do. The others were beyond his reach. Trying to cover for all the deadbeat, drive-by parents was an onerous burden, and he was ready to lay it down. Test scores and Ritalin were problems both vague and esoteric. What could he do? If the boys' parents didn't fight, why should he? Indeed, no victim had come forth—just Stan, who complained about everything. When Richard talked to Sasha, she'd been evasive. Apparently, her son was getting some special help he needed, and she didn't want to cause trouble.

The truth was, the battles had worn him down. He suspected they'd taken a year or two off his life—hopefully off the back end, when he wouldn't miss them so much. He was tired of Malliford, of caring, of being pissed off. He just wanted the school year to end. He needed to build his business and pare down the mountain of debt he and Anna Lee had accrued. If they had another child, money would be even tighter.

When he got to Malliford, he signed in and proceeded to the cafetorium. To accommodate the honors ceremonies, it had been cut into front and back halves by an off-white floor-to-ceiling accordion partition. Richard stood in the door and sniffed an overpowering, yet bland scent. Meatloaf? Chicken nuggets? Fish sticks? Country steak? Did it matter? They breaded everything that walked the earth or swam the seas.

Mrs. Little's bright-eyed, expectant students were the first of three third-grade classes to line up for the procession. Half wore nice clothes. Nick looked like a little preppie in blue slacks and a beige-and-brown argyle sweater, though the formal look was offset by his well-worn sneakers. Mrs. Little ordered a black boy wearing long baggy denim shorts to tuck in his T-shirt. Richard assumed that next year would bring uniforms, more discipline, better living through chemistry, higher test scores, and maybe even German accents.

The mainly white, female audience was thinner than at Nick's past honors assemblies. A dozen black parents and grandparents were scattered throughout the room. Miz Rutherford sat beside Cassandra Hardwick onstage, where they would spend the entire day shaking hands and issuing congratulations to students who received certificates and pins for making straight A's or all A's and B's, behaving themselves, or just showing up every day. In first and second grade, all kids got some sort of award, even if it was a certificate for Trying Your Best. Last year, most of Nick's second-grade classmates got the top award. Third grade was tougher.

"It's where the rubber hits the road," according to Mrs. Little.

Nick was first in line to receive his award, which seemed odd to Richard, since teachers were devoutly alphabetic. He knelt in the center aisle and aimed his camera; Nick beamed proudly as he crossed the stage and accepted his awards.

As it turned out, only three of Mrs. Little's students made Principal's List—a testament to the tougher third grade workload, Mrs. Little's unyielding standards, and the class's challenging demographics. Ten students made the B-average Honor Roll. The Citizenship Award went to well-behaved students regardless of grades. Three black girls got that and nothing else, as did Ahmad Henderson, a friendly, quiet boy Richard had tutored since December. Then there was Perfect Attendance, the last hope for some kids, i.e. Devonious, who snatched his certificate with a grin on his face. Richard had to admire the boy's persistence in showing up every day to cause trouble.

After the ceremony, Richard took a photo of Mrs. Little and Nick. In past years, he'd included Miz Rutherford. Not now. He didn't want her withered old face hovering like a bad moon rising over his pride and joy. Candace Josey volunteered to take a father-son picture. Nick gave her a goofball pose, then returned to class, flapping awards like bird wings.

Stan McAllister caught Richard on his way out. "Hey, wanna be presidential and stick around for the second-graders?"

"Sure." Richard said uncertainly, fearing Stan wanted to bring up the Ritalin issue.

They took their seats on the aisle, near the back of the audience. Stan surveyed the crowd and said, "Well, at least they got rid of the chain gang, now that they've got better living through chemistry." He raised an eyebrow, but Richard had nothing to say on the issue.

Moments later, the procession of second-graders began. First Mrs. Leland's class, then Ms. Bradford. Finally, a stern-faced Mrs. Vandenburg marched in her second-graders and sat them on the front three rows right of center. She gave Stan and Richard a look to let them know she would separate them if they caused trouble. The last child in was Alicia Rodriguez, who wore a frilly pink dress with matching ribbons in her hair. While her classmates beamed, Alicia looked like she'd been crying. Richard nudged Stan. "Whenever I see her, she's suffering."

Stan grimaced. "She's quite unpopular with the powers that be. Undocumented. Too diverse for their tastes. Her mother is a hotel maid. Her father drove a cab. Shot to death in a robbery."

Richard recoiled. "My God, I didn't know that. That's horrible."

"She's always in trouble, but I've never seen her do anything wrong. She's from the apartments. At least the beatings stopped after you walked in on the riot. Good thing you busted in on that. Now she just stands in the corner when she forgets to speak English or acts impolite."

"Anybody else get treated that way?"

"That would be a big No."

Stan's daughter went over to console Alicia. From the stage, Mrs. Vandenburg ordered her back to her seat.

"Karen is her only friend," said Stan, glaring at the teacher. "Well, her and the Keller girl."

A hitch in Richard's breathing. "Teresa's daughter."

"Yeah." Stan glanced around and whispered, "All Vandenburg cares about is test scores. That and kissing the principal's ass."

The assembly began. Miz Rutherford addressed the audience with all appropriate pomp, then turned to Mrs. Vandenburg, who called out names and awards. Richard was outraged when the boys who had beaten Alicia received Citizenship awards. Michael Gunther bounded across the stage clutching both his academic and conduct certificates, smiling smugly as Susan photographed his shining moment. Stan took a picture of Karen as she stood center stage holding her Principal's List and Citizenship awards. Hearty applause met every child until the awards were all gone.

One child was left behind. Alicia stood forlornly in front of her chair by the aisle.

"Sit down, Alicia," Mrs. Vandenburg snapped. "You're not getting anything. I already told you that. Sit down!"

Richard felt like *he'd* been slapped in the face.

"Well, look at that," Stan said loudly. "Publicly humiliating a little girl on Honors Day. Par for the course."

A little girl had been turned into a human sacrifice to test scores, offered up to her tormenters *and* their parents as a bad example.

It was a paralyzing moment. Ice cracking underfoot. Then a hush.

Alicia sobbed and looked around. She saw Richard and gazed at him plaintively. He'd coaxed her off the bus on the first morning of school. How could he allow such a horrible thing to happen when he was the one that got her into this mess?

He'd made a deal with her. It was time to keep it.

Something strong and wounded roared up from the bottom of Richard's soul. Quietly, he muttered, "This is the hill."

A book's worth of thoughts would cross his mind later, but right then it was simply a Popeye moment. If he'd had a can of spinach, he would have chugged it down in a single gulp. Instead of a whistle blast from a corncob pipe, there was a squeak of chair legs as he stood.

"I can't let this go on," he declared. "I can't stands no more."

He took a deep breath. His knees quaked and his stomach flew up into his throat as he stepped into the aisle and walked toward the little girl. He didn't know what he was going to do, but those dreadful women on stage had dared him to do it. This was the day. He was the guy.

He stooped beside her. "Hi, Alicia," he said softly. The whole room strained to hear. Miz Rutherford gripped her walkie-talkie in white-knuckled fury. Any hope she held that this was an innocuous Kleenex run would be dashed quickly "I am president of Malliford's PTO."

"El Presidente," she sniffed, her face streaked with tears. "I know."

He smiled. "You're special and we're glad you're here. The PTO has an award for your bravery and for trying your best."

He fumbled in his pocket for a quarter to solve the problem with a bribe, but his hand was wise and found his Duncan yo-yo, the truest thing in his world. The PWCs ridiculed him with it. What fools they were to confuse mockery with magic! Now it was time to transfer its power. He pulled out his prized possession. "This is for you," he said. She looked up at him with watery eyes. "On behalf of the Malliford PTO, I present you this yo-yo for doing your best—and to remind you what goes down can come back up." *All it takes is the right jerk.*

She stopped sobbing and reached for the trophy. He handed it to her, acutely aware of the near-perfect silence that surrounded them. A flash went off as Stan took a picture. "It has magic, I remember. *Gracias.* Thank you." In a heartbreaking and holy moment for him, she grabbed his hand and kissed it.

"You're welcome." Applause rippled through the crowd, escalating as second-graders picked up the beat, thinking it the proper thing to do. Now Alicia beamed, too.

The sentiment was not unanimous, however. "Mr. Gray." Miz Rutherford was having a Brutus moment of her own. "That's enough. Return to your seat and cease this disruption."

The applause died as she and Mrs. Vandenburg glared at Richard like he was a ten-year-old vandal holding a can of spray paint. He bent down and hugged the girl. "Be brave, Alicia. Let no one break your spirit."

She gave him a bright, defiant look, then turned to glare at Mrs. Vandenburg through her tears. She held up the yo-yo and said "Ha!" *A magic yo-yo is better than a stupid piece of paper. Even fools know that.*

The principal thundered, "Mr. Gray, I will not tolerate your disruption or your insolence. Leave the building now!"

He looked up and grinned. "Off with their heads!" he said with a wave, and then strode toward the exit.

Some parents and grandparents murmured approval—or condemnation. He couldn't tell and didn't care which right then. Susan Gunther gave him a withering look. Stan stood and gave him an ovation. The solo hand-clapping reverberated weirdly, making the cavernous room seem empty for a moment before someone else joined in. Then came a smattering of applause, a gust-driven rain that died down quickly. Rita, there to see the Delgado twins get their awards from Mrs. Leland, stood in the door, slowly clapping as he approached, wearing an expression of adulation and awe. She grabbed his arm, her eyes shiny with tears. "I love you," she whispered.

Feeling both brilliant and mad, Richard whirled to face the crowd. "You should know," he boomed, "Two boys who beat up Alicia got Citizenship Awards."

"Get out!" Miz Rutherford shrieked, surprising everyone with her loss of control.

"You should also know that black and Hispanic boys are being given the choice of Ritalin or special ed. They also get Jim Crow lectures about the importance of standardized tests. We say we celebrate diversity, but that's not true. We simply don't object to people who look different as long as they act, speak, and think like us."

Miz Rutherford came down from the stage and advanced on Richard, holding her radio like a can of mace. He turned to go and something caught his eye: the star-spangled "Celebrate Diversity" banner hanging near the door. He gave it a yank. It came down with surprising ease, as if it didn't want to be there. He draped it over his arm and faced the principal. "Put it back up when the phrase means something," he declared.

"That banner is school property. Bring it back right now!" Miz Rutherford cried out. She stepped toward him but thought better of it and returned to the stage while she struggled to regain her composure. "My apologies for that rude behavior. Mrs. Leland, please proceed."

Having captured the flag, Richard absconded with the school's symbol of humbuggery, storming out into the hall. Rita hustled after him and caught his arm. "Thank you, thank you, thank you. That's the most beautiful thing I ever saw."

"I just kept a promise I made. I'd better get out before she calls the police. Take this." He handed her the banner and walked outside, still in a daze over what he'd just done.

With the cold air came self-doubt. He'd have to live with what he'd done. He knew people would say he stepped out of bounds. And they would be right. But what could Rutherford do? Ban him from school? Make Mrs. Bailey escort him everywhere? Worse things could happen. Maybe he'd have to endure a vote of no confidence, resign, and get the hell out of town. Actually, that didn't sound like such a bad idea.

His stomach was tied in a knot when he got home. He sat at his desk and threw himself back in his chair, breathing deeply as he spun around, hoping that a combination of oxygen and vertigo would help his perspective in this topsy-turvy world. Had he turned into some kind of mutant aberration? Probably not. Maybe he was just another individual with a private agenda. But he'd done *something*, by God. Perhaps that was his purpose in life, to be that brave Wounded Child who found courage in time to turn back and rescue his comrades from the chain gangs of this world. And in the process, win that age-old fight with the principal—and his father. Or maybe he just didn't like adults much, anyway.

When the phone rang, he told himself to answer it, even if it was Barbara Hodges, calling to rip him a new one.

"Mr. Gray? I'm Deanna Richardson, education reporter with *the Sentinel*. I want to discuss some issues concerning Malliford Elementary. I hear you're the man to talk to."

FIFTEEN

Anna Lee stopped chewing and set her bagel on the table, missing her plate. She was staring bug-eyed at the headline atop the *Sentinel's* local front page: "Does 'Chain Gang' School Plan Target Blacks?" She looked at Richard with her mouth agape as he sipped coffee. "Did you do this?"

He shrugged. *Who can say these things? Who can explain them, who can tell you why?*

Actually, he'd merely elaborated on Stan's news tip about pep talks and Ritalin. There had been no mention of Richard's actions at the assembly, which were both too sacred and profane to discuss with strangers—or his wife.

As he contemplated what to say, the phone rang. He figured it was Barbara—who had called yesterday to chew him out for "pulling that stunt with that Mexican girl"—with more to be pissed about, since he hadn't told her about his interview with Deanna.

Feeling feisty, he took the call in the family room. It wasn't Barbara, though. It was Cindi Lou, calling to congratulate him for getting his name in the paper. "She's mean to everyone, not just blacks," Cindi Lou said. "Remember how ugly she was to me about paint for V-Day?"

"That makes you a person of color," Richard pointed out.

"I just think she's a bitch."

"There's that, too."

When he returned to the table, Anna Lee asked, "Your fan club?"

"Just a concerned parent who feels the way I do."

"One of the few." She shook her head. "I can't believe you're backing up Stan McCallister and giving him credibility. Get real. He's a crank."

Nick came in and glanced at Richard. "Are you mad at Mommy? You sure look like you are."

The phone rang again. Richard got it. "Go get 'em, Tiger," a sexy voice purred.

"Hi." He stuck a finger in his other ear in an attempt to keep Teresa's voice to himself.

"You're my hero. Can I have your autograph?"

"Stop."

"You let her have it. Said what needs saying. Did what needs doing. You were so *you*."

"I was pissed. Wait a minute. How'd you—"

"I was there. Caitlin, remember?"

"Oh, yeah." How could he have not noticed her? He truly had been wrapped up in the moment.

"Giving the yo-yo to Alicia when the world had forsaken her was the most beautiful thing I've ever seen. I know how much it means to you. You really stirred up the henhouse."

"Duck pond," he corrected.

"The place is split down the middle. But the cool people like you."

"Enough."

"Speaking of what needs doing, I've got checks to sign. How about this morning?"

"I'm not sure the school's safe any more."

"Carl left yesterday afternoon for the West Coast. Yay! ... I was saying Yay for your daddy, hon. Now go get ready." She paused. "I'll be back from taking the girls to school by eight. Why don't you come over? The sooner, the better. It's time to pick up where we left off. It's been so *long*. See you, sweetie."

What needs doing—and who needs doing. Well, well.

He returned to the breakfast table with an acceptably blank face. Anna Lee regarded him suspiciously. "Was *that* your Number One fan?"

"I thought Mom was your Number One fan," Nick said.

"I did, too."

"Jesus," Anna Lee muttered in exasperation.

"Thou shalt not takest thy Lordeth's namest in vainest," Nick said.

"Amen," Richard said, excusing himself from the table.

"I just don't think you should have publicly attacked her," Anna Lee called out.

"Attack who?" Nick asked.

"Nobody," Anna Lee said.

"Fine. Don't tell me. I'll find out. I always do."

The Grays got ready for the day ahead. Five minutes after Anna Lee left for work, father and son stepped outside. The sky was clear, the air chill. Richard felt Nick's forehead: normal. The boy said he felt fine. He'd memorized Dad's cell number. Richard made him repeat it. The phone's battery was charged; all systems go. "I'm driving you today. I've got some stuff to do with Mrs. Keller."

"I like Mrs. Keller. She's pretty."

"I hadn't noticed."

He dropped off Nick. Only after the cadet shut the car door did Richard remember to pick up *Duck Call* at the printer's. He was late; this was the day they had to go home with students. He pounded the steering wheel in frustration as he drove off. He called Teresa with the bad news.

"I'll be here waiting for you," she cooed.

It took him an hour to fight through traffic, get the newsletters, and return to Windamere Heights. Once he was back in the neighborhood, Richard decided to deliver them later. When he got to Teresa's house, the garage door was open. He drove in and it slammed shut, swallowing man and car whole.

"Sure took you long enough," Teresa said, embracing him as he crossed her threshold. "Three months. I missed you terribly."

Wasting no time, they ran up the stairs, passing the photo of Carl in a bodybuilder's pose. Teresa was surprised and pleased at his passion; he was delighted by her blue thong. Socks still on, they flopped like fish in shallow water on the king-sized bed. "That would have made a good movie," she gasped just after his climax, which followed hers by ten seconds.

The doorbell rang while they were still panting.

"Shit!" Richard cried. He heard a thud as he groped for his inside-out pants. She peered out the window and giggled as he hopped around trying to put them on.

"UPS."

"Damn. I didn't hear the truck."

"You were busy." She slipped on her clothes and retrieved the package. He lay dazed on the four-poster. When he went downstairs, she was sitting at the kitchen table.

Over coffee, they spent ten minutes on the PTO. "We spent more time fucking than funding," Teresa said with a giggle.

When Richard returned to Applegate, the answering machine held no

terrible news. After lunch, he drove to Malliford. He lugged his box of newsletters up the sidewalk and wondered about the reception he'd get now that
he was a pariah, a delinquent-coddler, a self-righteous, overweening helicopter parent from hell who thought working with kids three hours a week
made him an education expert. A fool. Asshole. Butthead. Stinky cheese guy.
But there was no turning back from what he'd done. He owned it.

Miz Rutherford's light was off when he signed in. He suspected she was
on the carpet at Central, explaining the latest chain gang crisis. Polly didn't
seem alarmed by his appearance or order him to leave. No doubt the latest
story saved his hide. Marine Antoinette couldn't exact retribution when she
feared the next headline would say, "Chain Gang PTO President Banished
for Befriending Latino Girl."

It was too late for Polly to distribute the newsletters, so he asked if he
could hand them out. "Guess so," she said. "Better you than me."

His new sneakers squeaked as he made the rounds. In the front all,
some teachers smiled as they accepted newsletters. Some pointed to a spot
they wanted him to place them. Others frowned, either at the interruption or in judgment of him. A hall camera tracked him as he passed the
cafetorium. He figured Polly was under orders; he stopped and gave her a
grinning salute. Mrs. Little gave him her *What-Are-You-Up-To-This-Time*
look. Nick grinned at him.

Down the hall, Mrs. Vandenburg's door was open. Students sat quietly. The TV was off. Richard knocked when he saw the teacher at her desk.
"What do you want?" she said, her face as friendly as a mug shot.

Feeling like a trespasser, he gingerly stepped into the room.

"Newsletters. Got 'em out late. We'll do better next time."

Karen McAllister waved. Mrs. Vandenburg glared at her. *What a troll!*
Caitlin Keller watched him. *What did she know?* Alicia was barely able to
control herself. She wriggled like a puppy and grinned, showing him a missing tooth. She proudly held up the yo-yo.

"Alicia, I warned you. Put that away, or I'll take it and keep it."

Richard strained to keep his mouth shut. He reminded himself to buy a
spare yo-yo—or maybe two dozen, one for each of the poor, unfortunate kids
in her class, except the Gunther-Hodges gang. He set twenty-four newsletters on the teacher's desk and backed out of the room, bumping into the TV
cart. He mimed losing his balance, provoking laughter.

"He's funny!" Alicia shouted.

"I warned you about yelling, Alicia." the teacher said. "Go stand in the corner."

Richard felt like he'd been stabbed in the gut. He stopped in the door and started to say something, but remembered his *Malliford Manners*. He shook his head in disgust and walked away, angry at the evil woman who ran that room and at himself for clowning around and betraying his most vulnerable admirer.

He heard a thump behind him—newsletters hitting the bottom of a trash can, no doubt. He hesitated for a moment. *Don't go back in there. Let this be her mistake, not yours.*

As Richard was signing out, Stan arrived to fulfill his Friday afternoon ritual of reading to second-graders. After the December smackdown, Mrs. Vandenburg had to accept her least favorite parent's unwanted help, given during the old TV time. Richard saw Stan's scowl and thought: *This is too easy.* "Your article is on page five: 'TV Contributes to Attention Deficit Disorder.'"

Stan brightened. "Great!"

"You'll have to get it from the trash. I think Mrs. V threw the newsletters away."

"Do what?" Muttering oaths, Stan stomped off.

If it's a battle they be wantin', then it's a battle they be havin'. Arrrr.

That afternoon, Nick had blood on his shirt. Richard feared he'd gotten in a fight with Devonious again, but his son said he'd gotten a nosebleed after lunch, and Ms. Hardwick gave him a Kleenex to stick in his nose. Spontaneous nosebleeds were new. As Richard tried to get the stain out, he realized this was the first time he'd heard of the counselor doing anything useful.

*   *   *

Devonious behaved poorly during Monday's tutoring session. Antonio, fresh from his triumph of achieving the "B" honor roll, wanted to tutor Devonious, while D was intent on teaching Antonio a lesson he wouldn't forget. Richard turned from helping Simeon to see D's fist raised above Antonio's head. "Put that thing down," he commanded. Devonious obeyed reluctantly, though the glower on his face suggested Antonio's reprieve was only temporary.

Nick complained frequently about Devonious's bullying, but Richard knew his son's troubles were nothing compared to Antonio's. Devonious had opportunities to torment Antonio on the bus, in the apartment parking lot, or by showing up at his latchkey neighbor's door. When Richard mentioned D's behavior to Mrs. Little in the hall, she said Ms. James and Ms. Hardwick were matching Devonious with a mentor in hopes of improving his behavior and prospects. "Otherwise," she said. "He's on the road to prison. Or worse."

On that grim note, Richard left. His mail check revealed a memo mixed in with badge catalogs and check requests. From Mrs. Vandenburg to faculty and staff, it outlined plans for Support Our Principal Day and all but branded Richard an enemy of the people:

> … Due to recent attacks on our school and its good name, it is essential for us to show our community how well-run Malliford Elementary is run (sic). All faculty will show their support and respect for our beloved principal by wearing black on Wednesday. We will hand out American flag lapel pins to wear. Black armbands will be given to teachers who forget to wear black. Parents are very strongly encouraged to participate. We look forward to a great day of celebration for Malliford and all the people who love this great school!
>
> P.S. This event is voluntary.

To Richard, the event seemed more like a funeral than a celebration. But he had to admit the flag pins were a nice touch, showing everyone which side was which—terrorist or patriot—if they needed a reminder. Also in his mail was Mrs. Vandenburg's resignation from the PTO.

Fine, but she wouldn't get her money back, because terrorist groups don't give refunds.

* * *

Support Our Principal Day was bright and sunny, cold but not bitterly so. That afternoon, Richard hiked up the hill in blue jeans and a yellow-and-black-checked flannel shirt, just in case the fashion police were making arrests. Polly looked especially dour in a black business suit.

"On you it works," he said, eliciting a sneer. Miz Rutherford came into the office wearing her trademark blue suit, faltering slightly when she saw Richard. "Hey, you're out of uniform!" he teased. "Didn't you get your memo?" She gave him her insecticide look and stiffly walked out. "I heard Mrs. Vandenburg is wearing a ski mask today!" he added.

Polly's eyes grew wide. "You are a bad, bad man. You should get a penalty for taunting." Then she burst out laughing; tears came to her eyes. "Thank you," she managed to say. "It's been a morgue around here. Morale is low, and it's not *entirely* your fault."

"How kind of you to say so. Now, if you'll excuse me, I've got a funeral to attend."

Not all teachers wore black, and some who did sent mixed signals. Mrs. Bailey wore a form-fitting black dress—which he could forgive, given her form—*and* a yellow PTO button. She winked when she ran into him in the back hall. The four teachers who had been scapegoated with apartment dwellers and now had a constant supply of PTO volunteers in their classes didn't wear a stitch of black. Mrs. Little wore a bright yellow pantsuit that made her look like a balloon, and she laughed at Richard's double-take. He noticed several more yellow buttons that afternoon. Not only was he divisive, but he was good at it! *The resistance lives!*

"To hell with peace!" said blue-jeaned Rita, marching down the hall, fist raised. "We want victory. Fight the power! Stan was dressed entirely in white—like an orderly in a mental ward. Which was his point. He's circulating a petition to get Lizzie Warden fired."

"Which you signed, I bet."

"Just once. For me, that shows remarkable restraint."

*   *   *

Thursday, January 18, brought cold, hard rain from the northwest. Richard worked for paying clients that morning; in the afternoon he drafted the agenda for that night's board meeting. The big issue: his teacher-training plan. Miz Rutherford had been noncommittal last summer and failed to respond to his November letter. However, Alicia had re-energized him and he was determined to push for change. After all, he was the elected leader of the ultimate sovereign—the people. If the principal believed she owned the school, she had another thing coming. And to think he'd considered becoming a lame duck!

Still, he was nervous. PWCs might call for his ouster. Add survival to his agenda, then.

As he slipped on his yellow rain slicker to go to the meeting, Anna Lee said, "Don't get in any more trouble."

"I'm not the one in trouble."

"Don't cause any, then."

He had nothing to say to that, so he left. He drove through heavy rain to school and parked in the back lot. He swallowed his anxiety and marched into the library, which was already set up for the meeting.

Teresa, sitting by the podium, gave him a smile that dimmed when she saw his anxious expression. "What's wrong? You look troubled."

"I do? Well, I'm cold and wet. That's troubling, I guess."

Barbara breezed in and buzzed by his ear, whispering, "Not a word about the assembly. Let's just pretend it didn't happen."

"Viva Alicia!" he cried out and raised his fist. Before the mortified ex-president could regain her color, Miz Rutherford arrived.

Richard smiled and said, "Good evening."

"Why, thank you," she responded, acting surprised he'd spoken civilly. She took her place beside Ms. Bailey. Only then did Richard notice Stan sitting wet and alone in back, glaring at the principal. Such a resentful muskrat. He was creepy, sometimes.

Richard reviewed his papers and waited for stragglers to arrive, but he didn't expect a big turnout—not on a rainy winter night. He called the meeting to order, affirmed everyone's patriotism with the pledge, attended housekeeping duties, and asked if Miz Rutherford wished to address the board.

"I'd rather make my remarks at the end of the meeting," she said.

Ah. The better to rebut. He shrugged and said, "Fine. On with business." As he spoke, board members looked over the treasurer's report. "We've done well this year, thanks to our elves, especially our main elves, Jane and Susan." He hated giving Susan half the credit when she did two percent of the work and ninety-eight percent of the complaining, but that was politics. Maybe his kind word would keep her off his back for the duration of the meeting. "We've got extra money, about five grand, and we need to spend it."

He explained his heroic plan for optional teacher training funds. He was relieved and gratified when board members supported the concept, though the principal remained mum. He needed an additional $5,000 to fully implement the program, so he asked for fund-raising ideas.

A few were bandied about before one took hold. "Computers," Brenda Carroll said. She knew a guy who refurbished old computers and sold them through PTOs to parents who wanted a cheap spare. "Beecham Elementary made two thousand dollars last year off it."

The idea swept through the room like a stadium wave. "My sister's PTO got fifty dollars for each computer. They sold a hundred over at Highbrook." Everyone was quite impressed, but everything was better at Highbrook. *Those snobs.*

"Do I hear any motions?" Richard asked.

Brenda: "I move we, uh, run a computer fund-raiser—the man is Aaron Roberts, I think—and use the money and what we have extra to fund advanced teacher training. That the teachers agree to."

Richard couldn't believe his good fortune: The motion supporting his plan came from the Table of Trouble! Moved, seconded, approved. So much for his reputation as a raving anarchist. *Vote of No Confidence. Not!*

"New Business," he said with a self-satisfied smile.

Stan stood up. Amid murmurs, he said, "I have a petition I want to present. It calls for new school leadership. It's signed by fifty parents."

Bedlam ensued. People started shouting. Susan told Stan she knew where he could put his petition. Miz Rutherford asked to see it, sending a chill up Richard's spine. Now *she* was giving him the creeps. Richard ruled Stan out of order and told him the PTO was not the appropriate forum for personnel matters.

"Let's move on," he said, grateful that Stan didn't press the issue.

Richard hastily finished up the regular business and turned to Miz Rutherford. "I believe you reserved time at the end of the meeting for principal's comments."

"I have nothing to say except that I'll be here a long time."

"Well, then. There being no other business—"

"Excuse me, Mr. President."

"Teresa." He felt betrayed. The one person he could count on was prolonging his agony.

"We need to give our president a new yo-yo under the line item Student Morale."

"Out of order!" Richard said.

"I just had to say that."

"I give up. All in favor of adjourning please stand."

People left quickly. This was not a night for after-meeting chit-chat, though Miz Rutherford and Barbara huddled in a corner. The principal jabbed Barbara in the chest with an index finger. If that's the way the old crone treated friends, Richard was glad he was her enemy.

"I wish we could go somewhere," Teresa whispered in his ear as he packed his satchel.

"A lot of people wish I would go somewhere," Richard said.

"But I'm the one with your new favorite destination." She left him blushing slightly.

Miz Rutherford approached Richard as he rolled the podium down the hall toward the cafetorium. "Congratulations," she said with chilly formality. "Your agenda carried the day. You should contact Mrs. Baines to implement this big plan of yours. But this is only one day."

"I know, I know, tomorrow belongs to you, right?" he said, but she'd already turned away and was busy ignoring him.

Stan was still in the media center when Richard returned and caught a whiff of something musty and sour—clothes damp with sweat. Richard recalled that Jane Baumgartner had complained about Stan's body odor that morning. "You need a ride?"

"Yeah. I was hoping to talk with you," Stan said.

"OK. Let's shut this place down."

Stan shuffled out of the library toward the front door. Miz Rutherford had already vanished, so Richard helped Ms. Bailey turn off the lights and secure the building. She dashed off under the protection of a blue umbrella. Richard pulled up the hood on his slicker and sprinted through pelting rain to the Audi as Stan thumped along behind him.

Once inside the car, Stan exploded in anger. "They're gonna pay!" he shouted and hit the dashboard with his fist. "Damn them! They're ruining my life!"

Richard paused before tuning the key. "What are you talking about?"

"Rutherford and her 'mental health professionals' reported me to Family Services. I can't prove it, since everything's anonymous. Vandenburg, Hardwick, James, and of course Dear Leader decided Karen was being mistreated at home. I should have seen it coming. A Family Services caseworker called Janet at work today. She was all upset when she called me. I told her it was bullshit, but they have to check it out, anyway."

"Jesus, Stan. What kind of evidence—"

"They don't need evidence. You know what they did? They called it in after Skate Night! Karen told the psychologist she got bruised falling down. Not only that, fifty people saw her! She's just learning to skate. That didn't matter to them, not after the petition. They're attacking me for my beliefs! I'm not going to be silenced. I'm not going to let them beat me down."

Richard stared at him in disbelief. "This can't be happening."

"Oh, it's happening, all right."

Richard felt sick. This was terrible. Mind-boggling. "Let me know if there's anything I can do to help."

"Got a spare bedroom?"

"Sorry, no. Not with my wife—"

Stan held up his hand. "Just kidding."

Richard started the car and drove through the driving rain. After reaching Stan's house, they sat in the car and talked for a few minutes. Richard sympathized with him and tried to calm him down. But there was too much going on for that.

"You have no idea what this is doing to me," Stan said. "A false charge is destroying my family. I'm all torn up inside, Richard. It's like they took a butcher knife and just—"

"It will be all right. They'll wrap it up, close the case, and no more trouble."

"You don't understand. My wife hasn't been happy." He shook his head. "It's just ... I don't know." He puffed out his cheeks. "What they did *worked*. They lobbed a grenade into my house, and I come flying out in bits and pieces."

"Janet needs to back you on this."

"Easy for you to say. Look, I've taken enough of your time."

"No, no. If you need to talk, we can talk."

"You be careful," Stan warned. "You're next on her shit list, my friend. It's a badge of honor and a world of hurt. You know, in the meeting I realized everyone on the petition was in danger if she got hold of it. Maybe I should tear it up. What do you think?"

"Give it here." Richard pulled out his pen and signed. "The county should see it. It might help."

"Probably not." Stan took the petition and opened the door. He climbed out. "What a fucked-up day."

"Tomorrow will be better."

"I doubt it," Stan said, slamming the door shut.

Driving off, Richard glanced in the mirror and saw Stan walking away from the house. He made a U-turn at the stop sign and drove back to check on his beleaguered friend, but Stan had disappeared into the darkness.

Rita had warned Richard a year ago that the principal was a vindictive bitch. *Come on, it's just a grade school. This stuff isn't supposed to destroy peoples' lives.* Maybe Stan had other issues. Nothing to warrant this, though. No, they'd done something abominable. Something unforgivable.

For that, they would pay.

SIXTEEN

R ichard did a quick "bitch-count" as he perused the crowd of friends and neighbors—neighbors, anyway—at January's general meeting. *Here a bitch, there a bitch.* Only four from the Table of Trouble, and they were spread throughout the cafetorium. Barbara the Inconstant, huddling in the corner with the principal; Helen, on the front row with a legal pad; Flora and Bessie in the middle. Bake Sale Brenda Carroll was there, but she was his new best friend after her fund-raising motion. No sign of Susan. *Excellent.*

He stood at the podium holding his glasses between thumbs and index fingers, moving them closer, then farther away, struggling to read the budget's eight-point type, wondering if it mattered. No one paid attention. Teresa watched him intently. She cared, thank God.

Stan came in, looking grim. He slouched into a seat on the back row, beneath the fascist duck. He'd called Richard that morning with ugly news: "You might be contacted by Family Services. You know the deal. Innocent until proven accused. It's bullshit. That doesn't matter to my wife. Janet was looking for an excuse, and the school gave her one. She's filing for divorce."

"That's terrible. Uh ... where are you staying?"

"Here and there. Look, somebody else needs to use the phone. I want to say one thing: They made a big mistake when they fucked with me. I am *not* going away."

Sure enough, an hour after he'd talked to Stan, a Family Services caseworker called. Richard told her he'd never seen any signs of abuse. He also said the accusation's timing was suspicious, since Stan was trying to get the principal fired.

Was he saying the allegation was an act of retribution?

"I think so," he said. "You've got to know these people."

"Interesting," said the caseworker.

"Like an old Chinese curse," Richard replied.

And yet Stan still made it to the PTO meeting. Well, he *shouldn't* go away. It was important for him to be in Karen's life—and to torment the principal. Richard looked at Rutherford as she took her place onstage with that smug, plastered-on smile. What would it take, he wondered, to break her like a rotten branch?

Richard turned to the audience, mainly parents and grandparents of fourth-graders who would sing that night. "Welcome." The microphone screeched. Stripped of his yo-yo, he was forced to rap the podium with his fist as he called the meeting to order. Following the pledge, he moved quickly through the agenda. After his budget amendments were approved, he yielded the podium to the principal with what he considered gracious civility. As he took his seat stage right, Richard noticed the Celebrate Diversity banner in its old position—only it was off one hook and hung listlessly, a broken promise.

Parents got Miz Rutherford's typical blue skies report, which neatly ignored the late unpleasantness. Then she switched course: "I have an important announcement. We are on the verge of forming a major partnership that will enhance the Malliford experience even more." She paused to inhale some of Malliford's excellent air. "It's an ambitious program to help our at-risk youth. To tell you more, I'd like to introduce our very own Jack Desmond, or as we know him, Christopher's dad. He's a relative newcomer to our community, but he's making quite an impact. Please give a warm Malliford welcome to Jack Desmond, executive director of the Southern Freedom Foundation!"

Richard sat dumbfounded as Desmond rose from his front-row seat next to Barbara Hodges. What the hell was going on? People were applauding the asshole! Outrageous! And furthermore, *not* on the agenda! Richard watched the real estate agent beam at Desmond as he stepped up and tapped the mike, which yielded a satisfying *pop* instead of the nasty screech it had given Richard, who now believed that even the school's sound system had joined the conspiracy against him.

"Thank you, Miz Rutherford," Desmond said. "I want to tell you about an exciting new program I'm personally piloting here at Malliford. You're going to hear a lot about The Mentoring Initiative in the days to come. Southern Freedom has selected Malliford because, quite frankly, I'm running the program and I'm doing the selecting." He paused to let the laughter die down. "But first, let me tell you about the foundation."

As Richard's blood boiled, Desmond gave his audience a brief, glowing description of the ultra-conservative advocacy group. After that, he got down to business: "This school is facing challenges with changing demographics, but there are ways to overcome these hurdles. What we're doing, in a nut-shell, is making up for the lack of positive male role models for at-risk youth. I know you're wondering, 'What does this mentoring entail?' Well, I'll tell you: After-school care, one-on-one tutoring, sports programs, scholarships for young boys ... and girls, especially those from single-parent families ... and other under-served youth without regard to race, creed, or color. Did I leave anything out?" He smirked. "I don't want to be politically incorrect."

"National origin," Richard suggested from behind him.

Desmond gave him a warning smile. "Yes, national origin."

"And religion."

"I think I covered that with creed."

"OK. How about sexual orientation?"

"I'm sorry. What?" Desmond's face crinkled in distaste.

Richard stood up. "Your organization has made homophobic claims about parenting that disparage several of the fathers in this room, including me. Your group's so-called *research* was discredited at the time. I wonder if you'd care to offer an apology to stay-at-home fathers."

"I didn't come here to talk about that." Desmond's tone was a mix of superiority and bile.

Murmurs swept the room. *Could men have a catfight?*

Richard didn't want to push the issue, since he already had a rep for killing a perfectly good assembly and worried the crowd might turn against him. Still, people needed to know this guy was bad news. And this was the wrong place for his program. Hundreds of schools needed it more. He gave Desmond the back of his hand: *You are so full of shit. Don't make me explain.*

Desmond waved back like he was shooing a fly and returned to his spiel. "I'm talking about major corporate involvement to benefit the community. It will *dwarf* your parent group's modest contributions—"

At that point, he and Richard exchanged venomous glares.

"—and I will personally oversee this program in its first year."

Desmond gave the crowd a smile. Richard wanted to wipe it off his face. What an arrogant little SOB! He wouldn't call the PTO by name, then chal-lenged the president's manhood! Richard wanted to kick him in his incongruously oversized balls. To compound the insult, parents applauded loudly, no doubt hoping Desmond's proposal meant they wouldn't have to buy over-priced gift wrap next year.

"If you want to know more, there's information on the back table, or you can visit our website, southernfreedomfoundation dot com. We're looking at an April kickoff to sign up kids for summer programs."

Richard sat bolt upright, realizing the plan tied in with the principal's weird behavior toward black boys. Of course! This was a way for her to get that elusive fifth star and gain recognition—maybe even sainthood. Once in danger of getting canned for her Gestapo tactics, Marine Antoinette was now on the verge of entrenching herself as Principal for Life.

Desmond left the podium to hearty applause. A beaming Miz Ruth-erford remained seated. Richard, feeling both ambushed and pissed upon, jumped up to adjourn the meeting and introduce the night's program, *The Song of Music*.

Some parents stared at him quizzically as he came offstage and took a seat beside Anna Lee and Nick. Others seemed perturbed. Richard caught a glimpse of Rita, who looked like she'd had a stroke. Of course she did. Her champion had been vanquished by Malliford's new Alpha Male.

"You could have handled that better," Anna Lee whispered. "Didn't you see this coming?"

"Guy's a major-league asshole." Heads turned. He glared and motioned for the transgressors to get out of his face.

"I hope they have baseball," said Nick.

"*Shhh.* The show's starting," Anna Lee admonished.

Richard was too furious to pay attention, however. The thirty-minute program seemed like three hours, since his kid wasn't in it.

Afterward, as the Grays rose from their chairs and moved toward the exit, Anna Lee said, "Come on, admit it. The Mentoring Initiative is great, don't you think?"

"I'm trying not to, right now," he said as he picked up a copy of the twen-ty-eight page TMI plan, complete with color photos, pie charts, bar graphs, and glowing endorsements from conservative heavyweights.

"My God. You're doing that thing with your tongue in your teeth. You're pissed because somebody else—"

"No I'm not."

"Are too."

"Drop it."

He leafed through Desmond's proposal, which contained buzz phrases like "Leave no child behind," "hands on," and "bold new thrusts." The highlighted passages bothered him. It just seemed ... a bit too hands-on, behindish, and *thrusty* for his tastes.

The list of sponsors included several heavy hitters, including Cablesync, the cable TV giant. One of TMI's plans involved wiring rooms for educational programming. Richard bet the principal's beady little eyes had lit up at that. He also noticed several Internet and new media companies had climbed aboard the conservative train, along with a major architectural firm, a chemical manufacturer, a regional bank, and a soft drink company. Big money. Empty calories.

"I'll take Nick home," Anna Lee said.

"Fine. I'll walk. I need a breath of fresh air after all that."

She shook her head. "Just get over it."

She left him to ponder her lack of loyalty. His mood soured further when he saw Desmond and Miz Rutherford together in the hall, surrounded by admiring parents.

Meanwhile, Aaron Roberts, having anticipated PTO approval of his company's fund-raiser, sat at a table in the front hall and took orders for refurbished computers. He was chubby, with short brown hair and the defeated air of a guy who'd been kicked around a lot. He wore a badly wrinkled shirt, an old tie, and scuffed shoes. Although his references had checked out, Aaron's threadbare appearance did not inspire confidence. Too late to worry about that, though.

Richard needed to help drum up seventy-five more orders for the poor guy. Then he would move on to the glorious long-term goal of Advanced Teacher Training! He had to admit his puny plan seemed cheesy compared to Desmond's. He wished he'd come up with a cool-sounding acronym like TMI. *Wait a minute ... wasn't that a nuclear plant that almost blew up? Or was it just Too Much Information?*

Stan approached. "You doing OK?" Richard asked.

"Yeah, I'm fine. And don't worry. I'm on top of No-TV Week."

"No-TV Week is the least of my worries."

"I appreciate your confidence." Stan mustered a cheerful smile.

Richard hadn't meant to be reassuring, but he saw no need to correct his friend.

"I saw Dear Leader's eyes light up obscenely at the prospect of big money," Stan said. "There'll be billboards all over and TVs blaring commercials in the halls before she's through. She'll turn this school into a whorehouse, though that might be better than the prison camp she's got now. Nah, it'll still be a prison camp. Just with whores."

"Shhh," Richard said, but it was a half-hearted effort.

He watched Stan waddle off and realized the anti-TV activist had a couch-potato butt. How did that happen?

Barbara came up to Richard and whispered, "Stan's wife kicked him out of the house."

"That's terrible."

"Know why?" Before he could respond, she said, "Internet porn and child abuse."

Linking the two accusations was pernicious, implying Stan was guilty of child molestation by conjunction. "Where did you hear *that*?"

"I know *everything* that goes on around here. Didn't anyone tell you? I'd be extra careful if I were you." She squeezed his arm and walked away, turning her head to show him her positively wicked smile.

She had to be lying. Had to be. He turned his attention back to Desmond's proposal, reading it closely for fatal flaws. A minute later, Teresa tugged his sleeve. For some reason, she seemed slightly radioactive right then.

"Whatcha think about this new development?" she asked.

"I think our principal is the comeback kid. Gotta hand it to her."

"You didn't even know this was in the pipeline?"

"Didn't have a clue."

"It's a deal with the devil, I'm sure. And speaking of the devil ..." She bit her lip and lowered her voice. "I miss you. I'll call you in the morning. Maybe we can do something."

After watching her sashay off, he decided her radioactivity had a half-life of five seconds. By then, only Aaron Roberts, Stan, Mrs. Bailey, Miz Rutherford, Richard, and hardcore gossips were left in the building. Stan was helping Aaron break down his demo computer. While Aaron was carrying the monitor out to his van, Stan trotted up to Richard. "Guess what? I got a job helping rebuild computers!"

"That's great." Richard had already concluded that his rumpled friend looked like Roberts's separated-at-birth twin. "Just great."

He couldn't shake the image of Stan as a grungy elf in a basement workshop, cobbling together an old computer. And then giving it a spin on the Internet. He shuddered. Barbara had to be full of shit. Otherwise, it could make an unimaginably nasty headline: "Chain Gang PTO Computers Packed with Porn!"

He walked home, reconsidering his life and concluding for the hundredth time that the PTO was a waste of time. Lame was the best kind of duck to be, especially for a president who was going bipolar on the job. Shortly after he walked in the door, he told Anna Lee it was time to build up his business.

"That's the best news I've heard all year!" she said, flashing a radiant smile. "Got any leads?"

"I'm sure I can come up with some. I'll get on it first thing tomorrow."

That night she made a pass at him. "Wanna make a baby?" she said as Richard crawled into bed. "This is the year, you know."

When he heard it phrased that way, he suspected she'd cut him off again as soon as she was pregnant. However, he had options with Carl out of town. "I'm real tired," he said and rolled away from her, marveling at this strange new power—radioactive or not—that Teresa had granted him.

* * *

Friday morning, frost dusted the lawn. Fifteen minutes after he'd returned home from driving Nick to school, Richard looked up from the kitchen table to see Teresa standing on the patio, smiling and stamping her feet. A surprise, but more than welcome.

"Is it safe?" she whispered as he slid open the door.

"Wow. Uh, yeah. She's got a luncheon on the other side of town."

Her rosy cheek chilled his face and their hair crackled when they embraced. She kissed him tenderly on the mouth, and then held him at arm's length, beaming. "I haven't been here since last summer." She glanced around and a mischievous smile lit her face. "*Brrr*. I'm cold. I walked here from school. Can you start a fire? How about cocoa?"

He lit gas logs as she took off her brightly colored knit cap and red wool scarf. "It's fun, sneaking around," she confessed.

A minute later, she sidled up to him as he poured milk in a pan. "Not very talkative today?"

"It's just that you reminded me of someone I used to know. Playing on a winter's day."

"Tell me."

"No. A long story for another day." Or never.

The fire roared as they sat cross-legged on the family room's tan Berber carpet and drank cocoa. He told her about Stan's troubles.

She was shocked and appalled. "If it's false, isn't there something he can do to clear his name?" she asked.

"There are other problems. An avalanche, actually. He got kicked out of the house."

"Where's he staying?"

"I don't know. Rita said he's sleeping in his car."

"Poor Stan."

They observed a moment of silence for Stan before going at each other like beasts in heat, rolling around on the floor, tearing at each other's clothes, kissing with tongue-twisting passion. For the first time, Richard made love in front of the fireplace. Teresa was loud, passionate, greedy, and athletic. If it had been a wrestling match, he would have lost several times. At last he was spent, sweating and panting before the raging fire.

"Men sound like a car breaking down when they come," she said.

"Just us older models."

"I came. Twice. I don't ever come ... well, you know. The camera is a turn-off." She patted his cheek.

"Uh, what camera?" He tensed up as he looked around.

"Carl likes to record his posterity. But you're the best. I wish we could do this every day."

"Every day would be nice."

"Or," she said, her sly smile returning, "twice when we can."

"Don't know how long I'd hold up under those circumstances."

"I accept your challenge."

She did her best to arouse him further, and her best proved good enough. The second time they made love in the master bedroom, at Teresa's insistence. Richard suspected she was marking territory. He felt guilty about taking another woman in his wife's place—and feared the luncheon was canceled and Anna Lee would walk into the bedroom. Didn't stop him, though—just made him finish sooner.

"I treasure every moment I spend with you," she told him afterward.

"I've just got you overly impressed," he said, pulling her off the bed.

"Damn right you do." She kissed him sweetly on the lips.

They showered together. Afterward, he watched her slip on her clothes and dreamily wondered what life would be like if she was his wife. When Teresa was ready to leave, she grabbed his hands. "You're the most wonderful man I know," she said. She ran her fingers through his hair when she kissed him, then left through the front door.

Richard thought it was good to be wonderful, but there was work to do, starting with washing the sheets.

* * *

On the eve of Groundhog Day, Richard's mind turned to shadows and long-lasting winters as he sat as his desk, unable to write anything past "At Smith Insurance, we—"

Who were these Smiths, anyway? Greedy bastards who specialized in ethnic redlining? He had no idea—and a financial duty not to care. Long-term debt, unpaid Christmas bills, income tax liabilities, and Anna Lee's lust for another child obligated him to take such clients. She'd given him some doozies. He'd agreed to flack for a semi-shady real estate developer but drew the line at printing takeout menus. Did she really want to see his work on windshields and blowing across parking lots? If *that* made her happy, what kind of a wife was she?

He didn't feel ambitious right then. No, he was in need of cheering up, or perhaps *naughty* would be a better way to describe his mood. He called Teresa.

"*He's in the house,*" she hissed like a horror-movie babysitter. "I'll be tied up all day."

"Not literally, I hope."

"God, I hate him. I'd be better off without him. I'd have my college degree. Maybe even a master's. My own company. Being treasurer has convinced me I've got a head for business. I've been thinking about your newsletter operation, and I've got some ideas—branching off into webpage design."

"Yeah, I'm planning on moving in that direction next year. I'm already writing posts for corporate websites. And the newsletters are moving online, too."

"I'd love to be your partner."

"By the way, don't tell people you didn't graduate from college. Everyone thinks you're an accountant."

"I'm close to not giving a damn what those bitches think."

"Me too, but I'm not there yet."

Richard hung up and looked through the slats of his office window's cheap white mini-blinds into the backyard at the crabapple tree, horribly naked without blossoms or Nick in its branches. Small clouds scudded across the sky in a wispy regatta, reminding him of time-lapse photos of storms and seasons passing. He could see Nick growing up, himself aging, dying, turning to dust, the sun going nova, the end of the universe. His time would be gone all too soon.

Therefore, happiness mattered. Why shouldn't he take what he had with Teresa? So what if it dissolved the glue of his world? Why shouldn't his life with Anna Lee be dust? Well, Nick, of course. If there was a way ... well, there simply must be. Yes. He could walk out of this time-lapse frame before the shutter came crashing down again. People did it all the time. He'd read of such things, and not just in murder mysteries.

Enough of that. Get back to work.

For the next several hours, he struggled to write Smith Insurance's mission statement and sales pitch. He debated the relative virtues of term versus whole life and decided survival was the only benefit he really cared for. Before he knew it, it was time to pick up Nick. Frustrated and desperate to get the flyer done, he let Nick watch TV after doing homework. Richard regretted using neglect as a parenting tool, but what else could he do?

That evening, when Richard checked his e-mail, there was a message from Teresa with an attachment. He jumped up and locked the door, fearing she'd sent him photos of herself in various stages of undress, since she'd done it before. He read the message:

> Hi,
>
> You're so fine you blow my mind, Hey Ricky!
>
> We should run away and be free. I say let's move to Hawaii. It would be better than the Bahamas. Further away and still in the U.S. We could write newsletters for pineapple growers. Do they grow mangoes in Hawaii? I want to herd mangoes with you at your earliest possible convenience. Let's do each other for lunch.
>
> Love you, T

The attachment was an animated hula dancer. He opened it, then deleted it in mid-undulation, along with the message.

The doorknob rattled. He clicked on the word processing icon and opened the door. Anna Lee cocked an eyebrow and gave him the up and down. "You're not doing porn, are you? Save some for me!"

* * *

Groundhog Day was sunny. Anxious to escape the school's shadow that Friday afternoon, Richard eschewed routines and chitchat while picking up his son. As he rounded a hall corner with Nick in tow, he nearly ran into a large black woman who was busy chewing out Donzella James. The woman had straightened hair and wore a dowdy black suit. Her eyes were flamethrowers.

"He needs to get over his father," the woman said, repeatedly poking her index finger at the psychologist's chest. "I don't need you diggin' into his brain and pullin' up that old stuff. His daddy's no good. More importantly, man's gone. I don't want you talkin' to the boy. I got a minister I can go to. I don't need a bureaucrat who never met me haulin' my boy out of class and givin' him the third degree about none of your business." Her arms rested on her hips. She seemed not only to dislike every feature of the smaller woman who faced her, but also appeared ready to rearrange them all.

"He told me you whipped him," Ms. James said. "I can report you."

Richard stopped in his tracks. The words chilled his blood, but they had the opposite effect on the outraged parent. "So what if I do?" she huffed. "Spare the rod and spoil the child. That's what the Bible say. I guess you wouldn't know about that."

"Go out to the front and wait for me," Richard told Nick. The boy hesitated, but his father vehemently shooed him away. The counselor came out of the office to join the psychologist. Ms. Hardwick did a double-take when she saw Richard standing in the hall.

"I'll tell you both. Stay away from my boy and leave him be, you hear?" the woman said.

"Mine too," Richard said.

"You just failed the attitude test, Mr. Gray."

"Is that what happened to Stan?"

Both educators fixed him with icy stares.

"They the ones flunkin'," the angry parent said, waving them off with a pointed finger.

"You got that right," Richard said.

The woman turned on her heel and walked away with a grunt of disgust. Richard followed. What could they do to him? He was made of stronger stuff than Stan, with better cards to play and more game. *Bring it on.*

When he went outside, Nick's nose was bleeding profusely and Mrs. Leland was stanching it with a Kleenex. The nosebleeds had become more frequent. Nick's pediatrician said they were nothing to be alarmed about, but the boy had to carry tissues in his pocket to school, and Richard now carried a small pack of Kleenex, too—a sorry substitute for his magic yo-yo.

On the way home, Nick asked for advice on how to deal with "someone who shall not be named," who was cheating in school and demanding help on tests and homework.

"Give him the wrong answers," Richard quipped. "That'll fix him."

* * *

Monday brought rain. Richard was scheduled to tutor Devonious, Antonio, and the others that morning. Polly handed him a sheet of paper when he checked in. He walked into the hall and bumped into Rita. "*Ooof*," she said, bouncing off his chest. "What you got there?"

He read aloud: "Important Emergency Revised Guidelines for Volunteers."

"I don't need them to tell me how to do my job. Let's go raise some test scores. Or hell. Whichever comes first."

He, too, planned to ignore Miz Rutherford's latest edicts, whatever they were. He folded the paper and slipped it in his pocket as they headed to the computer lab. A line of kindergartners passed them, index fingers to lips. Richard acted frightened and splayed himself against the wall to make way for silent ducklings, who giggled at his antics. Mrs. Patterson waved a "naughty" finger at him.

They entered the computer lab, empty except for Mrs. Smalley, a short, round, hyperactive woman who seemed unhappily surprised to see them. "May I help you?" she asked in a *What the Hell Are You Doing Here?* tone. This seemed uncalled for, since both volunteers showed up at least twice a week.

"Ask not what you can do for us, ask what we can do for the kids," Richard said, glancing around. Since the start of the second semester, D and his cohorts had been there when he arrived, usually searching computers for non-educational games. "Speaking of which, where are they?"

"We're not doing that any more."

"'Scuse? What do you mean by '*we*'? Because here *we* are."

Mrs. Smalley brushed her gray hair from her forehead and set her screwdriver down by a computer. She went to her desk, eyes darting to locate ... *Ah*. There it was, atop the pile. She cleared her throat and read: "Parents are asked not to be at school during the day during February because they would be a distraction from test preparation."

"Are you saying that language arts tutoring doesn't help kids prepare for tests?" he asked in disbelief, then turned to consult with Rita, who looked like she'd been hit on the skull with a brick. She was shaking her head so rapidly it appeared to be vibrating.

"I don't make the rules. You're welcome to read this." She handed him a memo to faculty and staff on the principal's letterhead, initialed by the counselor and psychologist.

It said what she said it did. The change was effective "for the time being, until further notice."

"Apparently, volunteerism has been cancelled," he said.

"So those two set school policy now," Rita managed to say.

"We discussed this in a staff meeting," said Mrs. Smalley. "Generalized instruction isn't focused enough. There's no writing on the standardized tests. Just mark answers with a good old Number Two." She meant a pencil, but since the exam was the Standard Hightower Intellachievement Test, Richard was thinking something else.

Rita started to argue; Richard touched her arm and told Mrs. Smalley, "We'll trouble you no more."

He pushed Rita out of the room ahead of him.

"No trouble, no trouble," Mrs. Smalley called out after them.

"I don't believe this," Rita grumbled as anger replaced perplexity. "I mean, Lizzie Warden never liked volunteers in the classroom, anyway—other than to serve cake and cookies, but this is just too incredibly stupid for words. What the hell is going on?"

As they walked by the office, they saw Jack Desmond enter Miz Rutherford's office. "I bet he has something to do with this," Rita said. "I'm irreversibly pissed now. Let's go in and demand to know what the fuck's going on."

"No," Richard said, grabbing his black, stubby umbrella from the corner by the door. "Right now the less I say, the better." They exited without signing out and paused in the alcove outside the front door. "I don't talk to her much any more," Richard said. "We're completely dysfunctional." He zipped his coat and stared out into the rain, listening to the whine of car tires zipping up the street.

Rita stared out into the schoolyard. "What a dreary day," she said, then turned to Richard. "What are you gonna do about this?"

"I've got work to do. I'm going home. The good news is, I just got part of my life back."

She looked at him in disgust. "Where's the piss and vinegar? This is not the man we elected to fight the power."

"You're such a radical. I can't stay constantly outraged. I'm not Ralph Nader, for God's sake."

"A month ago you stormed the Bastille, throwing yo-yos like grenades, ripping down banners, challenging Marine Antoinette. Now you're giving up."

"You are not the boss of me," he said, using the simple logic of a third-grader.

"Oh, God. You're bipolar, aren't you? I should have known."

He ignored the question. "There are limits to what I can accomplish. I thought we had her on the ropes, but now it's rosy for her. Rope-a-dope and we're the dopes. I have to step back. Do what I gotta do. I've got to start making money. Think of the family. Anna Lee wants another child."

"I bet *that* keeps you busy."

He ignored her comment. "I can't let this place consume me."

"You're not backing off because of Teresa, are you?"

"Do *what?*" Richard squinched up his face in shock and distaste.

"Come on. The way you look at her, it's obvious."

"What the hell are you talking about?"

"The fact that you've got a woman on the side."

"Whoa. Stop right there. I don't need you, of all people, spreading vicious rumors."

"You crazy fucker!" she hissed. "I'm trying to stop them! People are saying this is what happens, why it's stupid to put a man in charge of the PTO. The last man in your position—and I use that term loosely—had an affair with the principal and his wife was the treasurer. She ran off with all that money, and that's why the PTA got disbanded and we got a PTO and She Who Shall Not Be Named. So *Hell-o.* Things don't always turn out well, in case you didn't know."

"You're absolutely full of shit, Rita. This has nothing to do with that."

"Did she show you her tattoo?"

"She doesn't even have—"

"Busted."

He shook his head at his own stupidity. Horndoggery will out, eventually.

"You're human," Rita said. "I should have seen it coming. Hell, I'm tempted to make a pass at her myself. I'll speak of it no more. Just be careful." She patted his shoulder. He walked into the rain, and she followed. After a few steps, she stopped and turned around to face the school. "I sent three kids here. I've been on the PTO board for ten years. I'm more a part of this place than she is, damn it! She kicked me out of my own school!" Muttering obscenities, she stormed off.

Richard walked away slowly, realizing that he wouldn't give up the fight even though he knew he should, even if he was weakened and compromised. He would not be his father's son, not on this issue.

The rain slacked off and the misery index fell slightly. Richard had decided to confront the principal over her latest dastardly deed, but when he went to see her that afternoon, she escaped from the rear door of her office and slithered away—marking a new low, even for her. Richard figured that Polly had hit a silent alarm button, like a teller does when the bank's getting robbed. Next time, he'd post Rita on the exit.

When he went to get Nick, Mrs. Little hung her head. "I don't know what to say."

"About the volunteers?"

"For years, I dreamed of havin' parents do what you're doin'." She shook her head. "I've been respectful—tried to be, anyhow—prayin' what to do. I can't be the teacher I need to be with those two breathin' down my neck all the time."

"You mean the counselor and psychologist?"

She nodded. "I told them *they* should tutor Devonious after they chased you off. This time they pushed too far. He ain't gonna run this school."

"He? Devonious?" *Why, that little gangster.*

"Oh, no. Not Little D." She laughed and shook her head. "I shouldn't be talking like that. I do apologize. And you didn't hear it, either."

"Fair enough." Shaking his head, he left and walked home through the drizzle with Nick. That afternoon, he wrote a three-page, single-spaced letter to Superintendent Johnson about diversity, race, Ritalin, a little girl, and traffic lights that didn't work despite a dozen complaints, among other things.

He never got a response. Then again, that *was* a response.

SEVENTEEN

D ue to federal mandate, learning was put on hold in February. The Better Schools initiative—or BS, as teachers called it—required high-stakes, curriculum-based testing. For reasons known only to bureaucrats, the state examined students on their cumulative grade-level learning with three months still to go in the school year. The state's Department of Education had adopted the unfortunately but aptly named Standard Hightower Intellachievement Test to measure progress. Its acronym was never used, for obvious reasons. County educators referred to it as DESI (Don't Even Say It), and some irreverent teachers called it DUMP.

Though often ridiculed, the test was no laughing matter. Pride, money, stars, and housing prices rode on the results. Teachers in schools with improved test scores received bonuses; schools with declining scores faced sanctions. In the past, Malliford had nothing to fear. But now the influx of underachievers from Chantilly Arms threatened to lower scores and put the school on the state's Needs Improvement list (often called the SHIT list, for obvious reasons). This would be an unmitigated disaster, but it could get even worse. After a school languished for three years on the Needs Improvement list, its teachers were taken out behind the trailers and shot. At least that's how Mrs. Leland explained it to Richard.

With its status as a good school on the line, the stakes were terribly high. Since December, Mrs. Baines did little besides what she called "testprep." No one took DESI more seriously than reigning Teacher of the Year Sarah Vandenburg, who gave her second-graders practice exams the first day of school and tested them weekly thereafter—and let them watch TV, until she got caught.

Despite the newly challenging demographics, Miz Rutherford demanded that test scores rise. She also suggested heads would roll if they didn't. She'd already picked heads, having established scapegoats like Avon Little by filling their rooms with Underintellachievers.

Thus motivated by the principal's shrill cheerleading, teachers masked their desperation with pasted-on smiles as testing week drew near. They tried to create a festive air in their classrooms, handing out balloons, promising parties for high-scoring classes, and sending brightly-colored notes home to parents with tips on "how to get your students on the winning team." Miz R's "Secret Formula for Success" called for an 8:00 p.m. bedtime and a hearty breakfast on testing days. She also suggested kids watch TV to relax.

Richard considered this last idea a terrible one, and he would have said something to the principal had they been on speaking terms. Instead, he editorialized against it in February's *Duck Call*, urging kids to read a book instead, and quoted Stan to piss off the principal even more. Unfortunately, Richard no longer knew how many newsletters actually made it home to parents, since some other teachers now followed Mrs. Vandenburg's lead and threw them away.

Richard thought testprep was senseless. Back in August, he'd tried to schedule a Black History Month program, but the faculty-dominated School Improvement Committee shot him down. Apparently, black history lowered achievement. Miz Rutherford later regretted this decision; she needed a forum to tell African-American parents how to optimize their kids' DESI scores. She sent Mrs. Baines to parley with Richard on February 6, the day after he'd been fired as a tutor. The vice principal chased after him so furiously he thought Rita was coming up from behind to tackle him.

"Mr. Gray," she said when she'd corralled him, "we thought you might call a general meeting this month. Before the tests."

"Why would I do that?"

"Ms. James and Ms. Hardwick would like to present a program for *diverse* parents."

He stared at her like she was crazy. "Diverse? You mean a black history program?"

"Well, future black history."

"What's future black history?"

"What we make of it." She gave him a bright, brittle DESI smile.

"I proposed a Black History Month program, remember? No one liked the idea."

"We changed our mind."

"Mind? Interesting use of the singular. The problem is we'd have to have the meeting this week, and that's not enough notice. Sorry, can't help you. Too late. Ta-ta." He walked away.

Though appalled at the school's excessive zeal, Richard did hope Malliford would gain a top-ten ranking on his watch. A home in a five-star school district was worth $30,000 more than one in a four-star zone, according to Barbara. If he was ever going to get out of town, he wanted cash from the deal. This made him one of many "whores for scores," as Rita so indelicately put it.

*   *   *

"Devonious copied off my test today," Nick told his father as Richard chopped carrots for stew. "I told him not to, and he said I'd better let him, or else."

"Or else what?"

"*Duh*," Nick said emphatically. "Or else I'll get hurt."

"I'll talk with Mrs. Little."

"I wish he didn't sit next to me. He stinks and he cheats. Stinky cheat man."

"Enough."

"You know he smells."

"We don't talk about it like that, though."

"Why not?"

"You'll understand when you're older."

"I doubt it. At lunch, he said every cuss word he knew and didn't get in trouble 'cause Mrs. Little wasn't around. Dad, you know what? A lot of black people are bad."

"No. Why do you say that?"

Nick pointed to the television. The local news happened to be on, showing police subduing a young African-American robbery suspect.

"They wouldn't look so bad if we turned it off," Richard said. "There are millions of black people, and that guy went out in the street with a gun. So he's the one who gets on TV. A lot of white guys in suits and ties rob banks without guns."

"How do they do that?"

"Computers. Lies. Conspiracies. However, it's the guy with the gun who gets on TV. It's what they call *sensational*."

"That doesn't make sense."

"Exactly. A lot of crime gets ignored because they can't show the arrest. Being good or bad has nothing to do with what color you are."

"OK." Nick thought for a moment. "Are there more good people or bad people?"

"More good than bad, I hope." Richard shrugged. "It's a theory."

Nick crunched a carrot. "You wanna know what's stupid? At lunch today, Ms. Hardwick and Ms. James went around the cafeteria waving cardboard clocks over their heads that said 'Eight p.m. is time for bed!' Nobody likes them. It's not like they teach us anything. They bother me all the time. I wish they'd leave me alone."

Richard wasn't listening. He was staring out the window, wondering how badly he'd bungled his Atticus Finch moment.

* * *

Miz Rutherford devoutly believed a diet of grapes and bottled water for test-takers would help her win that elusive fifth star. She'd been preaching this message for months and needed the PTO's help to get the word out to parents of test takers.

"It's scientific," she'd previously explained to the PTO board. "Grapes assist the brain in the hydration process, which speeds up decision making, as anyone familiar with brain-based learning models understands." She'd finished off with an imperious glare at Candace and Cindi Lou.

"So kids still get wrong answers, just quicker," Richard quipped from the podium.

"You're missing the point," she said.

Then again, he'd missed every point she'd jabbed at him. Richard turned to the Drug Awareness chairperson and said, "This grape thing explains why people who drink a lot of wine think they're smart."

This prompted titters, but the overall mood was sober and serious. Some board members worried about allergic reactions and frequent bathroom breaks brought on by this brain-hosing. However, most believed in trying anything that might improve test scores, so they ignored warnings about poop and pee on first-grade floors from Candace, who glared back at the principal as she spoke.

A motion calling for the PTO "to make necessary arrangements to assure an ample supply of grapes during testing" was quashed by Bessie Harper, mother of all room mothers, when she said the magic words every president longs to hear: "Don't bother. I'll take care of it."

Bessie's first e-mail to room mothers called for green grapes and half-liter bottles of water. After Mrs. Baines yelped "Wrong grapes! Wrong grapes!" in the hall to Richard, e-mail corrections went out calling for red grapes. A parent wanted to know if purple grapes were acceptable. More checking, another e-mail: "Due to lack of research on purple or black grapes, those varieties should not be used. Parents should send red grapes, seedless of course."

Richard referred to these in his e-mails as *The Grapes of Math.*

A question arose: What brand of water was best? Another flurry of e-mails: Miz Rutherford declared Hydrate the brand of choice. Its parent company happened to back The Mentoring Initiative and planned to install soft-drink machines in the school. Richard tried to start a rumor that top schools used Perrier, but his pernicious claim never took hold.

"What if scores go down?" Bessie asked him during the second round of e-mails.

"Then we sell the information to Hydrate's competitors," Richard replied. "As a fund-raiser."

* * *

On February 12, parents and teachers held their collective breath as students began taking DESIs with all the earnest zealousness of a "Duck and Cover" air raid drill. With rankings on the line, every other school and student in the state was their enemy, while sharpened pencils and childish wits were their only friends. One way or another, they would fulfill the BS mandate.

What kind of test-takers were these Mallifordians? Would the world bow down before them, or would they be Underintellachievers, road kill on the superhighway to tomorrow?

Deep in the bowels of Malliford, someone already had an idea how it would turn out.

Come, let us test now, said the spider to the flies.

* * *

So far it had been an off-month for Richard's affair with Teresa, since Carl was sticking close to home. On the morning of Valentine's Day, Teresa dropped by Applegate with a Valentine's card, Frenched Richard when he answered the door, and while running back to the van, shouted, "The kissing bandit strikes again!"

After savoring its lilac scent, Richard tore up the lover's card and disposed of it properly, watching the garbage men that afternoon to make sure they hauled it away.

He spent that evening arguing with Anna Lee over housework. Despite the fight, Anna Lee made a pass at him that night. "I don't think so," he said as he shifted away from her. She didn't remember that line, but he'd never forget it.

"This isn't for you or me," Anna Lee said. "It's for the baby."

She tried again. This time, he succumbed. Who can argue with a baby?

*   *   *

The DESIs ended on Friday, February 16. Results would be published in April. Perhaps Malliford would be rewarded with a fifth star, but Richard suspected it would lose its fourth. With a note of deep concern in her voice, Rita told him she'd heard the sixth grade hadn't done so well on the tests, and the *Sentinel* ranked schools based largely on sixth-grade scores, tut-tut.

"I'd hate to think that my son's class was the weakest link in the chain gang," she added.

The following Monday, the principal named Cassandra Hardwick and Donzella James Co-Teachers of the Year. Richard was sure this was their reward for tirelessly advancing Miz Rutherford's agenda. That evening, Richard drove by the school and saw Desmond's beige Lincoln LS parked in front. There were only two cars remaining in the faculty lot. No doubt they belonged to Tweedle-Donzella and Tweedle-Cassandra, which meant the two of them were plotting something evil with the rich white guy.

*   *   *

Wednesday afternoon, Rita was hanging around the school's front door. "Didn't you tell the psychologist to stay away from your son?" she asked Richard as he approached.

"I did, indeed."

"Well, I saw Nick go into Donzella James's office right after lunch. I was bringing Bert back from a doctor's appointment." Richard looked like he'd been hit with a brick. She waved a hand in front of his face. "*Hell-o.* Say something."

"Words cannot express what I'm thinking right now," he said, then rushed inside the school.

When he came back out with Nick, Richard waited until they were out of earshot of Mrs. Cates, on bus duty, before asking, "Have you been seeing Ms. James?"

"Yeah. Twice a week."

"*What?* When did this start?"

"Day after Honors Assembly. Sometimes I talk to Ms. Hardwick, too. They told me not to tell you, but I figured you knew. You know everything that goes on at school."

"Not really. When do they do it?"

"On days you aren't tutoring."

Oh. "What do you talk about?"

"You, mostly. I think she's trying to trick me. So I trick her. Just like the black kids do. Every once in a while I tell her a joke about how mean you are, but I quit 'cause she doesn't think they're funny. Then she asked if you touched me ... in a ... in a—"

"Inappropriately?"

"Yeah. I told her you stuck things in my bottom. Inna butt." Nick laughed at his joke.

"You told her *what?*"

"You know. That thing. When I was sick."

"What about it?"

"I told her it didn't feel good and I didn't like it and we agreed we weren't going to talk about it to other people. She wanted to know all about it. She's a butt person." He laughed again.

Richard blanched; a wave of nausea came over him. First they came for Stan. Now him. While he hated Rutherford and her evil twins, he was also irritated at the boy's behavior. Nick should have simply given the psychologist his name, grade level, and lunch access code. Instead, he'd ratted out his father, identifying him as a sodomite. What kind of loyalty was that? The boy should have told him that bad women were trying to suck out his soul.

He told Nick to wait and went inside. He found Mrs. Little in her classroom. "We have a problem," he said, struggling to keep his voice under control.

"What's that?"

"Who put Nick in counseling? I never agreed to that."

Sensing hostility, she stiffened. "You don't have to. You send your kid to school, you give up certain rights. I don't have anything to do with that. You should talk with Ms. James and Ms. Hardwick."

He left before he said more—a wise move, given his mood right then. He took Nick home and started coaching him on how to deal with the mental health professionals. "You're a good kid," he explained. "There's nothing wrong with you."

"They're not worried about me."

"They're not?"

"No. They think I'm great. They're worried about you. What you do to me. They think you're sick or something. Anger is a disease. That's what they're always saying."

"They'll tell you you're great as long as you say what they want."

"They say they're my friends and want to help."

"They're lying, Nick. And they're not trying to help you."

"Yeah. I don't feel better when I talk to them. Worse sometimes, like when I told on you even though you didn't do anything real bad."

"About what?"

"Just being mean. I don't want to talk about it. They gave me candy."

"Didn't I tell you not to take candy from strangers?"

"They're not strangers, Daddy."

"Some people are always strangers. The more you know them, the stranger they get. That's who you're dealing with now." He thought for a moment. "I'll get you out of this. Let's not tell Mom what we talked about today. Otherwise, I might not be able to help you. All right. Go on and play."

"You mean do my homework."

"Yeah, yeah," said Richard, distracted. "Do that."

"Dad, you know you're doing that thing with your teeth."

"What?"

"That thing you do when you get real mad and act like you're trying to hide it."

"I'll be all right," Richard said, but he wasn't really sure if this was true.

*　　*　　*

Richard returned from a business appointment Thursday to find a phone message from Donzella James. She wanted to set up a meeting to discuss Nick's "low self-esteem and lack of communication." It seems Nick had refused to talk to her during their session that day.

"Attaboy!" Richard shouted, pumping his fist in the air. However, he also knew that "low self-esteem" was a buzz phrase used when opening child-abuse investigations, so there was a possibility the psychologist was upping the ante.

He didn't return the call. Instead, he phoned Polly and asked for a meeting with the principal. They would be on speaking terms, if only for a moment—and perhaps a loud one, at that. Polly called him back and said the principal could meet him Friday.

When he showed up for the appointment, Miz Rutherford was nowhere to be found. Richard suspected she'd ducked out again, and he cursed himself for neglecting to post Rita on the back door. Polly summoned Mrs. Baines as Miz Rutherford's proxy. Richard would have none of this second-rate treatment, however, and sent the flustered vice principal on her way.

He went home and called district school supervisor Curtis Blodgett. The woman who answered said Blodgett was gone.

"What do you mean, Blodgett is gone?"

"He's not here any more," she explained.

"What is he doing now?"

"Looking for a job, I imagine."

Richard was sure they'd fired good old Blodgett because he was marginally competent, making him far too qualified to work for the school system.

Where else could Richard turn? He wasn't sure he could stop a Psy Ops attack on his family, but he had to put up a fight. Unfortunately, things were rotten at the top, too. Superintendent Johnson, worthless to begin with, was under investigation for financial improprieties. The *Sentinel* called for him to get out of town at least once a month. School board members had been stung by an outside audit accusing them of micromanaging the system, so they were reduced to sitting on the sidelines acting outraged, doing nothing. (That might have been for the best, since there was danger in riding into battle with idiots on his side.)

Nick's interim grade report came home that afternoon. Richard was aghast. The boy should have low self-esteem! How had Nick plummeted so quickly from the bright-eyed, brilliant boy of last semester? And how had he failed to actualize in Ms. Landistoy's art class? He also got three unsatisfactory marks in conduct. It was time to go Chinese Mother on his ass.

"Your grades are slipping," Richard said, scowling. "Conduct, too. What's going on?"

"Nobody behaves. It's a rotten class and everybody knows it."

Under questioning, Nick admitted he wasn't always doing his homework, since Devonious copied it when he did, so why bother? He also said he taught Devonious not to cheat off him during tests by putting down wrong answers, and both boys' grades suffered as a result.

"That's foolish," Richard pointed out. "You're hurting yourself."

"I just did what you told me to do," Nick countered. "So if it's not working, don't blame me. Anyway, can we move? I'm tired of the cheating and the bullying and calling names. There's been fights, too, but Devonious is better than me 'cause he gets more practice. Aren't you supposed to talk to Mrs. Little about him?"

Hmm. Mrs. Little hadn't mentioned any problems, other than sending notes home. *Oh yeah. Those. At least the ones that made it.* Still, it bothered him that he hadn't heard anything from Mrs. Little about the fighting or Nick's general malaise. He suspected that the psychologist was handling those matters—and that Donzella James would rather build a case against the father than help the son.

Obviously, this so-called counseling was hurting Nick. How could it help, with soul-destroying bitches from hell running the show? *Wait a minute. Didn't his nosebleeds start when he began seeing those two?*

There were further repercussions that evening, when Anna Lee saw Nick's grades and blamed Richard for their son's failures. Well, C's, anyway. "Aren't you supposed to be watching him?" she asked, shaking her head in disbelief. "Isn't that your job?"

* * *

On February 28, Nick shuffled out of the classroom and looked up forlornly at Richard. Mrs. Little called out, "Make sure your father gets the note."

They took a few steps down the hall. "What note?"

"I got in trouble again. I always get in trouble. I hate school."

Richard waited until they were outside to ask for the note. Nick fished around in his backpack and found a crumpled piece of paper several weeks old. Erased and scratched over in pencil, it had taken Nick three tries to properly confess: "I compared myself to Hitler in class today. Hitler was a bad man. I should not have done this. Nick Gray."

A forced confession. Richard shook his head. *Absurd.* "What's this about?"

"She asked if anyone would help clean the whiteboard. I said, 'I'm your Hitler!' You know, from *The Producers*."

"*Whoops*. Probably shouldn't have said that. Not everyone gets it."

"Mrs. Little doesn't get any of my jokes."

Richard knew it wasn't fair. At least the boy offered to help. Would Hitler do that? He thought not. "It's best not to joke about Hitler."

After they got home and Nick went to his room, Richard called the school and talked to Mrs. Little, who said that comparing himself to Hitler showed Nick had serious role-model issues. Richard tried to explain, but she wasn't familiar with *The Producers* and had no intention of watching a comedy about a Nazi.

"We're under orders to be tough on inappropriate behavior," she explained. "Security and discipline, you know. I can't give your son special treatment."

"Special treatment? Let me tell you the problem I see." He proceeded to give her an earful about the nosebleeds during counseling sessions and Nick's problems with Devonious. *Finally*, Nick would say.

"I don't know what I'm going to do about D," she said. "He's got problems at home. His mama's not returning my phone calls. He's on his own when he's there. I filed several reports, but no one has followed up. Ms. Hardwick matched him up with Mr. Desmond as a mentor."

"Really. That's interesting."

"Now, about your son—there's something not quite right about all this. I don't think the counseling is helping. I'll pray on this."

Right then, apparently.

"Mrs. Little. Mrs. Little."

He waited for a minute, and then, just when he was about to hang up, she said, "We'll just take care of Nicholas between us from now on. It will be better that way. I'll talk to Ms. James."

"I appreciate that."

"And you can teach him some discretion," Mrs. Little said.

"Of course. I shall take due notice and be governed accordingly."

"You do that."

On that note, they said goodbye. Richard felt better. Mrs. Little was an ally. Maybe God was, too. He had to believe that, or all hope was lost. He went to Nick's room. The door was open. Nick was at his desk working diligently on something. Richard hoped it was homework. "I just talked to Mrs. Little and we both agree you need to do better," he told his son.

"Yeah, right," Nick said. "Now leave me alone."

What a surly little dude his boy had become! Thanks very much, Chain Gang Elementary!

* * *

The counseling sessions ended abruptly the next day. There had been a fight about it. Nick told his father Mrs. Little wouldn't let him go to the counseling office. Mrs. Baines came and they went out in the hall and then Miz Rutherford came and Nick found out the principal and Mrs. Little didn't like each other very much. Mrs. Little might be in trouble and Devonious was involved, but Nick didn't understand how, except D was in the middle of every mess. Nick was aware of all this because he sat by the door and knew to listen, being a kid. "Mrs. Little prays a lot lately," he said. "You can tell because she bows her head. I think she's just talking to herself."

"Let's hope that's not the case," Richard said.

EIGHTEEN

March 1 dawned cold; the weatherman promised a sunny day and the outlook was even brighter for Richard. Teresa was driving Carl to the airport. He would be gone two weeks to sell heavy equipment in Texas and "party down in titty bars," as Teresa put it. Richard had missed her terribly since their last tryst and longed for her athletic lovemaking in improbable places, including those they hadn't tried yet: office, sofa, minivan, Audi. *Hee-Yaw!*

Shortly before noon, the woman he desired dropped by Applegate with mischief in mind. She wore Capri pants, high heels, and a tight red sweater that showed her nipples to great effect. He looked out the door over his treasurer's nicely rounded shoulder to her van across the street.

"Who cares?" she said, reading his mind. "PTO stuff, right? Let no busybody tear us asunder." She walked in and threw file folders on the kitchen table. "There's your cover. Happy?"

He was, but just to be safe, he called Anna Lee at work to verify her whereabouts. "Hey, I got a new client for you," she said. "Dunaway Auto Detail wants five thousand promotional flyers."

"I'm working for guys who wash cars now?"

"Money is money."

Teresa pulled off her sweater and cupped her breasts. He gave Anna Lee a curt goodbye.

"If I was your wife, I wouldn't let any other woman near you," Teresa said and squinched her nose. "You're so sexy." She ran a finger down the buttons of his blue oxford shirt, kissed him lightly on the lips, and proceeded to engage in the sort of debauchery one might expect from a woman of her background, providing one was very nice to her—this time in his swivel office chair, which nearly toppled as he climaxed.

Afterward, still on his lap, she bitched about Carl, "a self-proclaimed stud—is there any other kind?—whose obsession is making home sex videos." She shook her head. "The stuff's worth a lot of money. I'm that good, as you know. I'm too young to be a MILF, but I guess that's how they'd classify me. I could make a living at it. I mean, I did that sort of thing at The Leopard's Spot back in college. Not the sexing, just the dancing."

She gave her head a dramatic toss. "My stage name was Candy. Not with an 'I' because I was the real thing. Candy Storm. I guess that's a good porn name, eh? Of course you've already got one. Maybe change 'Gray' to ... I don't know, maybe 'Slate.' Yeah, Dick Slate."

He grimaced in response. "Makes me sound like an obscene pool table."

Still naked, she jumped up and showed him some moves. "Likie?"

"*Um-hmm.*" Richard was entranced by the thought of having his own exotic dancer, which beat the hell out of Internet porn.

"That's how I met Carl. He came in to The Leopard's Spot with some of his whoredog clients. He was a big tipper, such a big tipper I went out with him after a show and never came back, not even to clean out my locker." She sighed. "Another time and place." Then she laughed. "Anyway, his day's coming. He's got no idea what I'm capable of," she said with an intriguing twitch of her brow. "Don't be surprised if I show up at your door one day with a bagful of money and say, 'Drive.'"

The look on Richard's face suggested he would be astonished.

"Whatsamatter?" she asked, patting his cheek. "Not ready to run away with me? You don't even say you love me." She pouted. Having failed to get the desired response, she said, "You're emotionally constipated, you know. But loveable."

As she dressed, she asked, "Wanna do it again tomorrow?"

"Unfortunately, I'm on deadline."

"I can help. More work, less screwing. Now *there's* a concept." She kissed him. "Making myself useful to you. Indispensability. My new job." She put a finger on his lips. "You'll be mine, all mine."

As Richard watched her drive away, he chuckled at her cockeyed plans. Running away from home? He was forty-one years old, for crying out loud! Even so, imagining his flight to freedom with an exotic dancer quickened his pulse and made him feel like he was capable of doing strange and dangerous things. And alive, for once.

He worked for an hour before school was dismissed. As he rose from his chair for the walk up to Malliford, he recalled it was Nick's day of independence. It had been decided between the two of them that Nick was old enough to walk to and from school himself, so Richard sat in the living room and waited. When Nick bounded triumphantly into the house, Richard congratulated him, then gave the boy graham crackers and milk.

"Dad, can I go over to Christopher's? His dad said I could."

"Christopher Desmond? He's not in your class any more." Surely Nick could see this created an impenetrable barrier.

"He's in my PE class. Everybody in third grade is. And now he's my only friend. Him and Antonio. Antonio rides a bus so he can't do anything after school."

"Maybe we can invite Antonio over." Antonio had visited twice but not recently. Richard liked Antonio, and missed tutoring the kid.

"Christopher has the best stuff," Nick whined. "Devonious said so."

"Devonious goes to Christopher's house?"

"Yeah, all the time. Oh, he doesn't smell so bad any more."

Maybe Richard had Desmond pegged wrong. Maybe this Mentoring Initiative was all right, after all. Nah. Desmond was evil. He could smell it, even if the boy couldn't.

"Do your homework. Then it will be time for soccer."

"Then can I go to Christopher's? 'Cause his dad keeps asking."

"We'll see," Richard said, meaning: *We'll see if you bring it up again and I'll keep saying "We'll see" until you quit asking.*

Richard worked until nearly five, dropped off Nick at soccer practice, shopped for groceries, and returned to pick up his son at six, impressing himself with his hyperparenting skills.

"I don't like my team," Nick said as he climbed in the back seat. "They're buttheads."

"That's no way to talk."

"I don't care. That's what they are. Oh, Coach might call you. I got in a fight with his kid. Beat his butt. All that practice with D is paying off. No white kid my size can beat me now."

The lecture that followed—mixing weight classifications with brotherhood and sportsmanship—lasted all the way the Applegate.

At dinner that night, Anna Lee was shocked to hear Nick brag about walking home alone. She'd never agreed to the deal Richard and Nick had worked out. Why wasn't she consulted? Didn't Richard understand? Didn't he watch the news? That child, abducted in California. No one was safe.

"Mrs. Perkins can see him from school until he turns onto Applegate," Richard said. "And I coached him on what to do if a stranger approaches."

"Tell them 'Your pet's on fire,'" Nick said, nodding.

"By then it will be too late," Anna Lee said.

The argument degenerated into a shouting match. Nick was sent to his room—for protection rather than punishment. Later, his parents sent themselves to their rooms, too.

Friday, Anna Lee walked Nick to school. When she returned to the house, she complained about her child's hatefulness: "He called me a 'stupidhead.'"

"You got off easy," Richard said. "Relax. He just wants to be independent. Let him grow up. Nothing bad is going to happen. It's only a quarter-mile. He knows to cross at the crosswalk, and Mrs. Perkins is always there."

"The warning light doesn't work. It's not safe." There was danger everywhere, and she would remain on high alert until they found that girl in California alive and well, not chopped into pieces with a pervert's DNA sprayed all over her. She gave Richard an angry glare and left for work.

An hour later, Teresa arrived. Richard was too far behind in his work to play, so they spent the morning on Brycedale Corporation's newsletter. First the laptop, *then* the lap.

Teresa had a knack for organizing information, and she could write passably well. Consequently, they finished before noon. She fixed Richard soup and a sandwich. He almost slipped up and told her he loved her while she was loading the dishwasher. But the dangerous truth was that he could now see her replacing Anna Lee, who, after all, didn't love him, at least not much, and made him do the dishes.

"You're not growing tired of having me around, are you?" she asked as she sat down with her own bowl of soup. She looked at him wide-eyed, puckered up and blew across a spoonful of minestrone.

"No. Among adults, you're unique in that respect."

"Sometimes I want to give myself to you in a dark and shameful way."

"I'm certainly open to suggestions," he said.

"Well, I have an idea."

She made the dark, shameful offering on the sofa fifteen minutes later. Who could turn down such a thing? Not him. She made so much noise he was afraid the neighbors would call the cops. He was gratified and disturbed (as well as impressed and appalled) that she would do this for him. That anyone would do this for anyone. That she would carry the tools, equipment, and other paraphernalia—call it tackle in this case—in her handbag to do it. Amazing.

He felt like a pervert afterward, yet strangely satisfied. He suspected she probably had Carl-produced Raspberry Beret videos of just such an act locked away. Yes, someday her love life would be for sale: *NAUGHTY HOUSEWIFE, JUST $1.95 FOR A THREE DAY TRIAL!* Was it possible to make a decent living off a porn website, or was that a contradiction in terms?

A few minutes after she slipped out, Nick came home with more problems. He had *not* finished his homework the night before, and there was yet another note about misbehavior buried in his backpack. This time his crime was "disrespect to a classmate," according to Mrs. Little. Obviously, Devonious was rubbing off on him.

"What am I going to do?" Richard asked.

"Nothing," Nick suggested. "That's what you do best."

"Watch your mouth."

"You watch yours."

"Go to your room."

"That's where I was going, anyway."

Richard shook his head in disbelief at his son's insolence. He also did that thing with his teeth, to check his anger, though he thought it might be a good idea next time to let it out and embrace his inner rage.

*   *   *

Tuesday afternoon, right when he expected Nick to walk in the door, Richard got a phone call: "Mr. Gray? This is Bill Scroggins. Your boy's here at my house. Some punks beat him up. I chased 'em off. You know where I live?"

"Yeah." Richard hung up and rushed out into the chilly, grey afternoon.

Scroggins, an older man, stood on his front stoop towering over Nick as Richard jogged up the sidewalk. The boy sat on a step, a sandwich bag filled with ice cubes pressed to his left cheek, tissue stuffed in both nostrils, bloodstains on his ripped shirt. Richard touched his shoulder; the boy flinched in pain.

"Looks bad, but I think it's all little stuff," Scroggins said. "I heard him yelling and came outside. Two nig—blacks were walin' away on him. Never seen 'em before. A lot bigger than he was. Too old for elementary school. I showed 'em my Glock and they ran off, that way." He pointed to a side street that cut through to Eastwood Avenue. "They come around again, I'll—"

Richard put his finger to his lips, but Scroggins wasn't through. "Gotta stand up for our rights, too. It's time he understood."

Richard turned his attention to his son. "You OK, bud?" Nick nodded. "Who was it?"

"Devonious said he'd pay someone to beat me up. That way it couldn't be traced to him."

"Sounds like his plan backfired," Scroggins noted grimly. "A fight's a fight, but if they jump out of the bushes and attack you, that's something else. Especially if it's two of 'em. They looked like they were thirteen, fourteen years old. Too big to go to school here unless they flunked a couple of years, but I guess that's possible. You ought to call the police."

"You're right," Richard said. He pulled out his cell phone and dialed 911. To Nick he said, "You're sure it wasn't someone you know? A dispute from school?"

"It *was* a dispute from school. D hired 'em. Cause I messed up his grades."

Scroggins shook his head. "This neighborhood used to be safe. I'll tell you ... that school, it's going to hell in a handbasket ever since ... you know. You see it up close every day."

A 911 operator answered Richard's call. He spoke briefly and hung up. As his son continued his account, Richard glanced over his shoulder toward Malliford.

"I fought back and yelled for Ms. Perkins, but they knocked me down and dragged me behind those bushes." Nick pointed to the scene of the crime and pulled off the ice bag, revealing bloody abrasions on his cheek. "I think they were going to kill me. Then Mr. Scroggins came out, and they ran off. I fought bravely, I tell you."

"Good for you, son."

Scroggins went inside and returned with a Coke. He raised an eyebrow to Richard, who nodded. Nick took it and smiled. "Thanks."

A police cruiser pulled into the driveway five minutes later. A stocky cop with a butch haircut hitched up his pants as he got out. "What do we have here, gentlemen?"

"An assault." Richard glanced at the officer's nametag: Llewellyn. "My son was attacked by two older boys. Black kids."

The cop glanced over at the school, calculating distances, angles, ramifications. "You sure this didn't happen on school property?"

"They were on the sidewalk, then my front yard," Scroggins said. "Two big black kids—"

"Not Malliford students," Richard added.

"School system's funny about crimes on school property," the cop interjected. "Don't want us involved. Messes up their statistics and inflates the crime rate. Son, what's your name?"

"Nick Gray."

"Nicholas," Richard corrected.

"Where did the attack occur?"

Nick pointed to the sidewalk just outside the school zone sign. The cop flipped open his clipboard and started taking notes. "You know anyone who would want to hurt you?"

"Yes. But if I tell, it will happen again."

"It won't," Richard said. "I'll be walking you from now on."

"Devonious."

"Saunderson," Richard said. "He's in Nick's class. Tell the officer about the threats."

Nick said he'd refused to let Devonious copy from his homework. Devonious said he needed it and that he'd make sure Nick got hurt real bad if he didn't let him. The scholarship angle was a new one to the cop. He asked questions, took notes, and suggested that it could be gang-related, since it was Chantilly Arms apartments. He would look for two black males, thirteen to sixteen years old, approximately five-six, wearing baggy pants and football jerseys, one red, one green.

"By the way," Richard told him, "The school zone lights don't work. Not that it would have helped my son."

"You should report that to the school."

"Yeah, right," Richard deadpanned. "I'll try that."

After the officer left, Richard took Nick to the pediatrician's office. Physically, there was nothing more serious than bruises and scrapes. This left Richard free to worry about future attacks.

On the way home, Nick complained of hunger, so Richard got him fries at McDonald's. They returned to Windamere Heights shortly after 5:00 p.m. Richard drove through the school's loop, but Miz Rutherford's car wasn't there. He'd write a letter, including the police report number, and give it to Polly in the morning. "Don't talk at school about the attack," Richard told his son.

When they got home he hugged Nick, who said, "Dad, you're squeezing too hard.".

Nick went to his room and Richard tried to work, but before he could get started, Anna Lee came home. He knew what she would think about his failure to protect their son. He realized how much he feared her judgment. That's why he hated her. Did he really hate her? He checked: Why, yes he did—but only in self-defense. She hated him first. He wandered out into the hall with an I'll-Be-Damned look on his face and told her what happened.

"What?" She contorted her face in disbelief.

He told her again.

"Goddamnit," she said. "Didn't I tell you it was a bad idea to let Nick walk alone? Why couldn't you see that? Don't you understand there are bad people out there? What part about evil do you—of all people—not get? Oh, they found the California girl this morning. Dead."

It would have been a fight if Richard had bothered to defend himself. But he didn't. He was whipped, having failed in the one thing he was supposed to do—his prime directive, taking care of Nick. Yes, he'd deal with it correctly this time, not like he'd done everything else, and he'd walk Nick to school, follow up with police, hire an attorney, call the FBI, alert the media, declare holy war on the sinister forces attacking their son, and not rest until the evildoers were safely locked behind bars, tortured, and executed.

"If those apartments weren't in the district, this wouldn't have happened," she declared. "This is your wake-up call. You know what they say: A conservative is a liberal who got mugged."

She turned from him and went to check on Nick. Meanwhile, Richard's resentment toward her festered. After an uninspired supper of pork chops and mashed potatoes, Richard helped Nick with his word problems in math. He couldn't help working up one of his own: *If I add five clients and sandbag half the money, when will I be free?*

*   *   *

The next morning, Richard resumed bodyguard duties. He dropped off his letter in the school office, unable to stomach the prospect of talking to the principal. The counselor and psychologist watched father and son walk by on their way to Mrs. Little's room. They both called out greetings to Nick, who did not respond—failing the attitude test, just like dear old Dad.

Richard told Mrs. Little about the attack before the morning bell. She promised to kept Devonious and Nick separated. "I think we're losing that boy," she said, speaking of D. "I'm not sure what I can do." She shut her eyes.

Pray, that's what. *Great. Just great.*

Devonious entered and sat down, avoiding Richard's glare, thereby convicting himself. On his way out, Richard whispered in D's ear, "The police are on to you. Leave Nick alone, you hear?"

"Mr. Gray, that's enough," the teacher warned. "He's got counseling to-day." That reminder ignited a smoldering fire in D's eyes as he glared at Richard, who realized it was only a matter of time before the kid killed someone or died trying, the little motherfucker.

* * *

The next day, Richard answered a knock on the door and found a FedEx deliveryman standing on the stoop with a letter for him from Donzella James. *FedEx? Where'd they get the money to do that?* She could have saved the expense by handing it to him. The letter warned him to stay away from Devonious "due to perceived threats you've made. ... Failure to adhere ... will result in referral to proper authorities and possible prosecution."

He paced the hall, cursing loudly, fuming about "mental health professionals" and how they blocked him from helping Devonious, and then blocked him from protecting his son *from* Devonious. Their solution: get a restraining order *against the PTO president!* Unbelievable. He could smell their stinking trap. *Why didn't they just call 911 and get it over with?* Or were they waiting for him to crack? He looked in the hall mirror: Hair disheveled, eyes wild. It wouldn't take long.

The phone rang. Out of morbid curiosity, he took the call.

"I'm so sorry to hear about Nick," Barbara said. "I hate to say I told you so, but now you know why I fought against them."

He slammed down the phone on the desktop so hard that he cracked the receiver.

* * *

Although police never found the boys who beat up Nick, Officer Llewellyn's visit to Chantilly Arms apparently helped persuade D to leave Nick alone. Meanwhile, Donzella James's letter to Richard convinced him to pretend Devonious didn't exist.

Nick's problems were not over, however. Polly called Richard at noon on Tuesday, March 13, and asked him to attend a 1:00 p.m. conference at school.

"And on what day would that be?" Richard asked.

"Today."

"You all love jerking me around, don't you?"

"It's extremely important."

"That you jerk me around? Of course. Are they going to address the attack on Nick?"

"I'm not allowed to say."

"Ah, but you're not saying it's not about that."

"That's one of the many things I'm not saying."

"Then maybe I'll come."

Despite misgivings, Richard showed up in the school office an hour later, hoping justice would be served. It was odd that no one other than Barbara had mentioned the beating, but then again, Richard hadn't gone around talking about it, either. No point advertising the fact your kid gets beat up—too much like wishing for bad luck.

"They're in the conference room," Polly said.

They? Richard got an uneasy feeling in the pit of his stomach as he walked down the hall to a room the size of a walk-in closet. He knew it was used mainly for disciplinary meetings involving students who didn't behave or wouldn't learn. A Mexican kid with ADD and gang affiliations would draw a standing-room only crowd.

So would a banner-yanking WASP PTO president with a bad attitude. Several people sat around the dark wood-grained table that dominated the room, barely leaving space for chairs. The same obese guard Richard saw during the Art War was there, slumped against the wall near the door. The principal sat at the table's far end, flanked by Ms. Hardwick and Ms. James. Two blondes—one large, lumpish and black, the other rail-thin and white—faced each other. The black woman wore a county ID tag. The white woman's tag lay on the table.

Richard took a seat opposite the principal, who caught his gaze before looking down at some papers. Mrs. Baines entered, squeezing past the guard to take the last chair. Miz Rutherford cleared her throat and motioned to the guard. "Close the door, please." She glanced again at her papers, then at Richard. "Good afternoon, Mr. Gray." The door closed with a sharp *click*.

"Is it?" He looked around. Strangers smiled uncertainly; the people he knew sat stone-faced. The guard picked at a thumbnail. The black blonde introduced herself as Sarah Royston and said she'd replaced Curtis Blodgett as area supervisor.

"I miss him," Richard said. "He fixed problems."

"Well, I certainly hope I fix problems," said Mrs. Royston.

"So what's the problem?" Richard asked. "Why are we here?"

"Ms. Ramsey, could you explain policy to Mr. Gray? Jennifer Ramsey is the county's vice coordinator for student conduct."

"You're *vice* coordinator for student conduct?" Richard asked. "I like the irony."

The thin white woman coughed and shifted uncomfortably. "Mr. Gray, last year the Board of Education unanimously adopted a Zero Tolerance discipline policy."

"I know." He'd thought Zero Tolerance was a joke, but he was glad to see they were finally taking it seriously. Now maybe D would be expelled and shipped off to Alternative School or wherever they sent social deviants. He'd be happy to testify. Those punks could have killed Nick. At least the Grays wouldn't be completely—

"Then you'll understand we have no choice but to suspend your son for violating the system's drug and alcohol policies," said Mrs. Royston.

Richard was incredulous. He wore a pained expression and his voice came out as a near-screech: "*Say what?* Are you claiming my son uses drugs? That's ridiculous."

"Actually, it's the alcohol policy."

"He was drinking at school? Whose fault is *that?*"

"Yesterday at lunch, he told children at his table he was drinking wine."

It seemed like a joke, except for the twisted feeling in his gut. "Was he? I demand to know." Richard pounded the table in a fit of mock histrionics.

"Of course not. We don't allow alcohol on the premises."

"It was fruit punch," Donzella James offered.

"So what the hell is the problem?"

"Please don't swear, Mr. Gray. This is hard for all of us as it is."

"We had concerns that you'd be difficult," the counselor explained.

"Concerns about your reaction," said the psychologist.

"That it may be inappropriate," the counselor agreed.

"He has anger issues," said the psychologist.

"Anger is a disease," said Ms. James.

"Anger is a logical response to the intolerable," Richard said. "Hence my anger."

"Nick's behavior has been deteriorating all year," said Mrs. Hardwick.

"As has yours," added Mrs. James.

"Unbelievable," said Richard, shaking his head.

"Let's get back on track," said Mrs. Ramsey. "In the county's *Student Code of Conduct*, page twenty-nine, section seven, Drugs and Alcohol, paragraph three-c, it says, 'No student shall possess drugs or alcohol on school property *or act in a manner as to lead others to believe he or she possesses drugs or alcohol.*'" She raised her voice to emphasize the last part and pushed the pamphlet toward Richard, but he felt no need to edify himself.

"By pretending to drink wine, your son acted in such a manner," Ms. James noted.

"That can be very misleading to the other children," Ms. Hardwick added helpfully.

"I doubt it," Richard responded.

"We don't want to argue the point."

"I'll bet you don't, since you're using my boy to get at me."

"We have a confession," the psychologist said.

"Good," he barked. "It's about time you came clean."

"From Nicholas," she said, producing several copies. Richard picked up one. There it was, in Nick's scrawl, on Malliford letterhead: "On Monday March 12 I pretended I drank wine in the cafeteria. (signed) Nicholas Gray."

This was an outrage, of course. Obviously, they'd been looking for an excuse to come down on his family, and once they heard about Nick's joke, they pulled him into their little hellhole to sign the confession. "I see these forced confessions all the time," he said. "They're invalid and un-American. Unconstitutional. Totalitarian."

"Nick has many problems," said the psychologist. "We've been concerned about a detrimental situation at home. That he may have inappropriate role modeling and physical contact."

"My God, you're parroting Jack Desmond!"

"No, we're not," said the psychologist.

"No, we're not," echoed the counselor.

Miz Rutherford curled her lip into a sneer. "Mr. Gray, don't be ridiculous."

"And *this* is how you improve his self-esteem? You're the ones who are sick! You're suspending my boy for drinking fruit punch—that you *SOLD* to him—and you're telling *ME* not to be ridiculous? If he's going to get suspended for drinking it, you ought to go to prison for selling it to him. This is pathetic. Pure, unadulterated chain gang."

"There's no cause for name calling," the psychologist said.

"Anyone who would kick a kid out of school for this is worse than a bully. Punks with badges, that's what you are. Punks!"

"You can appeal this suspension," said Mrs. Ramsey.

"It may not be such a good idea, however," said the principal. "Considering."

Richard slowly pivoted his head toward her and saw something dangerous and evil in her eyes. He just wished he could match her, evil for evil, but he suspected she had something on him: Teresa. He was a weak man, and Nick was paying for it. But they couldn't get away with this. He had to say something. "The administration at this school is out of control. I saw what you did to Stan. I should have spoken up more loudly then."

"We're not going to talk about that," Ms. Hardwick said.

"Now you've come for me. There are real abuse cases out there you're ig-noring, and instead you're making another mountain out of a molehill. Nick is a good kid, a *great* kid, a straight-A student. We know what the problem is. Go on, ask me what the problem is. Show me you really want to know what's going on."

"Mr. Gray—"

"See? You don't want to know. Since you've declared war on my family, I can no longer support this school or this system. But I will say this: You'll be sorry."

"Is that a threat, Mr. Gray?" the principal asked. "Do we need to notify the authorities?"

The amount of scribbling on notepads would have been alarming even if all the women in the room hadn't simultaneously looked up at the wall clock and made note of the time.

"Don't be stupid. Oh, I'm sorry. It's a bit late for that, isn't it?"

"Believe us," said Ms. Royston. "We don't want to do this."

"I *don't* believe you. My son was beaten up last week, and now you're throwing him out of school on a spurious charge. On a first offense, no less. You're doing this because I'm a dissident PTO president who embarrasses you, and you've got a lot to be embarrassed about."

"We understand you're angry," said Mrs. Ramsey. "However, Zero Toler-ance leaves us no choice. If you feel this is in any way unfair—"

"In any way unfair? Have you not heard anything I've said?" He fought to control his temper. "What part about this being a bunch of unmitigated ... *crap* do you not understand?"

"Please don't raise your voice," the counselor said.

Anger issues, the psychologist mouthed.

Anger issues? He wanted to kill them! A special place in Hell awaited them all—the sooner, the better!

"If you feel that this decision to suspend is in error," the bureaucrat contin-ued, "then you may appeal the decision to the Student Conduct Appeal Board."

Richard knew he'd need a lawyer for that, which would cost at least a couple grand. And Nick wasn't the perfect defendant—there was com-promising information he'd given the two mental health professionals, notes home, and bad conduct marks on his six-week progress report. The boy had turned into an informant, squealing about anal insertions, calling himself Hitler.

Richard could see clearly enough to realize there was a chance that this battle could push him off the cliff he was standing on, especially if word leaked out about his relationship with Teresa. Besides, he was behind on his work; he couldn't juggle a protracted conflict and his increased business workload, too. Even if he fought and won, what was the prize, three more days at Chain Gang Elementary for Nick? *Whoop-de-do.* Better to walk away from the edge and patch the nail holes in his wrists.

"If you appeal, the suspension will not begin until after the appeal is concluded," Mrs. Royston said. "Otherwise, it starts tomorrow."

Richard took a deep breath and exhaled. "This is too stupid to appeal. Too stupid to be a part of."

"What do you plan to do?"

"None of your business. I'll fight this on my terms, not yours."

"Don't do anything rash, Mr. Gray."

"I suggest *you* don't. You're making a huge mistake. Just stop this idiocy."

"I'm sorry," said Mrs. Ramsey, shaking her head. "We can't."

Richard broke out in raucous laughter. As others in the room tried to explain that she meant they were only following orders, he stood up and lurched out, pausing in the door. "And get the damned traffic light fixed."

When he was in the hall, Richard realized he was trembling with rage. He started to go to Nick's classroom, then spun around. The guard followed him and took a position just inside the front door as Richard went into the office. Its tomblike silence was broken by the big wall clock's humming. Polly, who knew nothing and everything, gazed at him expectantly.

He pulled out his pen. "I'll take my son home now," he said softly, signing the log book.

She went to the antiquated intercom console and hit the button for Mrs. Little's room. He stared at the wall and considered the missing stars. He wished he had a can of spray paint to give the school the rating it deserved.

A few minutes later, Nick appeared, dragging his backpack and singing, like he didn't have a worry in the world. Hadn't they told him he was in trouble? How could they hope to break a child's spirit if they didn't make him afraid?

How can you have any pudding if you don't eat your meat?

Wordlessly, Richard took Nick's hand and they walked into the dark corridor, past the dim guard, and into the brilliant afternoon. A small plane droned overhead.

Nick looked up at him and squinted. "It's about the wine, isn't it?"

"That's what they say, but it's really about me."

"Am I kicked out of school?"

"Yes. For three days."

"I didn't do anything wrong!" His frown of worried innocence was a work of art. "I was just pretending."

"Turns out they have rules against pretending. Except about how good the school is."

"Devonious told on me. Then they gave me a paper and told me to write down the words and I'd get in trouble if I didn't sign it. I thought it was like, *whatever*. It isn't fair." Tears welled in his eyes. "I figured they'd just send the note home to you, like Mrs. Little does."

"It's all right, Nick. I don't blame you," Richard said, although he wasn't really sure that this was true.

"Good," Nick said. "I'm tired of school. D can pick on Antonio for a change."

"He hasn't been bothering you this week, has he?"

"No. He said someone told him to lay off me. Antonio says he's Mr. Desmond's little bitch. That's why he gets away with everything."

"Nicholas!"

*   *   *

After ordering Nick to do his schoolwork, even though it wouldn't be due for several days, Richard went to his office and plotted revenge. A bright, shining light cut through the fog just as Nick came in to complain about the extra assignments he'd received because he was both Gifted and High Achiever. "I'm telling your story to the *Sentinel*," Richard said.

Nick's face lit up. "Cool. I'll be famous. Make sure to tell everybody I get extra homework."

Richard sent the boy away and called Henry Dobbs, a *Sentinel* editor he'd worked with years ago, figuring the gruff, anti-authoritarian journalist might want to cause trouble for principals as karmic payback. When he told Dobbs he was writing a piece on Zero Tolerance policies, the newsman said he'd look at it. "Localize it. If it's good, we'll use it."

"Oh, it'll be local. You can count on that. And it will be good, I assure you."

"We pay two hundred. Don't go over seven fifty words." *Click.*

An hour later, Richard heard rustling outside. Fearing the punks had returned to finish the job on Nick, he grabbed an aluminum baseball bat from the front closet and charged outside. There was something in the azaleas. He used the bat to poke the thick bushes.

"Hey, ouch!" a voice cried out in protest.

When he looked closely, he saw a familiar face. "Antonio! What are you doing?"

"Hiding." The boy looked up wide-eyed at Richard, who gestured for him to come out. "Devonious gonna beat me up if I don't let him copy my homework. And I want him to stay in third grade next year. So I ain't ridin' the bus no more." He rubbed his arms where branches had scratched him.

This was crazy, of course. Chantilly Arms Apartments was four miles away. But Richard couldn't deny the boy's logic. He picked up Antonio's frayed red backpack, patched with duct tape and held together by safety pins, and escorted the boy inside. He ordered Antonio to call his mother, who said she'd come pick him up after she got off work.

Nick was delighted to have company and bragged about being suspended. He was disappointed to see that Antonio wasn't impressed.

"Everybody at Chantilly gets suspended, at least the older kids."

"Devonious should be suspended," Nick said.

"He would be every week, 'cept for Christopher's dad takin' his side all the time. D gonna end up worse than suspended. His mama's a crackhead and she ain't never 'round. He gonna end up *dead*. And I'd be better off if he was."

"That's a terrible thing to wish," Richard said.

"I didn't wish it," Antonio said. "Just sayin'. It's a matter of fact."

*   *   *

Antonio was gone when Anna Lee came home. Richard, working on his article, slowly rose from his chair and trudged out into the hall to give her the bad news. "Nick got suspended from school for three days."

"What?" Her face froze in disbelief. "What happened?"

"They caught him drinking fruit punch in the cafeteria." He paused to let this sink in. "He said, 'Let's pretend it's wine.' Devonious diligently alerted the authorities. And because some people are who they are and I am who I am, Nick will spend some quality time at home."

"That's ridiculous!" Fire filled her eyes. She looked like she could kill somebody. "We've got to fight this!"

"I am, in my own way."

"*In your own way?* This is happening because of you! Our child has been kicked out of school because you declared war on the principal." She shook her head vigorously, as if to rid herself of an ugly thought. "This ... is where your rage gets you. You think you're so diplomatic, so political. But you're angry a lot of the time. Most of the time. I see you work the inside of your mouth the way you do. You've got problems from way back. Your dad, that pervert principal, your brother trying to run your life, our marriage—"

"*What marriage?*" he wanted to say. Instead, he worked the inside of his mouth.

Nick stepped into the hall. "I didn't do anything wrong. Dad said so. Not my fault."

When he stepped back into his room, Anna Lee followed and Richard trailed behind.

"And you're not going to fight this?" she asked Richard over her shoulder.

"I'd rather be suspended," Nick said, fluffing a pillow for his head. "I can use the time off."

"I can't believe this," Anna Lee pulled Nick close and stroked his hair. She kissed his forehead, then told him, "Finish your work."

When Nick turned away, she brusquely gestured at Richard's office. *You. In there.*

As soon as the door shut, she said, "Richard, I can't figure you out."

"Here's what I figured out," he said. "I don't want another child."

The conversation went downhill from there.

* * *

Untroubled by his outlaw status, Nick sang in the shower and fell asleep soon after he went to bed that night. Afterward, Richard brewed a pot of coffee to start his day's third shift while Anna Lee sat on the same sofa Teresa and he had despoiled just a few days earlier.

"I don't care what you did," she said. "They can't take it out on him—"

"What do you think I did, exactly?"

"You know what I mean. I'm more pissed off at them right now. It's some kind of criminal conspiracy. That bitch is pure evil."

"Log on at bitchispureevil.com and you'll see her picture there, along with Attila the Hun's second wife, Leona Helmsley, and Nurse Ratched. Not necessarily in that order."

"We ought to pull him out and put him in private school."

Richard didn't want to go through this again. There was the principle of ... well, not giving in to the principal. Also, they were broke. Anyway, it was too late in the year for a fresh start, especially with a war on. Retreating now, beaten and bloody, would be a craven act. Exactly what bitchispureevil.com wanted. "No."

"*Come on*. Getting expelled over fruit punch, being beaten up by thugs who face absolutely no consequences. It's like that Kafka fellow you like so much."

"Yeah. What a guy. Oh, by the way. You know how you say a conservative is a liberal who got mugged? Well, a liberal is a conservative who got arrested."

Richard went back to work on his opinion piece, pounding the keys furiously. At the rate he was going, he'd have a book by the end of the week.

Anna Lee defied his churlish refusal to procreate and made a pass at him that night, rolling over and snuggling him in bed. "Make-up sex," she said, though she couldn't fool him, since her tone wasn't the least bit friendly. This was procreative sex—fundamentalist Bible sex, the very worst kind. He turned away, but she rejected his refusal. "If we can't make love, we shouldn't be married."

No fair. That was supposed to be *his* argument; now it came to him as an ultimatum. However, having Nick at home meant he wouldn't see Teresa for the rest of the week, so he succumbed to the unfriendliest make-up sex he'd ever had. Any baby born of such a union would surely turn out ugly and ill-humored. *A chain-gang child.*

Afterward, lying in bed and listening to Anna Lee snore, Richard thought about Nick. *If he's been mugged and arrested, does that make him an anarchist?*

The next morning, Richard was determined to make Nick remember his suspension: no computer games or TV. He tossed a copy of the school system's rule book in front of Nick while he ate Cap'n Crunch. "Read it," he said.

"I know the rules," Nick protested.

"There's also a fifth-grade math worksheet for you to do."

Nick reached over and opened up his backpack, which lay on the floor. "I still have homework."

"I thought you did it yesterday. What happened?"

"Antonio and me got trainsided."

"Sidetracked." *In addition to being railroaded at school.* "What did you do?"

"We traded Pokémon cards when you weren't looking." With an incredibly poor sense of timing, he chose that moment to pull out yet another note from Mrs. Little. This one, a follow-up, stated that he'd been talking in class Friday and had apparently lost the previous note he was supposed to have signed by a parent. A minor matter, except there had been so many notes—and a steadfast refusal by the boy to get his act together.

After receiving a severe scolding, Nick bolted to his room and gave his father wide berth for the rest of the day. This was fine with Richard, who was busily honing his editorial knife, aware but untroubled by the developing irony. Publicly, Nick would be *Martyr Boy Sacrificed on the Altar of Stupidity Embodied in Zero Tolerance*. Privately, he was turning into something much less heroic.

That afternoon, the school's automated notification system left a message to say that Nick had been absent from school that day. *How nice of them to notice.*

Healthnet's director of communications called and left a message demanding the newsletter, which was already a week overdue. "I'll get it done when I get it done!" Richard yelled at the machine. "I've got more important things to do!" When were they going to go paperless, anyway?

* * *

Thursday, Richard worked several hours to finish his smackdown of the bureaucratic smackdowners. He did not mention vendettas and constant conflict, or a demented old crone who believed a reformer should be punished— which was, in his mind, the hard and bitter truth. No. According to his piece, Nick Gray was suspended *even though* he was the PTO president's son, not *because* he was. Instead of a blood feud, he wrote about ineptitude, misplaced priorities, hypocrisy, pushing Ritalin on kids, ghettoization.

In a way it was the truth, but the motive, the intent, was that of a liar, to mislead readers into seeing a big picture when the all-important fact to him was that it *was* all about Richard Gray. And he was pretty sure he'd get away with it, since it sounded like the truth and he had credibility. Miz Rutherford's bosses would wake up Sunday and read: "This just in, the latest dispatch from Chain Gang Elementary, where basic civil rights are not allowed to interfere with 'the Malliford experience,' or to put it more bluntly, not allowed."

Richard finished the piece that afternoon despite interference from Nick, lonely and bored on his second full day of house arrest. When Richard hit the final keystroke, ending his crescendo of calculated rage, the world was deathly quiet. He rubbed his face in his hands, took a deep breath, and e-mailed his article just as Malliford's dismissal bell rang in the distance. He heard it from his office for the first time ever. Fascinating. What fluke of barometric pressure caused the sound to carry that far? Or had it tolled for him?

Nick found him there, worn and weary, and tried to cheer him up, hugging his neck and kissing him on the cheek, but Richard's emotions were crashing down—anger at Nick, resentment toward Anna Lee, and despair over his life—making him inconsolable. He felt an overwhelming need to tell someone how badly he felt. He pushed Nick away—whether gently or brusquely, he wasn't sure—and closed the office door. He tried Teresa's home number, cooling it on the cell phone usage, since he didn't want to leave a trail (a thought that might have occurred to him earlier, if he'd been thinking). The line was busy. Carl must be home, working. Or—

No, he didn't want to think about that. He decided to call his brother in Ridalia. Not that Reggie would sympathize or empathize, but he might have a few new jokes.

"Bro," Reggie said when he answered the phone. "I'm glad you called. Have you thought about moving back to Ridalia?"

"No. Why?"

"I need you. Mom does, too. The town does."

"What am I supposed to do there?"

"Run my paper. I finally bought it."

"Your paper? Talk about funerals."

"Nah, it's profitable. It's the big papers that are folding. Anyway, I need an editor to move the *Independent* toward the center from the doofus right wing. Can you do moderate Republican?"

"There's no such thing any more."

"Well, think about it. Job's yours whenever you want it."

"Thanks."

After Richard hung up, he shook his head. Reggie never bothered to ask him why he called—as if everything existed to serve him. And how could Richard go along with such a plan? Still, his brother was offering him an alternative to his current situation, which seemed increasingly untenable. *Hmm.*

He rocked in his chair for a few minutes, then called Teresa's number again. This time she answered. "I feel bad," he said, sounding mournful.

"Oh, baby. What's wrong? Are you sick. Hurt?"

He told her what was going on—without mentioning Reggie's job offer—and concluding with a sigh, said, "I wish I could start over."

"There's a whole world out there. You can start over with me any time."

He could feel a blossom growing on the rocky mountainside of his volcano. "I love you," he said, feeling both startled and relieved at what seemed more like confession than profession.

"I love you, too. But you know that."

"I gotta go," Richard said.

"I long for the day when you don't. Goodbye, sweetie."

He hung up and stared at the wall, sniffed, and fought back tears.

There was a knock on his office door. "Yes, Nick."

"Can I tell you something?"

"Yeah, sure," Richard said, struggling to control himself.

"Ms. James kept asking me if you ever hurt me. Then she wanted to know if you were going to be PTO president again. Are you?"

"No way," Richard said, silently cursing the psychologist for trying to destroy his family.

"Good, 'cause I forbid it."

Richard laughed and reached out to hug him.

"I don't like Malliford. I want to go to another school," Nick said from inside the embrace.

"Yes," Richard agreed. "Getting away would be good."

NINETEEN

Nick's suspension ended in warmth and sunshine at 3:00 p.m. Friday. He and Richard had just returned home from Wyckfield Natural History Museum, and they were both in a good mood. Actually, Richard was exhilarated after Dobbs had called him on his cell and said, "Great piece! It's running Sunday."

Then, just a few minutes later, Richard got a call from *Sentinel* reporter Deanna Richardson.

"What did we do this time?" he asked.

"Do you know Antonio Jarvus?"

"Yes. Why? What happened?"

"He was hit by a car yesterday afternoon on Windamere."

"Oh my God. How is he?" Richard asked, immediately wondering why he hadn't heard. He glanced down and saw a blinking message light on his answering machine.

"He's going to make it, but he's in bad shape. He was in the crosswalk when his backpack broke. He stumbled and fell and the car came over the hill. He was scrambling out of the way when the driver ran over him and hit a utility pole. Amazing that she only got one of his legs, and it's a miracle he survived. This was about three-twenty. The driver was cited for going too fast in a school zone, but there was no crossing guard—"

Even as she spoke, Richard knew that, rightly or wrongly, Mrs. Perkins was doomed.

"—and no flashing lights."

"They haven't worked all year."

"Interesting. They should have been on until three-thirty. So the speed limit should have been twenty-five, not thirty-five. Police estimate the driver was going forty. Since this is Malliford, I got it. It's a chain gang thing. I figured I'd call you."

"What's the driver's name?

"Mildred Givens."

"Don't know her."

"Back to the lights. What can you tell me about those?"

"I've tried all year to get them fixed. Hang on a minute." He looked through his calendar book and gave her several times and dates when he'd called or written the school or county about the light. She asked him to fax her copies of his letters. "No problem," he said.

"So you know Antonio? Tell me about him."

"He works hard and made honor roll first semester. He writes poetry and plays baseball. I tutored him until the school shut down the program."

"They did *what*?"

"The principal shut down the PTO's tutoring program in February. She claimed it interfered with the Intellachievement tests."

"The SHIT."

"Yeah."

"No shit. We're covering Antonio from the too-much-homework angle. Neglect, too, since no one bothered to make sure he was on the bus. Police say the backpack weighed twenty-five pounds. And he was trying to walk home. How is a third-grader supposed to carry twenty-five pounds four miles?"

"There are some bullying issues, too. I found him hiding in the bushes by my house after school a few days ago. He refused to ride the bus after another child threatened him."

"His mother says kids call him Erkl."

"There's that, too. What hospital is he in?"

"Eastside Children's. So, other than that, how are things at Chain Gang Elementary?"

"I wrote a column for Sunday's paper."

"Chain gang stuff?"

"Pretty much."

"It doesn't quit, does it?"

"Not yet," he said.

After he hung up, he faxed the reporter copies of five of his complaint letters. Then he went to Nick's room and told his son about Antonio.

"I want to see him," Nick said eagerly.

"We'll go this afternoon. You can make him a get-well card."

A half-hour later, they left for the hospital. On Windamere, a county crew with a cherry picker worked on the school zone lights.

Nick paid close attention to the route they took. "I need to remember in case I get shot and have to get myself to the hospital when the ambulances break down or get attacked, like in a zombie takeover," he explained. "The first thing they go for is ambulances. They smell the brains of the injured people."

After learning Antonio's room number at the information desk, they went to a bank of elevators.

"Is that kid dead?" Nick asked his father as an orderly wheeled a gurney by them.

"*Shhh!* I don't think so. Head's not covered."

Nick strained to see how alive the child was. Richard pulled his son into an open elevator car. They got off on the third floor and passed the nurse's station on their way to Room 312. Richard poked his head in the open door. Antonio was asleep, suffused in sunlight, small and broken. A large gauze patch covered the side of his swollen face; two fingers on his left hand were splinted together. One leg was in a long cast. His glasses were gone. Beside him sat his aunt, a dusky woman of indeterminate age, holding a copy of *Guideposts*. She regarded Richard warily.

Richard introduced himself and Nick. Antonio's aunt warmed a little then, saying that Mrs. Little had visited the day before. She pointed to a red-and-silver balloon on the bedside stand, alongside daisies from the PTO, the work of Corresponding Secretary Cindi Lou (who had left a message with Richard about Antonio). Nick handed her his get-well-soon card, which was illustrated with a traced picture of Pokémon Pikachu. Richard told her to let him know if there was anything he could do to help and gave her his business card. During the visit, Antonio never stirred. The aunt returned to *Guideposts* as Richard and Nick left the room.

"He was pretty messed up," Nick whispered on the way to the elevators. "Remind me not to get hit by a car."

When they returned to Applegate, the work crew on Windamere was gone. There was a phone message from Deanna Richardson. "I read your column," she said when he returned her call. "My editors decided the car wreck and suspension together deserve front-page treatment. You should have told me about your son. It's wire-service worthy, as you—a former *Sentinel* staffer—would know."

"Emphasis on former. And for good reason."

"Point taken. So tell me about your son's drunken escapade at school. I'm all ears."

* * *

Richard awoke early Saturday, instantly alert. It was Butt-Kicking Day, and a new pair of boots awaited him outside. He slipped on clothes and retrieved the newspaper, a white bump in the driveway faintly irradiated by the streetlamp's effulgence. He thumped it on his thigh as he hurried back to the house. The world was quiet, but soon screams of outrage would rise throughout the land, punctuated by the shrill cries of the damned.

Inside, Richard pulled the *Sentinel* out of its plastic wrap like sword from scabbard. The blood of his enemies would foul the air like an orc's when its head was severed cleanly by a mighty stroke of his battle-ax. The gory image cheered him even though it made him a dwarf. He could see Rita dancing around the pike upon which the Evil Queen's head was impaled. He'd be dancing, too, of course.

Yes, Rutherford had gone way over the line when she tried to destroy the Gray family. She thought she'd whipped him, but he'd taken her best shot and survived. And then he'd roared back to deliver a blow that just might take down the old crone. Surely, the superintendent would now see that he must rid Malliford of its horrible bitch infestation.

He turned on the kitchen light, spread out the paper, and took a deep breath. There it was, along the bottom of the front page:

Does School Have Zero Tolerance for Safety?
News Analysis by Deanna Richardson
Sentinel Staff Writer

Two events this past week show how a suburban Gresham County school has earned and kept the nickname "Chain Gang Elementary." While the son of Malliford School's Parent-Teacher Organization president was serving a suspension for drinking fruit juice, a classmate was run over and nearly killed while walking in an unguarded crosswalk beneath a malfunctioning school-zone signal.

The light, out since August, was a hazard PTO President Richard Gray pointed out to school and county officials ten

times. Gray provided a reporter copies of several letters on the
issue. None of them received a response, he said.

As for his son's suspension, Gray called it "a case of a complete lack of discretion or common sense." According to his
supporters, Mr. Gray is too kind. Other parents call it "a vendetta by a vengeful woman" that started last summer, when the
new PTO president refused to spend $10,000 in PTO funds
to furnish Malliford Principal Estelle Rutherford's office with
a Persian rug and cherry furniture.

Ms. Rutherford refused to comment, referring questions to
Gresham Superintendent Harold Johnson, who did not return
phone calls.

And so on. The article jumped to page 6A and continued its savaging of
school and county. Ritalin, racist pep talks, star counts, and out-of-control
homework policies were covered, along with the criminal assault on Nick
and the messy story of Stan-I-Am, who surfaced to deliver some especially
heavy-handed comments that would have lacked credibility if printed on
their own. Deanna had learned about Alicia and the banner, so Richard felt
compelled to give an account of the Battle of Yo-Yo Me.

It was a brutal, first-class hatchet job. By the end of the article the average reader would think the people who ran Malliford and Gresham County
schools should be rounded up and thrown in jail. An editor's note told readers to look for Richard's "Different Viewpoint" column Sunday.

Anna Lee shuffled to the breakfast table, and her eyes bugged out when
she saw the article. News to her. Being out of his loop was the price she paid
for disloyalty to his cause. She glanced up from reading to say, "I'll never
understand why you didn't fight the suspension."

"We couldn't win. I didn't want to fight on their terms and justify the
process. Wait 'til you see the column."

"It just won't stop, will it?"

The phone's ringing cut off his response. Anna Lee answered. Stunned,
she turned to Richard and said, "It's *The New York Times*."

*   *   *

Richard stopped work on the overdue *Healing Time* newsletter to watch Nick
play soccer Saturday afternoon. Little Green Men lost their second game by

an even more lopsided score than the first. Parents grumbled afterward. They hadn't paid $200 in league and uniform fees to watch their kids lose 15 to 1. Nick complained that no one passed him the ball so he could score. Of course, he didn't pass the ball to anyone else, either.

Richard didn't like what he saw. The coach obviously didn't know his players, the game, or the difference between his butt and a cave. Richard was sure he could do a better job, if only because he wouldn't insult his players. Alas, Hyperdad could only do so much. Still, it helped to complain. "That team needs a new coach," he told Anna Lee on the way home. "Don't look at me that way. I'd hate to be in his shoes. Really."

"Nobody likes him," Nick said from the back seat. "Not even his own kid."

Richard stopped at a convenience store to buy an early edition of Sunday's paper. His op-ed piece ran across the top of the page, the headline borrowed from Dickens: "Gresham's Zero Tolerance Law is an Ass." The *Sentinel* also ran a short editorial, "Zero Tolerance, Zero Wisdom," which served as its monthly call for Harold Johnson's ouster. Miz Rutherford was "a sad example of an educator who put students last."

Ha! They'd been completely discredited. They couldn't come chasing after him now, not with freshly kicked asses of their own. He'd landed a mighty blow. Hell yeah. Surely they recognized the error of their ways and would fuck with him no more, amen.

*   *   *

Richard couldn't wait to take Nick to school Monday. Anna Lee gave them a brave smile and kissed both husband and son goodbye. There was a nip in the air as Richard stepped outside with Nick, who held a copy of Dad's article for the week's current event. *I am the news today, oh boy.*

Spring was in the air. They walked past blooming cherry, plum, and dogwood trees. Yellow dust was everywhere; pollen counts would be intolerable. People would be disabled by allergies. Still, it was good. Rebirth and all that. *Sure beats December, right?*

With grim satisfaction, Richard noted that the school zone warning lights on Windamere were working properly—for the first time in seven months.

Mrs. Perkins was gone, a casualty of war, replaced by a middle-aged woman with brown hair.

"You OK?" Richard asked Nick as they stepped on school property.

"Yeah. I'm not the one who did anything wrong."

"You got that right. You're a brave guy. Let's get 'em."

Mrs. Baines, working bus duty, wore a black paper armband. She looked apprehensively at Richard and gave Nick a creepy, pasted-on smile as they walked by. This was too much to ignore. Richard stopped. "Is that armband to show support for the principal?" he asked.

She nodded reluctantly, as if she knew that it would cause cancer.

"That insults Antonio and you know it," he said. "Have you visited him in the hospital?" She looked away. Poor, empty woman. He didn't want to taunt her, and yet—"Well, I did." *Nonny-nonny-boo-boo.*

Feeling manic, he entered the building and walked the halls with his son, searching for enemies. *Ye shall know them by their armbands.* The lovely Ms. Bailey wore a sleeveless red dress and a yellow ribbon, which could mean she supported the troops, but since yellow was the PTO's color, it could mean something else. Richard considered her move both brilliant and provocative. Was she gunning for Rutherford's job? Hell, he'd back her.

Miz Rutherford's least-favorite sixth-graders stopped Nick in the hall and gave him high-fives. "Way to go, dude! Don't let them get away with that crap!" said Spencer Hadley, the original Chain Gangsta.

"Fight the power!" yelled Bertie Malloy, Rita's son.

Richard watched with unalloyed amusement as Spencer handed Nick three joined paper clips and proclaimed him a lifetime member of the Chain Gang. Both older boys promised to toast Nick with fruit punch at lunch. As they took their leave, they cried out, "We're not worthy! We're not worthy!" and kowtowed in unison as they backed away. Nick beamed, while twenty feet away, Mrs. Vandenburg stood and glared at the dissidents, dull hatred in her eyes. She said nothing, however. This was not the time to mess with Nick Gray. Richard gave her black armband a contemptuous glance and gently prodded Nick to get him started down the hall.

When they reached Mrs. Little's room, Richard stood at the door and peered in. The teacher beckoned Nick to her desk. "You've got some catching up to do, Nicholas." She handed her top student some papers and said, "I heard you and your father saw Antonio in the hospital. That was nice." She looked up at Richard. "Mr. Gray, if I might have a word." She stood and stepped into the hall, closing the door behind her. "I wanted to call Nick last week, but I was forbidden."

"Forbidden?"

"That's all I should say." She turned and went back into her room.

"*Awk-ward,*" Richard said softly. Puzzled, yet satisfied that a semblance of normalcy had returned, he went to the office to check his mail and look for a fight. Polly held out an envelope. He tore it open and read a *mea non culpa* from the principal about the traffic light. Attached were letters—backdated, surely—to the county. (Where were the dated e-mails, eh? Those would at least be credible.) All lies, he'd be happy to swear under oath.

"I bet your fingers burned when you typed this," he told Polly.

"I turned in my two-week notice today. That's all I've got to say."

"Oh. Too bad on both counts," he said as he backed out the door.

He glanced back and wondered what was going on with the principal's secretary. After a moment's reflection, he decided that she was taking what was left of her humanity, dignity, and self-respect, and getting the hell out of Hell.

He wasn't ready to leave the building just yet. People *needed* to see him. Donzella James didn't want to, however. When she came out of her office, she saw him walking toward her. She turned and dove back into her room so quickly Richard didn't get a chance to see if she was wearing her armband.

His voice boomed after her: "Like I said, stay away from my kid!"

Someone cleared their throat behind him. He turned to see Teresa in the foyer with Jane Baumgartner. Teresa held a copy of Sunday's opinion section. "We need you to serve another term as president," Teresa declared in a straight-faced stage whisper.

She had to be kidding. Then he glanced toward the office door and saw Susan Gunther glowering at them. "Oh, yeah," he said, nodding. "Of course I will."

As Jane turned to tend the PTO's school supply cupboard, Teresa whispered in his ear, "We won't be here then, will we, sweetie?"

"Uh, where will we be?"

"I'm thinking New Mexico or Oregon. I wish we could hook up right now, but Carl's in town."

Too bad. Richard could have used a victory lap-dance.

Jane returned to the conversation, having sold a pencil to a third-grader for a hefty fifteen-cent profit. "The school's in an uproar, you know," she said. "There's talk of decertifying the PTO on one side and of starting a petition drive to fire the principal on the other."

"Yet another petition drive, you mean," Richard said.

"Something's got to give. The teachers are shell-shocked. It's like *High Noon* around here. They think you're a gunslinger, Richard."

"I thought I was the sheriff."

"Maybe there's too many sheriffs."

Ouch. He'd always considered Jane his friend, but he had to remember that her sister was a teacher, so there could be pressure on her to be a double agent. Maybe a hostage or a human shield. Sometimes it was difficult to properly assess allegiances and loyalties.

"Anything else I should know?" he asked.

"Avon Little is being suspended."

"Do what?" he blurted. "Why the ... heck for?"

"She pitched a fit over Nick's suspension, and Miz R told her to walk the plank."

"I didn't know. I've been out of the loop the past few days."

"More like you've been busy tying a noose," Teresa said.

"Everyone was surprised when you accepted your son's suspension," Jane said. "But they knew it wasn't the end of it. Now they're seeing the escalation and wonder what you'll do next."

Me, too. He thought for a moment. That was terrible, trying to destroy Mrs. Little for sticking up for Nick. And people thought she was the worst teacher in the school! She was the only one with an ounce of courage. Correction: She had a ton. And they couldn't handle it. Clearly, the school was coming apart. And that meant he'd have to keep swinging his sledgehammer. Tearing down this place was an essential part of building a new and better school to replace it.

"Tell 'em a coup's in the works," he said, hoping to start a rumor that would sprout wings and breathe fire and maybe, just maybe, become a real live dragon.

On his way out, he saw Desmond in a blue suit, carrying an attaché case into the principal's office. *Already planning a counterstrike, eh?*

That day he spent a lot of time on the phone, taking three calls from reporters. At noon, he picked up newsletters from the printer's and dropped off 5,000 copies of *Healing Time* at Healthnet's headquarters with deepest apologies and promises he'd never be tardy again.

That afternoon, between on-camera interviews in his driveway, Richard got a phone call from Superintendent Johnson. "Mr. Gray, I just got back from Malliford," he said. "Fine school, fine school. I understand you're unhappy with the way things are, however." Johnson spoke in a slightly surprised tone, as if any problems would be news to him.

"Ya think?" Richard was unsure Johnson even had a firm grasp of the obvious. "What exactly do I have to be happy about?"

Richard would later claim they went at it "like caged dogs," exaggerating somewhat. In a testy exchange, Johnson said he wasn't in the mood for Richard's jibes and that rules were there for a reason. Richard said he didn't care

what kind of a mood Johnson was in and suggested a public forum at Malliford to discuss the three Rs: Rules, Ritalin, and Racism. Johnson demurred
and denied Richard's claims of segregation and ghettoization, which were
"most likely illegal." Johnson wouldn't apologize for anything "I either did or
didn't do, since I always do my best."

"More's the pity," Richard replied.

After ten minutes of raised voices and interruptions, Johnson got to the
real reason for the call: an offer to transfer Nicholas to Westover Elementary—the top public school in the county *and* state. "All the teachers there
are gifted certificated," Johnson said. "And Nicholas certainly qualifies."

"Or you could make all the other schools better," Richard suggested.
"Nah. That would be too much like work. Hey, I've got an idea. Why don't
you replace our principal immediately, instead?"

"Estelle Rutherford broke no rules, and she has our backing. She's an in-
novator. Take The Mentoring Initiative—"

"Please. She's an aberration. She's a living, walking *Kick Me* sign for the
county, and you know it. At least you should."

"That's enough, Mr. Gray. We want parents to be involved, but you
crossed the line."

"What line?"

"The petition."

"Which petition? Not that I care. In case you don't know, petitions are
part of the democratic process. So are the letters you never respond to. And
what's up with the phones, anyway? Would it kill you to hire someone to
answer them?"

"It's clear you're not part of the team."

"Which team? I have a job to do for parents. It's a sacred duty—"

"It's a vendetta."

"—and under these circumstances that means advocating for new school
leadership, and to hell with your chickenshit line. As far as *investigating* is
concerned, don't make me laugh. I'll tell you what's over the line: those black
armbands they're wearing today. It makes it look like they believe in running
over kids and suspending straight-A students. Hell, maybe they do."

"The armbands are gone."

"They're *divisive*," Richard hissed, aware that Johnson considered division the most hideous mathematical process ever.

"Mr. Gray, I'm trying to make this a win-win situation."

"I don't think you know the score."

"I'm wondering if you do."

"Oh, I think it's pretty simple. You want me to abdicate."

"Well, if your child went to another school—"

"Even if he did, I could stay as president. Look at Evangeline Dombry at Bonaire."

Ha! Richard mentioned the name because he suspected that Johnson hated the grey-haired African-American woman who had served loudly and proudly as the PTA president at one of the county's worst performing schools for five years—ever since the Grays had moved away. A reporter's delight, she was a constant source of grief to Johnson, who once publicly suggested she shouldn't run the PTA because she wasn't a parent of a student at Bonaire, ignoring the fact she had three grandchildren there—and that several PTAs at schools with low parental involvement had teachers at the helm.

Johnson didn't bite, however. "Your resignation would have to be part of the deal."

"I should resign over the school system's failings. Amazing."

"I'm offering you a chance to put your son in the best school in the state! What part of that offer do you not understand?"

"The part where you think you're not insulting me. And the part that's cowardly, weak, and evil. Oh, wait. I know, I know, I know! The part where you think you can use sarcasm effectively. No, Dr. Johnson, I understand. I just don't like it. I've got a motto: If it's not good enough for my child, it's not good enough for anyone else's child, either. Like I said, I'm not the one who should go."

Well, now you've done it, Richard told himself, realizing that the rest of the school year was simply a beating he'd have to take. Anna Lee would kill him for turning down the offer, so he decided against a hard line. "Look, put it in writing and make it starting next year. I'm serving out my term."

"I'm afraid I can't do that, Mr. Gray."

"Didn't think so. Promise them anything, but don't put it in writing. We're done."

"I'm sorry it has to end this way, Mr. Gray."

Richard laughed. "It's not over, Dr. Johnson."

"It would be better for you if it was. You should know Miz Rutherford shared some information with me."

What the hell was that supposed to mean? There was so much shit out there, it was hard to keep track of it. He reached for his digital tape recorder and turned it on. "All right, Estelle Rutherford shared some information with you. So?"

"I've instructed Miz Rutherford not to share it with anyone else. As a courtesy to you. In return, we expect—"

"She can talk to anyone she wants about anything she wants. She'll just dig a deeper hole for the school system."

"I'm not sure you understand. We're talking about your ... uh ... personal situation."

Beep.

"It's already gotten personal, in case you haven't noticed. You're using my son to punish and reward me."

"Hmm. Yes, but I understand you have a rather sensitive situation."

"I've heard the rumors, too. Don't deal in rumors, Dr. Johnson. They've been spreading trash about me since before I became president. There's nothing I've done I can't live with." His throat was so dry that when he gulped, it felt a little like a razor going down.

"Really, Mr. Gray?"

The bastard was no better than a blackmailer, and not a good one at that. "Really, Dr. Johnson. Do I need to memorialize this conversation for the school board members?"

"Have you been taping this call?" he asked in alarm.

"No. This is digital. The better to download."

The ensuing silence was broken by a *beep.*

"Does that mean you don't have anything more to say?" Richard asked. He listened to the silence on the line for a moment, then said, "Hit me with your best shot. And when you're through, I'll take my turn. We'll see who's still standing when it's all over. That sounds sporting to me." More silence. Richard started humming the *Jeopardy* theme.

Finally the superintendent spoke. "I'm sorry you've got the wrong impression. That's not the way we do things. "

"No. You just punch people in the face and expect them to go down. I've seen you destroy a friend's family already and now you've come after mine. You're one family away from a class action lawsuit and with a hundred thousand kids in the system, I'm sure I can find a few more plaintiffs."

"There's no merit—"

"I'm not the one who called it a vendetta. There are plenty of witnesses."

"I'm sorry this conversation took a wrong turn. I promise—"

"I don't want or need your promises. Do your worst. You try to blackmail me and you'll just prove my case. And one other thing. Leave Mrs. Little alone. You mess with her, you mess with me."

Click.

"Well, fuck a duck," Richard said after he'd hung up, then chuckled nervously. "That went well."

He held out his hand and watched it tremble.

Later that afternoon, Rita called. She'd been at school during lunch and seen Johnson and Desmond huddling together. "Oh, they ran out of fruit punch, so many kids were drinking it. Sixth-graders made a toast to honor Nick while Johnson was in the cafetorium. He turned beet-red. I wish Nick had seen it."

"You love this," Richard said.

"That part I did. Is Nick all right?"

"Yeah, thanks for asking."

When Richard went to pick up Nick that day, there was not a black armband to be seen. Mrs. Little wasn't in the room. Too bad. He wanted to ask her how *her* suspension was going.

Once outside, Nick told him, "Mrs. Leland and Mrs. Vandenburg got into a fight over me. Mrs. Vandenburg stopped me in the hall and told me I should apologize to everyone in the school for all the trouble I caused. Mrs. Leland came out of her room and told Mrs. Vandenburg to leave me alone. Then they started yelling at each other. Coach had to break it up."

Richard bristled. Vandenburg had no business doing that. Nick had served his time and wasn't her student, anyway.

"Just behave yourself," he said.

"I'm famous now," Nick said. "Hey, did you know the entire sixth grade is getting detention tomorrow because of me? I feel bad about it, but Devonious is impressed. He said he wished he could be suspended like I was, but Mr. Desmond wouldn't let them do that to him."

At home, Richard sat down and crafted an e-mail excoriating Vandenburg for her heavy-handed attempt at thought control. He sent copies to Miz Rutherford, Dr. Johnson, and all school board members. Just to make them nervous, he sent a copy to Deanna Richardson, too.

The reporter called Richard that night with something else on her mind, however. She was covering of the school board meeting, which had just concluded. Johnson, in hot water, told outraged board members he would rethink the application of Zero Tolerance and "perhaps inject some common sense into the situation."

"A bit late for that, isn't it?" Richard asked.

Deanna also said that the policy on Ritalin—which Richard thought was a Chain Gang anomaly—was countywide. "Board members denied all knowledge," she added.

"That works for them. On any subject. At any time."

* * *

In all, Richard talked to a dozen reporters. Another *Sentinel* editorial ran Wednesday: "Zero Consequences for Educators' Bad Behavior." Eventually coverage died down, and Nick's fifteen minutes passed. Interestingly, his nosebleeds stopped after he'd served his suspension. And in the end, there was one minor reform. The county pulled the zero-percent-juice fruit punch from school cafeterias. Nutritionists rejoiced.

TWENTY

This is what Richard knew: Mrs. Little entered the Board of Education hearing room at 4:30 p.m. on March 20 flanked by lawyers—one each from the Gresham NAACP and the teachers' union—and walked out ten minutes later. She had come to fight her proposed suspension for insubordination. This action came on the heels of a heated argument she had with her principal over disciplinary measures taken against Nicholas Gray. Though a teetotaler, Mrs. Little opposed the boy's harsh treatment so adamantly that the principal reported feeling "physically threatened." As soon as the teacher took her seat, the chairman of the personnel board announced that all charges had been dismissed. He read a memo from the superintendent stating: "Gresham's Zero Tolerance policy is currently under review and may not have been properly implemented." The chairman told Mrs. Little the case was closed and that he hoped she hadn't been put in fear of her job. "I fear no man," she replied. "And if you'll excuse me, I have papers to grade."

Richard heard this from Jane Baumgartner, who heard from her sister, who heard from Ms. Bailey, who heard from Mrs. Baines, who attended the session in the principal's absence. The vice principal's indiscretion seemed like the latest crack in the Rutherfordian wall encircling the school. Of course the news leaked to Deanna Richardson, so it was covered in the *Sentinel*.

Anna Lee grew angry when she heard Richard's account, since she believed that, had they fought the suspension, Nick would have been vindicated, and this would have restored Nick's faith in the system. This was nonsense, of course. Richard knew better. Mrs. Little had two lawyers and God on her side—that was a lot more game than he could bring. Actually, he was part of her game, having given her the winning edge with his opinion piece (not to mention his recorded warning to Johnson about messing with her). Richard told Anna Lee that, lacking news coverage, Mrs. Little would have been drowned quietly. He insisted that he was right to refuse to play a rigged game and work to un-rig it, instead.

Besides, he didn't want Nick's faith in the system restored. Not this system. Not yet. Better to raise a radical lawyer than a Chamber of Commerce tool. But he didn't tell that to his wife.

Despite Mrs. Little's victory, Richard feared his new heroine's days were numbered. He didn't see how having God on her side would help her within the walls at Malliford, due to special circumstances currently prevailing in that underworldly place.

Sure enough, Mrs. Little was soon in hot water again. On the first day of spring, she refused to allow D to go home with Chris Desmond, claiming Devonious didn't have parental permission. When Richard came for Nick after school, Cassandra Hardwick and Donzella James were arguing with the third-grade teacher in the hall. Devonious was all up in it, insisting he had given his teacher the note from his mother. Mrs. Little said she didn't have one, and she doubted Dashika Rowan (D's mother) would have written a note, anyway. D had already missed his bus and the mental health professionals told Mrs. Little she'd have to take him home. The teacher said she'd be glad to, or wait with him at school until his mama got off work or whatever it was she did, which might be midnight or 4:00 a.m., it didn't matter to her. D said he didn't want to go home. His mama wasn't ever there.

"I don't work for Jack Desmond," Mrs. Little told the two younger women. "And neither should you." This put them in a rage—or rather, made them sick, anger being a disease.

As the Grays were leaving, the principal stormed down the hall toward them, a hardened sea captain on her way to quell a mutiny, her face grim and lined, looking like a cut-rate version of death itself. She passed them without speaking. A few seconds later, shrieking rent the air like a rake on a chalkboard. Whatever it was that got to Miz Rutherford, Avon Little had a ton of it.

*　　*　　*

Thursday evening, Richard arrived to pick up Nick from soccer practice ten minutes after it was scheduled to end. His son was playing one-on-one with Joshua Bancroft on a scarred brown field that had yet to recover from the torment of fall league play. All the other Little Green Men were gone. In the distance, under bright lights, in-ground sprinklers sprayed silvery ribbons of water on the new sod of Field One, where Gresham Youth Soccer Association's elite teams played—the field of dreams for ambitious soccer parents.

Joshua's plump, redheaded mother popped out of her blue BMW. "Where have you been?"

"Sorry I made you wait. Traffic." A lame excuse, and they both knew it.

"You missed quite a show. I'm afraid there's some bad news."

"Did somebody get hurt?"

"Coach Gilford had a breakdown."

"What? During practice?"

"The boys were doing their scrimmage thingie, and he was trying to set them up for a throw-in, but they weren't cooperating. Two of them started fighting. The coach's son plopped on his butt and started pulling up grass. That's when Coach Gilford started screaming. I don't mean yelling like coaches do to be heard. He was stomping around, calling them little bastards. He even used the F-bomb. I thought he was going to hurt someone. I went out on the field to calm him down. He told me, 'Blank it. *You* coach these rotten little blankholes.' Only he didn't say 'blank.' He stormed off and drove away, so pissed off he forgot his son. He came back and got his kid, then drove off again, yelling all the way. No apology. No nothing. It was very upsetting."

"Wow. I'm sorry you had to go through that."

"I don't want him coaching my son. No one does. Now we're in a pickle. We need a coach. We wondered if you could take over. You're the only parent I know of who's free this time of day."

She meant *man*, of course. He wanted to scream "No!" But instead, a small "Yes" squeaked from his mouth like air from a pinched balloon. "I'll do it."

"Good man. You're PTA president at Malliford, right?"

"PTO."

"Well, if it doesn't work out, you can always put them on the chain gang." She laughed.

Ha, ha. Such a cheery prospect, taking over a team that had been outscored 28 to 3!

He didn't have time to consider life's latest twist right then, since he had a PTO board meeting that night. He especially dreaded this one, which he'd been forced to add after he forgot to appoint a nominating committee in February. What he really wanted was to call off the rest of the year, screw it, and go home—or better yet, fall into Teresa's arms. After all the gut-wrenching madness he'd gone through, just walking into the schoolhouse made him nauseated. What if he fainted at the podium and keeled over like a big pussy, filled with puss? *Please, no epic fails tonight.*

He took Nick home, fed him a PBJ sandwich, and shuffled papers with one eye on the clock. Anna Lee came home at 6:50 p.m., so late it seemed deliberate, but by then insult had become habit.

"Guess what, Mom? Dad's our new soccer coach."

Richard left for Malliford with her laughter ringing in his ears. He arrived in the library at 6:59 p.m., neatly avoiding chitchat. It was a small crowd, barely a quorum. The principal sat at her table, exhaling foul, frosty air. No longer a person, she was now a concept, a disease, a disorder—like evil, psoriasis, hemorrhoids. The primary carrier of smackdown syndrome. Not long ago, he'd thought that people would rise up against her, but now it was 11 o'clock in *High Noon*. The time had come; the town's good people had fled. He could hear a rusty saloon door squeaking. *It creaks for thee.*

"Hi," said Teresa from her seat between the two antagonists. The smile he gave her in response was so strained that it wiped hers off her face. He thought she was too sensitive to his moods, especially with people watching. By then, he'd come to the conclusion that his enemies didn't really have anything on him; they were just making up a bunch of stuff that happened to be true. He was sure the principal would like to hint at "certain details" about his life—and suspected that the superintendent had warned her not to. And having recorded the superintendent's clumsy attempt at blackmail, he believed he had the upper hand. Nevertheless, he and Teresa had to be very cool from here on out.

After the pledge, he made announcements and gave an "Antonio update," thanking Cindi Lou for sending flowers. The boy was due out of the hospital any day, though it would be two weeks before he'd return to school. He lingered on the subject: It was sad, even tragic, that it took a near-fatal accident to get the traffic light fixed. Such a shame. So preventable. Sigh. As he spoke, members watched Miz

Rutherford, who showed no emotion, even though Richard practically accused her of running over Antonio herself, hitting the brakes, and then running over the poor boy again in reverse.

When it came her turn to speak, Miz Rutherford didn't mention Antonio and said nothing of consequence, although she kept glancing over at Richard. Whenever she did this, he grinned back at her.

The rest of the meeting was conducted in an icy calm. Nuclear winter, Rita called it. The nominating committee was picked. It included Jane

Baumgartner, Mrs. Cates, and four people from the Table of Trouble, including Barbara. Clearly, the pendulum was swinging back to the PWCs.
Richard told himself it didn't matter who the next president was, so long as
it wasn't him. And why should he care? His best-case scenario called for getting out of town, one way or another.

He breathed a sigh of relief when the meeting adjourned. Feeling drained,
he left without taking time to chat with Teresa, who gave him a hurt look as
he slunk away. Four more meetings—two board, two general—and his oc-
cupation of enemy territory would be over. That would be a relief, even if his
achievements turned out to be nothing more than graffiti to be erased once
the PWCs regained power. He could live with that, as long as they didn't tear
down the benches he built.

*   *   *

Friday afternoon, Aaron Roberts showed up at Malliford with thirty used
computers. Over the next two hours, buyers trickled in and picked up their
machines. When the computers were all paid for, Roberts wrote a check to
the PTO for $1,500 and handed it to Richard. It was less than a third of
what was needed to fund the PTO's teacher-training scheme.

Oh, well. Maybe next year. Then again, what did he care?

Stan showed up to help Aaron. The exiled board member looked more
disheveled than ever. He said he'd moved into an apartment and was thinking about going back to school.

"To be a teacher?" Richard asked.

"God no. Law school. So how are things with you?"

"About what you read in the papers. It's a fucking war now."

"Well, you'll never run out of ammo with the crowd you're fighting. Thing
is, you have to worry about being a target, too, eh?"

The less said about that, the better. As Richard turned to go, he wished
Stan good luck.

Stan said, "Have a nice day."

Obviously, something was wrong. Stan wasn't a "Have a nice day" kind of guy.

*   *   *

After three seasons sitting idly in the stands and second-guessing coaches,
Richard was in charge of a soccer team in a game for the first time Saturday
afternoon. He'd spent all morning at a licensing clinic, where he was told

to teach skills, stay positive, and make sure the players had fun. "And don't touch the kids," the director of coaching shouted as newly certified coaches ambled out the door of the cinder block Gresham Youth Soccer Association clubhouse wearing blue caps and GYSA polo shirts.

Two hours later, Richard hoped for the best as he drove Nick and Anna Lee to the field. Unfortunately, his unhappy team's goal appeared to be driving the coach mad. Richard was short two players besides the coach's son, who had quit the team along with his father—news that brought impolitic cheers from parents. Players who showed up complained bitterly of the cold, though it was fifty-five degrees, balmy by Richard's standards. As the game progressed, he exhorted his Little Green Men: "Challenge the ball!"; "Play your position!"; "Don't eat the grass!"

They responded by stumbling, standing around watching the ball, yelling at each other when the Raiders scored a goal, and, in one case, grazing—despite Richard's dire warnings of benching and purging. The high point came when Nick scored the team's only goal—while the defender was tying his shoelace. The low point came immediately thereafter, when Nick taunted the boy. There were three water-bottle fights on the bench. The sweeper declared he was too tired to play the fourth quarter. Throughout the match, parents yelled advice contradicting the coach's instructions.

Richard had been ready to forfeit by halftime—didn't they have a mercy rule?—but the game went on and on. He asked the teenaged referee if his watch was broken. Finally, after what seemed like five hours, three whistle blasts put Little Green Men out of their misery.

"We beat you thirteen to one," gloated a stocky redheaded opponent with a demonic glint in his eye, who intentionally missed Little Green palms during the after-game handshake. "And you wouldn't have scored if our goalie hadn't been tying his shoe."

"At least I know to keep my shoes tied!" Nick yelled over his shoulder.

Some parents approached the bench while snacks were distributed and congratulated Richard for a good effort, thanking him for taking on the task. One of them called him Dick.

"Richard," he corrected.

"Looks like the team needs extra practice," said Brandon Logan's father.

"Thanks for noticing," said the new coach. Richard heard Logan's wife arguing with the man on the way to the car, saying coaches were hard to come by and not to be obnoxious or he'd end up having to run the team. "Don't forget to take your kid!" Richard called out, giving Brandon a gentle shove in their direction. No child would be left behind—not with him, anyway.

Nick ran to the concession stand to get a slushie. Anna Lee smirked as she helped Richard stow his game gear. "So, how's it going, *Coach*?"

"It's embarrassing."

"Well, they didn't win either of their first games. Anyway, the other team was good."

"And mine's got the chemistry of a toxic waste dump. I ought to call them the ADDs. We're getting beat by an average score of ten to one. Who dealt this mess? What did my predecessor do to piss off the league commissioner so badly that he decided every misfit had to be on this team? I mean, Nick's all right, but the others ... *sheesh*."

As they walked toward the car, Richard said, "I need a plan."

"What kind of plan?"

"One that works, dear. One that works."

*   *   *

In Sunday's paper, occupying the same space Richard's op-ed piece had run the week before, was a guest column headlined "Spoiled Brats and the Children They Raise," by Jack Desmond. "People in prominent positions are not entitled to escape the consequences of the law," Desmond declared in defense of Miz Rutherford and the school board. "...Whatever happened to obedience to God and country? If we don't teach our children to respect the law, what good are we as parents? Not much."

Desmond also touted The Mentoring Initiative in all its high-tech and compassionate conservative glory, but mostly he made fun of Richard and his ilk: "helicopter parents who hover over their own children and don't care about the rest." At least he didn't say Nick was gay.

Richard told himself he was a big boy and could handle some bad press. After all, if he threw punches, he had to take a few. His attempt to calm himself didn't work, however. He was pissed. Moreover, he wanted to track down Desmond and disembowel him with the dullest tool in the shed. And now that they were in an official pissing contest, Richard was quite curious about Mrs. Little's confrontation in the hall over Desmond with Dear Leader and the mental health professionals.

When Anna Lee read the article, she said, "Two sides to every story. Get used to it."

He slammed his fists on the table and pushed himself away. As he stormed off, she said, "Barry wanted to put a resolution backing the Zero Tolerance policy on the Chamber board's agenda this month!"

Richard turned around and regarded her carefully.

She finished quietly, barely above a whisper. "I had to talk him out of it."

"Good thing you did."

"I shouldn't have to do things like that."

"Yes, you should. Zero Tolerance is a horrible, brainless policy whether we take it personally or not. Think of it as your civic duty to fight it."

"You've got to stop this ... this grudge match of yours. I'm too embarrassed to admit my son goes to that school!"

"Got to stop something, that's for sure."

When he went to his office, there was an e-mail from Teresa: "I saw the paper. Think New Mexico. Oregon. Maybe even Alaska. The further, the better."

You betcha.

* * *

There was something wrong when Richard went to pick up Nick Monday afternoon at school. The place smelled bad—as if a stink bomb had gone off, a toilet had backed up, or the principal had a massive personality leak. As he walked down the hall, Mrs. Leland gave him a strained smile and ducked into another teacher's room without speaking. Odd that the woman who fought in the hall to defend Nick's honor would avoid him. Everyone's radar was up. Even though he wore his sneakers, Mrs. Little was staring at him when he entered her room.

She gave him a terse greeting and had a favor to ask. "I need you to take Antonio's lessons to him. He's home now, but he won't be back in school for a while. I don't want him to fall too far behind. I'd do it, but I have a doctor's appointment. I know he'd like to see Nick."

"Sure."

She walked over to a bookcase and picked up a sheaf of papers, which she handed it to Richard. He was about to ask about Desmond and D when she held out an envelope with his last name on it. As he took it, he gave her a questioning look.

"We've been ordered to send these home," she said. "I don't think it's right, but they're looking for a reason to fire me right now. I'm sorry." She sat down and leaned on her fists, making herself into the glummest bullfrog in the world. "Even if you resent this ... and I understand if you do, please help Antonio."

"I understand," Richard said, even though he didn't. "Let's go, Nick."

As they walked down the hall, two teachers ducked into doorways; Ms. Bailey turned on her heel and skittered off.

"I must have radioactive cooties," Richard muttered.

"If you've got to have cooties, those are the best kind," Nick said.

They stepped outside into the balmy afternoon; Richard opened the envelope. Stapled to Desmond's article was a letter to parents from Superintendent Johnson. All this just a day after Desmond's vitriol had run. Remarkable speed for a bureaucracy. Richard stopped walking and read:

> ... I urge all parents to support Gresham County schools, not try to tear them down. ... I reiterate my unqualified support for Principal Estelle Rutherford, one of the finest educators I have ever had the pleasure to work with. I fully support her 1,000 percent in her efforts to make Malliford Elementary a five-star school, which includes the upcoming Mentoring Initiative ...

"A thousand percent," Richard grumbled. "Asshole doesn't even know how to do math."

"What asshole?"

"No, I said *Ask Cole.*"

"Who's Cole?"

"Some guy I know." *A lot of them, actually.*

Richard was still livid when they got home. He filed the letter. No way would he show it to Anna Lee, who would agree with that dumbass. He paced, stopped to begin writing a nasty response, realized it would no good, and returned to pacing.

He needed to do something in response. *And make it look like an accident.*

"Through with your homework?" he asked Nick as they passed in the hall.

"Yeah. It only took me an hour even though I get twice as much as the other kids."

His story never varied. Richard had to admire that. "Show me."

"I will if you stop pacing."

Richard did so and checked Nick's work. Satisfied that it was indeed done this time, he said, "Let's go see Antonio. I've got some stuff to take him."

* * *

As they drove to Chantilly Arms, Nick said, "Antonio deserves a medal for living there."

"What about Devonious?"

"He should pay for the medal."

Richard pulled into the lot and saw kids playing tag on the playground. A skateboarder sans helmet zoomed toward them. Apparently, all the crack whores had taken Monday off. Then again, maybe Susan Gunther had terrified them, though Teresa had unkindly suggested that her methods of intimidation worked only on suburban housewives who quit being women long ago.

They found Antonio's first-floor apartment. Richard knocked on the door and glanced around, wondering where Devonious lived. Then he saw a beige Lincoln LS parked in front of the next building. Desmond owned such a vehicle.

The *Guideposts* aunt, whose name was Lucinda, answered the door and graciously ushered them in with an offer of tea, which they politely declined. Not wishing to torment Antonio, Richard handed her the schoolwork. "How's he doing?"

"Better," she said. "You go ahead and visit." The Grays walked through the kitchen and saw Antonio in a recliner, bathed in late afternoon sunshine flooding through the sliding glass patio door. He wore a bulky sweater; a blanket covered his leg cast. He politely turned off the TV when his guests walked in, disappointing Nick.

His eyes widened in appreciation at the Pokémon books Nick had brought him. As Aunt Lucinda hummed in the kitchen, Richard sat on a plain green couch with straight lines and thin cushions. "How ya been?"

"I'm doin' better. I gotta wear this cast for another month." He nodded at the aluminum crutches on the floor beside him. "I should be back at school this week. It's boring here."

"I don't see how," Nick said. "You've got cable."

Antonio shrugged. "I'd rather be playing baseball. I'm gonna miss the whole season. I went to three practices and never got to play in a game 'cause of the accident." His splinted left hand clicked when he rested his hand on the lamp table beside his chair.

"Wait 'til next year," Richard said. "That's what baseball folks always say." He tried to be nonchalant as he switched the subject. "I think I saw Mr. Desmond's car at Devonious's place."

"Probably."

"Is he picking up Chris, you think?"

"That ain't the way it works. He don't bring Chris over when he comes. He got a key, too. I see him lettin' himself in like he own the place." Antonio lowered his voice to whisper to Nick, but Richard heard. "I told you Devonious was his bitch. That's how he makes his money. D's mama don't have no money. I've seen the manager over there arguin' with her about the rent, threatenin' to kick her out." Antonio turned back to Richard and said, "D told me never to come over to his place when Mr. Desmond's car was there." He shook his head. "They ask me I want a mentor, I say no, leave my booty alone."

Richard struggled to keep the shock from showing on his face. Recalling Mrs. Little's fight with the principal and the mental health professionals, he realized she also must have had some nasty suspicions. Well, *something* was going on. It certainly would screw up The Mentoring Initiative if a horrible secret was revealed, wouldn't it?

Richard said, "You may be wrong. Be careful what you say and who you say it to."

"It's true."

"Especially if it's true."

"I don't think he can hurt me worse than that car did." Antonio let the truth of that sink in, then added, "Wouldn't nothin' happen if he did somethin' to me. Nobody does nothin' when a grown-up does wrong."

Richard heard a challenge in the child's voice, an ancient echo that called to him from decades ago. He saw no other choice when it was put that way. With a grim expression, he said, "I'm going to do something about it. But don't talk about it, OK?"

The boys nodded.

Realizing he was sounding sketchy, Richard added, "If you see something you know is wrong, you should tell Mrs. Little."

Soon afterward, Richard and Nick left. The Lincoln was gone when they stepped outside.

"Don't tell what Antonio said to anyone," Richard reminded his son. "And don't go near Jack Desmond."

"Is he a bad man?"

"There's always that chance."

After dinner that night, Richard searched the Internet for background on Desmond and found several of his adversary's ratlike political utterances but nothing predating his appointment as executive director of the Southern Freedom Foundation. There had to be more, because there is always *something*.

*   *   *

The next morning, in willful and wanton violation of *Malliford Manners*, Richard walked into Mrs. Little's room and reported that he'd made his delivery to Antonio. He also mentioned that he saw Desmond's car at D's apartment and found it odd. Even stranger, Antonio didn't.

Mrs. Little snorted in disgust. "I reported my suspicions," she said. "Even put it in writing. I said there's something improper going on. They nodded and acted all serious, but they didn't do a thing. Said I didn't have any '*evidence.*' It was like I told 'em I saw a UFO. They wrote the boy off long ago. That man got power and money and he can do as he pleases. The devil walks this world." She paused to collect her thoughts. "D doesn't talk to anyone anymore. He's closin' off. This so-called 'mentoring' don't make a lick of sense to me."

Devonious entered the room and threw his backpack in the corner. He eyed them both suspiciously. A few seconds later, Mrs. Baines came in, surprising them when she blurted out, "Mrs. Little, I need to go over something with you."

"The camera," Mrs. Little whispered behind a sheet of paper. "They saw you comin'."

"Hello, Mrs. Baines," Richard said on his way out the door. "How are you today?"

"Mr. Gray."

Thoughts churned in his head as he left the building. *They turned in Stan after his daughter got a bruise on skate night. They worked for a month to get Nick to turn on me, then they turned on him. They'd go after me harder if they didn't think I had a recording of them trying to blackmail me. Now they ignore a teacher's concerns when there's actually something going on. This is worse than the Catholic Church. Is this how the principal and her minions build a reputation? Then again, with five stars within their grasp, what's one apartment kid? Leave No Child Behind was the mantra these days. What was Rutherford's slogan: A Child's Behind is a Terrible Thing to Waste?*

A contrary thought flashed through his mind: What if his hatred of the racist homophobe was making him paranoid and delusional? It turned out this wasn't an overwhelming concern. After all, he had to do something, and at this point, a certain amount of craziness was called for. When he got home, he called an old acquaintance from his reporting days: Thomas Skelton, an attorney and state representative. Skelton laughingly thanked him for throwing gasoline on the fire in Gresham County. "That school system needs to burn to the ground," he said. "I can't work with them any more. When I asked the chairman to get the school board to endorse a bill I sponsored, he autosigned every member's name on a letter, and then half of them ran around behind him denying the issue ever came up."

"There are too many fires to count right now," Richard said. "I've got one in particular I need to put out." Without naming names or political philosophies, he told Skelton what appeared to be going on and what he needed—a thorough background check.

"You could call Social Services, if you wanted to do it on the cheap," the politician said.

"I think it goes deeper than that. I want the truth, not accusations and denials."

"Then you should talk to Randall Wyatt," Skelton said. "Best private investigator in town. He's also an attorney. Pricey, but he'll find what you're looking for, if it's there."

"How much will it cost?"

"How much you got?"

"This is why people hate lawyers."

"Ha! They love us when they need us, and they need us all the time."

TWENTY-ONE

He would regret his pledge to Antonio—and later regret regretting it—but such was the life of Richard Gray. He certainly couldn't tell Anna Lee of his plan to dig up dirt on Desmond. She would forbid it, without understanding or caring that it was his solemn duty. While his moral math dictated his course of action, the finances were trickier. In any case, Wounded Child had declared class-action revenge on Desmond. Certainly not just for Devonious. That little gangsta was hardly worth it. No, D was not the hill he wanted to die on.

He had to talk to someone, so he called Teresa Wednesday morning. "Can we get together—"

"Sure, sweetie," she cooed. "I was thinking about what we did at your place. Maybe—"

"Just to talk," he said. "Privately."

"Sure," she cooed. "How about HyperCafe?"

"See you in an hour."

* * *

The log-walled, plank-floored, pseudo-rustic coffeehouse sat in the parking lot of a strip center six miles from Malliford—distant enough to minimize sightings by gossips, close enough to seem innocuous if the lovers were spotted there. Teresa brought a treasurer's report, and Richard entered with his laptop a few minutes later. He sat down beside her on a brown leather sofa, and since the coast was clear, kissed her on the lips.

"You sounded like you had the blues," she said. "I was so pissed at the letter from Johnson I chewed out Vandenburg this morning on general principle—or lack thereof. God, I'm starting to sound like you."

"It was a slap in the face, wasn't it?" Richard sounded glum.

"Poor sweetie," Teresa commiserated. "I want to cheer you up, so I planned something. Let's get our drinks to go. It's a beautiful day for a road trip."

"Where?"

"Lake Willow. I packed a lunch."

"Today?" Work was piled up on his desk. On the other hand, he needed a break from his quotidian hell. "All right. Why not?"

They got coffee, slipped on their shades, and left. "I love this car," Teresa said as she got in the Audi, setting a picnic basket on the back seat. "So sporty."

"The odometer will hit 100,000 today."

"Carl drives an Infiniti, just so you know."

"Dark green. Sanford County tags."

"You're getting good at this. You sure I'm the first?"

"Yup." He was grinning when they pulled out of the lot.

He drove carefully, knowing that a car wreck under such circumstances would be impossible to explain to Anna Lee—and probably not worth surviving. They took a state route north, eschewing the main highway, and escaped the suburban sprawl, climbing into low-lying mountains that were still a few weeks away from a full blanket of greenery. Along the way, he shared his suspicions about Desmond. She listened quietly as he told her his plans.

When they arrived at the park, there were only a few cars in the main lot. Richard drove past the ranger's green pickup and the log cabin office, then pulled into a parking space near picnic tables and a boat ramp. Across the green lake, a solitary fisherman in an aluminum craft puttered around in a cove.

It was chilly. The bright sun in the cerulean sky held more hope than heat, but at least the bugs weren't out. They sat atop a picnic table with their feet on the seat and clung to each other. Richard observed the table's scars, its carvings the archaeology of love: Jimmy and Carla, Jimmy and Jessica, Bobby Reid and himself many times, in graphic terms.

"Let's walk," she said. She grabbed his hand and gripped tightly, pulling him along as they hiked the well-worn trail, shuffling through pine needles down to the lake. "I love early spring."

"Yesterday, I told a Bradford pear tree to get a room."

"We need a room." She pulled him close and kissed him.

Richard picked up a flat stone from the shore and threw it across the water, bouncing it four times before it sank. Teresa, watching the ripples, said, "Have you missed me?"

"Whenever you're not around, I do."

"And?"

"I love you." They kissed lightly on the lips. He reached down and picked up another stone, a smooth oval brown pebble with white stripes, and gave it a fling. It sliced through the air, bounced three times atop the rippling water, and disappeared. He picked up another one.

"I'm leaving Carl."

The rock flew out of his hand and missed the lake completely.

"Look at you. You shouldn't be surprised. I never loved him. And now he's screwed up everything. After the stock market crash, he took what we had left in savings and lost that, too, just before the market rebounded. We're like the only ones with nothing now."

"You're not the only ones."

"Well, we lost a lot more than we should have. That is one high-risk bastard. I hate him. I'd like to ... No, I don't want to go there. I don't want to even think about him, especially not when I'm with you. I wanted to come here and get away with you for a reason." She took a deep breath. "And so I'll just blurt it out. Here's the deal: I love you. And you've got to decide whether all this sneaking around is worth it. We either call it off, or we move forward."

He licked his lips, suddenly very dry, and regarded her carefully. The sun reddened her auburn hair. She was beautiful. So was Anna Lee, though a bit familiar-looking after all these years. Teresa loved him. Perhaps Anna Lee did, too, once upon a time. Now that factor no longer seemed like a crucial part of their marriage. Teresa was spontaneous, impetuous. Anna Lee was calculating, businesslike. And a bit shrewish.

Marriage vows could do nothing to balance these inequalities and offered no hope of salvation for him. It seemed more like a choice between life and death—or life and death-in-life. It was a world-destroying moment. He stared out over the water to the pine trees on the lake's far bank, trying to think how he could keep walking the line.

"I'm in this for keeps," she said. "I want to be with you. I'll always be there for you. I'll help you any way I can. Will you do the same for me?"

Nearby, birds chirped.

"Do you want to marry me?" she asked.

"I think ... I do."

"You don't sound too sure."

"Yes. Yes, if we can figure out a way."

"We will, OK? That makes your problems my problems, which means Jack Desmond is our problem." She took a deep breath. "You want to hire a private detective and prove he's a pervert who's setting himself up with a harem of boys. I say do it."

"I don't know if I can afford to do a full background check."

"How much is it?"

He threw up his hands. "A bunch. I'm not exactly sure."

"I'll let you in on a secret. There's plenty of money. And I can't think of a better use for the Treasure of the Sierra Malliford."

A hawk flew high overhead. A crow taunted it from a pine branch. A squirrel stood up and nervously eyed the humans. Time stood still; Richard was dumbstruck.

"You heard right," she said, flashing a conniving smile. "I found the Treasure."

"For years I have heard of this theeng," he said in a *steenking-badges* accent. "It is too much to *bee-leeve* it is true."

She grinned. "Si, señor. It is true. I am very proud of myself for finding thees thing."

"How much?"

"Twenty-five grand. We doan need no steenkin' vote to spend it. Because you and I are the only ones who know about it."

"I am a simple man. Please explain to me how it is that you have found the long-lost Treasure."

"OK," she said, dropping the ersatz accent, "just after we moved to Summerwood, I met a woman from Ohio who was visiting a neighbor down the street. She was on the PTA board at Malliford twenty years ago. Rita may know her, Rita and maybe Mrs. Baines—"

"Or Ms. Bailey."

"I never think of her as being around a long time."

"Me neither."

"She's had surgery."

"So have you."

"Not on my *face*," she said. "Anyway, here's the story: I'm working in the yard because Carl never does and I had to let go of the service almost as soon as we moved in because we're not doing well, thanks to Carl's so-called investments. This woman is out for a walk and stops to chat. I mention my daughter's starting first grade at Malliford and she says, 'Did they ever get the gym built?' I'd seen the gym, so I said yeah. She says that's good, they raised twenty thousand dollars for the gym. And I say that's good, and I don't think about it again until I hear the *county* built it as part of a bond issue. And of course a gym costs more than twenty grand."

"Somebody said something about some PTA money sandbagged to furnish it, but nothing ever came of it."

"That's what she was talking about. Anyway, I met Rita, and she said you were going to be president even if you didn't know it yet. I had this teenage crush on you and wanted to do something about it, so I started talking about the treasurer's position, and I asked her about some fund-raiser for the gym and she says she heard something a long time ago, but she didn't know what happened to the money. There was a PTA president and he had an affair with the principal, and his wife was treasurer, so maybe everything got screwed up then."

She laughed. "Men screw everything up. Anyway, that's how Rutherford came to the school, I guess, after the shit hit the fan. Now everyone thinks she's a lez. I wish. At least then she'd be something instead of Lizard Woman. Anyway, I got to thinking about finding the money."

"And being the big hero."

"Whatever. It was something to do. So I snooped around and tracked it down, just sitting there collecting, like, one percent interest in a passbook account."

He gave her an incredulous look. "You found the passbook?"

"A woman who lives in Kentucky was the treasurer fifteen years ago. I located her, and she mailed me a bunch of stuff and the passbook was in it, just lying at the bottom of the box. I don't think she knew a thing about it. Presidents, treasurers, principals come and go. Schools and banks change names. Things get lost, forgotten. One day, thanks to a clever girl's digging, it turns up—more than twenty-five grand in an account they quit depositing money in twenty years ago in a bank they quit doing business with fifteen years ago. But it was the PTO account, not the PTA account, and that's important, because access is everything. And only you and I know about it. So there should be more than enough to pay for this investigation. I've updated the account so we can withdraw it any time."

"What about the signature card?"

"You already signed it."

"I did?" He scratched his temple in puzzlement.

"We could use that money for the detective," she said.

"I may be able to pay for it out of my own pocket."

"Come on, the Queen Bitch opened her withered old legs to corporate

America and told the PTO to piss off, remember? So what's it going to go for, office furniture?"

Richard looked out across the lake. The stocky man with brushy blond hair scrambled around in the boat with his net. "I don't know. It just seems ... wrongish."

"We could give the rest to charity, or to some school that needs it. Anonymously, of course. I mean, the karma's the same as long as we use it to help kids, right? Actually, we'd be making the world better. Come on." She grabbed his hand and pulled. They turned and walked back along the trail. The birds were noisy, wind rustled the grass, and twigs snapped beneath their steps. Richard dropped behind her when the path narrowed. He loved the way she moved, especially when watching her from behind.

And she was willing to give him everything. It was overwhelming. He started to choke up.

They returned to the bench and sat quietly. Teresa curled her knees up to her face. "What will it take to start over? How much money, I mean, to move to a new town and start a new life?"

"With or without a job?"

"You'd be setting up your business. Maybe you could keep your clients."

"Not likely."

"Should we buy a house in Oregon?"

"Not these days."

"Or maybe New Mexico. I think I'd like someplace sunny."

"Scary thought, starting over."

"What do you fear the most?" she asked, tracing a pattern on his jacket sleeve, and then raising her gaze to stare into his eyes.

"Losing the boy."

"The boy." She looked away and sighed. Under her breath, she said, "Three. That's a lot of kids to pack for."

"What?"

"Nothing."

"Look, maybe—"

"*Ut.* Don't go there. We're getting married. You proposed."

He thought she'd been the one to propose, but it didn't seem like something to argue about right then, being newly engaged. Anyway, he should divorce Anna Lee or at least separate before he made such a commitment. She deserved that much. "Uh, I don't think—"

She pressed his lips with her index finger. "Shush. Busting Desmond is

our going-away present. The PTO is fat, dumb, and happy, and we'll be so the
fuck out of here." She applauded her logic; the echo of her clapping carried
through the woods, silencing the crinkly song of a brown thrasher. "Here's
what we do. We're going to get divorces, but first we leave. Carl won't mind if I
take the girls. He'll be ecstatic that he can go back to uninterrupted whoring."

"I've got to work out something for Nick. To keep him with me."

"You know my position. I'll give you a boy." She spread her legs. For her,
everything was negotiable. "Of course, I'd be proud to have him as my son.
Maybe you can get him uncontested—or, you know, joint custody wouldn't
be too bad. We could use the Treasure for lawyers' fees."

But that wouldn't work for Richard. Taking the Treasure was stupid, of
course, yet not necessarily wrong—not if they used it to capture a predator and gave the rest away. He'd told Antonio he'd do something; he didn't
intend to bankrupt himself doing it. No, taking the money wasn't really so
horrible after all. Those kids it had been raised for two decades ago were
long gone. The mission it had been raised for was accomplished. And Rutherford might go down with Desmond. For the good of the school, then.
When he looked at it this way, just a little outside the box, there was no
better use for the money. Yes, he could do this thing. Still, he felt like he was
about to smoke his first joint—in front of a police station. It would be best
if he didn't use it to pay for the divorce, although he could see that being
PTO president had damaged his marriage. It certainly had poisoned Anna
Lee's attitude toward him.

"No," he said. "We use it to get Desmond and give the rest away."

"Great. Fine," she said with a sarcastic edge to her voice. "Just give it all
away. That's OK. Just par for the course. My money situation's been strange
since the day Carl stuck a hundred-dollar bill in my G-string. After he convinced me he was wealthy—and I convinced him I was pregnant—we got
married. Then I found out he was broke, but me, I kept my word and had
Caitlin. When Carl got himself out of debt, we moved to Summerwood, just
in time for the crash. Caitlin went to private kindergarten, you know. Wish
I had that money back. We're great at looking prosperous, but we owe a lot
more than the house is worth, and I'm never going to get ahead with that
loser around my neck. I've got to get out before he takes me down with him."

She picked up an acorn, tossed it away, and glanced at her watch.

"I was just thinking about teacher training. You know—"

"You're talking about Malliford, right?"

"Yeah."

"Enough about that place. It's a public school, so it sucks, OK? We're in the middle of recession, married to people who don't love us, and what we've got is each other. We can only save ourselves. This is Vietnam, baby. The war's over. You'd best take the last flight out, sweetie, and I'm that chopper. *Wooka-wooka-wooka.*" She patted his cheek. "Now let's eat."

She got her basket from the car and set up a meal of chicken salad, strawberries, pita bread and sparkling cider. Richard stared into the piney woods, lost in thought.

"I love you," she said. "You love me. That's all you need to know. That will get you through the days to come. And don't be a fool. The PTO was silly and irrelevant the day before you took office, and it will be silly and irrelevant the day after you go. They'll do something stupid if they get their hands on the money, so if you can do some good and save some kids from horror, that's what you should do. Throw this guy's ass in the slammer. Here, try the salad. It's got a touch of Dijon."

They ate for several minutes before she broke the silence. "Understand this: I'm really tough," she said, waving her fork. "So don't fuck with me." Tears welled up her eyes, and she abandoned the tough-gal act. "I always wanted a good man's love. And now I have it. You mean everything to me. You have no idea what it's like in here." She patted her chest. "You're the only thing that can make it better."

He grabbed her and held her tight, burying his chin on her shoulder, not sure what to do. He was caught between two women, between obligation and opportunity, between being kept alive and being alive—perhaps for just a short time. Nick had always been the compass that guided him home, but after this terrible year, Richard wasn't sure that his being around Nick was the best thing for the boy any more. Maybe he could make a clean break with Anna Lee and have joint custody. Then, after a decent interval, marry Teresa.

What was Anna Lee losing, after all? Certainly not money. At best she was a friend, and not an especially good one these past few years. More of a long acquaintance. He shook his head. On the other hand, he was troubled by Teresa's attempt to position herself between father and son. If things could just go on the way they had been, undiscovered—or only suspected and hinted at, kept under wraps by some kind of reverse blackmail. The more he thought, the less he knew. No matter what his choice, perhaps it would be best if he got out of town.

Teresa pulled back and gazed into his indecisive eyes. "So this is what we do," she said. "We go back to our little families and our little school and our little PTO and pretend we're happy and work to get out of this pit."

"Sounds like a plan," Richard said.

*   *   *

The next day, Richard drove to Wyatt Investigations, PC, on Dexter Avenue, near downtown. Randall Wyatt's well-appointed office had the look of a successful lawyer's, complete with wheatgrass-papered walls, brown leather chairs, and walnut bookcases filled with law texts. Wyatt was the go-to detective for the city's silk-stocking law firms. He handled investigations of CEO candidates as well as high-profile, messy divorces. Plaques and awards covered the wall: Kiwanis Club, Police Officer of the Year. This wouldn't be cheap.

Skelton's referral carried a lot of weight with Wyatt, and he had cleared his calendar for the meeting. The sandy-haired man had tufts of grey on his blond sideburns and wore a tan suit with a red tie. "How may I help you?" he asked, gesturing for Richard to sit down in a wing chair facing the desk as he took his seat behind it.

Richard breathed deeply. "I want a background check on someone."

"Why?"

"I'm concerned about the propriety of a man's relations with boys he works with."

"Who are we talking about?"

"Jack Desmond."

Wyatt whistled. "I've heard of him. What makes him interesting?"

Richard shared his concerns.

"*Hmm.* The Southern Freedom Foundation. Excuse me a minute." Wyatt turned to his computer. He ran a search while Richard strained to see what he was doing. After a few moments, Wyatt turned and said, "Heavy hitters. The state Republican chairman is on the board, along with CEOs of some Fortune 500 companies."

This only served to confirm Richard's fears that Desmond was too well-connected to tackle.

"And parents want to check him out. I've never heard of a PTA—"

"Not the PTA. The PTO. Look, let's leave the PTO out of this. Liability, you know."

"I see." Wyatt pursed his lips. "You've taken this on yourself. What's your basis for suspicion?"

"A teacher reported her concerns about Desmond's relationship with a young boy he's quote mentoring unquote. The school's administration failed to follow up on her concerns. That's why I'm here. The system isn't working. When I took some schoolwork to a boy with a broken leg who lives next door, he said his classmate told him never to come over while Desmond was there. From what I gather, the visits are frequent and unsupervised, and the boy's nickname is 'Desmond's bitch.' The kid's behavior is out of control since Desmond got involved with him. The mother is barely on the radar, and his father is unknown. I worked with him until the principal shut down the PTO's tutoring program. Control freak."

Wyatt's eyes lit up. "Chain Gang Elementary."

"Yes. Is it that notorious?"

"You've been in the news a bit. So you're a PTO president in a public feud with the principal, and there's a program run by a man you're in a pissing contest with, and you want to bring him down. Is that it?"

Richard gulped. The guy *was* good. "I admit there's nastiness, but that's not the issue."

"What is the issue?"

"I made a promise." Richard stood to leave. "But if you're not interested—"

"Please. Sit down. I'll take the case, Mr. Gray."

"Oh." Richard sat down. "Good. It is important."

"I require a retainer of two thousand dollars. That covers a basic background check—infinitely better than the stuff you get over the Internet. Didn't find anything that way, did you? I thought not. The deeper I go, the more it costs. Sometimes a basic check reveals what we need—an arrest record, a restraining order, the sort of thing that would be sufficient to make your point. I caution you not to talk about this with *anyone*. People have been known to behave poorly if they find out somebody's digging around, especially if there's something there. It's best done quietly. And don't use the investigation as a threat. That can backfire."

"I understand."

Wyatt asked for background information and took notes on a legal pad, underlining with his rollerball. "One final thing: If there's something under this rock, it better not be you."

"You'll have to look under a different rock for that."

Wyatt grinned appreciatively. "Fair enough. I assume time is of the essence. I'll get on it right away. If what you suspect is true, this will be a pleasure, Mr. Gray. Perhaps pleasure isn't the right word. Well, you know what I mean. I should have a preliminary report soon and we'll know where we are. Leave a check with my secretary. One that doesn't bounce. Good day, Mr. Gray."

In the outer office, Richard wrote a check from his business account and gave it to Wyatt's secretary—an older woman almost as fine-looking as Ms. Bailey. He hurried off to find five hundred dollars to make it good.

* * *

Saturday morning, Little Green Men roared onto the field and played like fiends. In an inspired effort, they won their first game, trouncing their opponents 7 to 4. Forward Chad Johnson exulted: "We finally won!"

"Wow!" Anna Lee said to Richard as Mary Bancroft distributed Hi-C and Ding-Dongs to the triumphant team. "What'd you do to turn it around?"

"It's a secret," Richard said, shouldering his coach's duffel.

"Fine. Be that way. Nick, what's going on?"

"Deep dark secret," the boy replied. "Double super secret."

"You're both just full of secrets, aren't you?"

"Yup," Richard said. He grabbed his wife gently around the shoulder and turned her away from the field for the walk to the car, hoping she hadn't noticed Teresa and her girls standing by the opposite fence, watching them.

TWENTY-TWO

When Richard passed by the school office Monday morning and saw Polly's replacement behind the counter, he nearly froze in mid-step. *Goddamn. This has to be a joke. Ha, ha, ha. After all, it's April 2 and April Fool's Day fell on a Sunday, so ... yes, that's what it is. Yeah. Good one. Whew.* After all, he was PTO president. Someone would have the decency to tell him Susan Gunther—

"Can you believe Susan got the job?" said Jane, standing beside the hall closet where she sold pencils for profit.

"*Shhh.* You're ruining my state of denial," he said.

"Oh, they didn't tell you? I just assumed—"

"That would have spoiled the surprise, o worthy volunteer."

She gave him a pained expression. "Is the communication that bad?"

Richard backed away from the office, spun around, and burst out the front door. Mrs. Baines, pulling bus duty, nodded as he quick-stepped away. There was one thought on his mind: *Seven more weeks and I'll be free/From this school of misery.*

That afternoon, having worked through several more stages of grief—but still far from acceptance—Richard returned to school with his video camera to record *Malliford Idol,* the student talent show, a new event that almost became a casualty of the parent-principal war.

PTO Student Activities chair Sasha Bramblett had begun organizing the event in August. In March, right after Nick's suspension, the school's mental health professionals had tried to cancel the show, claiming in a memo that it "would damage the self-esteem of non-participants." By then, Richard knew that the two women simply wanted to kill all PTO initiatives. He battled them and prevailed after threatening to rattle chains publicly—"just like he does with everything else," according to Sarah Royston, the unhappy county school official who was ordered to come in and mediate the dispute (and who had seen quite enough of the PTO president's chain-rattling capabilities as a result of Nick's suspension).

As soon as he entered the school to watch the talent show, Richard felt uncomfortable. Unwelcome. How could he even set foot inside the building next year without the protective mantle of the PTO presidency around him? A transfer for Nick wasn't such a bad idea, but Richard was fairly certain the offer was off the table. Unless he wanted to make more trouble. Well, why stop now?

He tried to shake off the negative vibe the place was giving him. Nick was performing, after all. He was so proud of his son. Such a resilient kid. Living well—and playing well—would be his best revenge. To that end, Nick had diligently practiced his boogie-woogie piano piece all week. Richard stood along the wall near the stage in the darkened cafetorium, the only illumination coming from the hall and a spotlight on the stage. He saw Antonio, on crutches, leaning against the opposite wall. This was his first day back at school.

Nick, the third performer, drew chuckles when he took the stage wearing a trench coat, fedora, and sunglasses—a cross between Philip Marlowe and Blues Brother. He played the piece nearly flawlessly. At first, Richard hoped he'd win the grand prize, a fifty-dollar gift certificate at Eastwood Mall— then he realized Nick was the one kid guaranteed not to get it.

Following Nick there were bad guitarists, semi-accomplished pianists, karaoke singers, and even a brave and corny comic. The last performer on the program, a little girl with a purple ribbon in her hair, took the stage in the white dress she'd worn the first day of school. Mrs. Spinelli lowered the microphone for her. The girl pulled out her magnificent sparkling yo-yo and spun it up and down three times, then walked the dog with it. Some boys jeered her, but what happened next was even worse. The counselor stepped from the darkness and moved toward the stage, on track to halt Alicia Rodriguez's performance, which was running into the fifty-ninth minute of the program and threatened to put the assembly over its time limit.

Oblivious to the threat, Alicia pocketed her prize. Cassandra Hardwick stepped onto the stage. A hush fell over the crowd and Alicia started singing. The spotlight hit the counselor full in the face, freezing her in her tracks like a deer on a country road. When she recovered a few seconds later, she tiptoed down the steps, tracked by the spotlight, operated by stage manager Bertie Malloy.

The song was, *Lean on Me*, made famous by Bill Withers. Alicia sang perfectly, with no accompaniment except her own tapping foot. When she finished, the applause was loud and long, accentuated by hoots and hollers from both kids and teachers. Alicia's eyes shone in the spotlight as she bowed. It was a transcendent moment.

*   *   *

And what goes up must come down. That evening, Jane called Richard to tell him the nominating committee had chosen Susan Gunther as the next PTO president. To make things worse, she had accepted.

"And the children wept," he said.

"I gather you're not too pleased."

"That the PTO president will depend on Dear Leader for her daily bread? That the principal can run the PTO from her office, instead of running the PTO president out of her office? There are so many things to say, none of them civil."

Jane listed the other nominees, who also came from the Table of Trouble or its suburbs: Flora Frederick, vice president; the unpredictable Brenda Carroll, treasurer; Bessie Harper, corresponding secretary; and failed newsletter editor Danielle Morelli, recording secretary.

"A word of warning," Richard said. "You will have no minutes next year."

*   *   *

Tuesday afternoon, Reggie called. "Got big news," he told Richard.

"What?"

"We found him."

"Who?"

"Allen."

"Allen?" It took a minute to sink in. "Allen Boone? I didn't know you were looking. Where?"

"Right where Wilkerson left him. Or thereabouts. Yeah, I went out there a few times, but I realized, hey, this is an archaeological dig. So I hired a grad student—had to be bilingual, since I had a crew of Mexicans that had been working on the new office park. Anyway, it cost me, but ... *whoop*, there he is. His parents can't believe it."

"I can't either. This is taking a while ... actually, I'm not sure it's sinking in. You found him?"

"His bones, silver tooth and all."

"I'm just ... floored."

"And you knew where he was."

"Well, I remembered something, that's all. It must be sad for his parents."

"They're going through the grief all over again, but John Boone told me they were glad to live long enough to gain closure. He had an older sister, you know. She's still alive."

"I don't remember her."

"Well, the funeral is Saturday. Wanna come?"

"Hmm. Sorry. Kind of tied up here. Give my condolences."

"Come on. I'll give you a tour of the newspaper. Believe it or not, it's actually profitable. Small papers aren't getting hit like the big ones are."

"Not yet."

"You could put it online."

Time to change the subject. "So, what else have you been up to?"

"Talking to reporters for the last couple of days. But now that this chapter is finally closed, all I have to do is find Wilkerson."

"Come on. He's got to be dead by now," Richard said.

"Nah, Bro. Nothing that evil ever dies."

*   *   *

An hour after his conversation with Reggie, Richard got a call from Candace, who told him that Ann Marie Summers's house caught on fire. There was extensive damage, but the home wasn't destroyed.

"That's terrible," Richard said, although he didn't recognize the woman's name. "Should I know her?"

"Her kids go to Malliford," said the PTO's vice president. "Fourth and sixth grades, I think. Anyway, the fire started in a back bedroom, where they put the computer they bought from us."

"You mean from Aaron Roberts."

"She thinks the computer started the fire."

"I doubt it."

"The fire department is investigating. Does the PTO have insurance?"

"Yes, but doesn't she?"

"There's a deductible and she shouldn't pay it if the PTO sold her a bad computer."

"I've got another call coming in," Richard said. "Gotta go."

"But—"

"Bye."

* * *

Wednesday morning belonged to Teresa. Richard walked the mile to her house in the sunshine, jogging when he spotted a familiar-looking minivan coming up the street. It was no one he knew, but in his sleazy suburban world, all minivans were now part of a vast and vague surveillance network. According to plan, he went around back and let himself in the sliding door. The house was quiet. Teresa had told him she wanted to play Hide and Freak. He expected her to be waiting for him naked on the bed in her exquisite dungeon. He was half-right. She was propped on an elbow in a silver silk gown that draped her curves. He jumped on her, smothering her laughter with kisses, tickling her until they fell off the bed in a convulsive heap onto the plush, rose-colored carpet.

After they made love, they lay entangled on the floor. "Teresa Gray is a nice name. So tell me," she said, rubbing her nose along his neck. "Tell me, tell me, tell me what I long to hear."

"I love you. Did I guess right?"

She popped him on the shoulder with her fist. He laughed, then lay silent. Broken sunlight slanted through the tilted blinds and turned her smile golden. He loved her even though she forced him to say it. What he felt wasn't pure or absolute, but it was *something*, and the fact that it lived and grew in the rocky soil of his chest—that quarry cliff—made it special. Whatever it was, if he chose Teresa, it would have to do. And he knew that his day of reckoning was fast approaching. No point in worrying any more. He was caught in the pull of the waterfall. Which side of the river he landed on—which rocks he broke his back on—didn't matter. If he woke up in New Mexico with Teresa, that would be his life. As long as the boy was in the picture, life would be livable.

But there was no guarantee of that. Quite the contrary.

She poked him in the belly, then got up and looked through the blinds. He saw her eyes in the warm light, a strand of hair tucked behind her ear. She was so pretty. What if her scheme worked? Could they end up in Ridalia? He debated telling her about his brother's job offer, and decided against it. Better to go somewhere the ghosts couldn't find him.

* * *

Little Green Men won Saturday's game 4 to 3. Their second victory in a row fueled visions of glory in players and parents.

"I figured out your secret," said Anna Lee after the game.

"Which one?"

"How you got the team to perform so well."

"Simple, really. Tried-and-true coaching tactics, teamwork—"

"Pixie Stix. You pump them full of sugar during the game. That's why they dominated the second quarter."

It was true. They scored three points in the latter part of the first half and held on for the win. They'd run out of steam at game's end, giving up two goals in the last five minutes. If the game had gone on for another five, they would have lost.

"No rule against it," Richard said. He picked up his equipment bag. Three restaurant sugar packets tumbled out of a side pocket onto the ground. Anna Lee looked at him with amused disdain.

"What? What? It shut the parents up, didn't it?" He scowled. He'd had enough of her criticism and contempt.

They walked toward the Audi. Nick, trailing behind them, was already in a sugar coma. He ran into the side of the car without bothering to open the door.

* * *

Randall Wyatt called Richard Tuesday afternoon and gave him a preliminary report, interesting but incomplete: "Desmond isn't who he says he is. It's going to take more digging."

"I want to know everything," Richard said. "Dig all the way to Hell if you have to."

Wyatt laughed. "I've been told to go there before, not by anyone willing to pay my way."

"You'll find something there."

"Oh, I'm sure there's something."

"Fine by me. How much do you think this is going to cost me?"

"Hard to say. I could get lucky with my next phone call, or it could take a while. I'll give you a break on my fee, but it could get expensive."

"Give me an idea."

Wyatt gave him an idea. Richard whistled in stunned disbelief. "Whatever happened to fifty dollars a day and expenses?"

"Bogart died."

"OK." Richard sighed. "Let's do it. I've got money." As he said this, he felt like a trapeze artist in midair, reaching for a swinging bar. "It's worth it to see it through."

"I'm on it."

After he hung up, Richard tilted in his chair away from the desk and fretted over the hard choices he was making: Teresa over Anna Lee, crime over civic virtue, suspicion over faith. And he may have just lost his son. But there had to be a way to stay with Nick. There just had to be.

"What am I doing?" he groaned as he reached for the phone, but he did it anyway. He called Teresa and told her he'd committed the Treasure to the hunt for Desmond's past.

"We're in it together big-time now," his lover said, sounding quite pleased at the prospect.

*   *   *

After supper Thursday, the Grays played Scrabble. Both parents helped Nick so much that he won, inducing a bragging fit that lasted until his father picked him up by his ankles and hung him upside down. Nick was getting too big for this, however. The two of them tumbled to the floor in a heap and ended up wrestling. Anna Lee beamed at them.

She had been more affectionate lately, complicating matters for Richard. It was easier to contemplate leaving her when she was being bitchy. Richard thought she might be sorry for hating/nearly hating him so long. Or she'd reverted to mating mode, cruising for seed.

After they tucked Nick into bed, Anna Lee motioned for Richard to follow her to their bedroom. "Sit down," she said, patting the comforter beside her.

"What's up?" he asked.

"Relax," she said. "You've been so tense lately." She rubbed his shoulders.

"Lot of stuff going on, what with deadlines and all."

"I've got some news. Quite unexpected. Care to guess?"

"You tell me."

"'Unexpected' is a pun." He gave her a blank look. "God, Richard, you can be unbelievably obtuse. I suppose I should just say it."

"I suppose you should."

"I saw Dr. Taylor this morning. We're going to have a baby!"

He was dumbfounded. "You and me?" How could such a thing happen?

"Who else, silly?"

She hit him on the shoulder, jolting him out of his shocking news-induced daze.

"That's, wow, wonderful!" he touched her belly. "Shouldn't you be showing?"

"Give me time," she said, blowing out her cheeks and crossing her eyes. "There's so much to do. We've got to start planning. It's going to be hard to find a new place for what we can pay, especially with me at home. Or maybe we could convert the garage into an office."

"Or we could move," he said. One way or another he was getting the hell away from that damned school.

"I want to call my folks before Dad goes to bed. They'll be so excited." She hugged Richard's neck and reached over his shoulder to grab the phone. In her zeal to spread the good news, she hit him on the head with the receiver.

He went to his office, closed the door, and buried his face in his hands. A headache came with the rush of blood to his head. What the hell was happening? Everything that had been swinging Teresa's way had shifted back in an instant. He could never desert a pregnant wife. Especially not his. That would make him a major asshole, on par with Archie Gunther. Anna Lee had trumped him. She always won. No fair. He gulped; his throat was razor-dry.

His life had gone *clunk*; the car he'd been driving had shifted into reverse while roaring down the highway. Metal parts were shearing off and clanking on the asphalt as the vehicle disintegrated instead of slowing down. What the hell had he been thinking? Why had he told Teresa he loved her? It was a stupid thing to do, especially if he meant it. And he did. Now he wasn't sure what to do, or how to do it.

It was heartbreaking to realize he couldn't make love to his kinky treasure of a treasurer any more, no matter how hard she begged—and she was very good at begging. Excellent, in fact. Maybe ... no, it would only encourage her. For him, it would be like that one drink for an alcoholic. It was time to sober up. For the second time in his life.

Surely Teresa would understand he couldn't leave Anna Lee now. She had to. Then he thought about the Treasure. *Ewwh*. That would be tricky. But they had a deal: They'd pay Wyatt and give away the rest. This didn't change that, as far as he was concerned. Better yet, he'd cover Wyatt's bill somehow, and then he and Teresa would present the money—all of it—to Malliford's PTO as a fait accompli. Win-win. Teresa could take the credit. Brilliant!

On the other hand, what if his lover held a grudge—and a gun? He'd seen the Kellers' collection, which included a snub-nosed .357 revolver that could fit in a purse. She was always dropping dark hints about "getting rid of Carl." Maybe Miz Rutherford was right to want metal detectors at school.

When they went to bed, Anna Lee made a pass at him, which he accepted, since, as all men know, sex cures headaches. Afterward, she said it was the best she'd had in years. This also served to disprove his theory that his wife would freeze him out once she was safely pregnant, and made sticking around seem worth it. Sex could be so troublesome. It lured him away from home, and now it snapped him back. He was indeed the Yo-Yo Man, after all.

They broke the news to Nick the next morning.

"Do I get to keep my room?" he asked. "I don't see how, unless the new kid sleeps in your office. Or with you."

"We'll figure it out," Richard said.

"If it's a girl, I'm not sharing my room." Nick adopted a thoughtful pose. "I suppose this would be all right having a younger brother."

"Or sister," Anna Lee said.

"Brother," Nick said. "Yeah, it would be OK if he obeyed my commands."

"Babies don't obey commands," Richard said. "They give them."

*　*　*

Saturday morning, Little Green Men won their third game in a row, evening their record to three wins, three losses. "We're mediocre, we're mediocre!" Nick chanted, sharing a joke Richard thought was just between them.

Joshua Bancroft responded by punching Nick. Parents advancing across the field to offer post-game congratulations had to wait for Coach to break up the fight between his two stars. He told them both he'd bench them during the next game, but it was an idle threat, since they were his top offensive players. Each had scored two goals that day.

If the parents knew about Richard's coaching through chemistry, they showed no sign of caring, not after a 5 to 2 thumping of Benton's Bandits, one of the league's better teams.

"My guys are coming together," Richard told Anna Lee. "Their confidence and self-esteem are increasing. I think it's working out OK."

That afternoon, he cut the grass, obsessing about Teresa as the Briggs and Stratton engine roared and the lawn mower handle vibrated against his crotch. He tried to convince himself everything would be just fine. After all, what was happening was sane. Normal. He was saving his life, that's what he was doing. He shuddered when he realized he'd almost jumped off a cliff with that woman. But damn, she was fine.

*   *   *

Richard ventured into the office at Malliford Wednesday morning to check the mail. In and out quickly—hopefully without Susan noticing him, although the truth was that she ignored him most of the time, anyway.

In the hall, Jane stood by the school store closet, grinning. "I saw Anna Lee at Kroger last night," she said. "Congratulations!"

"Thank you." He glanced around to see if anyone had heard her and saw Teresa approaching, wearing the red sweater he so loved to pull off. He'd been avoiding her the past few days, and now he felt a noose tighten around his throat.

"Congratulations?" Teresa looked at him quizzically. "For what?"

"Haven't you heard? Tell her, Richard!"

"Anna Lee and I are having a baby!" he said, trying not to sound like a lookout spotting an iceberg off the starboard bow.

Teresa's stricken expression—a mixture of shock, pain, and betrayal—was a dead giveaway. After an incredibly awkward silence, she managed to say, "Oh, that's great," without bothering to smile.

Jane's eyes widened. If she hadn't suspected anything before, she did now.

Ms. Bailey, stopping to say hello, said, "Are you OK, Teresa? You look like you saw a ghost."

"I'll be all right," Teresa said through clenched teeth.

Ms. Bailey gave Richard a worried look as she moved away.

This was beyond awkward. Did she know, too? Did everyone know now? His gut told him they'd always known. *Run!*

A second-grader approached the store. Jane turned away to tend business.

Teresa whispered to Richard: "I need to sit down before I fall down." She plopped on the sofa in the foyer beside a chubby black pigtailed girl wearing a dark green skirt. A few seconds later, Teresa struggled to her feet. "I've got to get out of here."

"I'll walk you to your car."

"No! Stay the hell away from me!"

Susan glanced out from the office at the disturbance in the hall.

"You said 'hell,'" the girl noted.

"Damn right I did. Get over it."

Richard watched Teresa storm off. *So much for stringing things out.* He considered following her, then remembered the gun that fit in her purse and decided to let her go.

When he got home, the phone was ringing. The caller hung up when the machine took the call. A minute later, it rang again, and he picked up.

"That was rude, hearing it from Jane."

"I'm sorry you had to find out that way."

"How long have you known?"

"Just a couple of days."

"And you didn't tell me? Any chance it's yours?"

"Who else could it be?"

After an awkward pause, she said, "We need to talk, face to face."

He didn't want to talk. He wanted the affair to end. He wanted Teresa to understand. Accept. Move on. Balance the books.

But life couldn't be that simple. "HyperCafe in thirty minutes."

"Fine," she said. "I love you."

"See you soon."

*   *   *

Teresa arrived at the coffeehouse few minutes after he did. She had changed into a red dress, which seemed oddly formal. She'd been crying. He hoped this meant she knew it was over.

She knew no such thing. "Do you love me?"

"Yes." He said in a matter-of-fact voice, like he was answering a census-taker's question. "Let me get you a cup of coffee. What do you want?"

"Something strong to keep me going."

He went to the counter thinking she was in denial, but then realized he hadn't given her anything to deny. As far as she knew, the next thing they'd do would be to call an apartment-finder service in Albuquerque. He got her a cup of HyperCafe's famously strong blend and fixed it with cream and sugar. A cup of black coffee for him.

He set the white cup before her. She looked up at him, forlorn and hopeful. "I don't know why I'm upset. I mean, we have a deal."

"I have a child, and one on the way. I can't—"

"You *can*. We can do this. Believe me," she said with the tiniest of laughs. "If you think money's a problem, it's not. We can wait until the end of the school year, if you want."

He looked at her like she was crazy. "It's not going to change."

"It changed when you started loving me."

"It changed when you decided to leave Carl, before we even met. I'm just an accessory after the fact." He'd worked on that one while he was driving over, and that seemed like a reasonable way to look at things. Surely she'd understand.

"You're the man I chose. I didn't choose lightly. I need someone for the girls. They need a daddy. Carl's worthless as a father. As for your boy, you'll always ... I mean, we can have children."

"I'm not going to leave him. Or her." Or the other him or her, for that matter.

"This happens all the time. And we have a deal." She set her jaw and gave him a hard look.

Again with the deal. He shook his head. "It's funny... I disprove your point about how good I am if I go with you. How could you love a man who'd desert his wife and kids?"

"You're not deserting. You're switching to something that's better for you. You're not happy with her, and you deserve to be happy. It can be better for Nick, too." she said softly. "Come on. Be brave. Be strong. It can work out. I promise. I *need* you," she pleaded. "God, you've kept me alive this past year. I die a little each time he walks in the door." She started sobbing. "He hurts me and he doesn't care. I try to be all bright and shiny, but inside, I'm just one big bruise."

He sipped his coffee. Behind them, cups clanked in the sink.

He had to kill this thing, strangle it dead. He shook his head. "Nick."

She waved her hand. "Grab him and let's go! You're not doing him any favors leaving him here! God, this place is sucking out our souls!"

If that was true, it was already too late. His soul had already been sucked out. He'd just gotten it confused with the other thing since he'd met Teresa. Now here he was, saying goodbye, when he still wanted her as much as ever. But he couldn't tell her that. He had to be strong and let that thing inside him die.

Teresa leaned over and whispered, "Let's go to my house. We can have some privacy. He's out golfing today."

"No." He pulled his hands away. "It's over."

A storm swept over her face. "Really." Her expression hardened as the sleet turned to ice. "Did I miss something? Did I give you the impression that I'm some stupid little bitch? Did I give you permission to fuck me over? I told you I was in it for keeps, and I don't bullshit. If you leave me, you're going down!" She shook her head and gave him a disgusted look. "That's right. If I go, you're ruined. Ruined, do you understand? There's no going back," she hissed. "You're an embezzler."

"No. We'll tell the board about the Treasure Thursday night."

She slammed her fist on the table. "Don't be a fucking fool!"

"Hey!" called out the barista as other customers turned their heads. "Chill out."

That was enough for Richard. Chair legs screeched on the floor as he stood.

"Where the hell do you think you're going?" Teresa demanded.

"Down."

He walked out, marveling that he was more pissed off than broken-hearted. An ugly way for love to end, if love it was.

TWENTY-THREE

R ita called Richard an hour before the board meeting and said, "I'm resigning my position with the Harpy Valley PTA rather than endure Susan as president."

"Come on," he cajoled his steadfast and often annoying ally. "Bertie will graduate before she takes office anyway, and you'd forfeit your chance to outlast Lizzie Warden if you quit."

"You're right, damn it. I withdraw my resignation. But my only hope to see my dream come true is some kind of medical emergency." She made a choking noise, then hung up.

When he entered the media center just before seven o'clock that Thursday night, Richard searched the room for a friendly face without much luck. Rita was absent, and even more troubling, Teresa was a no-show. Jane, the double agent on the verge of defection, refused to look him in the eye. Candace and Cindi Lou, those cowards, were nowhere to be seen.

Meanwhile, the Table of Trouble was packed. Richard was sure the PWCs knew his secret. Apparently, his enemies smelled blood (or some other body fluid). He could see animosity in their eyes and feel their loathing across the room—breathing, alive, growing stronger every minute. They went on the attack before the meeting started. Susan said she was "deeply concerned" about Teresa's absence and had some questions about the budget. Did Richard know where she was? No, he said. She laughed derisively at his reply, but Richard had more pressing problems to worry about than what Susan thought of him, which wasn't much to begin with.

The PWCs had another reason to hate him. Antonio's mother was suing the school system for negligence. The mountain of evidence Richard could provide her might cost taxpayers dearly and serve to reward personal irresponsibility—all because some minority kid's single mother didn't pick him up at school or teach him to look both ways before he crossed the street.

Stan showed up, only to be heckled. The whisper campaign against him had escalated into open contempt. Susan muttered about child molestation, and Flora Frederick accused Stan of arson. "We're gonna be sued for that computer fire," she said from the Table of Trouble, where she sat wedged between Susan and Bessie Harper. "He may as well have set the Summers house on fire himself with gasoline and matches."

"An overloaded circuit started the fire," Stan said, brandishing the fire marshal's report. "A waffle iron would have the same result."

This claim outraged Bessie, who shouted, "Why the hell would she have a waffle iron in the bedroom?"

To shut them up, Richard banged his fist on the podium (how he missed his yo-yo!), calling the meeting to order three minutes early.

All day, Richard had felt queasy about being there, and now, looking out over a not-too-friendly crowd, he decided against announcing Anna Lee's pregnancy. (From a public speaking standpoint, it's more than a little awkward to be caught between an expectant wife and a jilted lover.)

The meeting would turn into a humiliating waste of time, but at least the principal wasn't there. Ms. Bailey stood in for her, announcing that Miz Rutherford would hold a 4:00 p.m. news conference on Tuesday with Superintendent Johnson and Jack Desmond to officially kick off The Mentoring Initiative.

"She's bringing TV cameras to the school during No-TV Week?" Stan cried out in anguish. "That's sabotage! I move we pass a resolution to protest."

"Out of order," Richard said, raising his voice to be heard above the catcalls coming from Susan's crowd. "I will not consider any resolutions tonight." *Count the votes, dude.*

Ms. Bailey also said Standard Hightower Intellachievement Test results would be released soon. "We're hopeful Malliford will improve its standing, or at least hold its own." Wearing an anxious, hopeful grin, she crossed her fingers. "Think good thoughts."

On to business. When Richard's proposal to downscale his heroic Teacher Training plan was tabled on a motion by Barbara Hodges, he figured his presidency was over, for all practical purposes. He was now the lamest of ducks.

No-TV Week was on the agenda, and Stan gave an impassioned plea for everyone to get involved, "even if the principal thinks watching TV improves test scores"—a dig at Miz Rutherford's advice to students back in February.

Susan interrupted Stan to say, "How long is this going to take?"

Richard cut her off sharply. "You're not president yet and you don't have the floor. Let him speak. This is a good thing, he's doing, and he deserves our help and support. Is there anyone here who thinks turning off the TV every once in a while is a bad thing?" When no one raised a hand, he said, "Yeah, that's what I thought. We'll endure Tuesday's news conference, although it is undiplomatic and ill-timed, considering No-TV Week is an annual event and we were pushing it this year."

"You two were pushing it this year," Susan said.

Barbara Hodges whispered something to Susan, causing her to shut her mouth. Apparently she'd gone too far for PWC sensibilities. Meanwhile, a few unaligned board members murmured support for Stan's efforts.

All in all, it was an ugly mess of a meeting. After adjournment, everyone quickly left the building because a storm was in the air. When Richard got home, he didn't go inside. Instead, he hopped in the Audi and drove around for a while, pitying himself. The lights were on at Teresa's house each time he passed by. When it started raining, he returned home. Both Nick and Anna Lee were asleep. The Seth Thomas wall clock in the living room said 11 o'clock. *Wow.* Turned out he had a lot of self-pity.

He sat in the recliner in the family room and turned on the TV, hoping to find distraction from his troubles, but all it did was remind him about No-TV Week and Stan, the sorry bastard. He turned it off and paced, worrying about Teresa. Where was she? Why hadn't she come to the meeting? What had she done with the Treasure?

The phone rang. His heart rate shot up. He let the machine answer the call, realizing his mistake too late. He sprinted to his office, closed the door, and listened in horror as Teresa bawled and babbled incoherently. He erased the message, turned off his cell phone, and went around the house, unplugging phone jacks. As he fumbled around in the dark to disconnect the bedroom phone, Anna Lee rubbed her eyes and said, "Who was that?"

"PTO stuff," Richard said. "I'm sick of that shit."

"Bad meeting, eh?" She pushed herself up, resting on her elbows.

He sat on the bed and slumped against the headboard. "They're all bad. I can't wait for this year to end. I want to move away."

A tear trickled down his cheek, shining in the soft light from the street.

She reached up and stroked his face. He clasped her hand and thought they could still manage to have a happy marriage if he could admit they were stuck with each other and make the most of it. He'd learn to love Anna Lee again. Maybe, just maybe, things would turn out all right. There was always that chance.

* * *

Richard awoke from a fitful sleep and immediately sensed a disturbance outside. He closed his eyes hard, blinked twice. The clock's demon numbers told him it was long past midnight. He strained to hear what was going on, hoping it was nothing more ominous than the wind playing with tree branches but knowing that a bill had come due. He padded to the window and looked out. Through the light rain, he saw mist rising from the pavement underneath the streetlight. In the middle of Applegate stood a forlorn figure more terrifying to him than any bogeyman.

He dropped the cell shade back in place with an unnerving *clunk*. He couldn't let her stand out there; come morning, she would turn to stone. Or worse, she would knock on his door. What if she was crazy and had a gun? In any case, it was his withered heart's duty to respond—and to at least spare his family the madness he'd brewed. This was the moment they should have had the other day, if only they'd kept their tempers, but maybe this was a good thing. More *Casablanca*, less *Pulp Fiction*.

He slipped on jeans and sneakers, found a sweater on the floor, fumbled for his glasses. He peered out again. Where was her car? *Oh God. Carl threw her out. Wait. Wasn't he a thousand miles away?* Richard couldn't keep track. He really wasn't good at this sort of thing; perhaps that came with practice.

He snuck through the house, accompanied by the clunk of the icemaker and the tocking of Seth Thomas. He clicked the deadbolt open, stepped outside, and squished softly toward her. A balmy Gulf breeze whispered through the leaves.

Teresa wore a trench coat and tennis shoes. Her hair was wet, and she looked jaundiced in the streetlight's pale yellow glow. A motorcycle screamed up Windamere and wailed off into the distance. Anna Lee was a sound sleeper, but if she woke and peered out the window there could be no explaining what was going on.

"Drive," Teresa said softly, lightly touching his arm.

Her breath smelled of gin. He moved out of the bedroom's line of sight, forcing her to follow him. When they stopped, he looked into her face, a mixture of hope and desperation. "I can't."

She lifted her arms in the air. "What have you got here that's so important? She doesn't need you. She doesn't want you. I do. I do, I do, I do." She poked him in the chest to hammer home her point with digital exclamation marks.

"I have my family. My home. I can't keep doing this."

"It's broken. You broke it, loving me. And you do love me. You're not taking that away. I'm not letting you lie to me, not about us. I'm not letting you break us."

"This hurts."

"Well, *duh*. Welcome to the world of the living, you bastard." She thumped him on the chest with both fists.

He grabbed her wrists tightly. "Shush."

"I need you," she said. "Not like she does. She needs you like Carl needs me. Somebody to put their world in order, nothing more. You're not happy. You deserve better. This is your last chance. You've got to take it," she said, sobbing. "Please."

"The Treasure—"

"I am the Treasure." She pushed against him, opened her coat, and nuzzled him. No bra. "Don't tell me you don't need me."

He pulled away. "Carl's not home, is he? You should be with your kids. What if something happened?"

"God, you're such a putz. It's the boy. It's always been the boy. Bring him with us. Get him now. This house is on fire; they're all on fire." She spread her arms to include the whole of Applegate. "Carry him out and save him from this suburban nightmare. We'll drive all night. We'll be three hundred miles away by daybreak."

"I can't. I've got a baby to think of. I can't stay out here. It's over, Teresa."

Her shoulders slumped. "I'm sorry, then."

"You don't have to—"

"No. I do. I did something. I thought it would help us be together, but I guess it's too late for that." She reached into her pocket and pulled out something. "You're it."

For a second, he thought she was going to shoot him, but she handed him the item instead. She turned and walked away. He thought for a moment that he should give her a ride home, but he couldn't move forward. All he could do was retreat. He watched her until she turned up Windamere, heading toward the school, and disappeared.

It's done, then. It's done.

Under the streetlight, he looked at what she'd given him—a passbook from Superior Savings. The Treasure. She was a good person, after all, turning it over to him. Draped in the passbook like a page marker was a set of miniature fetters: a chain gang keychain.

He slipped back into the house and clicked the lock shut. All quiet, except for the tick-tock of time slipping away. His hair was damp. He went into the master bathroom, danced through the familiar darkness, found a hand towel, dried his head, and pulled off his clothes. He stood in the darkness, his silhouette in the mirror. *Soccer game Saturday. Was that tomorrow?*

He took his keys, muffled their jangle, tossed his clothes in the hamper, and returned to bed.

Anna Lee's eyes opened. "Where were you?"

There was a painful silence before he answered. "I heard a noise outside, so I went to check."

"What was it?"

Think, think. Something with a bit of truth in it. "A small creature."

"A possum?"

"Maybe."

"My hero. Fighting off the possums that threaten our home."

Anna Lee rolled over and went back to sleep. She spent much of the rest of the night groaning her way through what sounded like a long, erotic dream with a cast of thousands.

He lay in bed until dawn, pondering imponderables. What would life have been like if he'd run away in the rain with the woman he loved? He imagined their son, the new boy she promised him, and mourned their stillborn chance at happiness, cursing himself for being so weak and allowing himself to dream, when he knew that dreams eventually turned into nightmares, and his only hope was to wake up.

* * *

In the morning, after Anna Lee and Nick were gone, Richard looked at the Superior Savings Association passbook and saw the account balance: $25,642.69. Hallelujah! He tucked it away in his desk drawer. He'd spring it on the general membership next Thursday, giving Teresa full credit for her great achievement, of course. Then he'd spend it on teacher training before Susan and her boss could say "Persian rug." He did hope that Teresa had come to her senses and quit wandering the neighborhood like a zombie, bur really, at this point, what could he do?

He worked on a new client's newsletter, enjoying peace and quiet until he realized he'd shut down all phone service. He switched on his cell and plugged in all the jacks, but no one wanted to talk to him. Well, the feeling was mutual.

In the afternoon, he took a nap, waking up just before school dismissal.

When Richard arrived at school, Nick was sitting alone in the classroom. No Mrs. Little. Strange. Richard felt the world receding. People were avoiding him. Fair enough; he would return the favor. As they exited the door by the Dumpsters, Nick chided his father for the breach of etiquette and looked back at the safety cadet, who wagged an admonishing finger at them.

They went home, and Nick settled in at the family room computer to play games. Richard heard a car stop on the street and the mailbox door clang shut. When he went outside, the car was gone. In the box he found a memo dated that very day, April 20, from Miz Rutherford to all faculty and staff. "Malliford Elementary will not participate in No-TV Week," she wrote. "Do not hand out event materials to students. Please collect any materials that any other organization, individual, or entity has tried to distribute."

Was the memo's delivery intended as a heads-up by an ally—or a boastful taunt from his enemy? And did Miz Rutherford consider Stan an individual or an entity? He could see the principal driving down the wrong side of the street and sticking her withered old arm out the red Cadillac Seville's window to deliver this lowest of blows. Hell, he wouldn't be surprised if she put one in every mailbox on the street, just to make sure the message got delivered.

Poor Stan had busted a gut all year planning the event, hoping half the kids would participate. Richard had seen the gratitude in Stan's eyes for his support during last night's meeting, which had not gone well for either one of them. And now this, on top of that. Did the principal really hate Stan so much that she'd wreck a scheduled event just to spite him? Hell, yes, although she'd prefer to pretend that Stan didn't exist. Since she couldn't do that, she'd blow up his big event just to show him who's boss—after she and her minions had destroyed his family. This was a certifiable outrage. Inexcusable. No wonder she skipped last night's meeting. She couldn't stop cackling!

But there was another motive at work. Richard recalled two of the sponsors for The Mentoring Initiative were CableSync and Gamerstores. *Ah.* She wanted no vestige of anti-TV activism during her news conference Tuesday, when cameras would record her greatest triumph. TMI gave her the perfect excuse to grind her high-heeled jackboot into Stan's face and sabotage No-TV Week.

And her timing was impeccable. Obviously, she'd learned her lesson from *Malliford Idol*. She wouldn't give Richard a chance to go over her head this time. No, she'd jerk the rug out from underneath them at the last minute!

And next year, it would be a Persian rug. All hail Estelle Rutherford, Queen of the Damned!

"Fuck you!" he screamed, flushing sparrows from the oak tree across the street.

With his gut tied in a knot and his head pounding, Richard stomped back to the house and stood in the foyer, folding the memo over, pressing the fold, trembling, pissed beyond belief. How could he even talk to her about this? She'd give him that smug smile. It was hard enough looking at her evil old wrinkly face to begin with. He wouldn't be able to stand the sight of her after this.

Nick's backpack was lying in the middle of the foyer. He dug through it and found a note about No-TV Week along with a pledge card—like the ones Stan distributed last year, not this year's. A day-old photocopied note by Mrs. Little told students to complete their pledge and have it signed by a parent. Then they would get a fifty-point bonus in social studies.

Well, somebody wasn't with the program. Maybe she didn't get Rutherford's memo. Then again, Mrs. Little had a tendency to lose correspondence that offended her sensibilities. *Good for her. Maybe she'd give her boss a stroke.*

Soon after that, the phone rang for the first time that day. It was Stan, upset because he'd called Karen and learned she didn't bring home a No-TV pledge card. "Is it just Vandenburg or is it—"

"Orders from the principal," Richard said. "With Mrs. Little being a notable exception." He proceeded to read the memo to Stan, who frequently interrupted him with screams and curses.

Richard tried to calm him. "I'll talk to her and tell her I'll write another column in the *Sentinel* if she doesn't back down." That sounded like a lame threat because it was.

More yelling from the other end of the line: "That fucking bitch has gone too far!"

"Stan. Calm down. I'll meet you at the school at eight sharp Monday, all right?"

Stan hung up on him.

Shit. Richard called the school and left a voicemail for the principal. Then he tried her cell phone with the same result, and finally—for the first time ever—left a message at her home. Not expecting to hear back from her, he was shocked when the phone rang a minute later. Gearing up for confrontation, he went into his office to take the call.

"Mr. Gray? Randall Wyatt here. I've got results."

Richard was caught completely off guard. "Say what?" He had to think for a moment before realizing this was a good thing. Maybe. "When can I see them?"

"As soon as—let's see, the balance is ... twelve thousand, six hundred dollars. We're closing for the week. Can you bring in a certified check Monday? I should be in the office all day ... Mr. Gray?"

Richard was literally floored. His back slid down the wall and he landed butt-first on the office carpet with a dazed look in his eyes. He touched his right temple with his free hand and felt a vein throb. For a moment, he thought he was leaking blood but then saw it was only a trickle of sweat. "That's a bit more than I thought it would be," he said.

"I understand. I spent a lot of time on it. Believe me, you got your money's worth."

"I'll be there." Richard hung up.

And there went half the Treasure, along with his heroic plan to reveal it at the next meeting.

Nick came in a few minutes later and asked if he could watch a movie. Richard still had his back to the wall, with his legs splayed out on the floor. The boy picked up his hand, checked his wrist for a pulse, then dropped it. "I need to watch a lot of TV before Monday, because after that I can't watch it for a week."

"OK," Richard groaned.

When his body chemistry had recovered enough for him to function, Richard tried to rally the troops for No-TV Week, sending out e-mails and making phone calls, trying to sound both reasonable and betrayed. He made some headway, but he knew the damage had been done. No TV-Week was the latest casualty in the Chain Gang War, but it would not be the last, for the real carnage was yet to come.

* * *

Saturday afternoon, Richard sat at the kitchen table in his blue coach's shirt and GYSA cap, penciling in the lineup for the game. "What's wrong?" Anna Lee asked. "You look unusually somber for a soccer coach going for his fourth win in a row."

"Buncha stuff." A moment passed. "Shit." He scratched out a name and drew in another. "Gotta keep the lineup even, quality-wise."

"You're taking coaching much too seriously, dear." She kissed him on the back of the neck. "Nicky!" she sang. "Are you ready for the game?" When there was no response, she went to check on the boy.

The phone rang. Richard cursed, and then, moving like a seasoned snake handler, snagged the call. "Is this Gray?"

"Who's calling, please?"

"Do you know what I'm calling about?"

"I'm sorry. Who did you say you were?"

"Carl Keller. I hear you may know where my wife is."

Richard told himself to remain calm. "Oh. Carl. No, I haven't seen her the past few days."

"I heard you been seein' a lot of her. Now she's gone."

"Gone? She didn't come to the meeting Thursday night, but—"

"Cut the shit. Do you know where she is?"

"No. Sorry. Wouldn't know."

"Like I said, that's not what I'm hearing."

"I don't know what's going on, OK? So you tell me."

"Yesterday, between the time school let out and when I got back from Denver, she took off with the kids, the van, a trailer, and our bank accounts. She also maxed out the credit cards. The bitch cleaned me out."

"Don't talk about her that way."

"You're lucky I'm talking at all. I should put a bullet in your fucking face, but here's where you get lucky, you little fuck. She took my guns. Otherwise, I *would* blow your brains out. I might still, if I could find a credit card *that fucking worked*!" He screamed the last few words.

"Stay away from me!" Richard snapped.

"Be a man. Tell me. Have you been fucking my wife?"

"I don't have to sit here and listen to this."

"I'm going to ruin you, you fucking son of a bitch. Then I'm going to kill you. Tell me where she's going. I need to find her."

"I understand you're upset," Richard said, hoping to calm the man down. "You want your family back."

"I want my money back, asshole!"

So she was right all along about her husband. In that case, he didn't owe Carl anything—not the time of day or even the general direction Teresa was heading. "I don't know where she went."

"I want those videos she took, too. And if I ever find out you're in any of them, I will hunt you down and kill you in front of your fucking family!"

"You're talking nonsense. I'm not going to listen to this filth. You come near me and I'll swear out a warrant."

"You better watch your back, asshole."

Richard hung up; his hand trembled. When he turned around, he saw Anna Lee standing three feet away, her eyes bright with tears. A twisted smile played on her lips.

Richard had a horrible realization. "Were you listening in?"

"So tell me," she said, her voice quavering, "How's your little possum? Or should I say *where*?"

"It's nonsense. A misunderstanding. I can explain, uh, after the game."

"*Now*." She fumed, arms crossed, muttering under her breath, "I knew she was trouble from the get-go, wearing those fuck-me outfits to PTO meetings."

"We'll talk after the game." He stood up and brushed past her. She threw an elbow, a hard shot that hit him under the ribs. He doubled over and winced in pain.

Nick had trouble finding his socks, his shoes, his shin guards and his ball. Richard helped him search like he'd never helped before. And where was his water bottle? No time to find it. They'd buy water at the concession stand. They were already running late when they climbed into the van. With a deep, empty feeling in his stomach and a headache pouring into his skull like a load of Ready-Mix cement, Richard took the wheel. His face felt like it was on fire.

Anna Lee stared straight ahead. Halfway to the soccer fields, she burst out sobbing.

"What's wrong?" Nick asked. "Did you hit her, Dad?"

"No," Richard said. "Don't be silly."

"Worse than that," Anna Lee muttered. "Worse than that."

That's ridiculous. Who'd prefer a beating? Someone who's never gotten one, that's who.

He stared straight ahead and tried to concentrate on soccer. Alas, Richard had neglected to give Nick his sugar boost. He could only hope that oversight would pay dividends in the second half. He'd have to shuffle playing time accordingly.

On the field, he discovered his players had prematurely self-medicated themselves into oblivion. Nick was the only Little Green Man who wasn't in a sugar coma the first quarter, and they were down by two points soon after the game started. Richard was doing no better than his players. He was too distracted to coach, trying to come up with a way to rescue his marriage. It wasn't fair. It shouldn't blow up in his face now, after he'd chosen Anna Lee and his ride had left town without him.

During the second quarter, a mother confronted him on the sideline. "Tad's diabetic!" she yelled. "What are you doing giving sugar to kids?"

Richard didn't look at the woman at first. Instead, his gaze swept the field, the stands, and park grounds to see who else and what else might be coming to get him. Only then did he looked her in the eye and protest, "He never told me!" He reached in his coach's bag and grabbed a folder. He pulled out Tad's medical release form, which she'd filled out. There was no mention of diabetes. "Go back to the bleachers!" he yelled. "Parents aren't allowed inside the fence precisely because of this kind of thing! Look! They just scored on us again! I gotta coach!"

She wouldn't leave, though. Instead, she harangued him until the field marshal showed up and escorted her away. Richard never regained his composure after that, and Little Green Men took a severe beating. Final score: 11 to 3. Richard fled the field in defeat, hounded by harpies, demons, jealous husbands, hostile mothers, and angry wives, the most furious of which was his.

"The team sucked today," Nick pointed out.

"Some days are like that," Richard said, sounding even glummer than his son.

After they returned home, Nick took a shower and watched a movie. Anna Lee secluded herself in the bedroom and made cell phone calls. When Richard knocked on the door, she shouted, "Get the fuck out of my house!"

He retreated to his office. He looked up from the computer to see her standing in the doorway, staring at him with loathing in her eyes.

"I talked to some people," she said. "Turns out I'm the last to know. How long has this been this going on? Don't act like you don't know what I'm talking about. Fucking Teresa Keller."

"I don't see any point—"

"You know, you're right. So very, very right, as usual. There's no point. We're past the point. So tell me the truth or leave right now."

"OK. Come in." He offered her the spare chair. She refused to sit.

He told her a short version of the truth—very short. No point telling her he'd considered leaving her, since she was just about ready to make that happen on her own. No, he stressed that he'd broken off the relationship with Teresa. Which was why all this madness was happening. "Ironic, eh?"

"Fuck you," she replied. "I don't know what I'm going to do. I'm not going to forgive you just like that. God. I don't even know you. I should leave you. Or kick you out. I'm not some suburban housewife who has to cling to her husband, you know. I make a good living. What were you thinking—that I'd put up with this? Possum! Did you think you could play me for a fool?"

"I'd already told her it was over. She came back one last time—"

"Could you sleep somewhere else tonight?"

"I'll take the couch," he said glumly.

"I was thinking a different zip code."

"No."

"Fine. I will. And I'll take Nick with me."

"Settle down. Let's not drag him into this."

"You know what? I don't like being ordered around by a cheating asshole."

She exited, slamming the door. The rest of the evening, she practiced militant aversion, locking Richard out of the bedroom when she retired. He slept on the sofa and reminded himself to call Reggie and find out how long these freeze-outs lasted. After three wives, his brother would know.

*   *   *

Sunday, Anna Lee took Nick to First Methodist Church, seeking comfort and strength in a sanctuary that was safe from Richard, a place he could not enter lest his head bursteth into flames. *How worthy is the faithful spouse! How much weight his word carries! And how like a skunk-sprayed dog is he who is caught casting his seed in a bush far from home!*

Richard took his notebook computer to Java Joe's, a place not haunted by the ghosts of his affair. He tipped the barista three bucks, plugged his laptop into a wall socket, and proceeded to camp out for the day. He had Healthnet articles to edit, so he didn't have to concentrate, which was a mercy, since he was incapable of deep thought. Even so, he spent much of his time brooding on his plight. If Teresa had pulled up in front of the coffeehouse right then, he would have grabbed his computer and hopped in her van like he was being chased by a serial killer. How sad to be regretting regrets, but such was the life of Richard Gray. "Shit," he said. "Shit, shit, shit."

"Need to switch you to decaf," said the barista from behind the counter.

Richard shook his head to clear it. "You wouldn't believe the stuff I'm going through."

"Sunday mornings," the server said as he clanked coffee cups in the sink. "Weeks crash into Sunday morning, and you end up with rubble."

The cheating husband sadly agreed. "Rubble is exactly what I have."

*   *   *

Richard returned to Applegate Sunday evening and moved like a trespasser through the house until it was time to bed down. Once gloriously defiled, the family room sofa was now the loneliest spot in town. Burned out from worrying, he fell asleep on it almost immediately.

In the deep of night, he woke and saw a silhouette against the drapes. "What is it, Nick?"

"I want to sleep with you. Mommy's door is locked." Nick snuggled in. "I'm afraid you're going to divorce."

"No, no, that's not going to happen. I love Mommy very much, and she loves us, too—"

"She doesn't love you much right now."

"Well, she's hurt and angry. She has a right to be. I did wrong."

"Did you do like President Clinton? Mommy said he dated another woman while he was married, and that's wrong. She said if I ever did that to *my* wife, she'd disown me."

"Did she tell you that today?"

"No. Last year. Did you date another woman?"

Ouch. He licked his lips. It seemed inappropriate to confess to his son, wrong to be under an eight-year-old's jurisdiction. But there he was, forced to teach by bad example. "Yes."

"Why?"

Why, indeed. "When I look back, there's no good reason. You know how when you do something that's wrong, and you know it's wrong, and you just hope you get by with it, and then you quit doing it, but people find out about it anyway, and you just wish you hadn't done it and they hadn't found out about it and it would just go away, but it doesn't?"

"Yeah."

Richard was amazed his son had followed that, since he'd lost track himself. "Well, grownups make mistakes like that. That's what I did."

"I think you did it because you're president, and presidents think they can do anything because they're so powerful."

"I'm not so powerful," Richard said.

Nick giggled.

"What's so funny?"

"You're sleeping on the couch. That makes you not powerful."

"Let's get some rest, buddy."

Nick curled up beside him as he pushed himself into the sofa's cushions to make room. They lay quietly and listened to the distant rumble of an early morning train.

"I'm never going to be president because I don't want Mommy to disown me. It's not worth it to make her mad."

"No, Nick, it isn't. You'll be a better president than me."

"I'm smarter than you, too. I know not to make Mom mad and I'm eight. You're—"

"Old enough to be president. Now go to sleep. There's not much time left before tomorrow becomes today." Richard wanted sleep because he dreaded thinking about the coming day. There would be much nastiness ahead, starting with an evil woman and ending with an evil man, and somewhere in the middle he'd have to figure out how to pay for the hard, stupid choices he'd made.

TWENTY-FOUR

Richard awoke on the sofa to see Anna Lee emerge from the bedroom in a black business suit. Down to primal morning emotions, she grunted in distaste when she saw him. She retrieved the *Sentinel* from the drive while he started coffee. As he rattled around the kitchen, she eyed the Krups machine warily, as if debating whether or not to drink the man's swill.

"I'll take Nick to school today," he said in his most helpful voice, practically begging for the chance to re-enter the daily routine. "I've got some unpleasant tasks to do today."

She kept her gaze on the paper. "You *are* an unpleasant task."

"It would help if we could talk."

"Try talking to *her*. Oh, right. She disappeared. What's up with *that*?"

He glanced apprehensively toward their sleeping son. "How long are you going to act this way?"

Her eyes took in the walls and ceiling before fixing on him. "How long were you sleeping with her?" Her voice rose as she spoke, causing Nick to stir. "*Shhh*."

"How about this? Don't try to shut me up or put me down any more."

"Sorry." He held up his hands. He couldn't recall having done either of those things. In fact, he was sure that she was the one who dished out the abuse, but how could he prove it? How could he prove anything, when his life had been a lie?

"I thought you were a decent man. Now I've got no idea who the hell you are."

"Maybe we could get counseling."

"How about we cut off—" she couldn't bring herself to name his offending member "—you bastard!"

She grabbed her briefcase, stormed out the door, returned, brushed her teeth, kissed Nick, and stormed out again. Richard held the paper with trembling hands and tried to read. People were dying, cars were colliding, diplomats were failing, and most American high school seniors were unable to find Turkey on a world map. Things were tough all over.

Nick struggled into the kitchen, his eyes half-closed. "I think Mom's still mad."

"Eat your breakfast."

After Nick was fed and dressed, father and son trudged up the hill. Nick was burdened by his backpack, Richard by his file on No-TV Week, a celebration betrayed—*now there was a movie-of-the-week title!*—and his unconfirmed appointment with evil. As they neared the school property, Richard witnessed something exceeding strange: A police car rolled down the hill past him, traveling away from Malliford. Miz Rutherford sat in the back seat, making Miss Daisy gestures at the officer behind the wheel. It seemed too much to hope for, but there it was. Adrenaline rushed into Richard's bloodstream, causing manic glee: *They finally got the old bitch!*

"Did you see that?" he asked.

Nick looked around. "What?"

"Never mind." Richard considered it tragic that his son had missed the most joyful sight an oppressed schoolboy could ever hope to see.

They crossed the street. Mrs. O'Malley, the new white-haired crossing guard, gave Richard a perplexed look. "Wish I knew," he said with a shrug. Ahead, a cruiser and an unmarked police car were parked in the loop, creating a bottleneck. A bus driver edged her yellow Bluebird through the narrow lane. Near the building, Mrs. Baines tried unsuccessfully to break up a growing cluster of kids, and a burly white uniformed police officer stood next to a black detective in a suit who was writing on a pad.

"I bet the police shot D," Nick said. "He has a gun. That's what he told me."

"They didn't shoot anybody. There's something on the sidewalk." As Richard drew closer he saw a busted television. "Stan I am," he muttered under his breath. The bell rang. "Get to class or you'll get a tardy slip." Nick proceeded reluctantly, staring at the broken set as he passed by.

Richard asked, "What's going on, Mrs. Baines?"

She regarded him suspiciously. "Your friend threw a TV at Estelle."

"Oh, come on. That's ridiculous."

"Really, Mr. Gray," she said in her best cut-the-nonsense voice. "He chased after her with the set, but he could only throw it a couple of feet and it didn't hit her. Coach came out, and he ran away."

"Who are you?" the detective asked Richard.

Mrs. Baines pointed at Richard like she was viewing a police lineup. "He's the PTO president, Richard Gray. He's very close to Stan McCallister. They may be in this together."

Richard went into Detention Avoidance Mode: "I wouldn't say—"

"You know where he lives?" the cop asked. "They don't have a current address or phone number in the office."

He couldn't harbor a fugitive TV-thrower, could he? "I've got a number." Richard flipped open his cell phone. To Mrs. Baines, he said, "I can't believe you don't have his number. I bet it was lost on purpose." The detective shook his head as he wrote down the information and handed it to the white cop, who sauntered off with the note.

"Karen's mother is coming to get her," said Mrs. Baines. "We're concerned something bad is going to happen."

"Don't be silly," Richard said. "All year, he'd been planning to break a TV to start the week."

"He did it in anger," said Mrs. Baines. "Intending to harm."

"Oh, come on," said Richard in exasperation. "Cut the crap. His plans for No-TV Week are a matter of public record. That TV was heavy. I'll bet he just dropped it, and as usual, this school's administration is trying to criminalize his behavior." He looked the cop in the eye and said, "I'm not sure you should believe them."

"So you know what this is about?" the detective asked. "Why would he threaten the principal? She said she had no idea why he would have a grudge against her."

Richard laughed. "No idea? That's completely dishonest. They hate each other, but Stan's not violent. He was talking about doing this back in August and even wrote about it in a newsletter article. What happened was that we got double-crossed."

Mrs. Baines was outraged. "Are you calling our principal a liar?"

"Yes. And it sounds like she's making false statements to police."

"Well, I never!" And she wasn't about to, either, choosing to retreat from the dispute and move toward the schoolhouse door. Richard continued: "Today was supposed to start No-TV Week. It's a national thing. People go without watching for seven days." He showed the cop the principal's memo. "And then it got canceled without notice after the PTO planned it all year. Stan was the chair of No-TV Week."

"You're saying she killed his baby."

"And there was a child-abuse investigation against him in January, after he circulated a petition calling for the principal's replacement. Along with a couple of years' worth of stuff leading up to that, starting with dirty bathrooms."

"Bathroom?"

"Yeah that's where it started. I was going to meet Stan to talk with her this morning. I guess that's off, although I doubt if she would have met with us, anyway."

"What kind of car does Stan McAllister drive?"

"An old white Corolla. ... So where'd they take the principal?"

"She went to swear out a warrant."

"Wow. So it's down to that, is it?"

The detective asked Richard for the memo, so they went inside to make a copy. Susan Gunther charged into the workroom after them. "What happened to the Keller girls?" she demanded. "Carl's been calling everywhere, sick with worry. I told him you might know. I thought they were with you."

"Why would you think that?"

"Because you've been sleeping with their mother, Dick."

"My name's not Dick."

"It is now." Susan spun on her heel and left.

The cop let out a low chuckle. "Ah, yes. I remember now. Chain Gang Elementary."

"You got that right," Richard said. "If you don't need me, I'll be about my business."

After giving the detective his cell phone number, Richard went home and took a shower. The phone was ringing when he got out. He listened as the machine took the call: "I'm going to get a lawyer. I want a divorce, and I want you to move out. *Today.*"

Before he could towel off and put on his pants, the phone rang again. This time, the message was from Ms. Pettit of Windamere Bank: "Mr. Gray, we need you to come down and discuss some urgent matters as soon as possible."

In the midst of a rising panic, he pulled out the PTO finance folder, found access codes, and called Windamere's automated banking line. The voice declared that the checking account was overdrawn. Hyperventilating, he checked the PTO's savings account, which supposedly held $7,000, or more than $30,000 if Teresa had deposited—

"This account has been closed."

"*Noooooo!*" he howled. Blood rushed to his head. Everything would be all right. Well, maybe not all right but mostly all right, if—

"The bitch cleaned me out," Carl said. *Why should I fare any better?*

Wearing only a towel, he looked up the number for Superior Savings and made the call that confirmed his suspicions: The Treasure was gone. The account had been cashed out Thursday.

The PTO had no money. All gone.

He went to the bedroom and found the passbook under the bed, along with the tiny fetters. He threw both items in the kitchen trash can, then realized he needed to do a better job of destroying evidence. He pulled them out from amongst the coffee grounds and banana peels and stuck them in a baggie after wiping off his prints.

He finally got the message: He was going to jail. *She said she'd take me down. It's not over. She's going to frame me for this.* How could she, though? He wasn't involved in any embezzlement. She had to have forged his signature. That was the rule, after all: Never sign a blank check. The recollection came like a hammer stroke on a coffin nail.

Oh shit.

On Volunteer Day, out by the benches. There were two checks. She'd been nervous and defensive about it, hadn't she? Yes, because she was setting up her scam. She'd showed him receipts, paid by check. *Her personal checks, no doubt.* Next thing he knew they were lovers. She held the checks and found the Treasure of the Sierra Malliford—or vice versa—and plotted and planned. With him or without him, she was going to make it happen. His head spun. His knees buckled, and he grabbed the kitchen counter to keep from falling to the floor.

That little noir bitch! What was that book she bought the day we met?

He'd never know, but he expected he was living the plot. He gulped down a chilled bottle of water, feeling like a man stuck in the middle of a desert with no idea when he'd get more. What was he going to do? That depended on what happened. Best case scenario: Maybe they'd catch Teresa and force her to pay restitution. Then, he could quit the presidency and turn the reins over to Candace, who would shriek at the prospect like he'd dropped a horse head in her bed. Then, in twenty years, when all was forgotten, another man could be president. *Knock yourself out, dude.*

There was some money stashed away that he could get his hands on. It would be wrong to take it, and it wasn't enough to pay back all the money Teresa stole, but it would be enough to pay Wyatt. And since that seemed like the only thing within Richard's power to do, he set about the business of doing it.

He put on khaki pants and a button-down blue-striped oxford shirt. Then he drank a cup of coffee, just to jangle his nerves a little more. He tore down the cookie fortune that said, "You Can Let Each Day Build or Destroy You." After all, this was the day it had been waiting for. "Come on," he said, tucking the slip of paper in his shirt pocket, "You're coming with me. You get to watch."

He drove to Windamere Bank, still unsure of what he should do. Pulling into the parking lot, he noticed a black Crown Victoria with a government tag. No way was he going inside. He could spend the rest of the day tied up—or handcuffed. No guarantee Anna Lee would post bond, either. He kept driving, recalling wistfully that Teresa liked handcuffs. He never put them on, though. He didn't trust her to take them off. One stupid thing he didn't do.

On to the next stop, where he would pick up twelve grand to pay Wyatt. Easy pickings, really: Nick's college fund. He hated doing it, and stopped just short of hating himself for it. There were so many reasons to hate himself right then that stealing his son's future would just have to wait its turn. His mouth was dry as he pulled into the lot at Transnationbank. He went inside and conducted a simple transaction, closing out a joint money-market account that had been started with Anna Lee's inheritance from an aunt. They'd debated putting it in stocks or bonds, but they'd decided to play it safe. *Safe.* What an ironic word. Withdrawals only required one signature. The teller sent him to the customer service desk, where he asked the branch manager to make a certified check payable to Randall Wyatt.

With check in hand, he got into the Audi and sat for a moment, listening to the quiet dead emptiness of his life. He'd drawn his cards. Time to play them out. He would worry about the consequences later. Perhaps he could replace the money before Anna Lee found out, though he couldn't see how at the moment. He started the car, then turned it off. He pulled the chain out of the baggie and held it between his fingers for a moment before deciding to keep it as a memento of his pain. He got out of the car and threw the Superior Savings passbook in a trash can by the ATM. Then he moved on to the next station in his rolling train wreck of a day.

Richard stumbled into Wyatt's office shortly after eleven with his heart pounding and his thoughts a mix of curiosity and dread. Wyatt was expecting him, and the secretary waved him through.

"Have a seat." Wyatt said, eying him like a bright-eyed bird. "Chain Gang Elementary."

Richard wondered if Wyatt had heard any breaking news updates about an embezzler on the loose, but the detective seemed like a solid fellow, unlikely to let minor details stand between him and twelve grand. "So, you've got a report for me."

Wyatt tilted his head in a half-nod, half-shake. "There's the matter of payment."

Richard gave him the check. "I'm short eighty dollars. It's all I've got."

Wyatt regarded it for a moment, appeared to have a problem, then decided he didn't. "Close enough." He reached into a drawer and pulled out a thick manila envelope. He then gave Richard papers to sign. Wyatt put the forms with the check and handed over the envelope.

Richard didn't feel like reading right then, but he had to know, of course. "What did you find out?"

Wyatt adjusted his cuffs and straightened his name plaque on the desk before speaking. "Once upon a time, your man's name was Andrew MacGregor. As a child, he was involved with a lifelong pedophile named Waterston in Denver, Colorado. Waterston was the headmaster of a private school. MacGregor was teacher's pet. According to police reports, even as a student, young MacGregor was providing certain services for Waterston, working with younger students—I guess they call it 'mentoring' nowadays—and delivering them to the headmaster's private chambers for Waterston's pleasure. Waterston was busted in 1982. MacGregor, then in college, wouldn't testify against him. Such loyalty. Waterston was convicted on child molestation charges anyway. He was linked to a couple of missing-persons cases in other states but never prosecuted. Lack of evidence. A shame, really."

Wyatt produced a copy of an old newspaper article. Its photo caption said, "The Montgomery School's Valedictorian Andrew MacGregor accepts congratulations from Headmaster Simon Waterston."

"The master predator," Wyatt said. "His probation ended in ... let's see ... 1997. He must be in his mid-eighties, at least."

Richard stared at the photo and shook his head. What he was seeing was too much to deal with. *No*, he told himself. *You're imagining things.*

"MacGregor wasn't charged in that case, but he should have been, since he'd graduated from victim to co-conspirator somewhere along the line. He finished college, got a teaching certificate, got married, had a kid. A bright fellow, he advanced rapidly, becoming assistant principal at Pembroke Elementary in Boulder, Colorado. He had a slight misunderstanding with the neighbors involving their eight-year-old son. There was an incident report, lawyers lawyered, money changed hands, but no charges were filed. He moved to Arizona with his family and took a teaching job. Couldn't keep his hands to himself, unfortunately. Got arrested a year later following an incident in a library bathroom, this time with a nine-year-old boy.

"People weren't so forgiving this time. A warrant was issued, his wife divorced him, and he pleaded guilty to a felony. He served three years in prison, five on probation. He got out of jail and took a job in sales, but old habits die hard. A couple of years into his probation he was caught in the restroom of a Phoenix toy store with—surprise!—a partially dressed ten-year-old boy holding a fifty-dollar bill. It gets worse. Another boy in his neighborhood had been reported missing a week before that, and Desmond was questioned in that case. He didn't wait around for further interrogation. He jumped a fifty-thousand-dollar bond on the molestation charge and went on the lam, shed his old name like a snake skin, moved here, married a divorcee with money and an only child ... name of Christopher, adopted him, gave the boy his name, and became your problem. I think his wife is clueless about his past, and apparently he keeps his hands off the boy. Smart fellow. Doesn't want to foul up his own nest. Then again, the boy may not be his cup of tea. You see, all his victims were preadolescent African-American males. And that missing kid in Arizona was never found."

"Never found?"

"It's an open case, and your man is wanted for questioning."

Richard shuddered. "All this is nailed down?"

"Yes, sir. I got file prints, police reports, court records, divorce filings, and some interviews. I also listened to some cell phone calls ... but you don't want to know about that. A lot of it isn't admissible in court, but that won't matter. He's a bail jumper. They get special treatment."

"But he's a public figure. How did he avoid detection?"

"That's the big question. He had major reconstructive surgery, so he doesn't look like he used to. Prints match, though. I figure he took this job and angled it toward 'mentoring' so that he could get his hands on boys without going through the background checks a public school employee has to endure. Congratulations, Mr. Gray. You're saving your school a world of hurt. A word of warning, though. He suspects something is going on. One of my sources said he's been making calls. A little too late, I think." Wyatt smiled thinly. "I've contacted people in Arizona. The wheels are grinding."

"They told me you were the best."

Wyatt smiled. "What can I say? You got your money's worth, that's for sure. Look through it and let me know if you have any questions."

Richard pulled a folder from the envelope and glanced through the report. He had one overwhelming question. "Uh, Waterston—"

No, it was crazy. Too much to think about right now. "Never mind."

He shook Wyatt's hand, thanked him for his work, and left.

Outside, he leaned on his car, overcome by what he'd learned and what he now suspected. Yes, that photo, and the man who stood with Desmond. He had seen that face before. Deep in his bones, down to the marrow, he'd never felt right about Desmond, and beneath that, there was an even more longstanding and horrible antipathy he couldn't voice or understand. Maybe it was Desmond's smirk that reminded him of something or someone. *What goes around comes around.* And in this case, like a wayward comet, it involved an eccentric, decades-long elliptical orbit around Richard Gray. Then again, his mind could be playing tricks on this, the cruelest of days.

He drove away, knowing what he had to do next. He'd let Rutherford know, of course, for the sake of the school and its children, even though some people would think he was smearing Desmond to draw attention away from his own scandals. *You gotta admit it's a helluva diversion, though.* Then he'd resign as PTO president. But maybe not right away. He'd have to see how it played out.

As he drove up Windamere, he saw a large screw sticking out of a piece of wood in the road just before he ran over it. A second later, the right front tire blew out. Richard pulled onto a side street three blocks from Applegate and parked on a level section of pavement. When he opened the trunk, he found that the spare was flat, too.

"All part of my perfect day," he muttered. "I'll deal with this later."

He grabbed the folder from the front passenger street and began walking up the hill to deliver the news to Miz Rutherford, rehearsing the line he'd use: "I don't care what you think of me—"

Then he was struck by the obvious: He couldn't trust her. He had to make copies, which meant a detour to his house. When he was at the corner of Windamere and Applegate, he saw a black Crown Victoria sitting across from his house, so he kept walking up the hill.

He pulled out his cell phone and called the one person he could turn to. "Reggie," he said. "Look, I'm in a bit of a mess. Anna Lee is kicking me out of the house, my treasurer looted the PTO's bank accounts, and before I resign, I have to turn in an investigator's report on a child molester, but I don't trust the person I'm giving it to and I want you to hold a copy for me."

"Fax it over. I'll put it in my safety deposit box."

"Thanks," said Richard.

When he finished the call, Richard was on Rainwater Drive, in front of his back-fence neighbors' house. He cut across their yard and vaulted into his own and entered his house the back way, through the patio door. He went to the master bedroom and peered through the cell shades at the man in the black car, who wore a suit.

Richard whistled softly and said to himself, "This day is not going to end well."

Keeping the house darkened, he tiptoed to his office. The answering machine had been busy. There were five calls from board members who, after talking with Susan, wanted to know if Teresa had stolen the PTO's money. Candace's sobbing voice was gut-wrenching: "Should I take over? That's what Susan is telling me to do."

The air in the house was stifling. It was difficult to think or breathe. But there was work to do. He made a photocopy of Wyatt's report for himself, and then faxed one to Reggie. As he fed the last page into his machine, his cell phone buzzed. Feeling brave, he took the call, though he immediately worried he was being tracked or triangulated by the police.

"I heard somebody's been nosing around and I figured you were behind it, Gray. So what kind of lies are you trying to spread about me?"

The devil himself.

"How'd you get my cell number?" Richard asked, though he was sure Susan was Desmond's source.

"Word's out," Desmond said. "You're an adulterer and an embezzler. Your credibility's shot. No one's going to believe you."

Richard could see the man sneering. And suddenly, he felt a strange calm come over him. "No one has to believe me. It's a matter of record. An unbroken chain. Looks like the end of the road for both of us."

Desmond's voice turned anxious, jittery. "Look, we can make a deal. It would be a shame to destroy a program like the one I've built—"

"It's over."

So much for the charm. "I'm not letting some asshole ruin everything I've worked for. You're a dead man."

"If you want to kill me, you'll have to stand in line."

"Then I'll go where the line's shorter," Desmond said. "I'll kill your kid, instead."

And then, with a feeble beep, Richard's battery died. "*Gaaawww!*" He reared back to throw the phone against the wall, but restrained himself at the last instant and slammed it on the desk instead. No time for niceties. Nick was in danger, thanks to Dad. Richard wouldn't call the school when he could be there in five minutes. He grabbed the report, stuck it in the folder, and rushed toward the front door. As he reached to unlock the deadbolt, he remembered his car was gone and the police were waiting for him, so he slipped out the way he'd come in.

It was a nice day out, except for murder in the air. The trees had fluffed out in full greenery. A blue jay bitched about the decline of its neighborhood. A crow told him to get bent. Richard stopped running halfway up the hill to Windamere, gasping for breath, his lungs burning. *Just keep moving. You'll get there.* He looked over his shoulder to see if the black car was tailing him and returned to a jog. He crested the hill and crossed the street at the loop. It was after lunch and the early bus driver sat in her yellow Bluebird, infinitely patient, reading her Bible, as she had since Nick's kindergarten days.

Richard knew that Desmond's arrival at Malliford would not cause a ripple of concern, since he was there so often. Most likely he was just bluffing. After all, child molesters were notorious cowards, and Desmond was full of shit to begin with. Then again, there was that missing kid in Arizona and Desmond's high school graduation picture, where he posed with that master of evil who went by the name of Waterston that day.

Ahead, there was his old buddy, the underachieving security guard, ambling away from the building. For once Richard was glad to see him. *Wait.* The guy wasn't ambling. He was moving as fast as his pudgy legs could carry him. The fat bastard was running away! Something bad was happening.

Richard muttered an obscenity and sprinted toward the front door. He burst into the building just as Susan made a PA announcement: "Mr. Davenport, will you please report to the office. Mr. Davenport, please report to the office."

"Mr. Davenport" was the code for an intruder alert. Doors slammed shut up and down the front hall. As Susan stared at Richard, her face was a mask of dread, disbelief, and loathing.

"This is your fault!" she screamed out the office door at him. "Fix it, damn you!"

He heard a man yelling down the hall. Then Mrs. Little's booming voice filled the air. "If this is the day I meet Jesus, then it's a good day, sir."

"Nick!" Richard shouted, and took off running. Just as he hit his stride, he crashed into Stan, rounding the corner from the front hall to the office foyer, staggering both men. Breathlessly, Richard said, "Stan, help me! Nick's in danger."

Stan looked at Richard like he was crazy, then said, "You seen Rutherford?"

Even though Stan was holding an automatic pistol, it took Richard a moment to realize that his wayward board member was the intruder. By then, Stan was on the move, waving his gun like he was leading a charge. Over his shoulder, he said cheerily, "Come on, this is your lucky day! You get to watch the Queen Bitch die!"

"Stan! Don't!" Richard darted after him into the office and saw a shoe sticking out from under Susan's desk. Somehow, she'd managed to cram her ample bulk into the kneehole. "I never hurt my daughter, you lying bitch!" He took a shot at her, but his aim was off by three feet and he hit her computer monitor instead.

The stupidity of Stan's action stunned Richard more than the pop of his gun and the shattering plastic. "Stop it!"

Stan moved toward the principal's private office. The light was off. He tried the knob; it was locked. He peered into Miz Rutherford's darkened space like an Indian scout, hand over brow. Richard grabbed his shoulder just as he pulled the trigger. The bullet went through the window, but the wire-mesh glass didn't shatter.

"Stop it!" Richard shouted. "Don't make it worse!"

"Get off me." Stan struck him in the face with the gun barrel, and then hammered the window with its handle. Richard dropped his folder and tried to grab the weapon. On his back swing, Stan cut Richard's lip and chipped his right eyetooth with the hammer. Richard staggered backward, holding his bloody mouth as Stan haphazardly aimed the gun at Richard's face. Richard took a step back, and Stan started industriously banging away at the window. When he'd knocked out a large enough hole, he reached through with his left hand and, bleeding from several small cuts, groped for the door handle. Susan chose that moment to escape. Richard moved to block Stan's aim in case he tried to take another shot at her.

"My tooth hurts," Richard said. "Anyway, Rutherford's not there."

"I know she is. Stay out of my way. I'm going to retire the bitch right now." He opened the inner door and turned on the light. Richard stumbled in on Stan's heels. He was amazed to see Estelle Rutherford in her trademark blue suit, cornered and hissing, a feral gleam in her eyes, gripping a sterling silver letter opener in her right hand, prepared to go down fighting. *What a gal.*

"She's not worth the bullet," Richard pleaded, slipping between them. "I got some—"

"Put down the gun, you craven pervert!" the principal barked.

"Shut up!" Richard shouted at her. "Don't make it worse!"

Stan lunged forward and swiped at her face with the gun. Richard, still wedged between them, deflected the blow. Stan pointed the gun at her face, but when he pulled the trigger, Richard was in the way again and lurched backward onto the desk. He yelled in pain and managed to slam his right fist into Stan's nose, knocking him backward. He hit Stan again and shrieked in agony when he tried to follow with his useless left arm. Richard kneed Stan in the groin, knocking him backward, and kept moving, fighting like Monty Python's Black Knight, only with a crazed frenzy and with somewhat better results.

"Get out of my fucking way or I'll kill you, too!" Stan yelled as he straightened up.

With his left shoulder a bleeding mess, Richard grabbed a heavy textbook from the desk with his right hand and swung it awkwardly. The blow landed on Stan's head, stunning him. Richard hit him again. He grabbed Stan's gun hand and tried to push him out of the office. They reached the door. Richard kept pushing, using his legs. Even wounded, Richard was stronger, at least temporarily, and in a second they were both out in the hall.

They weren't alone. Alicia, locked out of her classroom during the intruder alert, cowered on the floor in front of the sofa. "Run, Alicia!" Richard shouted, but the child who had been left behind remained frozen in place.

Gathering his waning strength, Richard kept bulling Stan backward until they tumbled against the locking bar on an entrance door. It swung open, depositing both of them outside in a heap. The door closed behind them and Richard heard the click as it locked. Stan stood up and shot the door in retaliation; the bullet ricocheted and clipped off a piece of brick. Richard stood up in time to see the hunched-over principal scurrying like a rat back to her hole, leaving Alicia out in the hall.

Stan breathed heavily, palm on one knee, gun on the other, and gestured toward the office. "Look at that. She only thinks of herself. You shoulda let me kill her."

"Let's talk," Richard said, hoping to convince Stan to stop the madness. He tried to ignore the nova of pain in his left shoulder as he turned and walked toward the benches, waving his good arm for Stan to follow.

"You really fucked things up, asshole." Stan said. "As usual."

Richard felt a blow to his leg just as he heard a pop behind him. He kept his feet and tried to move faster. The next shot hit him in the back and knocked him down. He didn't think he could get back up, nor was there any point in it if the bastard just kept shooting him. He tried to focus on the benches, straight ahead. They were very important. He built them on a sunny day like this. People all around, friends. His best day ever. The day he signed those checks. The day that built and destroyed him.

He kept crawling, proud of his progress, which was marked by a thickening trail of blood as he slowed. He peered back at Stan, who plodded behind him, tracking his progress, as curious as a boy watching a turtle race. Stan looked up to the cloudless sky and then at the benches, as if to calculate the PTO president's odds of making it.

Richard heard a siren in the distance, then another even further off. The early bus driver was pulling out of the loop. A horn honked, brakes squealed. A crash and a tinkle of glass. Hell was breaking loose and raining car parts. "So this how it ends," he muttered. "A shooting and a bus wreck. What a fucked-up place."

Richard made it to the benches like a spastic swimmer, reached up, touched one, and felt a sharp splinter. His hand fell to the ground. With great effort, he rolled over on his right shoulder and faced the sky.

The siren grew louder. "My ride," Stan said.

Richard disagreed without being disagreeable. "Could be mine."

A strange look crossed Stan's face as the siren grew even more insistent and he stared at the laurels Barbara's crew planted on V-Day. Richard heard a car door slam and tried to turn his head. It wouldn't move. He moaned in pain. His throat was dry. He wondered if he'd ever see Nick again.

Stan looked at the school. "Why'd you get in my way? You could have watched her die."

Richard groaned. "Not my idea of a good time." He started to tremble. The world was turning cold.

Stan pointed the gun at Richard, then at the sky. "I can't believe I shot my best friend. My only friend. You're not much of a friend, really. *Hm-mmph*. Maybe that's why. Bad form to be so inconstant, Richard." He looked around. "They'll take me to jail. I'll never see Karen again."

Richard didn't argue. That sounded like a good plan to him.

Stan stuck the gun barrel in his own mouth.

"Don't put a curse on this place," Richard said. "Not any more than you already have."

Stan pulled out the gun and said, "Stan I am," then stuck it back in. He pulled the trigger. Nothing. "Shit. I should have brought more bullets."

And then he ran away.

The siren ceased. Richard's pain grew louder. He lay on the ground and listened to its roar. It turned him inside out. He looked at the inside of his eyelids and thought: *She won and I saved her. This is a horrible way to die, with Desmond on the way.* As he wondered where he'd left his folder, he sensed movement. A squirrel perhaps, or a crow come to pluck out his eyeballs.

He looked up and saw Alicia standing over him. He managed a smile. "Hello, little girl."

"Don't die. My daddy died this way. Don't die."

He was drooling; he wiped his mouth with his right hand. "I'll do my best."

"Be brave. I will pray for you, but you must take this. You will need it to be strong. Use it now." She handed him the yo-yo, bright and hard in the sunshine. He grabbed it and wouldn't let go, even though his bloody hand shook with a new and dreadful palsy.

A man stood over them and clicked a camera.

"I'm so sorry you had to see this," Richard croaked to Alicia. "So sorry."

"It's all right. I don't cry any more." Tears welled in her eyes.

A strident voice erupted: "Get away! You can't take pictures on school property!"

"I love you," Alicia said.

"I'm glad."

She was gone, swept up and away by a black cop who picked her up on the fly and stomped away on a dead run.

A round face came into view. "Mr. Gray? Mr. Gray, is that you? I'm Deanna Richardson. Hang on. An ambulance just pulled in. Just hang on. Who did this to you?"

He looked at her carefully, dispassionately. "I always thought you were thinner." A siren whooped. A car door slammed. Richard stared at a tire close up. The thump of footsteps grew into a tumult. A pair of blue pants hustled the reporter away. *Poor Deanna. Now she'll have to report that she's fat.*

People swarmed over the lawn. A giant Easter-egg hunt, and he was the egg. EMTs huddled over him, talking to him and about him like he wasn't there. Radios crackled. He tried to tell them evil still lurked, but they said the trouble was over and everything was going to be OK, and this was a lie he could do nothing about. "You don't understand!" he wheezed, each word precious for the effort it took to speak. "You've got to help the boy!"

He was loaded on a stretcher and placed in the back of an ambulance with strangers' assurances he'd be all right. If so, then why was the crew in such a hurry? He looked out and in the deepest darkest distance saw that dreadful woman throwing a folder in the Dumpster. The doors closed on his feeble protests, the siren wailed, and the ambulance pulled away.

It rolled down the hill by Applegate, past azaleas and a howling dog Richard knew by name and reputation, taking him on his final journey away from Malliford. The blaring siren called the neighborhood's attention to the sorry mess of Richard Gray's ebbing life, and now everyone would know his business, damn them. He hoped Nick remembered him well. The piggyback rides along Windamere to kindergarten. Ice cream cones and kites and always being there ... except now, with a bad man on the way to kill him.

"My son," he said. He struggled to say more, but no words would come.

TWENTY-FIVE

H e was lying in a pit, darkness upon darkness all around. Bats wheeled overhead in panicked flight. Rocks and boulders rained down on him. Wilkerson sat on his chest, furiously driving a stake through his heart. This was the forever dream, and there would be no waking from it. Dreaming ... dying ... damned. He was being taken; in a moment he would be gone. But when it appeared all was lost, he heard a distant voice, the one he loved above all others, faint but clear: *I am always with you, wherever you may roam.* He swam upward, away from bottomless death, through the depths of despair, and past the debris of madness, his broken heart filling with dazzling hope like sunlit glass to see—

Mrs. Little, in all her bullfrog splendor, sitting beside him. Stout and reassuring, she held an open Bible in one hand, his right hand in the other. Drowsy from drugs, he blinked, unable for an instant to recall whether he was man or child.

"Can't be Hell if you're here," he said, drooling on the white hospital sheet. He cast a bleary-eyed look around the room. "But this place is new. Can't move my arm. They got it strapped in this harness thing."

It was Wednesday, his first day out of Eastside Regional's ICU, and since Stan was no better at killing than he was at living, Richard had survived, though not in one piece. He'd lost part of his small intestine on the operating table, and he was still a mess, medically speaking. He was doped up on painkillers, awaiting surgery to repair his shoulder, hooked to a drip feed, pissing into a tube, and hoping they didn't switch containers, like the orderlies did in *Catch-22*.

Mrs. Little slipped a red ribbon amongst the Psalms and closed the battered book. She shifted her weight on the blue plastic chair and regarded him critically. "Coulda been worse. We almost lost you. But you made it."

Worrying about Nick had kept him alive in the ambulance. So had the yo-yo (which disappeared somewhere between the ambulance and his room). He had gripped it to keep from falling away from the world and bleeding to death, rallying the last brave corpuscles so that they wouldn't desert the fight along with all the weenie ones.

"Got some flowers from the PTO, too," she said, pointing.

He stared open-mouthed at the daisies on the bedside stand and wondered how the organization could pay for them. Cindi Lou would not be reimbursed, thanks in part to him. "Who sent the forget-me-nots?" he asked.

"Don't know. No card."

He saw a strip of red crepe paper taped across the wall-mounted television's blank screen. The severed ends of the coaxial cable and power cord dangled halfway down the wall. Mrs. Little gave him a defiant, innocent look worthy of the most pugnacious schoolboy.

"I hear you're a big hero," he said.

When she tut-tutted modestly, he asked her to tell him what happened. He had a general idea from police detectives and Reggie, who had flown in to help attend to his affairs. But the story would sound *truthier* coming from her.

"Can I get some air in here first?" she asked. "This place is stuffy and all full of hospital smell."

He nodded. She rose and adjusted a dial, then returned to her chair. She took a deep breath and let it out. She blinked her big eyes and stared past him, toward the hall. "Well, you already know Mr. McAllister wanted to kill Donzella James and Cassandra Hardwick for what they did to his family. And the principal, too. You were there for that. Do you remember?"

"All too well." Since then, it had been confusing, though. All the news and people and visions and visits blurred into each other, thanks in part to the painkillers that made him forget how much he should be hurting. Inside him, drugs were holding at bay a soul-crushing depression. And when the drugs wore off—well, that's what the buzzer was for.

"I happened to look out the classroom window and saw Mr. McAllister's car pull up by the Dumpsters. Actually, he banged into one of them. I got a bad feelin'. Things were really tense that day. A lot of teachers were mad at the principal for backstabbin' the PTO, and the police were lookin' for Mr. McAllister already. Plus that other stuff was goin' around, too, but you know a lot more about that than I do." She paused to give him the look she reserved for misbehaving boys. "So when I saw him I had an idea nothin' good was gonna happen, and it was gonna happen mighty fast. We were comin' toward each other in the hall, and he had a gun. I got to the counselor's office a half-second before he did. He said, 'I gotta get to them.' I told him, 'You'll get to them over my dead body. If this is the day I meet my Lord, then it's a good day.' I was wearin' the No-TV pin he gave me last year. He looked at me and said, 'You're the only one here I wouldn't shoot to get to them.' He turned away and ran into you. I turned to those two fools, still under their desks, and I said, 'That's what happens when you mess with people's children.'"

She fingered the pin. "I'm wearin' this every day now, just like my cross. When I saw Mr. McAllister with that gun, I prayed no one would get killed." She looked Richard over . "I should have asked for better, hunh?" She paused for a moment, then said, "You know the principal is gone."

"The last thing I saw before they closed the ambulance door was her throwing a folder in the Dumpster and ... I thought all hope was lost. I—"

"I saw her, too, so all hope wasn't. There's a reason I got Dumpster duty. A reason for all of this, but I haven't sorted it out yet." She shook her head. "I dug out those papers and gave them to the police. At first she denied ever seeing it. Then she claimed she thought it was about No-TV Week. But her prints, smeared in blood—"

"That would be mine, I think."

"—were on it, and they could see she'd turned the pages. So she knew. She knew."

"Busted."

"Susan Gunther got arrested, too."

"No!" That cleared his head. Somewhat. "What happened?"

"It hasn't made the papers yet. You know how the county hides bad news. It happened Tuesday morning, when the school police blocked Miz Rutherford from entering the school. I guess she saw her world fallin' apart and got crazy violent. She picked up a hole puncher and clubbed a security guard and clawed the district supervisor's face. That's going beyond loyal, you ask me." She shook her head and suppressed a smile. "But look at you. You're the real hero."

"I don't feel like one. I hit bottom, and I'm getting dragged across it. I'm in big trouble."

"Don't worry 'bout that. You didn't take any money for yourself." She paused and gave him the once-over. "Did you?"

"No, ma'am."

"Well, then. Got your head turned around by a pretty woman, though."
She sniffed. "Oldest story in the Bible. You have to answer for that, but not to
me. What you need to do is concentrate on gettin' well. Your boy needs you."

"How is Nick? I haven't seen him. They told me my wife came in while
I was in a coma to do insurance, but I haven't heard ... I'm sorry. I don't
mean to—"

"I understand you got troubles at home. Nick is transferring to Westover
next week. That's the best school in the state."

"Ha. They offered it to me to go away. I suppose it's for the best." He certainly wasn't going to fight the move, since it meant he wouldn't have to set
foot in Malliford again. And Anna Lee would consider the shooting a small
price to pay for such a glorious result.

"We got DESI test scores today. Nick did just fine. Well above grade
level in all subjects. If he could just stay focused, he's capable of great things.
I told him so."

"That's good to hear."

"He did a whole lot better than sixth grade, that's for sure." She rolled her
eyes. "You don't even want to know what happened with that bunch."

"The Chain Gang," he mused. "No, I probably don't. Say, did you see Alicia at school today?" Somewhere in the haze of the ICU, Alicia had visited
him, he thought, but now he wondered if it had been a dream. She proposed
marriage on behalf of her mother, who scolded her in Spanish. They didn't
stay long. Or he woke up.

"No, I didn't see her. I've had other things on my mind. I need to tell you
about Devonious. You earned the right to know, puttin' that man in jail. I
hear he's wanted in a missing-child case in Arizona."

"The police told me bounty hunters caught him Monday afternoon as
he was getting into his car. He had a gun. I told them he had threatened to
kill Nick and was going to Malliford. That's why I came up to the school
Monday afternoon."

"Oh my Lord. He was on his way."

"He was on his way." That was Richard's story, and he was sticking to it.

"He would have had to kill me first," Mrs. Little said.

"You were all ready to die Monday, weren't you?"

"For me, it won't be dyin'."

"I tried to tell the paramedics about Desmond, but I was fading away."

"Now you're back. Partly, anyway." She took a deep breath. "OK. About

Devonious. Monday was the first day he missed all year, and I feared for him after I saw that report in the trash. I always knew that man had the devil in him. I had to answer questions from the police, but soon as I could, I rushed off to check on the boy, crazy with worry. I knocked on the door and D said, 'Come in, it ain't locked.' I stepped inside. He was sittin' in the dark pointin' a gun at me. The second time that day I got to deal with that. I flew back against the door."

She rubbed her wrist. "The assignments I brought him went flying, and I thought, *Lord, please don't let him shoot me over homework. I know it's a lot but it's for his own good.* But that bullet wasn't for me. I said, 'Child, what brought you to this, waitin' on someone to walk in the door so you can kill 'em?' He shrugged and acted the way he does. Cold and half-dead inside, a child who's spent his life bein' whipped for cryin'. He said, 'It don't matter, him or me. It ain't happenin' again.'"

She sighed. "I was heartbroken. I trusted those fools to follow up on my reports and they didn't do anything. I told D you found out about Desmond. He said you were a day late. After a minute he put down the gun, which belonged to his mama's boyfriend. One of 'em, anyway. I tucked the gun away in my purse and looked around. It was just terrible. Cigarette smoke, cognac. Cheap furniture, what there was of it. Blankets coverin' the window. There was a crack pipe sittin' on the coffee table. And a huge television four feet across. The woman doesn't have much, but at least she got cable." Her lip curled in disgust. "Desmond bought 'em that TV. But you know what? There was a red ribbon on it, one I gave him Friday even though they tried to kill No-TV. The boy was tryin'. Despite his troubles and the deck stacked against him, he was tryin'."

A tear trickled down Richard's cheek. She pulled a Kleenex from her purse and handed it to him. When she set her purse sideways on the floor, a pair of electrician's pliers clanked out. He looked at the disabled television, then at her.

"Mr. Gray, I know how people are. They come in and watch their shows cause you're sleepin', then you wake up and break your pledge. Besides, the news isn't any good."

"It's all right. Go on. What happened to D?"

"I hugged him. The phone rang and he broke free, but he didn't answer it—just turned away. I saw a dark spot on the back of his pants and I said, 'Honey, did you have an accident?' He said, 'Wadn't no accident.' I knew right then that Desmond had his way with him."

"Oh God."

"That's why he was sittin' with the gun. Hadn't even changed himself. Hadn't seen his mama in over a day. He said it happened at school—at school!—Sunday afternoon when nobody was around. Desmond had a key to the school and the combination to the burglar alarm. Some kind of sick fantasy, I reckon. Can you believe that?"

"For some strange reason, I can." Because he knew the man who taught Desmond how to do it. There was no denying it now: The man in that old picture was Wilkerson, and Desmond had turned a school into his playhouse, like his mentor had done before him. And that foolish woman let him do it, just as Mrs. Selck had a generation ago.

She squinted at him skeptically before going on. "I called 911. The police came. An ambulance, too. They took him to the hospital. I called Mrs. Baines and told her. She said, 'The cameras.' That's all she said at first." She paused. "Well, the police already had the videos from you being shot. And they checked back and saw Desmond take the boy in there. I don't know what else was on there, and I don't want to know."

She dabbed her eyes with a tissue. "My Lord, I cannot believe anyone could do such a thing even when I know people do it all the time." She took a moment to compose herself. "You were sent. I prayed, and you were sent."

"I came too late."

"You saved his life. Saved that worthless man's life, too. D would have killed him or gotten killed and either way ..."

"Where is D now?"

"Away from his mama. I got him."

"You? How—"

"I prayed. And I'm a licensed foster parent. I don't have any of my own. That makes all of 'em mine."

"Why am I not surprised," he deadpanned.

"God works in mysterious ways. You were doin' the Lord's will, Mr. Gray, without even knowin' it." She laughed. "I bet you're tired of hearin' me carry on."

"Not at all, but I worry about what's going to happen to you. They treated you poorly. Even if ... she's gone, I mean, I don't see how things would be the same."

"I decided to go back to Bonaire. It's time to start the healing."

"Bonaire? Why there? That's no place ... you know, we moved away after the shooting."

She laughed. "And look what happened to you."

He gave her a wry grin. "A casualty of war."

"That was my nephew got killed at Bonaire, you know."

"What? Your nephew? But—"

She held up her hand to silence him. "Justin was waiting for me to give him a ride to his Eagle Scout project. There were some other people there at the time. Someone drove by and didn't like the looks of him, picked the wrong victim, or else it was just a stray shot. Because the shooters were in a gang, all the TV news stations called it a drug-related or a gang-related shooting and my nephew became a gangster drug dealer after he died, and now that's what everybody who never knew Justin thinks he was. That's why I don't watch TV. It makes my people look like a bunch of stupid criminals. When it's not showin' a bunch of filthy sex and violence. Excuse me. I don't mean to go off like that."

"It's all right. I understand. My apologies for thinking—"

"You just thought what the TV told you to think, just like everyone else. Anyway, I decided I couldn't run away from my past. I gotta face it. So I'm goin' back. Those kids need their breakfast more than they do at Malliford. More of 'em do, anyway. Oh my. Look at the time. I'd better let you get your rest." She got up and moved toward the door. "I'll keep you in my prayers."

"Mrs. Little."

She stopped and turned. "Yes."

"You're a good teacher."

"Thank you. That means a lot, coming from you. Thank you for having faith in me. And for helping me as much as you did."

"You're the bravest person I know."

"I'm happy just being a good teacher." She looked out the window and pointed. "TV crews settin' up out there. I'll be glad when things calm down. I appreciate you trying to do right by Devonious. He's a troublesome child. I know sometimes it's difficult."

"It shouldn't be. I had something ... happen to me when I was a kid. I realize now that when I wrote him off as worthless, well ... what goes around, comes around, as you like to say. I got written off, too, once upon a time."

"I understand. I been around you too long, but I understand."

"It's a hard lesson to learn."

"Those are the ones we remember best. Goodbye, Mr. Gray."

"Goodbye, Mrs. Little."

She left. A dinner cart rattled by in the hall while the clear fluid the nurses called food dripped into his veins. Outside, reporters talked about him, but he was quite incurious about what they said—and rather glad Mrs. Little had taken her righteous vengeance upon the TV.

TWENTY-SIX

Wilkerson, naked this time, pounded away at the stake in little Ricky's chest like he was setting up a tent. The dead had congregated around him and waited for his soul with open arms and blank, expressionless eyes. Again, the voice called him back from their clutches.

"Daddy, Daddy!"

Richard woke and stared in wonder at his son, who was feverishly rubbing his right hand.

"You were yelling," Nick said, letting go, then hugging his father gently. "People said you were going to die."

Richard croaked, "Nope, I'm right here." He struggled to sit up, but his shoulder wouldn't permit it. After rising an inch, the bedridden patient collapsed and groaned.

"A safety cadet told me you died three times and they kept bringing you back with those paddle things and you saw God. Did you see God?"

"I saw Mrs. Little. That's pretty close."

Nick made an ugly face. "I'm not going to have her any more. They're moving me to another school. That's OK. I hate it now, anyway. I especially don't want to walk by the benches, because that's where ... that's where—"

"I know. I was there."

"I've already cleaned out my desk and said goodbye to Mrs. Little. She said you were very brave."

"She's very brave, too. Hey." Richard looked around for Anna Lee. "Where's your mom?"

"She's talking to a nurse. She's mad at you, but Uncle Reg and I are working on her. We tell her she can't leave you."

The idea that he had advocates was somewhat heartening, though Richard doubted Anna Lee would want to reconcile. "What does she say?"

"She tells us to shut up. She and Uncle Reg have been fighting a lot. She made him leave last night, after he brought us dinner. He didn't even get to eat it. When I told her that wasn't nice, she said he could afford to miss a few meals. She's being mean, I tell you."

"Well, she's hurt and angry."

"Not as hurt as you."

"In a different way."

"*Yeah-uh*. In a not-getting-shot kind of way. Maybe the baby's making her angry. Angry baby."

Anna Lee walked into the room, bringing with her an air of hostility.

"I hope it doesn't turn out to be a monster," Nick whispered in his father's ear.

Richard watched Anna Lee set her purse on a chair, brush hair back from her face, and stick her hands on her hips. She gazed at him steadily without speaking. With his good hand, he pulled the sheet up close around his neck, near peek-a-boo territory. "I'm sorry for this."

She laughed drily. "The one thing you don't have to apologize for."

"Everything else, too."

There was silence. Richard became painfully aware of the hospital room's semi-stink. Nick, having dropped to the floor, crossed his legs and rocked to and fro.

"Well," Anna Lee said. "I'll help out for the time being, but you're not my favorite person right now."

"You're supposed to say 'Get well soon,' Mom," Nick said, showing his irritation.

Anna Lee snapped, "Nick, wait outside in the hall." He hesitated. "Go." She stared intently into Richard's eyes as Nick scurried out.

Richard regretted seeing his ally leave.

"You almost made me a widow," she said.

"See, I *do* need to be sorry about this, too."

"Well, you are one sorry individual, I will say that." She looked around, as if to measure the room. "Do you need anything?"

"Maybe my laptop."

She shook her head. "May get stolen. Can't trust anyone these days, you know."

He chuckled. "Yeah. Maybe you should just leave it at Applegate for now. My car—"

"I saw it and got Dad to fix the tire. It's in the driveway now. So on top of everything, you had a flat. I'm sorry," she said, and started giggling. She sniffed and composed herself. "You're really screwing up the divorce," she said in a tone Richard couldn't decipher. "I want you to know that."

"Is that all you've got to say?"

She nodded, biting her lip. "For right now. I just wanted Nick to come see you."

"What about you?"

"I saw enough of you in the ICU. Ha. But you didn't see me, coma boy." She paused. "Get better, OK?"

She spun on her heel and walked out. Nick's head briefly appeared in the door. "Bye, Daddy." He waved, and his hand disappeared sideways, like he was being dragged off.

That woman made Richard nervous. Actually, at that point, they all did. With a trembling hand, he buzzed the nurse's station and asked for more painkillers.

*   *   *

When Richard awoke, Rita was standing over him with a teddy bear. "I love you," she said.

"That puts you in the distinct minority," he replied.

After they discussed his injuries, which were magnificent compared to most, Rita gave him the dirt on Malliford. "I don't know if you heard, but Stan's being held without bail. They caught him in a gun shop trying to buy more ammo. His court-appointed attorney told the media that the shooting was accidental, despite the fact he'd emptied his weapon and run off to reload. I hear he's on suicide watch ... I feel so sorry for him. They drove him over the edge."

"I feel sorry for his daughter."

"And Desmond faces murder charges in Arizona. Congratulations and thanks be unto you for nabbing his despicable ass. We should be taking up a collection for you, instead of—"

"*Ut*. Don't want to think about *that*."

Richard fell quiet and half-listened to her prattle about the fall of the house of Malliford. He flinched when she said she felt "an extreme closeness" to him. He didn't pass on what he knew about Desmond and Devonious, since he was growing more distrustful of her with every word she spoke. He refused to talk about Teresa, who was still at large with two children and an undisclosed amount of money.

"Have you heard the latest about Susan?" she asked. "They charged her with felonies under the Zero Tolerance laws for violence and set bond at ten grand. Archie will get the kids if she goes to jail, and he'll probably sell them to a sweatshop in Singapore."

"Gawd," he drawled. "What else could go wrong?"

"Well," she said, licking her lips, "led by Mr. Chain Gang, Spencer Hadley, our sixth graders took a dive on the SHIT. To protest the various and unending cruelties of Mrs. Cates et al., most of them filled in the wrong answers on purpose with their number twos. It was really quite a conspiracy. They should get credit for working so well together. But since the state judges schools on sixth-grade scores, Malliford will soon rank among the worst schools in the county, if not the state and nation. Barbara and her property values are screwed. Instead of leaving no child behind, Malliford is now one big behind."

When Richard cringed, she gave him a wicked smile and said, "I wonder if our principal ever learned the difference between a spider and a fly."

He realized that Rita was reveling in the destruction. Her long-term resentment was festering into malicious glee, which now seemed rather ghastly and ghoulish up close.

"Thank you, Richard, for finally getting rid of that dreadful woman. That was the most important thing in the world to me."

"But all I did was get shot."

"And give her the rope to hang herself with."

Richard couldn't get the DESIs off his mind. "You knew about the test scores all along," he said. "You set it up, didn't you? You sabotaged the school. Why?"

"She had to go down," Rita said in a cold, hard voice. "You knew it as well as I did. And face it, it wasn't happening. Quite the opposite, in fact, with that damned TMI plan they cooked up." Rita paused. "I did what I had to do. And it was working. If she hadn't been gone Tuesday, they would have yanked the chain on her when the test scores came in. Call it my parting gift. At least with my plan, nobody got shot."

"What a pity you won't get credit. If you don't mind, I'd like to be alone now."

*　*　*

Thursday morning, Reggie flicked water on Richard's face. "Wake up, King of Pain," he said, handing his brother a letter to sign.

"What's this?" the groggy patient asked.

"Your last will and testicles. Actually, your resignation as PTO president, 'for personal reasons,' of course. Not necessarily to spend more time away from your family."

"Fuck you. I didn't steal anything, but I take responsibility, since—"

"Damn right you take responsibility. We're cutting a deal whereby you pay back the money and avoid prosecution. I gave Acting President Candace Josey a check in exchange for an agreement not to press charges. I told her it was the only way the PTO would ever see the money. Fortunately, she likes you and just wants all this to be over. She hates that your girlfriend is getting away with grand larceny, but tough titty. They'll catch the bitch. Or not. Know where she is?"

Richard leaned over the bed rail and spit into a cup, then glanced at the forget-me-nots.

"Yeah," Reggie said. "Best if you don't. Anyway, it's only money. And don't answer the room phone." He dug through the duffel Anna Lee had left for Richard and pulled out his brother's cell phone and charger, then plugged them into the wall socket. "And screen your calls. I don't want you saying anything to blow the deal. The DA and police are receptive, but it's not signed, sealed, and delivered. They don't want to prosecute a hero, even a sleazy one."

This was all good, but there was one thing Richard worried about more than anything else. "What about Nick? I don't want to lose him."

"I'm working on it, OK? Making progress. By the way, Randall Wyatt is very good."

"The best," Richard said. "I bet he got a reward for turning in Desmond. Seems like I'm entitled to a share of it, since I paid for the job."

"Already being handled, bro," Reggie said. "That's what's paying for Phase Two of the investigation. Wyatt's good, but so am I. That's what she said."

"Please elaborate, except for the last part."

"That old newspaper clipping in the report you faxed me? I couldn't see it clearly, but I met with Wyatt yesterday. I figured out that man in the picture with Desmond—"

"Was Wilkerson."

"You knew?"

"I suspected it when I saw the picture. And the knowledge kept bearing down on me, even in my dreams."

"It's amazing, on top of pointing out where Allen was. How?"

"I never forget. There was something deep down about Desmond that bothered me. I can't tell you exactly what. I paid to have some rocks turned over, and Wilkerson was under one of them. Maybe it was an accident, or an answer to someone's prayer. Or it could simply be a case of what goes around comes around, and I was the one in charge of the coming and going."

"Well, Wilkerson is very old and very alive in Arizona. I made a phone call and they've drawn up a murder warrants in Ridalia."

"Wow." Richard stared at him open-mouthed. "That quick."

"That quick. We need to make sure you get proper credit. I mean, look at you. You need it more than I do." Reggie glanced at his watch. "Hopefully, they've busted his old ass by now. I gotta go."

"Park in a tow-away zone again?"

"Yeah."

"So what happens next?"

"Maybe I get towed. Oh. In *your* life. I forgot, it's all about *you*. Tonight Candace asks PTA members to accept the deal at the general meeting."

"PTO. What if they reject it?"

"I'll stop payment on the check and set up a defense fund. But they can't be that stupid. *Hmm.* Actually, having dealt with them, I take that back. Let's hope for the best."

"Poor Candace. Poor me. How am I paying for this? And how much are we talking?"

Reggie waved him off. "Don't worry about it."

"I need to know."

"Well, the two checks you signed totaled twelve grand, six hundred and change. That's what we're giving them."

"That's all?"

"You know something I don't?" Reggie regarded him warily.

"Rarely," Richard said, hoping the Treasure was still off the books. Perhaps it would remain a forget-me-not secret. "I just wonder about the consequences."

"Consequences? Well, there's substantial overhead on the kind of major-league clean-up and extrication I'm doing for you, in addition to what I've mentioned. And you *will* pay me back."

"With interest," Richard said.

"With interest, hell. With *flesh*. And it will be the best deal you'll ever get. That reminds me." He found some more papers in his attaché. "Sign these, and do it as fast as your addled mind permits. Don't worry about anything. Just get better. By the way, I saw a picture of that treasurer. Not bad. Heard she was a stripper."

"Exotic dancer."

"A distinction without a difference. More trouble than she was worth, eh? Who knew?"

Reggie left Richard alone with Thursday's *Sentinel*. Each morning since he'd gotten out of the ICU, Richard had received a used copy of the newspaper from Reggie. Sniffing a Pulitzer, the paper had assigned four reporters to cover the collapse of Chain Gang Elementary. (Eventually, it would win one, for the photo of Alicia handing Richard the yo-yo.)

There certainly was plenty to cover, but there was no triumphant Tuesday news conference at Malliford, since Rutherford was banned from school property and Desmond had been apprehended. By the time he got to Phoenix, it was canceled. Implementation of The Mentoring Initiative was "indefinitely postponed" while the Southern Freedom Foundation scrambled to explain why an escaped fugitive, convicted child molester, and accused murderer (but a good conservative) had been allowed to run its operations. By Wednesday, three board members had resigned.

On Thursday's front page, Deanna Richardson reported that Cassandra Hardwick and Donzella James, like Estelle Rutherford, had been suspended due to "unspecified reasons." *It's called pimping, fools.*

* * *

Shortly after nine o'clock Thursday night, his cell phone buzzed. It was Rita, calling in a breathless report on the PTO meeting. "There was a huge turnout, news cameras all over the place. So much for No-TV Week. Our would-be president-elect wasn't there, but I heard she made bond. The nominating committee refused to put her name before the membership, and because Susan headed the ticket, there *was* no ticket. Candace couldn't handle the stress and leaned on Cindi Lou, so our corresponding secretary ran the show. It was like one of those worse-case scenarios where there's a nuclear war and the postmaster general has to take over and all hope is lost." At that point, she broke out laughing.

It was more than a little unnerving to Richard. "You're having way too much fun with this."

"You had to be there. Cindi Lou read your statement that while you never profited from your position, you take financial responsibility for what happened and have already replaced the missing funds the treasurer took. Teresa's the villain. That's the spin. Cindi Lou said that settled the issue of money. So you're out almost thirteen grand."

"I'm getting screwed, that's all I know."

"Ironic, eh? Then someone in back asked who died and made her queen, and the meeting went downhill from there. That idiot with the computer said the PTO burned down her house and owed her money. And someone who didn't like *her* moved to disband the PTO so it didn't have to pay, and everyone wanted to know how to do it, how to kill this headless beast, and they asked for a parliamentarian. Somebody said you were, and someone else said that proved how screwed up the PTO was. Then someone else—none of them a board member—said the PTO should dissolve while it was ahead, and the woman who complained about the fire was crying, '*Nooooo, nooooo,*' and then there's a second on the motion, and before Cindi Lou can do any-thing—and she doesn't know what to do, anyway—everybody's shouting, "Disband, disband," like a mob, and that passes for a vote. It was nearly unan-imous, except for that woman shrieking about the fire. Don't you just love consensus? Mayhem. Absolute mayhem. I must say it was all very interesting. Then the first-graders come up on stage and start singing and dancing."

She paused for a moment to catch her breath as the gruesome collection of images collided in Richard's mind. "So that's how we killed the PTO and destroyed Rutherfordism in less than a week. I think our work here is done. I'm sorry. I can't help laughing. I just wish it had happened to someone be-sides you. Ring around the rosie, a pocket full of posies, ashes, ashes, we all fall down."

"A plague on both our houses," Richard said.

"I'll come see you when you're in a bet—"

"I'm thinking: Don't." His tone was curt.

"You're kidding. I mean I—" she started to choke up "—Richard, I did it for *you.*"

"Right now I feel like I got caught up in a monumental battle between bad and evil. Goodbye, Rita. Have a good life." He hung up on her.

*   *   *

"That school is crumbling to the ground," Reggie said. "I envy Nick. I tell ya, every boy should live to see his principal dragged off in handcuffs." He tossed Friday's *Sentinel* on the bed and told Richard, "You should write a book about it. Tell your story to the world: *I am a Fugitive from Chain Gang Elementary!*"

"I'm not the one to do it." Richard glanced at the lead story on the front page: "Malliford Principal Faces Charges in Molestation Case." There was another front-pager on the PTO meeting, and a story inside about Susan's arrest. "Poor woman can't make the front page no matter how hard she tries. And the PTO is dead."

"Yeah," Reggie said. "I seconded the motion to disband it. I figured it would be hard to sue you if the plaintiff didn't exist. Elementary school, my dear Watson."

"You're not a member of the PTO."

"They weren't burdened by a knowledge of procedure."

* * *

Friday afternoon, Richard was lonelier than he was cautious and picked up the room phone when it rang. *D'oh*. It was Deanna Richardson, wanting to know how he was doing. That wasn't the reason she called, of course. It was all about Chain Gang Elementary for her. For the record, Richard claimed he was fine.

"I was wondering if I could ask you a few questions."

"I'm afraid I don't have any credibility any more," he said.

"Are you crazy? You ought to write a book."

"I've been getting that a lot. On both counts. In any case, I don't have anything to say right now."

"Then let me tell you a few things. The county is revising its policy on Ritalin after the NAACP threatened to file a class-action suit."

"Good. What they've been doing is evil. I'll at least say that."

"Also, the school board is forcing Harold Johnson to resign. He gets a huge buyout as a reward for his incompetence."

"Par for the curse. I'd ask why, except he should have been fired long ago."

"I'll tell you: On top of high crimes and misdemeanors, including the Zero Tolerance policy and his blind backing of Malliford's principal, it turns out that Estelle Rutherford is seventy-five years old. Mandatory retirement age is seventy."

"Shit."

"May I quote you on that?"

"She should have left five years ago. And then none of this would have happened. Stan would never have met her. My presidency. Desmond, the devil she found to counteract the PTO uprising. None of it, if the county had just abided by its own rules. Sad thing is, it's not even hard to believe. We talked about it. We'd say she's incredibly old and this has *got* to be the year. Spring would roll around and we'd expect her to retire, but she never did. Drove Rita crazy."

"Rita Malloy? I wish she'd quit calling me about how bad the place is. I got that figured out. *Hell-o*."

"How old did the county think Rutherford was?"

"Fifty-five."

Richard broke out laughing. It still hurt. "She would have outlasted us all."

"Her lawyer claims she has Alzheimer's."

"It's so sad—" Richard sucked in his next words, because *sad* summed up everything so well that there was nothing else to say.

"OK. I mean ... I know the treasurer left town and everyone is pointing the finger at her, but my editors have to know this. Did you take any money from the PTO?"

"No," Richard said, "but I take responsibility. That's all I'll say, except this: never sign a blank check. That's rule No. 1, and I forgot it."

"There's one other thing I'd like to ask. Teresa Keller—"

Click. The interview was over.

*   *   *

Saturday morning, Anna Lee showed up, wearing khaki shorts and a white top. So far, her visits had been short, perfunctory, and awkward, since she was more pissed than pleasant. She hadn't exactly been an angel of mercy, and Richard was starting to dread seeing her, since she tended to talk ugly to him. He had hoped she'd bring Nick this time and the boy could act as his attorney. No such luck.

She sat in the plastic chair next to the bed without saying a word and touched her belly. Richard noticed her baby bump for the first time. Then she stared at him like he was stupid, which he was willing to admit he was. It seemed like a good start of his personal twelve-step program. *Hi, I'm Richard, and I'm dumb as a stump.*

"Good to see you, too," he said.

She shook her head. "Our money situation is truly a nightmare. I am so pissed at you for raiding Nick's education fund. Damn right I checked. I understand you used it to pay for a detective to catch that pervert."

"Wilkerson."

"Wilkerson what?"

"Never mind." Something to talk about another day.

"For that little faux pas, you can foot the entire bill for Nick's college, you hear me?"

"I hear you."

"At least your brother fixed that PTO scam you were pulling with that little whore. What were you thinking?" She grunted in disgust. "You're lucky no one's prosecuting." She sneered at him. "Were you actually going to run away with her?"

"No," he said meekly. "I broke up with her. I—I never could have left Nick, and ... the baby saved us—you and me—or so I thought. Family values." He thought that, as a Republican, she should appreciate the notion.

She grunted. "Maybe you should have gotten out when you could."

"No. Everything would be worse if I'd done that. It's not about me."

"*Now* you say that. I thought everything was about you and your sufferings since the beginning of time." She gave him a derisive laugh, then grew more reflective. "That was very brave, what you did at school. It took guts. Sorry. No pun intended."

"I did what I'm good at, getting in the way."

She reached over and touched his shoulder gently and smiled, then shook her head. "I can't believe how everything is working out for you. All right." She cleared her throat. "I've been thinking things over and I've made a decision that I may regret, but we'll see. There seems to be some general consensus that you won't make it without me." Her gaze was piercing now. "That somehow you'll die if I don't take you back."

She threw up her hands, as if this was a ridiculous notion, though Richard suspected she was baiting him. He looked out the window and said, "I read where half the men who divorce are dead before they hit the floor."

"Look at you. Just the threat of it—"

"Made me suicidal. Yes."

She laughed lightly, but there were tears in her eyes. She put her hand on his. Sniffling, she said, "Richard, I missed you for ... a long time. It's like you were going off somewhere, and I began to think you would never come back. And now this—"

"I thought you were gone a long time ago." Tears welled up in his eyes, too. "It was bad, and you know it."

"No excuses for you, though."

"No excuses. Right." He took a deep breath. "I don't want to live without you and Nick. And ... *her*." He pointed at his wife's belly. "Or him. But I'm thinking it's a girl."

She reached over and hugged him. "I may be a fool, but I'm willing to try. So," she said, blowing out her breath. "I'm taking you back, o Wounded Child."

"Don't forget Troubled Loner and Emotional Cripple with No Friends."

"Yeah, all that," she said, waving her hand dismissively. "On double super-secret probationary status. I don't know if this will work. And I'm still incredibly angry about it. But your brother, who's a magician with money if not people, has set something up that might work out. That's good, because I sure as hell don't want to live here any more."

"What are you talking about?"

"I'll let him tell you about it."

She kissed him on the cheek. "You'd better love me this time, you bastard. See where that gets you on a Saturday night, instead of all your whining. So ... earn my love or set me free."

"OK," he said meekly and gave her a wan smile. "That's what I want to do. Right now, I feel all broken inside." He grabbed her hand and kissed it.

She gently pulled her hand back. "It's a start, I guess."

*   *   *

A couple of hours after Anna Lee left, Reggie came by. "You're looking chipper. Anna Lee told me she was pulling your sorry ass back off the street, Yo-Yo Man."

"How about that?" Richard said brightly.

"Yeah, well, we'll see how that works out."

Richard couldn't help but notice the telltale cynicism in his brother's voice. "What do you know?"

'You have no idea. But that's a problem solved for now, and let's leave it at that. I want to talk about what you're going to do after they patch up your shoulder."

"Got any ideas?"

"You're coming back to Ridalia."

"'Scuse?"

"Didn't Anna Lee tell you? You're going to run the paper. She gets to stay at home, which means I'm going to have to overpay you."

Richard's expression was both puzzled and displeased. "That was never part of the deal."

"We talked about this. At least, I told you I wanted you to run the newspaper when I bought it. Well, I bought it and *dipso facto ergo*, excuse my Latin, you're going to be in charge. As editor. I don't trust you with the money, for obvious reasons. And I must point out your negotiating posture has deteriorated since then."

"*You* talked about this. I didn't."

"Just try not to be a Communist when you write editorials, OK?"

There was a long silence that entailed a drink of water by Richard, a trip to the bathroom by Reggie, a staring contest Richard won, and numerous glances out the window and into the hall by both of them. Finally, Richard said, "How about progressive independent?"

Reg scowled. "Sounds like a way to avoid the 'L' word."

"You listen to too much talk radio. I am what I am."

"All right, as long as you advocate personal responsibility."

"Personal responsibility. What a concept. When do I start?"

"As soon as you're fit to travel."

Richard mulled it over. "No prosecution. I owe you twelve—"

"Now it's about sixteen, but don't worry. It will be more."

"And you have a peonage deal for me to work it off as editor of the Ridalia *Independent*. Picking up where Dad left off nearly forty years ago. Wow. I just realized I've been shot, sued, and sold into slavery. Strange."

"Well, almost sued. Anna Lee didn't actually file, but she had the papers drawn up. Some lawyer named Archie Gunther."

Richard groaned at the mention of Susan's rat bastard husband.

"But you keep your wife, for the time being. She's not happy about this, but her other options suck even more. It seems there are some interesting conditions at your local Chamber of Commerce. *Huh*. By the way, you have no idea how close you came to getting arrested. No idea. As for the human bondage deal, based on what I've seen of your recent life, it's a step up. Except for the hot mistress part. Little Miss Grab and Go was out of your price range, though. You're coming out ahead, the way I see it."

"What, going from PTO president to slavery for debt? Not what I call a happy ending."

"Not even an ending," Reggie said. "Call no story over until it's in the grave."

"Not even then. There are ghosts in Ridalia."

"More than you know. But it beats what you've got here." You'll be the crusading editor. Fits you. Don't ask me why."

Richard shook his head. This was too much to deal with. "Funny if it works out."

"Oh, it will work out. You'll limp away from this and grow up. Go back to Ridalia a flawed hero and live somewhat happily ever after with your wife and your son at your side—if you keep your world intact, that is."

"Sounds like a plan to me. Although you left out the part where I'm sold into slavery."

Reggie squinched up his face. "That part is *so* misunderstood."

"OK," Richard said. "I'll do it."

"One more thing. Don't let Anna Lee push you around. Her position isn't as strong as she'd like you to think it is."

"What do you mean?"

"You screwed up, but you're not the only one." He grinned. "I told you Wyatt was good, didn't I? A few months from now, you might even be in the driver's seat."

Richard shuddered as a chill swept over him. "Are you saying—"

"Well, I gotta go. I'm illegally parked." Reggie then gave him a look similar to the one Anna Lee had given him earlier that day. "Grow up, you dumb sap. You're a sap, you know that? You're the husband who gets pushed off the train and run over by the next one and you *still* don't know it, even though you're staring at your legs on the other side of the tracks."

"Nice image."

"Thanks. I've been working on it. I'm just saying the child might be yours."

"It *will* be mine."

"I hear what you're sayin'. *I'm* just sayin' it may be your call, if you know what I mean."

With a sympathetic shrug, Reggie left his little brother to consider all these new possibilities and revelations. There were things people needed to know, and he would be the one to tell them. He would testify against Wilkerson, behave himself, win back Anna Lee, and keep Nick by his side. If that meant returning to the rubble of a past life and rebuilding its broken bricks into something lasting and strong, so be it.

And now he was intrigued by the idea that Anna Lee might be a different person than the one he knew. This made her much more *interesting* Kind of hot, too. *There was a chain-gang man, who had a chain-gang wife ...*

A nurse came in to check Richard's improving vital signs. "I married a dame," he told her with a touch of awe in his voice.

"Good for you." She patted his hand.

And I'm a sap. As he stared at the blank television screen, the crepe banner came loose and fluttered in the air. The nurse climbed on a chair to re-attach it. "No-TV Week," she said approvingly. "We do it at my house every year." With a frown, she added, "But you didn't have to cut the cord."

She left Richard to dwell on Personal Responsibility. A very specific issue, for there was a matter to resolve. He tried figuring the payment schedule in his head as the numbers floated around. Perhaps he could repay the

Treasure in eight years at $250 a month, more or less. Maybe he'd play Robin
Hood and give the money to someone else. Evangeline Dombry and the
Bonaire Elementary PTA came to mind—especially if Avon Little ended
up back there.

Dusk brought a storm. Rain pounded the window and lightning torched
the sky. After the storm passed, he dozed off. In the morning, an orthopedist
would operate on his wounded shoulder. In the meantime, he dreamed of
evil, but this time, it was Ricky Gray chasing the monster, not vice versa.
Indeed, Wilkerson's day of reckoning was coming, now that the boy in the
pear tree had tracked him down. There would be no more dreams of dying.

ACKNOWLEDGMENTS

It has taken a while to hammer out this book. Along the way, I joined the Atlanta Writers Club, which turned out to be an essential move for many different reasons. I had a great deal of help keeping my story in perspective from my fellow writing group members, who endured me while I polished the manuscript: leader Ricky Jacobs, (an expert linguist and grammarian), Angela Still, and Paula Buford. I also thank my editor, Alice Peck, who has stayed with me and graciously continues to offer advice and encouragement long after she finished helping me strengthen the links in my chain. (You can visit her at www.alicepeckeditorial.com.) Also, kudos to cover designer Michael Mullins at Anything Design, who did a marvelous job even as his assignment kept shifting.

On a personal note, I want to thank my PTA co-president at Evansdale Elementary, Jennifer Oliver, as well as the board members, elves, and worthy volunteers who made my stint in office very pleasant—not in the least "chain gangish." Thanks also to Evansdale teachers and administrators. Principals "Sam" Wyrosdick and Joseph D'Ambra were delightful to work with nearly all of the time. Special thanks to Helen Byrd, whose transcendental kindness on my daughter's tenth birthday will always be remembered. All three are retired now, and I wish them only the best.

Above all, thanks to my wife Judy, whom I cherish. In addition to keeping me alive, she has read more versions of *Chain Gang Elementary* than either of us care to count.